Train to Budapest

DACIA MARAINI

Train to Budapest

Translated from the Italian by Silvester Mazzarella

ARCADIA BOOKS

Arcadia Books Ltd
15–16 Nassau Street
London W1W 7AB

www.arcadiabooks.co.uk

First published in the United Kingdom by Arcadia Books 2010
Originally published by RCS Libri SpA, Milano under the title *Il treno dell'ultima notte*
Copyright Dacia Maraini © 2008
English language translation copyright © Silvester Mazzarella 2010

ISBN 978-1-906413-57-6

Typeset in Sabon by MacGuru Ltd
Printed and bound in the UK by CPI Mackays, Chatham ME5 8TD

Arcadia Books gratefully acknowledges the financial support of Arts Council England.

Arcadia Books supports English PEN, the fellowship of writers who work together to promote literature and its understanding. English PEN upholds writers' freedoms in Britain and around the world, challenging political and cultural limits on free expression. To find out more, visit www.englishpen.org or contact
English PEN, 6–8 Amwell Street, London EC1R 1UQ

Arcadia Books distributors are as follows:

in the UK and elsewhere in Europe:
Turnaround Publishers Services
Unit 3, Olympia Trading Estate
Coburg Road
London N22 6TZ

in the US and Canada:
Independent Publishers Group
814 N. Franklin Street
Chicago, IL 60610

in Australia:
The Scribo Group Pty Ltd
18 Rodborough Road
Frenchs Forest 2086

in New Zealand:
Addenda
PO Box 78224
Grey Lynn
Auckland

in South Africa:
Jacana Media (Pty) Ltd
PO Box 291784,
Melville 2109
Johannesburg

Arcadia Books is the *Sunday Times* Small Publisher of the Year 2002/03

I asked myself what I was doing there, with a sensation of panic in my heart as though I had blundered into a place of cruel and absurd mysteries not fit for a human being to behold.

He seemed to stare at me [...] with that wide and immense stare embracing, condemning, loathing all the universe. I seemed to hear the whispered cry, 'The horror! The horror!'

JOSEPH CONRAD, *Heart of Darkness*

1

The slow train struggles northwards. Amara sits composed and dignified, gripped by a sort of sleepy excitement. This is the first long journey of her life. The train stops at every station. Its seats are graced with handmade doilies and it stinks of boiled goat and permanganate soap. The smells of the cold war that has divided the countries of the West from those of the East, segregating them behind walls, barbed wire and soldiers armed with rifles.

'This separation bears witness to the assertion of a suspicious and aggressive form of communism. And on the other side is an equally suspicious and vehement anti-communism. Basically, neither side knows anything about the other. Surely we want our readers to know how people really live beyond the Iron Curtain? About what still may remain of the suffering caused by the Second World War? About what survives of the memory of the Holocaust?'

The voice of the editor of the newspaper she works for as he reminds her to notice details, to talk to people, to study the daily lives of those living in the East of Europe, and then to write. The editor is young and good-looking and completely bald. He favours her with an exceptionally charming smile as he adds that she cannot be paid very much for her contributions.

'But my dear Sironi, you are at the very outset of your career, you know how much I admire the clarity of your writing, but I could not possibly pay a beginner more. On the other hand, you will be able to telephone the paper free of charge and dictate your articles directly to a call-corder. This is the first time for years that the international lines to the East have been working, even if only for a few hours a day. We have good connections with Austria; as for Czechoslovakia and Poland, I don't know. We shall have to see. Do you good to try. Please collect your special journalist's pass from the secretary's office.'

He had provided her with a piece of paper with the phone

numbers of the Italian newspaper agencies in the various cities of Europe and, after giving her a fatherly kiss on both cheeks, closed the door behind her.

The train had been held up for hours at the border between Italy and Austria, and now it has reached the frontier between Austria and Czechoslovakia. Soldiers have taken away everyone's passport and left the haggard passengers locked in their carriages, only dimly discernible under a tiny service light.

The locomotive puffs impatiently, anxious to get going, but is held back by something with more energy than a mere engine: the dark, tenacious, mindless and obtuse power of frontier bureaucracy. Night has descended unnoticed by the travellers. Nothing can be heard outside but the tread of soldiers. It is hot in the locked carriage. Amara is sharing the compartment with two men and a young mother with a newborn baby in her arms. The older of the two men, in a blue windcheater, is trying to lower the squeaking window. When he stretches his arms fur armbands can be seen.

A gust of fresh air blows briskly into the carriage. Amara puts her head out to breathe a little better. All she can see is the gloom of a starless night. Far off, to the right, some tiny lights are flickering. A village? No dogs can be heard barking, no donkeys braying. It is like being suspended in the void. A soldier shouts. He comes up and beats on the lowered window with the butt of his rifle. Opening the windows is forbidden! There are no other openings or slits on this train trying to slink not so much from one country to another as from one civilisation to another, from one ideology to another, from one mentality to another. An old train with very few passengers on board, a chain of decrepit carriages struggling to force a way through the armour-plated barrier dividing the world. And who are these reckless travellers? How can they be so bold?

Inside the carriage, with its dim little blue light, they start talking. One of the two men is Slovak; the other half-Austrian and half-Hungarian, and they communicate in German. The woman holding the baby understands nothing but her own dialect from Gdańsk.

The man with fur armbands says he's on his way to see his family in Kladno. The other man, who has a line of gazelles running across his jumper, talks of a pregnant daughter expecting

him in Poznań. The woman just repeats the name Gdańsk over
and again. She cradles her pale silent child and murmurs Gdańsk,
Gdańsk.

'And where are you off to?' the man with the gazelles asks
Amara.

'Birkenau.'

'Auschwitz-Birkenau? And for what, if it's not too impertinent
to ask?'

'I have to write some articles for my paper. But I shall also be
looking for traces of someone who disappeared in '43.'

The man in the blue windcheater makes no comment. His fur
armbands sparkle in the half-darkness. What use can they be? But
the man with the gazelles seems impressed and interested. 'My
mother also died in a Nazi camp, at Treblinka,' he says in a small
voice, concentrating on Amara. 'Was your relative Jewish?'

'He wasn't my relative. But he was Jewish, yes.'

'And you want to try and trace a man who wasn't even a relative. Aren't you afraid?'

'It's something I promised myself to do.'

'Ah!'

In that 'Ah' is understanding and a discreet curiosity. To
Amara's ears his words do not sound like idle chat. They seem
shot through with an honest desire to understand. She looks more
closely at him: a man of about forty with thin arms and a very
long neck that emerges like a Modigliani image from a dark col-
larless shirt; he has wide eyes, high cheekbones and a soft mouth
marked by small concentric wrinkles. She would have liked to tell
him something about the child Emanuele and his passion for flying
and of the cherries that smelled of the wild and his illness and his
letters and his disappearance. But the man in blue, the one with
fur armbands, scares her.

Every now and then a soldier's helmet appears at the bottom
of the window and runs along the edge of the glass like a turtle's
back. First from right to left, then from left to right. The night
has freshened the air. Amara pulls her woollen cardigan round her
shoulders. She is beginning to doze. Maybe she'll be able to sleep
for a few minutes against the bald threadbare velvet of the seat.

When she opens her eyes the man with fur armbands is snoozing
in front of her, mouth wide open, hands lying abandoned on his

thighs. The young mother is still cradling her baby and humming a little song. The man with the gazelles on his chest starts talking quietly, his mouth nearly touching her ear.

'I'm afraid they won't let me go any further.'

'Why not?'

'I have an Austrian passport. My mother was Jewish-Hungarian, and I worked as a journalist for several years.'

'Is all that in your passport?'

'They have information and lists. The only thing that works in this country is lists.' He sounds like a conspirator, but there is mockery in his smile. A wisp of brown hair streaked with grey slips across his brow. His breath smells of dried figs and also a little of wine, as if he has just come from a cellar where they stack oak casks and baskets of figs. Something about him reminds her of her father: the timid smile, the thick smooth hair tending to slide over his forehead, the grey eyes edged with green. The pale figure reflected in the window is serene and attractive, even if marked by time with a few small wrinkles. Now he seems to have turned away from her to snooze, his head propped against his seat. He has such an abandoned, defenceless air that she feels an urge to protect him. In the same way as the young mother in the far corner of the carriage is supporting the heavy head of her little girl only a few months old.

Amara glances up at the worn and battered suitcase on the rack. Her father gave it to her years ago, saying: 'I took this with me to Venice on honeymoon – now you can have it!' At the time she threw it on top of the wardrobe without a second look. But later she came to appreciate it. Post-war suitcases are made of cardboard and fall apart at once, while her father's, even though old and worn, is made of strong, durable leather. It bulges, scarcely able to hold everything she has crammed into it: skirts, jumpers, light boots, books, and the packet of Emanuele's letters and his diary. She knows some of what he wrote by heart. Like the first letter, which reached her from Vienna in December 1939.

Dear Amara, our house is on Schulerstrasse. On the ground floor there's a clockmaker's where I always stop when I'm going out or coming in. All the clocks tell the same time. Isn't that funny? Even the ones marked with the names of distant cities, Shanghai, Tokyo, New York: they all say three in the afternoon.

What does your watch say? And what time is it in your head when I'm not there? The hours dance, you know, like in Ponchielli's *Gioconda* which I saw with Mutti at the Pergola in Florence last year. The dance of the hours, I never expected to see ballerinas come on holding hands. They made a circle and boys in black slipped into the middle to mime the slow regular movements of the clock's hands. My hours stopped in Florence. I ought to go back and get them, because here there are other hours I don't recognise. Hours not made from minutes but from jumps and strange backward movements. Why are you not here with me? I so much want to put my arms round you. From my window I can see a pancake seller who stops at the corner of Blutgasse and he's really good at making palacsintas: he spreads a little butter on his hotplate, then as soon as he takes his ladle to add flour mixed with milk, a jet of steam hits him in the face. He wipes his face clean on his sleeve, but never for a moment takes his eyes off the hotplate, where the flour is coagulating and beginning to curl up. As it sets, he spreads it out with a short wide knife. Then, with a quick flick of the wrist, he separates the thin palacsinta disc from the hotplate and turns it over. In less than a minute it's ready. Then he delicately places it to one side, on a plate smeared with butter. If a customer comes along he moistens it with rum, adds a spoonful of plum jam and folds it delicately like an expensive handkerchief before gracefully handing it over. Write to me soon, write to me constantly, even twice a day, please, your letters are like your kisses to me. I love you. Emanuele.

The linguistic virtuosity of little Emanuele makes her smile; that childish need to prove himself better than everyone else, to show off the adult observer living in the body of a child.

2

At last at about five in the morning the passports come back. A very young soldier is holding them in his hands, hardly more than an adolescent with his pink cheeks and bow legs. He returns them one by one, except the one that belongs to the man with the gazelles. The soldier looks at him scornfully and says something in Czech. The man replies timidly, but looks annoyed. The soldier turns and gestures as if to say what can I do, it's nothing to do with me. Then he sets off down the corridor to the sound of hobnailed boots.

'What did I tell you? Now they'll make me get off the train and hold me for two days. It's always the same.'

'If you know it's always the same, why expect anything different?' asks the man in fur armbands sarcastically.

'I've got to get to Poznań where my daughter's about to have her first baby. She's alone, her husband died in an accident. Her mother, my wife Ester, died of cancer eight years ago. I keep hoping things will change. They've been saying on the radio that relations between Austria, Poland and Czechoslovakia have been improving at the frontiers. But it's not my nationality that's the obstacle, it's because I'm listed as half Jewish and I've been a journalist, two things that make me suspect. As a businessman I'd have no problems.'

His German is precious, rather out of date and very literary, slow and polite. Amara wishes she could help him, but how? At that moment another soldier comes into the carriage, this time an officer with a haughty manner. Planting his feet wide apart in front of the man with the gazelles, he asks his first name and surname, then starts addressing him rudely in Czech. The other answers calmly if unhappily, then turns timidly to Amara.

'He's asking if we're related. I said yes. Please excuse me presuming on such a brief acquaintance. Would you be willing to act as my guarantor?'

Amara nods. She knows nothing of this man but feels she has known him for years. Let's hope he doesn't get me into any trouble, she reflects rapidly. The official gives her a form. She gestures to say she doesn't understand. The man with the gazelles reads, translates and helps her fill it in: 'I the undersigned, Maria Amara Sironi, daughter of Amintore Sironi and Stefania Bai, born Florence 2 December 1930, resident in Florence at Via Alderotti 102, declare that Hans Wilkowsky, born Vienna 4 July 1910, son of Tadeusz Wilkowsky and Hanna Paduk, resident in Vienna at Strobachgasse 6, is a cousin of my father on his mother's side and that I can guarantee for him. Signed and countersigned.'

Amara signs immediately. She hands the paper to the official, who goes away. Is that all? Is a signature all that's needed to snatch a potential 'enemy' from the frontier bureaucracy? The man with the gazelles answers with amusement as if reading her thoughts: 'Just regulations. Tiresome, stupid sometimes, but inescapable. None of the people who apply these rules believe in them. But they have to respect them, they have no choice. They have to fill in forms to prove how efficient they are. A totally useless efficiency, I might add. So sorry to have bothered you, but without you I would have lost two days. I'm extremely grateful to you for signing.'

Why does this man inspire confidence? Is it only because he vaguely resembles her father? Or because he speaks such good Italian as well as German, Czech and Polish? Or because of the mysterious grey reflections in his eyes?

'If you should need me,' the man goes on. 'I live in Vienna but for the moment I shall be in Poznań at my daughter's. I'll write the address on this piece of paper. I hope you won't be angry with me ...'

'Why should I!'

'I've memorised your address in Florence. You're lucky. You live in a warm city with ancient memories, with harmonious memories I mean ...'

Funny, that formal tone. So far from irritating her, it touches her. Perhaps it's those family traits: the high cheekbones and almond eyes, the soft, gentle smile. Now, superimposed on her travelling companion, she sees the image of little Emanuele perched at the top of the cherry tree waving to her to join him. Come on up, he says, come on, I'll help you! And she takes off her sandals so she won't slip on the bark and starts climbing the lowest branches. The bitter scent of the cherry leaves fills her nose, blending with the subtle odour of hot feet and grazed knees that comes with Emanuele, and which deep down she calls 'the smell of happiness'. She hears his laughing voice as he spurs her on: come on, come on, higher, higher! What are you scared of?

Emanuele Orenstein: an oversensitive child who is upset when the slightest thing crosses him. The neighbours say he's been spoilt by his mother who is too elegant and rich and owns houses in the great city of Vienna. Her husband owns a toy factory at Rifredi. No one understands how anyone can prefer Rifredi when they could live in Vienna. Emanuele has no use for his father's toys. These are mass-produced in sets, but he prefers unique things, like the Pinocchio carved from a single piece of soft wood which he gave his little friend on her birthday. With Amara he is easygoing, always ready to start a new adventure. He might seem fragile, but he isn't really. Together they climb the highest walls, braving the sharp fragments of pottery along the top to reach the wild pears that set their teeth on edge. Together they open manhole covers and go underground with a torch to explore the city sewers. Together they read books about fabulous voyages. Together they race through the avenues of Florence on two ramshackle bicycles with tyres that constantly get punctured. And no matter whether it's her tyre or his, they always stop and crouch together by the roadside to mend the puncture. They pull the patches and rubber solution out of their rucksack and get down to work: you hold the tyre while I pull out the inner tube. You open the rubber solution because my hands are full. Two heads close together, one fair and one chestnut brown. They have something in common. Like a brother and sister. No sooner is the tyre fixed than they're off again, hands sticky with rubber solution, pedalling at breakneck speed down Viale Michelangelo.

'Are we friends?' he asks from time to time, stopping in the middle of the road with one foot on the ground and the other on the pedal, as if seized by sudden fear.

'Friends in life and death!' she answers, repeating a formula they often use between themselves and which undoubtedly comes from one of the adventure books they've read together. Most of all they love sea stories. Ones in which a small boy (unfortunately small girls aren't expected to get into difficulties of this kind) goes to sea as a cabin boy and everything imaginable happens to him. Like the very young Redburn whom Melville describes as an awkward and naïve adolescent. The first time he is sent aloft up the mainmast to unreef the sails, he is seized by vertigo and grabs the shrouds so as not to fall, while the sailors on the bridge laugh with scorn and amusement. Another book they read with their four eyes tells of a ship wrecked on a desert island. In the disaster everyone is killed except one young adventurer who explores the island and learns how to survive, fighting ferocious animals at night and wandering about by day in search of water and food. He invents a language of his own that enables him to communicate with the clouds and the stones, sews clothes together with strands of grass and learns to swim like a fish.

'I've got a plan,' says Emanuele in a mysterious voice.

'What plan?'

'A secret. You mustn't tell anyone.'

'You can't think I'm a spy!'

'I've found out how to fly.'

'Like the birds?'

'Like the birds.'

'But how?'

'You need two light wings. And a small structure of wood that must be very strong but weightless. I know how to do it.'

'Did you find it in a book?'

'Just trust me.'

'But what if we fall?'

'We won't fall if we follow the logic of flight.'

'And how is it done?'

'Shhh, they'll hear us.'

When he squeezes her hand like that her tummy feels as hot as if a little stove was boiling inside it. She knows he can feel how hot the stove is too but they've never discussed it. He's the most mysterious child I've ever known, little Emanuele. He doesn't like chatter, except when he's writing, then he lets himself go. He knows lots of words, like someone who reads a lot and memorises the most difficult expressions for things. 'He writes like a professor,' Mamma Stefania says of him with admiration. 'A know-all!' comments Papà Amintore. Amara watches him walking confidently but cautiously, his grazed knees nimble, his supple back straight, expressing at the same time fear and defiance.

The first love of her life. She knows that now. She has told herself so at night as she watches the reflection of the street-lamp on her window. She has repeated it again and again: I love Emanuele and he loves me. And they will go on loving each other whatever happens because you can't choose who you meet; you just have to accept it as destiny, and once it's happened it's happened for all time.

3

'My mother, dear Miss Maria Amara, was tall, fair and strongly built. A woman who befriended her in prison told me that after only a few days in the camp the centimetre of hair sticking up on her head after she had been shorn, and the down on her arms and her eyelashes, turned white. Like the girl in the Chinese fable. Do you know the legend of the woman with white hair?'

'No.'

'Well, I'll tell you. A young peasant girl, in the days of the great estates, was persecuted by her master who wanted to force her to make love with him. Mei-Mei, that was her name, left home and ran away to the mountains so as not to have to give in to the fat proprietor who considered it his right to lie with the adolescent peasant girls on his estate. Everyone was in despair; they spent months searching for her and in the end assumed she must be dead. But one person never stopped looking for her: her mother Ching, the only person who still believed she was alive. For this reason she went on waiting for her daughter in the constant hope of seeing her return. Then one day, looking for mushrooms in the forest on the Jan Tzse mountain, Ching came on a wild young woman in ragged clothes. She had long white hair like an old woman and her hands were covered with cuts and wrinkles. At first the mother didn't recognise her daughter. But Mei-Mei recognised her mother and hugged her. She explained that for three years she had been living in a cave and eating plants. Ching told her they could go home now because the master was dead. But Mei-Mei looked like an old woman; how could she find a husband with that spooky long white hair?'

The train starts swaying more violently. Amara instinctively braces herself so as not to be thrown from one side of the carriage to the other. The young Polish mother is so intent on rocking her baby that she doesn't notice. Her hair is parted in the middle and tied at her neck with a red ribbon. A few strands have escaped and fallen untidily round her ears. She has a tiny mouth. There is something crazy about her. Why does she never for an instant take her eyes off her little baby? Why does she purse her lips as though terrified of the slightest breath of wind? Why does she never meet the eyes of her fellow travellers? Why does she keep slipping a hand in among the folds of her skirt to find a lemon-coloured sweet that she puts into her mouth, only to spit it timidly out again into a small handkerchief that she then folds and puts away in her pocket?

The two men have fallen asleep, the one with the gazelles huddled up with his head propped against the window; while the other has slithered down in his seat with his legs wide apart and his head lolling on his chest.

Amara silently pulls the package of Emanuele's letters out of her father's suitcase and lays it in her lap. She can't resist the temptation to read them again, as she has already done so many times since Emanuele disappeared. She has left the envelopes at home to save a little space. The pile of pages covered in tiny rounded hand-writing smells of dust and coal. She imagines him writing them, especially the last ones, by the light of an oil lamp with a pencil squeezed between dirty fingers. But this is one of his first letters and it breathes an air of everyday serenity.

Vienna. December '39

Mamma has a new dress I like very much with storks flying against a clear sky. When she walks the storks move, opening their wings and starting to rise. When I grow up I want to be a pilot. I told Papà this but he laughed in my face. He says I'll be an industrialist like him. We own a business, he says, you have to begin thinking about that. Papà doesn't know how to put on his tie. He twists about in front of the mirror and pulls funny faces. In the end he calls to Mamma for help. And with her tongue between her teeth, she makes him a perfect knot.

There are no trees to climb here, Amara my love. We're living in a flat in the centre of the city. From my window I can see a big grey building with friezes sculpted in stone. I can see vases displayed on balconies. I can see closed curtains. I've never managed to catch a head looking out of those windows. How I wish I could be with you in Florence, where people lean out from their balconies and call up from below, like in a village. In the morning I get up at seven and eat with Papà. Mamma sleeps till ten. Our nanny, Mariska, makes us fine breakfasts: fresh yoghurt with sliced banana on top, hot milk laced with coffee, slices of toast spread with fresh butter and jam she has made herself. Every day she complains that because it's wartime she can't get the ingredients to make food the way she wants. And Papà has to give her more and more money for buying things at the market.

The train sways. Now the young mother is asleep with her daughter in her arms. But even in sleep she doesn't relax. She grasps her child as though they might take her away at any moment.

The man with fur armbands seems to be having disturbing dreams because he keeps thrashing about, still stretched out in his seat. He has taken off his shoes. His big feet are enclosed in woollen socks threadbare at the heel. But the man with gazelles on his chest has woken up and is reading in a corner, his book close to his face. There is very little light, but he persists. His face shows intense concentration, almost as if he has forgotten where he is and who he is travelling with.

Amara pulls out another letter.

Why don't you come here to Vienna too? Yesterday I went for a gallop on a lion with a red mane. At one point I kicked his sides so hard he took off and flew, but my father said that's enough so he came down again all crestfallen. He's irritable these days, Papà. He says the business isn't going well. The SS are constantly under our feet. And they want to give the orders, he says. Mutti has promised to sew me a pair of wings with real feathers for Christmas. Why don't you come and see me for Christmas? I like the apple tart here in Vienna, but not the ice creams. They don't have good ice cream here, not like in Florence. What's good here is the cream. Almost as good as in Florence. Do you remember that day in the Cascine when we ate four wafers with cream and then we ordered a fifth and you dropped it in the bushes? I'm waiting for you, Emanuele.

The train moves off again. The new day has started, young and sunny. They are running through the middle of a birch wood. The tall slender white trunks flash past. When the man with the gazelles disappears to the toilet the traveller from Kladno with the fur armbands opens his eyes, turns towards Amara and says mysteriously: 'That man must be a spy. You should never have acted as his guarantor. They'll catch up with you. They'll take away your passport.'

'But I'm Italian. And I have a permit.'

'These days anyone crossing the boundary between the two worlds is suspect. Don't you know about the cold war? No one can avoid it. You also could be a spy.'

'What sort of spy?'

'The West needs information about the East. And the East needs information about what you call the "free" world.' The man smiles, showing bright red gums.

'So you could be a spy too.'

'Of course. Who says I'm not?' He sneers, his eyes still dull and very sad.

'May I ask you something: why do you wear those fur armbands?'

'Rheumatism in my wrists. My hands get paralysed if I don't keep them warm. Satisfied? But maybe that's not true at all. Maybe I tried to cut my wrists and want to hide the scars.'

There is something disquieting about this man who says things and then immediately contradicts them.

Now the woman is walking up and down the corridor with her baby, humming a lullaby. The child whimpers feebly with a low, tentative sound.

'May I offer you some coffee?' says the man with fur armbands. 'I've got a thermos full. Let's make the most of it now we're alone in the compartment. If I'd offered it to the others too my thermos would be empty by now.'

'I don't drink coffee, thank you.'

'Of course as an Italian you know what real coffee is. In fact all I have is a very poor Polish substitute. But still, it's hot. You're sure you don't want any?'

'No, thanks.'

'A biscuit, then?'

'A biscuit, yes, thank you.'

'Terrible Soviet biscuits. But they do help fill the stomach. They know how to make missiles, do our Soviet friends, excellent ones, but they don't know much about biscuits. Biscuits are a luxury, missiles a necessity, don't you agree? Always bearing in mind the nationalist point of view, of course. Defending ourselves from the

West, defending ourselves from your butter and ginger biscuits, that's what communism is all about.'

The man laughs, throwing two biscuits at once into his mouth. There's something simultaneously brutal and subtle about him. He seems to get enormous fun out of surprising her.

'Did you know about Comrade Stalin? He died three years ago, alone, sozzled with drink, terrified and out of his mind. I don't think it was living people he was afraid of, so much as the ghosts of the friends he'd had murdered. He saw an enemy in every shadow. Even his wife, Nadezhda Alliluyeva, was driven to kill herself in '32. And to think everyone thought him a good family man. Or better still, a father to every Soviet citizen, no, to every communist the world over. Did he not seem like a good, fatherly peasant? In fact he was a lunatic with criminal instincts. Perhaps not unlike Peter the Great ... In fact, I tell you, Peter the Great, in some ways, was more understanding and indulgent than Stalin ... Did you know that Tsar Peter had a passion for pulling out his subjects' teeth and would chase his courtiers down the palace corridors to do it? But there's nothing wrong with my teeth, the wretch he had managed to catch would protest. Just one tooth, what's that to you, then you'll feel better, the Tsar would reply. But they all took to their heels. Did you know that? Just think of the courtiers running about all over the place! What a laugh! When he died, they found a sack full of teeth under his bed. Did you know that?'

Amara looks at him in consternation. Armbands seems to have no interest whatever in any response from her. He continues undaunted, despite the presence of the man with the gazelles who has returned to the compartment and is now combing his disordered hair with the window as a mirror.

'My father got two years in prison,' went on Armbands, 'because he knew English and organised an exhibition of European painters. Accused of espionage. Locked up in prison, tortured. My mother was careful to distance herself from him, because the political police were after her. She was trapped into saying he secretly entertained American spies at home. Everyone round him believed the accusations, including my grandfather and grandmother. He instantly became an enemy of the State and as such had to be punished. Great Father Stalin couldn't be wrong.

communist Thought in its infinite greatness couldn't be wrong. The worst possible criminals took advantage of the wonderful illusion.'

'And didn't you believe in it?' asked the man with the gazelles.

'Of course I did. Like you, like everyone else.'

'I believed in utopia, but not in the practice of communism. I'm half Jewish and I won't stay anywhere where they persecute Jews. Stalinism wasn't kind to the Jews, remember.'

'Though the first tank to enter the death camps was Soviet.'

'But some of the worst persecution of Jews took place in Poland, with Stalin's consent.'

'That was what we believed in then ... I ask myself, what the hell did we believe in?'

'A new, just world, with no masters or slaves ... a world where the weak would be protected and defended, where no one would be able to buy the body and soul of another person ... To each according to his need. Isn't that what we believed in?'

'To each according to his need, what crap! And who decides what I need?'

'The Party,' says the man with the gazelles, smiling. 'That's the trouble, my friend. Once they start building pyramids, there's no hope. Imagine a pyramid of innocent and generous people tightening their belts for the sake of their country, while at the top of the pyramid a well-fed man is waving a red flag with a gold star on it. And so many have died for that flag, honestly and sincerely, in the belief they were making a sacrifice for liberty.'

'Whereas in fact they devoted their best energies to the will of others, to idolatry and dictatorship, is that what you're saying?'

'But even that was better than dying in the name of abuse of power, race hatred and worship of the superman, don't you agree?'

'Delusion bites, with the teeth of a shark.'

'Yet there's still a difference between that and governing by invading other countries and insisting on the supremacy of your own race, plundering and sacking and putting to death the weakest and those who have worked for equality.'

'But unsuccessfully, my friend, this is the problem. What's the use of a theory of equality and justice if both are then destroyed?'

'But I must insist that there's a difference between an ideology of death and an ideology aiming at freedom for all.'

'Freedom? Who was ever free under Stalin? And who is this stupid cold war setting free? In the West, dreadful crimes are being committed in the name of freedom. You're a Jew: just think of the Rosenbergs! And the American atomic bomb on Japan! And what sort of justice is being done in the East? The most disgusting things: think of the Stalinist massacres. A quarter of the Russian people were imprisoned or killed to humour the obsessions of a maniac. Is that what you call liberty?'

'Don't take me for a Stalinist. I'm thinking of all those who sacrificed themselves for the promise of a better world. Those who gave their lives freely for communism, without being driven by murderous fury or theories of racial selection as the Nazis were. People who simply wanted a classless world. It wasn't their fault they were deceived and manipulated and sent off to be stupidly slaughtered. People like my wife's father Amos, who kept a portrait of Stalin in his modest home in Budapest, I knew him well: a mild and kindly man, exceptionally honest. He worked hard all his life. He believed in communism as a system that had helped men to be equal and to be brothers. He never hurt a fly. But I despised his neighbour Béla Lukacs who was a spy. He was paid for denouncing a poor tenant who had accepted a phone call from abroad. He believed in nothing. He was a Stalinist out of self-interest.'

But Amara could not follow the two men any further because they suddenly switched from German to Polish. Not deliberately to cut her out, but in the excitement of the discussion.

4

Dear Amara, yesterday we went for an outing on the Danube with our teacher. We skated on the frozen water. I had a pair of brand-new wings with me, very wide and solid but the teacher wouldn't let me climb the hill. Then we sat in a sort of improvised tent and ate Prague ham and fresh cheese with black bread and salted gherkins. The child Kitty asked me if I'd like to be her fiancé but I said I already have a fiancée, who lives in Florence and I'm going to marry her when I'm eighteen. Do you remember my promise? Papà says I'll change my mind but I don't think so. Mamma gave me a hug and printed a fine red mouth on my cheek. I didn't realise at the time but when I got to school they teased me: 'Who's been kissing you, Emanuele? What an enormous mouth your fiancée has … It covers half your cheek. How will you manage kissing a fiancée with such a big mouth?' The child Kitty was angry. I explained that it was my mother who'd kissed me but they didn't believe it. Now they call me 'the boy with the big-mouth fiancée'.

One morning Amara had waited for little Emanuele for hours under the Villa Lorenzi cherry tree which they liked to climb every day. But he never came. So she climbed the tree alone and filled her mouth with ripe cherries and spat the stones as far as she could, filling her cheeks with air. At the same time she watched the path to the villa.

She suddenly felt so lonely up on those branches in the midst of the light leaves with their wild, bitter scent. She stopped eating and suddenly burst into tears. To stop her tears she daringly hoisted herself higher, ever higher, balancing on the slender, rocking branches. But it had not been climbing to the top of the cherry tree that had consoled her so much as the sight of a blackbird sitting on a nearby branch, and she had begun watching it with curiosity. The bird's attentive and fastidious expression transfixed her. She was no longer herself, but became the blackbird. A fragile little Amara completely absorbed in her own destiny, as only an animal can be. She had understood that to survive as a blackbird you must be quick to anticipate anything that may happen, as birds do when they sense the imminence of a storm or an earthquake. It had never occurred to her that Emanuele might move away and surprise had snatched away her breath. Why had he not come? And how could she have not even imagined the possibility that he might not come?

With her pockets stuffed with cherries, her legs scratched and her face grubby, she had gone to look for him at his home. At the gate she had met his mother leaving in a hurry. 'Emanuele's had a fall. One of his usual flights from the roof of the garage. He's hit his head. He's not well and we have to leave, what bad luck. Go up if you like.'

His mother kissed her, then climbed into a great black car with its door held open for her by a uniformed chauffeur.

Amara climbed slowly to the upper floor and pushed open the door of Emanuele's bedroom, where they had sometimes played together with puppets. She was hit by a strong smell of fevered body, of sweat and vomit and disinfectant. An intrusive disagreeable sweetish smell mingled with the delicate fresh scent of a little bunch of freesias stuck in a small vase on the bedside table. Emanuele was stretched on his back, face white as paper, his narrow shoulders in lilac and blue striped pyjamas, eyes shining and half-closed, as if his eyelids were heavy under his arching eyebrows. Amara moved forward on tiptoe, listening to the rumble of water boiling in a small pan on a spirit stove.

She stood in silence watching him and understood that she loved him with a love as unexpected as it was unalterable. A love that would last for ever, she was sure of it, because that little knot of nerves, muscles and blood that was Emanuele was part of her own body and nothing in the world would ever be able to keep them apart. She would have liked to tell him so, but his childish gaze was hidden under his eyelids. So she said nothing, just pulled the cherries from the pocket of her dress and put them on a corner of the great bed, hoping he would take one and lift it to his mouth. It would have been a sign of continuity. But little Emanuele, normally so greedy for cherries, never noticed the shiny round fruit lying near his feet. So, with awkward, timid movements she started eating them herself, one after another, without ever taking her eyes off him.

At one moment she thought he smiled. But it may only have been a grimace of pain. She could hardly believe such deep, raucous breathing could emerge from such a small nose, from such delicate nostrils. 'You're like a dragon,' she murmured. But he gave no sign that he had heard her voice.

As she was swallowing the last cherry, she saw the door open. She immediately identified the man who appeared as the doctor from the worn leather bag in his hand, the greasy hair slipping across his forehead, and the attentive yet blank look he turned on the sick boy. Without even noticing her presence, he began to auscultate Emanuele's tiny chest after helping him to sit up and roughly unbuttoning his pyjamas.

Finally Emanuele opened his eyes and looked at her. With a look she had never seen in him before: a look of fear but at the same time of surrender, of abandonment to something stronger than his own will. Afterwards, having often thought about that look, she had convinced herself that it contained a premonition of a precocious end. Had he wanted to anticipate it with that leap into the void with two wings of cloth and wire? Or had his flight been a way of trying to escape a departure he foresaw would be disastrous? Had he been aware of the trap they were about to fall into?

A yellow liquid issued from his mouth and his eyes showed their whites as if he was tired of studying the outside world and wanted only to turn towards the muddy black well inside his sick body. The doctor helped him to lie down again, pulling the sheet up to his neck.

'Is he dead?' she had asked in a tiny voice.

'He'll be fine in ten days or so.' Then, as if aware of her for the first time, the doctor pulled her by the hand towards the stairs. 'He needs rest now,' he added hurriedly, cleaning his hands on a wad of cotton steeped in alcohol. 'Come on, go home, off you go!'

Amara headed quickly for the door. As she turned to say goodbye to the sick boy she saw him give a slight smile. There was in that exhausted face a desperation greater than the body that contained it, deeper and more relentless than the illness at that moment serving him as a shield. He had used his feeble power as a child to attempt a last opposition to that foolish departure in the direction of death. Although probably well aware he could not escape and that, weak and exhausted as he was, he would have to follow his energetic parents who, victims of who knows what impetuous leap of Teutonic patriotism, had decided to return to Austria to 'face the enemy together at home'. Both felt entirely Austrian. For them, being Jewish was a fact of culture and religion that in no way interfered with their belonging to the country in which they had been born and grown up and in which they had their roots. Besides, they were used to being respected and admired for the intelligent use generations of their families had made of money, and for the loyal and faithful manner in which for a century they had served the Austrian state in these parts.

That smile was the last thing she had seen of him. A smile of grieving love. A smile of fear but of promise too. As though he wanted to say: I'm here, and even if I move I'm not moving. I'm waiting for you.

Instead it had been she who had waited, for days, weeks, months and years. Most often in the branches of the Villa Lorenzi cherry tree. That was where she liked best to wait. Perched on a branch, half blackbird half child. She had grown into a girl, then a woman. But she had never stopped waiting for him. Whenever she could she climbed the cherry tree with a book in her hand. She would read, content to stare at the branches. Every now and then she would raise her eyes and study the dusty little path along which she had so often seen Emanuele come, hopping and skipping in his sandals and kicking the dust up round his knees.

5

The bus drops Amara right in front of a tower she has often seen in photographs. A rail track overgrown with grass passes under her feet on its way to penetrating a massive building and high gateway crowned by the square tower with a long narrow loophole under its roof. Auschwitz. She steps through the damp morning grass, wetting her shoes. On the horizon are birch trees with shining leaves. New trees and new earth everywhere. As if the will to forget is emanating from the earth itself. An atmosphere of enigmatic peace resting on what still remains of the horror.

Then she walks along a soil path, towards the great gate of the main camp with the famous phrase in wrought-iron letters WORK SETS YOU FREE. A delicate script in capital letters, subdued and dark against the clear sky, framed by two metal strips for insubstantial, reassuring emphasis. The parallel strips are not brutal, but seem to follow an almost subtle path, broken in the middle by the dancing leap of a small arch. ARBEIT MACHT FREI. Along the camp the sun caresses the steel barriers, curved at the top, that hold metal nets and still taut barbed wire. The effect of the dark bars is softened by the many little white ceramic caps whose purpose was to maintain and control the electric current passing through the wire. The buildings that survived the mines with which the Germans did their best to hide their places of death, now have their doors wide open. A few tourists in coloured jackets move peacefully in and out with cameras and notebooks, hats pressed down to shield their heads from the sun.

'Through me you come into the grieving city, through me you come among the lost people.' Dante's words come spontaneously to mind as she climbs the stone steps to the main entrance. From the warmth outside she passes into a damp and disquieting darkness. This was one of the camp's clearing and assembly stations. A white arrow indicates the entrance to this sinister museum of memory.

Amara passes down a long corridor, its walls decorated with thousands of photograph portraits side by side, each protected by a sheet of glass and a slim wooden frame. Under each head is a name. Identification photographs that show the faces of men and women caught in a moment of confusion and total loss of all affection. At this very moment when their identity was fixed on paper, they were about to lose it. From that instant, a process would have begun to depersonalise them not only physically and psychologically, reducing them to bodies without gender or flesh, mere ghosts consumed by terror and the ferocious laws of survival, their names replaced by a number on an arm.

The expressions on their faces show they have not yet fully understood where they are and what is about to happen to them. They know their prospects are not good, that they have left behind all security and power of ownership. A strange and cruel process, this photography, bearing witness to the insane precision of the Nazis as they pedantically catalogued each new admission. A mania that lacerated the heart of the system of punishments of the Reich. The SS knew perfectly well they were acting as assassins and bandits and tried to conceal their crimes by exterminating those who had witnessed them. Even so they were unable to stop themselves cataloguing, registering and recording on paper names and dates that were to be unequivocal testimony to these crimes.

Amara examines the faces on the wall, one by one, slowly, trying to hear them speak to her. She has almost forgotten that the one face she is looking for is Emanuele's. These portraits are vivid proof of what it means to arrive in a camp after long days in an armoured train. They also tell of people not yet marked and wounded by camp life. People who have only just left their homes and their cities. People whose cheeks still carry the bloom of a normal life when they were still able to delight in an exam passed, a walk in the woods, or a letter sent by a distant love.

They have passed day after day crammed in a train with no food or drink, sitting side by side on the floor without toilet or water, forced to perform their natural needs in front of everyone. But their eyes still have a touch of confidence. They think they have reached a work camp, brutal perhaps but ready to give their thirsty bodies a home. They think they will have to work hard like others they have seen here dressed in pyjamas with vertical stripes. But they know nothing of the gas chambers, nothing of the fear which will transform them into living dead, or 'muselman' as they are called in the camp or, if they are selected to work for the guards, will transform them into ferocious and treacherous slave-drivers, often even forced to kill their own brothers.

There are workers' faces among these photographs, prematurely marked by hard toil: peasants in patched shirts, family women with discoloured headscarves. Poor Jews from the villages of Eastern Europe: Germans, Poles and Hungarians. And contrasting with them are the refined faces of prosperous citizens: girls with light fair hair and school-uniform collars, boys with proud frowns and open-neck shirts, old men in jackets with velvet lapels, eyes staring in astonishment.

As Amara turns away from the last portrait she realises more than an hour has passed without her coming across either the face or name of Emanuele Orenstein.

'Are these all the photographs of the prisoners?' she asks a guard who has been watching her. 'No, miss,' he answers in broken English. 'To begin with they photographed everyone, writing down first name and family name, date of birth and place of origin. Then they stopped. So many arrived they had no time to register them all.'

Amara has noticed some Italian names among the multitude of Germans and Poles: Ascoli, Padova, Levi, Roberti, Canepa, Sereni. In one corner, in capital letters, is a long list of the numbers deported in Europe: Poland 3,000,000, the Soviet Union 1,100,000, Slovakia 71,000, Hungary 550,000, Bohemia 80,000, Lithuania 140,000, Germany 165,000, the Netherlands 102,000, France 75,000, Latvia 71,000, Yugoslavia 60,000, Greece 60,000, Austria 65,000, Belgium 28,000, Italy 8,000, Estonia 1,500, Norway 762, Romania 350,000.

Vienna. April '40

Hitler and Mussolini have shaken hands at the Brenner Pass. Mamma has shown me the photo published in all the papers. 'See what good friends we are with Italy,' she said. 'No need to worry about the business at Rifredi even if Papà says they're virtually taking it from us. We have occupied Denmark and Norway,' says Mutti. 'Showing the world how strong we are. In fact, we're firmly in the

saddle,' she insists. She's happy. But I've no idea what saddle she's talking
about. A saddle on a flying horse? A friend of Papà in Florence has sent him
a book by a young poet called Eugenio Montale. In the evening, after supper,
Papà read us a poem from the book, the title of which is *Cuttlefish Bones*. I
didn't understand much. But now and then a phrase struck me: 'A gloomy air
weighs/ on an undecided world' it says in a poem called 'Sarcophagi', and I
seemed to see a black cloud descending very slowly on our roofs bringing scary
long shadows. 'Now let your step be/ more cautious' says another poem, and I
looked at Mutti with apprehension: her steps are far from cautious, in fact they're
headlong. Will she be able to hear this young Italian poet?

I'm building a wonderful machine, Amara my love, to bring me to you.
My inspiration has been the little planes the Wehrmacht have developed from
studying the relationship between the wingspan of a seagull and the body which
navigates the sky. The weight of its body including intestines, breathing apparatus
and reproductive organs relates perfectly to the span of its wings which have to
be three times more voluminous. Do you understand the secret? It's all there in
that proportion. And I'm working to achieve the same result. If only you could
see my room, it's full of sheets of paper covered with numbers. And there are
pieces of wood and boards of every kind, with cords, string, iron and copper
wire all over the place, on the bed and the chairs. Mamma says all this mess
prevents her tidying the room. But she doesn't get angry unlike Papà who just
dismisses the whole thing as ridiculous. Deep down she's happier if I stay at home
to work on my plane than if I go out.

On my way back from school yesterday I saw that a huge poster had
appeared right at the corner of our house. A man with a repulsive face and
thick dark hair over a low forehead and hairs growing out of a curved nose. He
is reaching out a claw to grasp the throat of an Austrian soldier over the words
'The Jewish Bolshevik has his eye on you. Give him a chance and he'll wring
your neck. Act while you still have time!' 'What does Bolshevik mean?' I asked
Mamma, and she laughed. 'Stupid rubbish,' she said, 'stupid propaganda by a
few blockheads.' But Papà is worried. 'I'm Jewish but I'm no Bolshevik,' he says.
'Listen, tonight I'll go and pull that abomination down.'

6

Other arrows point the way to other rooms. Bare floors made of inferior tiles worn down by visitors' feet. Suddenly Amara finds herself facing a mountain of dusty shoes. 'But, Mum, can dead people walk?' comes a voice from low down in front of her. A plump little boy is sucking a strawberry-coloured lollipop as he contemplates the sad pile of shoes long since reduced to a uniform shade of faded grey.

Shoes of every variety and size: big shapeless men's shoes, little high-heeled women's shoes, slippers, ankle-boots, tiny lace-up shoes for children; moccasins, bootees, clodhoppers, mules, galoshes, leggings, sandals, tight-fitting topboots, babouches.

Amara tries to fit the photographed faces in the corridor to the shoes piled at random before her. And fails. She can't make herself imagine bodies moving in those shoes hardened by time, their creases penetrated by dust. Single shoes that have lost their partners, scratched ankle-boots that may once have been red but are now almost black; lace-up shoes without laces that poke out tired tongues.

It is only when her eye is arrested by a down-at-heel shoe for a little boy that something stirs in her imagination. Beyond the greasy-fingered glass that divides the visitor from the mountain of private possessions, she can see the bare legs of a little boy in well-worn shoes. And next to him the robust ankles of a countrywoman. The woman is walking with difficulty, her knees wide apart. Why? Ah yes, she is pregnant, the baby heavy in her swollen belly. The little boy in his brand-new blue shoes skips lightly ahead, almost as if following some internal rhythm of his own. Now and then he stumbles and nearly falls, but recovers and hurries on, a little butterfly happy with the simple joy of being alive. The rest, men and women, follow in a crowd, their footsteps ever more confident. Thousands of feet on the move. But where are they going?

Mamma has sewn a beautiful yellow star on my jacket. She says I must always stay in sight of her. She has a star too. And Papà. I'll wear the star if you sew me my wings, I told her. So she did this on condition that I don't take off that mark of identification, because it's dangerous to do so. And what's more, please don't try to fly out of the window, she added. I won't. I shall throw myself off the barn at the Weisenbergs' house where we are going on a country outing on Sunday. I've already worked out how to collect hay and pile it on the ground so that if I fall ... but I won't fall. This could be the real thing, don't you think? And then I'll fly to you. To be on the safe side, keep your window open. I've read that there's a certain kind of glue strong enough to resist the wind, the cold and the heat of the sun. It's made with caoutchouc from the trees of the Ivory Coast, mixed with the resin of Siberian firs. I've asked for it everywhere but no one seems to know anything about it. So I shall make it myself. A cement strong enough to hold together the pieces of wood to which the long cloth arms of the aircraft will be tied. But where can I find caoutchouc and the resin of Siberian firs? Can you get me any caoutchouc? I remember once in Florence we came on a dark little store in Via dei Calzaioli, d'you remember? We went down four steps that stank of cat's piss, and came to a little shop with a tiny little man sitting on a stool gluing bits of leather together to make boxes, book-covers and belts. Remember? You were fascinated by the way he spoke, like Gepetto in Pinocchio. He had a little blond wig too. Maybe he was losing his hair. Or perhaps he really was Gepetto and didn't want to be recognised. But Pinocchio himself wasn't there. And this man, instead of working with wood, was using leather and skin: tanning, smoothing and tinting. Do you remember you said to me, 'What a wonderful smell this glue has!' And the man lifted his head in surprise. 'People usually say stink,' he said and you started to laugh. 'What's this fine glue made from?' And he answered, 'Caoutchouc from the Ivory Coast,' Do you remember? Get some and send it to me. I really need it. My darling little Amara, I think of you all the time, I never even for a moment stop thinking about you. If I shut my eyes I can feel myself squeezing your hand. You always have nice warm hands, and I love it when you grab my hands which are too big and always so cold. I dream of kissing you. Isn't it funny? When we were together all the time we hardly ever kissed and now I'm far away I never think of anything else! I can feel my mouth coming closer and closer to yours, closer and closer, till I can feel the warmth of your breath; then I shut my eyes and can't see you any more but I can feel the tenderness of your top lip on the skin between my mouth and my nose and I'm so satisfied I wake up all sweaty and happy.

Amara scatters the letters on her lap. There are so many of them. But there's a familiar break between those written before 1941 and the later ones. The early letters are all about excursions, good dinners at home, nannies, school, and that obsession with flying that kept Emanuele shut up at home struggling with ever more varied kinds of hand-built aircraft. After 1941 everything changes. Even the paper he writes on, even the ink that from being black and smooth becomes clotted and pale, and is finally replaced by pencil. His letters got less frequent, in fact they became so few and far between that she can remember the anxiety of waiting for them to come. 'Has the postman been?' she would ask the moment she woke, knowing perfectly well he never came before ten. Why can't he change his route, she would ask herself, when he does his round on his bicycle, ringing his bell when he gets to the corner of Via Alderotti. If instead of first going to Via Segato he turned round in Via Incontri, he'd reach her home at nine-forty. But postmen are mysterious, and choose routes no one can understand.

Vienna. November '41

Dear Amara, I haven't written for some time because I've had no paper or pen. Everything's changed since last time. The SS came to my school. They read out a list of names. Including mine. 'Starting tomorrow, you can't come to school here any more.' Our teacher, Frau Schadhauser, was furious and protested. They handcuffed her and took her away like a criminal. 'It's not that we're stopping you going to school,' explained a little soldier with short red hair, the nicest of them, 'it's just that you can't be with Aryans. You're Jews and you have to be with Jewish children, in a Jewish school, with Jewish teachers.'

Mariska has gone from our house. I've done all I can not to cry and I've succeeded. She was with us for so many years. She was my nanny and a mother to me too. She held me in her arms when I was little. The law says Jews can't keep Aryans as domestic servants. Mariska cried her eyes out. Mother gave her a ring with a precious stone which consoled her a bit. Before she left she made me the bilberry tart I like so much. She was crying while she beat the eggs. I think I ate Mariska's tears with the cream. Why aren't you here? I so much need to talk to you. To tell you I don't understand what's happening to us, I'm so frightened I can't sleep at night. Papà says we should go back to Florence. But he does nothing to get tickets, or to ask for our passports which they've taken away. Anyhow I don't think they'd give them back. They're Jewish passports. Mamma's more of an optimist, more self-confident. She wraps herself in her fur coat, puts on a worried frown and says we're more patriotic than they are, that her father was a general and the Emperor Franz Josef in person pinned a medal on his chest after he lost an arm in the battle of the Kolubara in Serbia, under the command of General Potiorek on 25 November 1914. 'What can they do to us? Are we or are we not Austrians? We've been Austrian for longer than any of them,' Mamma states, most of all, it seems, to convince herself. Meanwhile on the radio we hear Hitler's voice thundering and screaming that all Jews are communists and Bolsheviks, that the Jews are secretly arranging to hand over Austria and Germany to the Soviets, and at the same time conspiring with the world's great international bankers to accumulate in their own bank accounts all the money that belongs to honest citizens.

But was this really Emanuele writing? So grown up, so wise and serious. He had always been a studious child, with an adult mind, meticulous in his use of language, but now he seemed to have grown more mature. Nearly two years had passed since he left and he would certainly have needed to grow up quickly to understand and face up to what was happening in his country. If only he had stayed behind in Rifredi with his father, leaving the beautiful Thelma to set off in her furs by herself for the house on Schulerstrasse! He would be twenty-eight now. Who knows what he might be like? And would she recognise him if she saw him?

We're in Auschwitz, Amara tells herself, we're here to find out about Emanuele, stick to the point! She has lost herself in a letter. One of those letters she is never without, that she carries folded in her bag as her most precious possessions. Her feet move forward slowly, almost unconsciously, as if familiar with these corridors, as if she has walked here before.

Now Amara is in Hall number 5, facing a confused disordered mountain of prostheses: wooden legs, iron joints, halters, elastic belts, and hands made from ceramics, chalk and cork. Made-to-measure prostheses could hardly be of much use to the Nazis. They couldn't sell them as they could hair, but nonetheless prostheses had to be detached from the bodies and piled up to await orders from Berlin. To be accepted by death, even a mutilated corpse had to be stripped of all its possessions. Many came from soldiers wounded in the First World War when they had fought against Germany's enemies in the name of a country that now brutally tore away their prostheses as it sent them to be butchered. Certainly Frau Orenstein had some reason to be proud of her furs when she remembered that her father had received a medal from the Emperor. Emanuele's grandfather, Georg Fink, had climbed down alone under a bridge to disable an explosive just before it went off. In doing so he had lost an arm. Emanuele had told her the story several times: when he was little he had been fascinated by that empty sleeve that, always tidy and ironed, had been kept elegantly tucked into a jacket pocket. 'Grandfather, tell me the story of the bridge,' he would ask, and the old man would begin: 'We knew it had been mined, but we had to get across the river. No one dared to go and search for the mines because there were snipers watching. I waited for night. Then dressed entirely in black I climbed down under the bridge. The iron was smooth and slippery, and I was in constant danger of falling into the water from a height of sixty metres. I doubt I would have survived. But I was so quiet the snipers never heard me. Alone with a small pocket torch in my mouth. I could see where the TNT was rigged up, its cords not as thick as I had feared. Who would have thought it possible to climb all that way down! Directly above the dark water, on a starless night. Luckily I'd done a lot of rock climbing when I was young. I was wearing a sling to keep my hands free. I took my knife and, sweating and swearing, I cut the cords, releasing the dynamite which fell into the river. The moment it hit the water it exploded with a great roar. I felt something hit my arm, but paid no attention at the time. I managed to get back to my post safe and in one piece. Our men took advantage of the confusion caused by the explosion and firing of guns and crossed the bridge. Unfortunately my wound was infected causing gangrene and they had to cut off my arm.' Emanuele watched him with wide-open eyes. Was that heroism? Would he too be capable of doing something like that?

7

'The Nazis made full use of everything they could extract from the Jews, just as people do with pigs: their poor gassed, hanged or poisoned bodies were not thrown away until they had been stripped of clothes, shoes, watches, hair, gold teeth, prostheses, and sometimes even their skin, as is said to have happened in Buchenwald.' So says a survivor in a booklet Amara is reading in the camp bookshop.

All that remained was sad bones of no value. And even these were burned so as to leave no evidence. Besides, burying them would have caused more work and more trouble. The strength of young prisoners was needed for heavy work like cutting firewood, building huts, pulling the dead from the gas ovens and stripping the bodies of their possessions both natural and artificial. A few privileged prisoners, trained in some useful trade, worked on those poor tortured bodies: with skilled movements they would extract gold teeth, cleaning them of organic material and throwing them into bucketfuls of formalin. Later they pulled out the disinfected gold, melted it over small burners kept permanently alight and formed it into small rectangular bars that still preserve something of the hastily improvised work of those amateur goldsmiths who had invented a trade for themselves to escape the gas chambers and mass shootings. Unaware, or discovering too late, that they themselves must in any case meet the same end as witnesses of this infamy. Each gold bar was individually checked by the SS before they were carefully packed in cardboard boxes and sent to Berlin.

Vienna. December '41

Dear Amara, Papà no longer knots his tie. He says this is no time for ties. The roads are full of SS. The walls are plastered with gigantic drawings of Jews whose noses can piss into their mouths and whose hands are crammed with money. They say the Jews are busy destroying the country and must be hunted down. They are, we are, the greatest threat to our own country. There are murderous bloodthirsty Jews behind every street-corner, and if it weren't for Hitler's wonderful police they would be laying waste to the country and killing every living Austrian. Mamma laughs and says what stupid nonsense. 'We're more Austrian than they are, never forget your grandfather lost his arm in the First World War. Remember his parents were already living in this city before the goyim arrived from the southern provinces.' 'Mamma, you're always going on about the same things!' I tell her. She just shrugs her shoulders. She's so convinced of her patriotic immunity that she never stops making plans for the future. Papà seems more worried. They've taken over his firm's offices. And now it seems even the factory in Rifredi has been lost. Mamma says we'll be able to go back to Florence. I'd be happy to, but Papà daren't go and ask for permits, the thought of presenting himself to the police terrifies him. What if they stop him and arrest him just because he wants to go? A good patriot never leaves his country in time of war. But I'm not that Jew with a beaked nose and little snakes of dishevelled hair on a pear-shaped head. I don't have those claw-like hands that grab the necks of poor Austrians and squeeze and squeeze as if throttling hens. I'm a boy shivering in my shorts and with chilblains on my heels, like every other Austrian forced by the war to sleep and study in an icy-cold home. I am the Emanuele you know and they don't know. I have large hands red with cold, a little round nose and straight blond hair; and even if my arms are a little longer than most that doesn't mean I want to grab people by the shoulders and slam them against a wall. All I want for my hands is to be able to squeeze yours, and feel your breath on my closed eyes, and know you are close to me, darling Amara, why have we been separated? I don't understand it, I never will understand it...

Another great empty room. Another pile of objects: suitcases this time: little ones, big ones, cardboard ones, leather ones, suitcases with names on them: Klara Fochman, Vienna 1942; Peter Eisler, Berlin 1943; Maria Kafka, Prague 1943; Hanna Furs, Amsterdam 1942, and so on. Carried from all over Europe by men and women who didn't know they were heading for their last journey. Imagine the care with which they must have packed their precious possessions into those cases, trying to work out how to save them from greedy hands. Today, empty and battered, the suitcases simply seem bored with those long ago plans. Tiny plans, admittedly, in an age of mass plunder and humiliation, but still believing in a future of work, no matter how difficult and spartan. No one packs a case to go to the cemetery. What these suitcases prove is the deceit practised on millions of trusting people who could never believe that anyone would ever want to remove their faces from the earth and even obliterate their very names, trampling on their bodies and casting them for ever into the great oblivion of history. There were no credible reasons for it. It was simply implausible.

The Nazis were masters at creating make-believe life, precisely when preparing their biggest death projects. Next to the so-called little white house, a gas chamber camouflaged as a shower, stood a lorry with a red cross on it to reassure the prisoners as they queued up for death. And what can one say of that fictive bathhouse. 'Undress and leave your clothes here,' the prisoners would be told. And naked, embarrassed, each reaching for a humble piece of soap, they would trust those reassuring words, forcing themselves to trust, silencing their deepest forebodings, calming their fears as they faced those icy but clean and fragrant officials in their impeccable uniforms, as they directed the children, the old and the sick to the gas chamber.

'Emanuele has had a fall from the third floor. Luckily he landed in the black nightshade bush. Scratched all over but hasn't broken a single bone.' 'Lucky for him. He has more lives than a cat.' 'I'll wring his neck. One of these days there'll be an end to those wings.' 'Passionately interested in flying, we just have to accept it.' 'I'll give him flying!' 'His father's given him a beating, to add to the scratches and bruises he already has.' 'His mother's been crying like a sucking calf.' 'Gave him a kick as well.' 'Who did? Signor Karl Orenstein, that perfect gentleman who when it's raining pulls his trousers a bit higher and fastens them at the ankles?' 'Signor Orenstein has beaten his only son.' 'And even Emanuele's little friend, that awful Maria Amara, has been in trouble.' 'Really? Why?' 'Didn't you know? The two of them were planning to fly off together from the top of the fifteenth-century tower in Via Maffia.' 'In a plane, I hope.' 'No, on wings made of rags and paper fixed to a wooden frame.' 'Mad, both of them.' 'They're always together. No one can keep them apart. When Signor Orenstein locked the boy up in his room, he escaped through the window and rushed out to her. And his room's on the third floor.' 'Wings again?' 'No, this time he climbed down the drainpipe.' 'Utterly mad! Good-looking boy, though. Like a cherub with that fair hair and shining black eyes.' 'You'd never know he was a Jew.' 'Is she Jewish too?' 'No, she's just in love.' 'Even children fall in love.'

Amara walks on, down icy corridors. 'Through me you come into the grieving city. Through me you come among the lost people.' Her mind trips on these words that slip from her memory like the snaking tendrils of an obstinate creeping plant.

And what's this that seems to be shining and dancing before her like a great mass of dragonflies with vibrating wings. Thousands and thousands of spectacles, sunglasses, glasses for the short-sighted and the long-sighted, with aluminium or copper or Bakelite frames. Any gold ones had already been taken away and melted down.

How would short-sighted people have known where to put their feet when their glasses were taken from them? Or did they let people go into the shower in their glasses, and only rip them off after they were dead? When their eyes were no longer aware of the details of the misery that surrounded them. Eyes blinded and lost. Emanuele sometimes wore glasses, too. But would she ever be able to recognise his glasses in that shimmering, glittering heap? Walking eyes, dancing eyes, idling eyes, eyes raised to look at a mouth or an absent smile. They have all disappeared, those smiles. The mouths are closed, the corners of their lips turned down. And the eyes that saw those grimaces; perhaps they understood or perhaps they didn't. Times had changed; one had to adapt to a new reality. How could those soldiers, always so elegant and smart, keep their purpose in view: to slaughter every single person, down to the last child? Some of them had decent faces, like good family men. And indeed that was what they were. Along the road to Birkenau their wives and children were at home waiting for them behind embroidered curtains. And when they came home in the evening after doing their duty as slaughterers, the men would bend smiling over those children.

Amara sits in front of the ruins of one of the gas chambers. The Nazis blew it up before they left. The crumbling and collapsed roof is in a large room in which one can still see concrete walls marked with blue with a few pipes sticking out of them.

The book lying open on her lap has an eloquent photograph of hundreds of naked people on their way to the deadly bathhouse that is now lying smashed and motionless before her. The only sign of life is a lizard warming itself in the sun.

Someone is sitting next to her. How did she not hear him arrive?

'I wanted to see you ...'

Amara turns and recognises Emanuele's dark, intense eyes.

'So you survived!'

'I've thought so much about you.'

'Me too.'

But when she looks more closely she sees it's not the Emanuele she knew. The boy sitting on the stone beside her is a very thin child with furrowed hands and prominent veins. In fact, he's not even a child. More like a decrepit old man who has spent a lifetime digging and carrying heavy weights. He has stooping shoulders, eyes surrounded by wrinkles, rotten teeth that shift in his mouth and nails edged with black. Amara's heart tightens and contracts into an insubstantial lump.

'How did you survive, Emanuele, and why did you stop writing?'

'I had no pen or pencil.'

'And your mother?'

'I cannot separate myself from the words. They are like stones fastened to my ankles that I must drag with me. Listen.'

'I'm listening.'

'Now please undress and be careful to remember the number of the hook where you hang your clothes or you won't be able to find them again ... A soft voice speaking. There was nothing to alarm us and we were ready to trust that voice. After the shower there will be hot tea and fresh bread for everyone ... But on going into the shower please make sure you leave everything behind; if you've forgotten a ring or a little chain, put them here on this table near your clothes. You'll get everything back after your shower. Here's some soap, a piece for everyone; wash well, you are all filthy from your journey ... Gently, almost ceremoniously, they guided us politely towards the shower hall ... Mamma was smiling as we went in. I haven't washed for eight days, Emanuele dear, I really do need a shower, after that train without food or drink, sleeping on top of each other on that wooden floor, with the stink of shit ... Mamma was singing happily, she was Thelma Fink von Orenstein, singing as brainlessly as a goldfinch.'

'And you?'

'I noticed a disturbing smell. I couldn't relax. A smell I'd never smelled before but which seemed familiar all the same ... Mutti, what's this disgusting smell? We're all so dirty ... we have to wash ... don't you understand, they're giving us all a cup of hot tea afterwards? They're really nice. In my opinion, these men in the camp are clearly superior to the ones on the train, a different brand of SS altogether ... No sooner had we got off the train than they took us to the shower, an excellent idea, don't you agree? Let's hope the water's really hot ... I've never longed so much for a nice hot shower.

'But I knew it wasn't human filth I was smelling. It was some nauseous chemical related to that big room, something that made me think of bitter almonds gone rotten. The walls were impregnated with it. I didn't want to go in, I didn't want to go into that room with its wet, slippery floor. But I did go in, Amara, I did go in with her pulling my wrist as she sang. What a dreamy, absent-minded Mamma I have! They know it, she was saying, they know I'm the daughter of a general who lost his arm fighting for our country in the famous battle of the Kolubara in Serbia, they know that, they know everything, these people. She kept repeating it. She was still convinced, as we headed for the showers accompanied by that revolting smell, that she was privileged and would be respected, she really believed it, because her father had fought for Austria and lost an arm so our soldiers could cross the bridge over the Kolubara. The Emperor himself had pinned a medal to his chest and called him a hero. Even if in the end the Austrians had lost the battle and been forced to abandon the town of Ljig.

'When they bolted the doors noisily from the outside someone started yelling. Why are they locking the doors like that? And what's this horrible smell? But Mamma didn't worry. So much fuss about a shower! She encouraged everyone: you'll see how good we'll feel when we're under the water! ... But this blessed water isn't coming, it's not coming! I said, and I could see her turning the soap in her hand, rubbing it on her stomach behind me. She was hiding behind me out of embarrassment because she was naked. Everyone was naked there, old people, women and children. But why were there no young people there, where were they? Should we not have been suspicious that among all those bodies there was not a single pair of strong muscular legs to be seen, no head

— 36 —

of young hair, no calloused hard-working young hand? Only old people who found it difficult to stand, all twisted and swollen and tormented by hunger and thirst. And mothers, young like mine, each with a child or two. It was their job to reassure their children, and the children's job to reassure their mothers. My mother held me close tenderly, partly to hide her nudity and partly to reassure herself that we were still together. They had not separated us and this gave her a peaceful feeling.

'Suddenly the light went out and a cry of terror went up. Some narrow slits in the ceiling opened and a hissing could be heard, a disquieting rustle. Here's the water cried my mother happily, turning up her face to be hit by a shower of cold sand. My simple Mutti thought it was water. Good. Now we could begin soaping ourselves. But the sand raining from the ceiling no sooner hit the wet floor than it began to fizz and dance about. Meanwhile the light had come on again. Something strange was happening! When the bluish grains touched the ground they released blue bubbles that rose in a transparent cloud. A beautiful sight. But when it slipped up nostrils and between lips it made people cough, then spit, then vomit and then ... They struggled violently as they tried to climb, to get away from the rising clouds, to reach the iron mouths that seemed to be oozing water. Bewildered, Mamma looked around in astonishment. But only for a second. Then she fell to the floor, dragging me down with her. I couldn't shout, I had no breath. I clung to her; I wanted to say: Mutti, what's happening, but I couldn't speak, my voice had gone. My throat was tied in a knot. I was suffocating. Oh for a drop of water, just one drop, one single drop, and I licked the metal pipe sticking from the wall close to my cheek. I was immediately overwhelmed by another blue cloud, light and translucent. Then another and another. The fizzing had stopped but the bodies were still there, suddenly gigantic and very white, writhing and twisting. Those still on their feet fell, those still breathing began to wheeze and rattle. Silence had descended like a snow of ice on us all. Nothing but that writhing on the floor. Gigantic feet and huge hands near my eyes. Gaping mouths and stiff necks with bulging veins. I no longer thought of breathing. Only my eyes still existed. Those naked bodies were too shocking, too exposed, too silent. Like an ancient sacred dance with long naked legs instead of heads and fingers instead of hair, fingers revolving in silence. In all that whiteness there was only one colour: red ears. I don't know why the ears were so red, like small poppies growing from white flesh. They were so beautiful, those ears. I could not help gazing at them. I was utterly lucid. I could see children clinging to their mothers, making single bodies with many legs and many heads. The tiniest infants were trying to push their way back into the safety of their mothers' wombs, pushing and pushing like newborn puppies trying to get milk from the teats of an elderly bitch. A completely bald old gentleman was lying on his back a few inches from my head, his open mouth shooting out red fire. My mother looked surprised. I could feel her arm round my neck. Let her take me with her, I thought, let her drag me wherever she goes, I want to be with her. And she never let go, not even when she stopped breathing. Someone fell on top of me. Feet were beating on my side like a drum. My small stomach swelled and swelled like a football, it was incredible how it could keep swelling. Might I even have a child in my belly? But could it ever be born alive? Luckily Mamma hadn't had time to discover the trap. She had breathed in the gas rising from the floor so eagerly she had lost consciousness at once. I was happy for her. I looked at her face again: it was pale and tender; her eyes closed and her lips parted in a gentle smile. I wanted to kiss her, say a last goodbye and repeat the prayers people say for the dead but I fell head downwards.'

Amara reached out to squeeze the boy's wrist but her fingers met warm stone. She shuddered. 'Emanuele!' she whispered. The only thing occasionally moving anywhere near her was the lizard as it tried to find more sun.

8

'You move, please? With signorina in middle no can photograph ruins.' A guide comes up followed by a little group of visitors. Amara sees from their faces that she is in their way. She is sitting among the ruins of Gas Chamber number 3. But she can't make herself move. She sees the group with blind eyes. She hears the guide's voice explaining: 'Here shower room, really gas chamber. Nazis put bomb before they going away. But only part fall down. You see roof very broken? But walls still standing. Wait peacefully water. But no water, instead gas grains drop from roof touch wet floor become gas, poison. Zyklon B, death certain, in maybe eight, ten minutes. Death sure. And they all dead, all.'

Amara struggles to her feet, her head spinning like a top. She is still looking for the man who has just been talking to her, the person who claimed to be Emanuele. But only the tourists crowd round the guide who continues to explain: 'Forty thousands Italians deported, thirty-two thousands political and military and eight thousands Jews, only three thousands live. Less than ten per cent.'

You can tell from a mile off that they are Italians, from the disorganised and uncoordinated way they move, and the trouble the Polish guide is having trying to keep them together, constantly chasing some young man or elderly lady who has moved off to take photographs without listening to instructions. For several years now such groups have been able to come directly from Italy by bus.

'Now, signorina, follow the others, please!'

He has mistaken her for one of his party. Amara obeys automatically. The man has a pleasant voice despite his awkward, comic Italian. The group moves from place to place through Auschwitz and she goes with them.

The Polish guide, guardian of the dead, seems more real than anything else in the camp, with the warm crosswind seeming to sweep aside the ghosts like scraps of paper. 'Here: gypsy zone. Here: hospital men prisoners. Here, name Mexico, transit camp for Jewish women.'

Amara is holding a booklet published by the camp management with large reproductions of period photographs: a line of naked women, their flesh white with the pallor of skin stripped of clothing in winter. She has never before seen nudity like this. A nudity that in revealing itself terminal has become gentle, transparent and mute. The women's heads are shrunk into their shoulders and their backs hunched as they try to hide their sex under their hands. The damned moving meekly to final judgement though they know themselves innocent. They are branded with numbers that fix their destiny as martyrs. Their crime is that they are alive, that they are themselves and exist. Even if they never listened to the serpent or bit into the apple of temptation, they must now undergo the humiliation of divine rejection. For ever, say those curving backs, for ever. But why?

'Here SS homes,' says the guide, lifting his hand. Humble little houses though with some pretension to elegance. Lace-edged curtains carefully hung to form two waves in the middle, blue and white shutters. In the little front gardens daisies struggle with rubble and coarse grass.

'Here storehouse for things stolen from Jews, name Canada.' This was where Amara had seen the mountains of shoes, the piles of cases, the masses of glasses, the heaps of prostheses. She decides to go back into Canada: perhaps first time round her attention was so distracted by the unexpectedness of it that she failed to make a proper check of the huge number of dusty abandoned suitcases. Would she have been able to recognise Emanuele's? Of course she would; she had seen it often enough on top of the wardrobe in his room. Faded leather with brass bosses and a shiny hook-shaped fastening whose small tongue was made of silver-coloured metal. The lid stamped E and O in gold.

But she has hardly taken a step before the fatherly Pole intervenes: 'No, signorina, this way, please.' So she turns back, without even knowing why.

'Here platform for selection. If you young, can work, this way; if you old, child, mother with children, that way, to gas. Here dead bodies burned. When too many deads and ovens full. Then more ovens made, but later.' He shows a photograph of corpses hurled at random into a ditch. The tangled limbs make it impossible to tell one body from another. Not even an orgy could entwine legs, arms, heads and pelvises like that. They look strikingly different from the other inmates, from those circulating like spectres in pyjamas looking for something to eat or queuing for roll call early in the morning. The dead are still full and firm, with prominent muscles. They were gassed at once on arrival and it is hard to know whether to grieve over their abrupt extinction or to rejoice that they were spared the torture of camp life.

Vienna. January '42

Dear Amara, yesterday we opened the door to find two servants in uniform, complete with aprons. 'We've come to clean the house for the new owners,' they said. My mother, always polite, offered them coffee. 'There must be some misunderstanding,' she told them, and added, 'there really must have been a misunderstanding; this is our house, my father bought it before I was born.' 'But now it has been assigned to Consul Schumacher and his family.' 'Please, madam, don't insist, we'll sort it all out, you'll see.' 'Aren't you Jews by the name of Orenstein?' 'Yes, but Austrians first and foremost, my father lost an arm in the Battle of the Kolubara during the First World War and the Emperor himself pinned a medal on his chest.' 'Your house has been requisitioned, here are the papers. You must move out by tomorrow. We start cleaning now.'

My mother made telephone calls in all directions but couldn't reach any of her friends. Only an employee at the department of social administration who told her abruptly that her house had been requisitioned under the new anti-Jewish laws and assigned to an Aryan family by the name of Schumacher.

'Please come back tomorrow,' said my mother very politely. 'You will find the house clean.' The woman made a sign to her assistant and they left. Soon after the doorbell rang again. This time it was an SS squad. They searched the house saying they were looking for arms. Of course there were no arms. But when they left they took with them all my mother's silver, jewellery and furs, an eighteenth-century Venetian mirror and a nineteenth-century English silver teapot.

By now Amara knows nearly all Emanuele's letters by heart. The words of her little lover echo in her mind, his voice gradually growing more dry and desolate.

'This, first gas chamber. This, second gas chamber. Here,

crematoriums one, two, three, four, five. Bodies gassed by pipe here for burning. Body in, smoke and ashes come out. One load every half hour. Here toilets and baths.' The guide continues relentlessly, taking them rapidly from one part of the camp to another.

Łódź ghetto. February '42

They knocked on the door of our house in Vienna at four in the morning. Gave us an hour to pack our bags. One case each, not more than three in all. But where are we going? No answer. They were impatient and bad-tempered. Papà and Mamma began arguing about what to put in the suitcases. Papà wanted to fill them with food. Mamma with clothes: rugs, warm coats. Her furs, jewels and money had already been taken by the other SS. When they came back after an hour we weren't ready and they started shouting. Finally we left all loaded up; my father with a valuable mat under his arm and my mother with two cashmere jackets. But at the main door they took everything from us except the three cases. We were loaded onto a lorry and then a train. We had no idea where they were taking us. Four nights of hell in an armoured cattle-truck together with about a hundred other Austrian Jews and nothing to eat or drink. Luckily we'd brought some sausages and apples with us. My father kept saying: You see? You see I was right to bring food? We ate a sausage and an apple each, keeping the rest for later. But when we went to get more, Papà's case was empty. One of those starving people had stolen the lot. Even the Prague ham, the hardboiled eggs, the bilberry liqueur and the biscuits. We were parched with thirst. We arrived dirty and thirsty. Where? At the Łódź ghetto, another Austrian told us in a whisper. Why there particularly? No answer. Only my mother kept asking questions and protesting. My father seemed more dead than alive. They assigned us to a small room in a crumbling building, on the second floor, in an apartment where four families were already living. Only one kitchen. One bath for everyone. Mamma started again on her long lament about her father having won a gold medal for military valour in the Battle of the Kolubara, but no one listened.

The only thing that matters here is survival. Thousands of Jews are wandering about searching for work and food. They start at five in the morning. Any job, no matter how badly paid, can help to buy bread. They are pale and have difficulty walking. Even the young ones. 'When your face and your feet start swelling, you know you're going to die,' a boy called Stefan, to whom I had given a sweater for two kilos of potatoes, unexpectedly told me. Bread, said Stefan, costs twenty-five złotys a kilo. But they also accept marks which are worth twice as much as złotys. I'm writing to you with a pencil I stole from the directors' office where Mamma dragged me while she was going on about it all being a misunderstanding and that we ought not to be here. This is how I met Rumkowski, the leader of the ghetto, a strong man with glasses and a hat. Compared to the others we see around, hunchbacks with tuberculosis and legs reduced to sticks, he looks like a pasha. He too was forced to listen to the story of grandfather Georg Fink and the medal for military valour pinned to his chest by the Emperor. He didn't bat an eyelid. But he then said very coldly that in the Łódź ghetto all are equal, that no one has any special privileges and that everyone has to work to earn the złotys they need to survive. Then he asked politely, 'What skills do you have, madam?' Mamma was so offended she couldn't answer. But does she have any particular skills at all? Mr Rumkowski advised her to look for work in the textile factory where there are still a few places left for women, then shut the door on us.

Łódź ghetto. March '42

A month has passed, I'm sorry, I couldn't find any paper to write on. Now in our little room we also have Uncle Eduard, goodness knows how he came to end up with us. I've found a job in a carpenter's shop. There's always someone who wants a bedhead made into a table, or a shutter into a bench. Mamma didn't go to the factory to begin with. But after starving for two weeks she made up her mind. Father is in bed with a fever. We hope it isn't typhus. Lots of illnesses go around in the ghetto. Uncle Eduard hasn't found any work. Four of us living in one small room is hell. I sleep on the floor on a shabby little mattress so short my legs stick out, Papà and Mamma make the best of a rickety sofa with exposed springs and Uncle Eduard spends the night on a camp bed. We do have a cooker but often there's no gas. Worse still, there's nothing to cook. The potatoes only lasted a few days. Now we're waiting for Mamma's first monthly pay packet which will give us thirty złotys to buy a little meat and some sugar for our tea. We still have half a jar of sugar left. The only thing they didn't steal from Papà's suitcase on the train. I earn five złotys a day. Butter costs twelve złotys, meat forty-five złotys a kilo. Today the temperature sank to seven degrees below zero. I curse myself for giving away my warmest sweater for two kilos of potatoes. I won't say I wish you were here with me. That would be blasphemy. But sometimes at night I dream I'm in Florence in our tree, filling my stomach with cherries. Ciao, Emanuele.

9

Uncle Eduard hides the pieces of bread Mamma and I steal under the cover on his camp bed. Mutti doesn't complain, but says the war will be over in a few months. We just have to stick it out. Every morning at six she walks to the textile and uniform factory on Drewnowska Street. She puts on her apron and starts her sewing machine. Mamma is showing a courage I never expected of her. But Papà seems desperate. He can't get over the fact he ever left Rifredi. He spends half his time in bed. Uncle Eduard was deported on the same train as us and we never knew. He wanders about the ghetto picking up cigarette-ends. But he says there are no longer many to find. People have no money for cigarettes. What most upsets me is losing my books. I used to have more than a hundred. Most got left behind in the house at Schulerstrasse in Vienna. I only managed to keep the three or four I threw into my suitcase at the last minute. Picked up at random. Now I read them again and again. Dickens' *Great Expectations*, *Pinocchio* and *The Sorrows of Young Werther*.

Łódź ghetto. March '42

Dear Amara. Today my father came home with three passports bought from forgers. He used the last of our hidden money to buy them. Mamma screamed at him that he was mad. He's convinced we'll be able to use them to get out of the ghetto and go to America. But everyone knows all passports have been cancelled and no one is allowed to leave the Łódź ghetto for any reason. With or without a passport. Uncle Eduard is 'going off his head' as Mamma puts it. He collects fag-ends in the city and buries them under a loose floorboard. The other day he killed a mouse and said: you lot can eat this. I'll stick to pork.' But there aren't any pigs round here. The only little pig in this house is made of pottery and has a slot in its back for coins but it's empty now and its gentle sugary pink face looks over at the window with a disheartened expression. 'He's been driven mad by fear,' says my father, teasing him. But Uncle Eduard doesn't smile. 'We'll all end up dead, all of us dead!' he keeps shouting as he collects crumbs of bread round the house, hiding them in his pockets. The other day my mother sniffed the air and asked, 'What's this stink?' Then she discovered it was half a turnip rotting under Uncle Eduard's camp bed and giving off an unbearable stench.

It's snowing. It's cold. I sleep in my coat. Mamma looks like a whale, wearing all the clothes, both summer and winter ones, that she brought with her, three pairs of thick socks, and a now almost hairless fox muff that she wears on one arm even while cooking. The butter's finished. Lard costs ten złotys and we can't afford it. My father has run out of tobacco for his pipe. He's started smoking birch leaves which makes a nice smell in the house. But it also makes him cough like a consumptive.

Yesterday I saw two SS men beating up a boy who had no yellow star on his coat collar. The boy showed them that he had his star sewn in full view on the lapel of his jacket, which he was wearing under his coat. But they went on hitting his head just the same. The boy was holding his head in his hands. One ear began spurting blood which stained the snow all round. A very thin and decrepit dog came from God knows where and began licking the blood up as though it were redcurrant syrup.

Amara tries to imagine Emanuele in that dirty and overcrowded ghetto in Łódź, with the snow falling. She has always loved snow. It softens and refines houses and countryside. But what can it have been like in that dirty and overcrowded ghetto?

Łódź. March '42

I've found some paper. I swapped a silk handkerchief of Mamma's for an exercise book. Writing to you is like writing to the whole world. But I've no money for a stamp. And in any case I don't know if the post will take letters sent abroad. When we first came to the ghetto letters did go off. And sometimes they arrived, even if half blocked out. But not now, no longer. We're shut in, closed in a trap. But I'm writing to you all the same. One day you'll read the letters I'm writing in this exercise book. Or at least I hope so. The ghetto's getting more and more crowded. More Jews are arriving, some from Holland, some from Hungary. Bringing with them the odd bundle, or suitcases tied with string. Many have no shoes, just hungry eyes. An organisation here looks after them. Gives them shelter and something to eat. But only for the first few days, after that they have to fend for themselves, find some workshop to employ them so they can earn the złotys they need to buy a little bread and margarine or barley coffee and sugar which today costs forty złotys a kilo. Yesterday my mother gave her gold wedding ring for three pig's feet and two kilos of potatoes. When Papà heard they are deporting those without work, he too started looking for something to do. Yesterday nothing, but today he helped carry bricks for a bricklayer with frostbitten hands. Luckily he still has his pigskin gloves and carried bricks all day for seven złotys.

I've lost my job at the carpenter's. There are too many of you, said the manager. There are fifteen of us boys and he can't afford to pay us all. All the same, he let us have a portion of soup at midday. I don't want to think my family have been stupid. I don't want to think that. But I do think it sometimes, even if I don't want to. The stupid patriotic idea of returning to Nazi Vienna when everyone else was trying to get away from it. Why am I not with you now? I see our cherry tree again, I remember our games, I can feel your hand again in mine. The thought of you distracts me and helps to keep me going.

Łódź. April '42

Dear Amara. I'm writing to you from the shelter in the cellar of our block. There are hundreds of us crushed in here. Someone is singing a mournful dirge. A child is crying. Shots can be heard from far away. The good thing about a crowd is that it creates heat. It's warmer here than in the flat. I'm writing by the wavering smoky light of an oil lamp. The pencil is still working. My letter is in this exercise book. It'll be easier to write your name and your address on it and stuff it into a hole in the wall I recently discovered. Maybe it had something to do with the chimney of a stove that's no longer here. It had been stopped up with a piece of wood and whitewashed over. But I managed to get it open with a penknife. I'll leave my memories there for you, if we don't manage to get out alive. Otherwise, if the war ends in a few months, I'll bring it to you myself. How wonderful it would be to hug you again! An epidemic of typhus has broken out in the ghetto. There's no medicine and people are dying of fever. It's a miracle none of us is ill. Mother says all you need is to keep a pad soaked in vinegar between your lips. I'm not going to be able to stand the stink of vinegar much longer. Yesterday my father found some eggs for sale at a fair price. He brought them for my mother as a present, very proud of himself. How small and light they are! she cried. When she opened them she found nothing inside. Someone had pierced them with a needle and sucked out the contents and then sold them like this, empty. If you looked closely you could see the holes made by the needle, stopped up with transparent wax. My mother wept in despair. Those eggs had been bought with my złotys. Three days' work gone up in smoke.

Łódź. April '42

Dear Amara. I've started working at the carpenter's again. Every day more lorries arrive and pull up panting in the middle of the street. The SS grab whoever they see and make them queue up with others. Then they make a selection. They push the old, the ill and the infirm into the lorry and take them away. They let the others go, the young ones, especially if they're in work. It's said those in the lorries are taken to a camp and killed by a blow to the head after being forced to dig a ditch for their own grave. No one knows for sure because no one has ever come back from these expeditions. The story came from a Jewish cook who heard the SS talking about it while they were having a meal after an 'action'.

Yesterday I saw an old man refuse to get into a lorry with the others, so they tied his hands and feet and attached him with a hook to the lorry which set off at high speed with his body bumping and rolling behind. It made a strange noise like the rattling of an empty box. You know, I can't dream any more. What d'you think it means when you can't dream any more? I wake in the morning with my tongue burning in my mouth. I'm hungry, that's all I can think about. The bricklayer my father worked for has been taken away too. His hands were covered with sores. He kept them wrapped in two filthy rags. He was about thirty years old, so he told me, but he looked fifty. He had grown old suddenly, his neck wrinkled and his hands covered with ulcers. The Nazis grabbed him and pulled him towards a lorry. He shouted that he could still work, that his hands were only bleeding temporarily, that in a couple of days he'd be able to start working with bricks again, but they took no notice and lifted him bodily onto the lorry. I was watching from the window. I couldn't feel the compassion I would have expected to feel. In fact, I felt nothing at all. Perhaps this is the beginning of the great change. I am in the process of being transformed into a human being made of stone. Stone eyes, a stone brain, a stone tongue and even a stone heart. Even my love for you is becoming cold and mineral. Another stone in the little cemetery of memory. I must say a prayer.

How can that stone child have survived in that ghetto? Would he have had the strength to survive? Was turning to stone a way of holding on? And what if, after all, he had made it? A boy has his life before him. And it isn't easy to break a stone.

Łódź

Dear Amara, one day the ghetto fills with people and the next it's empty again.

They arrive in their thousands, some in good shape, from towns and cities newly conquered by the Führer. Many, already tried and tested, thin and with their stomachs full of parasites, come from other ghettoes. But they soon disappear. The SS bring their lorries every day, collect two or three hundred people and take them away. No more is heard of them. So when people hear the engines of the lorries making their way along the streets, they start running away. But the SS push their way into the houses and grab the children and the old. A monster who specially loves children. Do you remember when we used to read *Tom Thumb*? This is the great ogre, greedy for little people. In order to keep in condition he needs to swallow at least a hundred a day. And to make sure they'll be good about being eaten, and not shout or wriggle too much, he strokes their heads and gives them big friendly smiles and talks to them in a reassuring voice: now take off your little hats, no need for shelter, it's warm here even though there's snow outside; it's nice and warm in here. No, take off your little coats, you don't need them. There, that's right. Take off your shoes too and come to me. And the moment they get close, whoomph! he crams them into his mouth five at a time. And if at this point they start kicking what does he do? He crushes their bones with his teeth and swallows them at a single gulp. Little children are so tender!

I am a little stone man now, watching petrified from my window. My mother fusses behind me, but she doesn't bother me. Except now and then when I beg her not to move so much because she's causing a cold draught. She says Uncle Eduard was right, they're going to kill us all. Or we'll starve to death, like our neighbour Chaim Bobrowski who knew how to play the violin like a king. His feet and face swelled up till he could hardly walk. But he dragged himself to work just the same, his shoes full of holes, so as not to miss his soup ration. Then one morning he fell to the ground. No one stopped. No one picked him up. When someone dies, they die. We know the gravediggers will come in the evening and take the body to the cemetery. Every day my father risks his life trying to get a pass. He runs this way and that with the forged passports in his underclothes trying to find a way out. A mouse in a cage. I know we'll never reach America as he hopes. He paid so much for those passports but they'll end up like the eggs, empty and useless, fit only to throw away. But he's obstinate. Now all he has left is a single valuable earring of my mother's, hidden inside a pillowcase. An earring with precious stones with which he hopes to bribe someone to let us through, maybe at night, to make our way to the station. Two mornings ago they took Uncle Eduard away. He went out to look for a piece of coal. It was early in the morning and nobody seemed to be about. He had often done this. He thought he was safe because no lorries could be heard anywhere near. But there was one round the corner with its engine switched off and as soon as they saw him they told him to get in. He tried to run away but two bursts of gunfire landed at his feet. He wasn't hit but he stopped and climbed into the lorry with a heavy heart. Since then we've heard nothing. Stefan who lives in the corner house told us about it.

10

Kraków. Returning absent-mindedly to the Hotel Wawel, Amara doesn't see the partly rolled carpet, trips and crashes to the floor. A young porter with red hair runs to her rescue. 'Are you all right? Sorry about the carpet, we were just moving it out of the way.' Then she hears him shouting at a boy in trousers that are too big for him bargaining over other rolled-up carpets piled on a hoist.

'There's a letter for you,' says the porter after checking that she hasn't broken anything or needs medical attention. He hands her a buff envelope with the key to her room.

My dear Saviour ... Amara reads and rereads again but nothing makes any sense. Saviour from what? The letter is indeed addressed to her, but she doesn't recognise the sender's name: who's Hans Wilkowsky? She reads on: *I have such a vivid memory of your ears. Why particularly your ears, who knows. They seemed to me like two unbelievably graceful pink shells. Perhaps I remember them because I was trying so hard to make sure the profound and sincere sound of my voice would reach you through them.*

Now she remembers: the train to Prague. They had stopped at the frontier. The man with gazelles on his jumper. The guarantee she signed in such a hurry. The sound of the locomotive in the night. And next to him the other man with fur armbands, the mother with the young baby, and the smell of smoked herrings and birchbark.

I trusted you and you trusted me. You saved me from two days of bureaucratic torture. I reached Poznań safe and sound. I found my daughter Agnes had just given birth to a beautiful boy who will be called Hans like me. The child looks like my mother. I told you in the train my mother Hanna was Hungarian and Jewish, and died in the Treblinka concentration camp. My father is half Austrian and half Polish. I'm not sure the two young people did the right thing in coming together as a couple but, I assure you, they were really beautiful: a girl with honey-coloured hair, very long legs and a crystal-clear soprano voice, and a tall dark young man with shining eyes and a playful and well-formed mind. Tadeusz and Hanna. I have here a photograph of my parents at Graz. She is wearing a long light-coloured skirt and a pair of lace-up sandals; he has a jacket with wide sleeves and a pair of shoes with spats. They met in the first years of the twentieth century. My father was studying music at the famous conservatory at Vác. He wanted to be an orchestral conductor. My mother had studied singing in Budapest and had won a scholarship to Vác to follow a course at the conservatory which was reputed to have produced great singers. One evening they met and walked beside the Danube under a huge moon that made their eyes shine and silhouetted them against the long white riverbank. You may ask how I know these details. I answer that my father never stopped talking about it. It was a little piece of family mythology that made him intensely proud.

They spent all that night chattering. And in the morning, when the sun had warmed them, they decided to take a dip in the river naked. They never even kissed. Just lay close together in the sun without their clothes, then left each other, each going home. But they began writing to each other and after two years of lively correspondence they decided to get married.

They went to live in Graz, in a little apartment without water or lighting, because he had not yet found work as a conductor and she was singing in the theatre for next to nothing, just to get known. They were so deeply in love they could not bring themselves to separate for a moment. 'I was afraid of meeting you again after so long apart. We had grown used to that and I was afraid our separated bodies would not understand each other. But they understood each other perfectly and we have never felt any need to be unfaithful.' This was what my mother used to tell me when I was a child and too young to understand. It is only now I understand what their love was.

Then came the laws against the Jews. Tadeusz and Hanna had returned to Vienna where at long last he had found work with a youth orchestra. Until one day the city authorities discovered that my Austrian father had married a Hungarian Jewess. The guilty pair were summoned to the police and told that despite the long years they had lived together, and despite the fact that they had two grown-up children, their marriage was not valid under the new laws of the Reich.

Two weeks later an SS patrol came and took them to Heldenplatz to join other couples like themselves. They were forced to wear placards round their necks. On hers was written I'M A JEWISH WHORE AND I CORRUPT CHRISTIANS. On his I'M AN AUSTRIAN PIG AND I LUST FOR JEWISH MONEY. The SS photographed them in right profile and left profile, and made them stand in the square all day with passers-by staring at them. Some, encouraged by the guards, spat on them, particularly on the 'Jewish whore'. Others showed sympathy, but didn't dare to stop. I still have a photograph published in a Nazi paper. She is in a light-coloured dress, her curly blonde hair now touched with grey, wearing her hat at a jaunty angle, her head poised with a certain defiance despite the humiliating situation. Her face is serious, not exactly resigned, more ironic I think: it's easy to see how contemptible all this is, she seems to be saying; I'm here and you are there, you're free to spit on me, but you can't avoid seeing me and understanding the horror of my situation. My father seems much angrier, even disheartened. He is holding his placard by one corner; its chain is probably hurting his neck. With his other hand he is holding his hat against his leg; he has a white shirt and bow tie and his eyes are sad. Behind him are standing four SS guards in brown shirts, their collars tightly buttoned to the chin, bandoliers across their chests, swastikas prominent on their shirt sleeves, more swastikas stamped on their caps. They are standing stiffly, pleased with themselves. One is smiling; another sports a Hitler moustache though his manner is unconvincing. A nice souvenir photo ...

I was in Denmark at the time and so missed the whole wretched scene. It was nearly evening before the police let them go home. But after that nothing was the same as before. A few days later my father lost his job. My mother had to wear the yellow star on her chest. My sister died soon after of tuberculosis. When their friends saw them approaching, they would cross to the other side of the road and look away. They no longer had any right to go into shops, sit in trams, or go into a cinema or restaurant. I wanted to come home, I wanted to be near them, but they begged me to stay where I was. That saved my life because my mother was deported to Treblinka, where she died of privation a few months later. My father managed to hide until almost the very end of the war, when they found him and took him to Auschwitz. I did not know about this till later. For years I heard nothing. I went on writing to them thinking they must still be alive somewhere. But I never had any answers.

It was only after the end of the war that I found my father, who had miraculously survived not because he was an Aryan but because at the very moment when the Germans decided to burn the camp and exterminate all the survivors as embarrassing witnesses, Soviet tanks arrived and set them free.

When I met him again in '46 he weighed only thirty-eight kilos and had lost all his teeth. I took him in my arms like Aeneas with his father Anchises after the terrible sack of Troy. It was like embracing a little child. You can't imagine, my dear Saviour, what it was like for me to take home the featherless sparrow my father had turned into. He couldn't even speak and only chirped, just like a little bird. I had the joy of seeing him get back his health. A little at a time, stuffed with eggs, meat and apples, he recovered. I also bought him a set of dentures. We were happy together for two years. Then he fell in love with a Frenchwoman called Odette who had settled in Hungary and set up house in the centre of Budapest with her and his friend Ferenc Bruman, first violin in the city orchestra.

Please forgive me if I have bored you with my family history but you are the first person I have felt to be sympathetic and understanding, even though you are so much younger than I am. I know you are not only working as a journalist, but also trying to track down someone you love. I put myself at your disposal: Hans Wilkowsky, man of many occupations, resident in Vienna but temperamentally a vagrant, proposes to help you find the child who was deported so many years ago. Will you accept me as a companion in research?

What a strange letter. A man met on a train telling her such private things about his life. A man with a complicated and unhappy past, asking if he can come to her and help her. Should she trust him or not? Something she remembers in his smile inclines her to trust him, despite her doubts and a mass of unanswered questions.

11

Hans and Amara are sitting in the Cafè Mayakovsky on Izaaka Street. In front of them are glasses of white wine. Great drops of water are sliding down the window and lightly touching the amaranth-coloured damask tablecloth.

'Our glasses are weeping,' says Hans with a smile. Amara looks at the man with the gazelles who today is wearing dark trousers and a white shirt open to his long thin neck.

'What shall we drink to?'

'To research!'

'Have you discovered anything?'

'So far, no.'

'I'll help you in any way I can. I seem to know this Emanuele already: have you a photo of him?'

'As a child, yes. Nothing later.'

'When did he disappear?'

'His last letter is from '43. It's in an exercise book sent to me after the war. I don't know who sent it. He may even have sent it himself. This is another reason I think he survived.'

'So you don't know whether he died at Auschwitz or survived. What makes you think he might still be alive? They gassed the children at once. Useless for forced labour. In fact they caused nothing but trouble.'

'Emanuele was fifteen when he was taken from the Łódź ghetto, and he had always seemed older than his years. I found no trace of him at Auschwitz. But, as the guard explained to me, the later records are incomplete: too many trains were arriving and unloading in a hurry and the Germans didn't always keep a proper register of the new deportees, particularly if they were destined for the gas chambers.'

'And what makes you think he ended up at Auschwitz?'

'Everyone from the Łódź ghetto was sent there after '42. Before that they were sent to Chełmno. Or so I've read.'

'Wouldn't it make more sense to let it go and stop looking for a needle in a haystack?'

'I don't believe he is a needle in a haystack. And I've dreamed he's alive.'

'You believe in dreams?'

'When they're as sharp and vivid as that, yes I do.'

'Even if he is alive but hasn't been looking for you, might not that mean he would rather keep himself to himself?'

'I dreamed he was calling me.'

'Can you describe the dream?'

'I was at a railway station, a derelict one; the tracks had been abandoned and were overgrown with grass. I noticed a fresh red poppy growing in the midst of those rusty rails. When I went to get a closer look I felt a vibration accompanied by a hissing sound. Looking up I could see, in the distance, a locomotive belching smoke and struggling towards the station. But how could this be possible, surely the line was dead? How could there be a train arriving at that ruined station. I stood in a daze watching the engine advance down the ruined tracks. It was about to run me down and I needed to get out of the way. I wasn't afraid, just reasoning in the same way as I do when I'm awake. I kept asking myself: if this station has been derelict for so long, where can this train be coming from? And how can it run on these damaged rails?

'It still came on huffing and puffing and slowly reached the station. Then, squeaking and creaking, it stopped. And I noticed it was a train made up of cattle trucks sealed by planks nailed up in the form of a cross. I glimpsed a movement. I thought it must be animals, cows or horses being taken for slaughter. But, in a gap between the boards, fingers were moving. When I looked more closely I could see eyes shining in the dark. So there were people in those trucks. Even in my sleep I was astonished. Then a dirty little piece of paper fell from one of those hands. I quickly picked it up and pushed it furtively into my pocket for fear I might be seen. I knew danger was hanging over me and over these people. Looking round, I could see armed men standing pointing rifles at the train. Where could they have sprung from if until then the station had been deserted and derelict?'

'Did you ask yourself that in the dream?'

'Yes, I did.'

'A dream is only a dream, dear friend.'

'I suddenly realised it was a train full of people being deported to the camps. I don't know how I knew this.'

'How old were you when you were watching that train?'

'I don't know. Maybe the same as now. Or younger. I snatched that bit of paper with a rapid, agile movement.'

'What was written on it?'

'I didn't read it. I pushed it hurriedly into my pocket.'

'And when did you read it?'

'After the train left and the SS and their rifles had disappeared. I was alone again but the poppy was still there, a fantastic red colour basking in the sun.'

'And what did it say on the paper?'

'I didn't think about that. I was focused on the poppy. It seemed such a clear, unabashed sign of life that it made me happy. I wanted to pick it but when I went near it moved aside as though it didn't want to be picked.'

'And the bit of paper? Weren't you curious at all?'

'I was distracted.'

'So when did you read it?'

'I've completely forgotten.'

'Completely?'

'Completely.'

'So you never read it?'

'Later I did. Years later.'

'Years passed in your dream?'

'I knew my body had changed and matured and my walk had become less bold and secure. The paper was still in my pocket.'

'So in the end, even years later, you read it. And what was written on it?'

'"I'm here", that's what was written, "Emanuele".'

'Was it signed?'

'Yes, it was signed.'

'"I do not know if I was Tzu dreaming he was a butterfly or the butterfly dreaming he was Tzu." That's what Chuang Tzu says, and it seems to fit the case. The dream tells me nothing about the survival or otherwise of your Emanuele.'

'But I know he's waiting for me somewhere. And I'm here to

find him. If you can help me, Hans, I'll be grateful; if not let's just say goodbye.'

'All right. I'll help you. Give me more facts. His family name, the date of his disappearance, a photograph, whatever you have.'

'His family name is Orenstein. His father Karl was an industrialist, his mother Thelma Fink an actress. I have no photographs of them, only one of Emanuele as a child.'

'We must search the archives, Maria Amara, but where did your own unusual name come from? I've never heard it before.'

'My mother wanted to call me Marlene after her favourite actress, Marlene Dietrich. My father wanted me to be Mariuccia after my grandmother. They argued for a bit, then settled on Amara, which was the name of a little newborn bear in a caravan with Togni's circus, which had just stopped at Rifredi. It was in all the papers. It seemed a strange name, but also easy to say, so they settled on Amara.'

'Your grandmother Mariuccia must have been unhappy.'

'My name was registered as Maria Amara but they immediately started calling me just Amara. For my father, choosing such a strange name was also a way of cocking a snook at the fascists who only approved recognisable names, connected with the saints and above all, Italian. But on official documents I'm still Maria Amara Sironi.'

'Tomorrow morning at eight we'll go to the police where it seems they have some recently discovered camp registers. Agreed?'

'Agreed.'

Hans moves away. She hasn't even asked him where he lives. Does he have a telephone? She is on the point of calling him back but he has already turned the corner.

Amara sets off down Estery Street. The pavement is wet, but the grey stones are shining now in the fresh sun peeping out from behind thick, heavy clouds. The houses she passes smell of pork and boiled cabbage.

She touches the letters crushed into her shoulder bag. They are heavy, but she carries them everywhere. Every now and then she likes to pull them out and read them again. There is also the exercise book with its closely written pages in pencil, the handwriting light and meticulous but also distorted and full of crossings-out, as if written propped on bare knees when the writer was not at all well. A black school exercise book with squared pages. Something always leaps out from the letters to surprise her, like a novelty. The certainty that he is alive somewhere stays with her. She absolutely must find him! The dream comes back to her mind, bright and clear. The scrap of paper was addressed to her and carried a precise request: come on, look for me, find me, I'm here, I'm here, but where are you?

12

Hans ought to be at the corner of the market square; he phoned her at the hotel in the evening to make the appointment, but she sees no sign of him. Perhaps he's forgotten. Poor Hans whom she privately still thinks of as the man with the gazelles. But why 'poor'? He has the air of a slightly damaged young man, though basically robust and healthy. Hans, the man she met on the train, the man with a sad past, the man saved from the Nazis by the foresight of a loving mother. While Emanuele who if he had stayed in Italy would probably have escaped the death camps, was deliberately taken to Austria by an optimistic and patriotic mother. Who was blind, utterly blind.

It's just eight and the roller shutters of the shops are still closed. Amara's light footsteps echo on the wet pavement of Plac Nowy. The sky is opening over a city getting ready for work. Who knows how many families are sitting at table behind those misted windows over a breakfast of milk and barley coffee, toasted hard bread and home-made jam. Amara had tea in the empty dining room of the Hotel Wawel where a waitress in black stockings and lilac slippers, her maid's cap perched crookedly on curly grey hair, had served her unceremoniously with a spoonful of fresh yoghurt and tinned fruit in syrup.

But Hans is crossing the square towards her. She recognises his lean, happy walk. He walks like a youngster, she thinks, smiling to herself. Like a man who knows where he's going, not afraid of tripping and falling, advancing happily on a new day.

They shake hands without a word. Then, guided by Hans, they cross Miodowa Street and make their way to the police station where he has made an appointment for them.

'The Germans call it Krakau, the Poles Kraków. It has been the capital of the region of Lower Silesia since the fourteenth century. Doesn't it make you think of the croaking of crows, this name

stuffed with k's? Kra kra … you can almost hear them. But no,
It was founded by King Krak,' explains Hans, walking beside her
and giving her arm a friendly squeeze. 'They say that in the reign
of King Krak a dragon infested the banks of the river. An enormous dragon that ate all the animals in the pasture, destroyed the
crops and often even attacked people and tore them to pieces. He
had a particular taste for virgin girls, so to keep him in a good
mood the villagers would leave a naked girl each month in front of
the cave where this revolting beast had his lair.'

Amara half-closes her eyes to savour the story. She loves being
guided through a story. She cuddles up mentally in a corner of her
body like when she was little, and listens in bliss.

'The king was fed up with this nuisance so he issued a proc-
lamation promising half his kingdom and his daughter in marriage to anyone who succeeded in suppressing the dragon. Knights
came from all over the kingdom and beyond to kill the monster
and marry the princess. But the dragon was very strong and very
clever and had lots of heads and legs, and scales so tough that no
lance could pierce them. When he was hungry he would whip out
his long rapacious tongue and grab an animal or a man by the
waist, flicking them deftly into its mouth where he would crunch
them up with teeth as sharp as knives. People would throw pikes
and javelins at the dragon and attack him with swords and knives
and hurl enormous rocks, but no one could get the better of him.'

Hans stops at a kiosk to buy a bag of dried fruit. In among
the figs and apricots are some cherries, shrivelled but extremely
sweet and with a wild smell. The man with the gazelles pays for
the bag and passes it to his companion who picks out the dried
cherries and puts them in her mouth one by one. The bitter flavour
reminds her of the tree she used to climb with Emanuele when
they were children in the garden of the Villa Lorenzi at Rifredi.
Can you stop time for love? Can you force a mystery? Can you
take a secret by surprise to rescue it from the folds of the past? You
have embalmed love, a voice says inside her, you can't just snatch
a dead body from the silence of the past. It's not allowed, and you
know it. But the desire to go on searching is stronger than every
other consideration. The desire to hear that voice, to see that body
again, is pulling her towards a future she knows will be full of
dangers and delusions, like when the knights set off to fight the

seven-headed dragon. But despite her fear and the uncertainties, she can't resign herself. Is this a serious fault?

'Don't you want to hear how the story of King Krak ended?' asks Hans, interrupting her thoughts.

'Yes, of course.'

'One morning a young cobbler called Szewczyk Dratewka appeared before the king and said he could solve the problem. When the king looked at him he saw a thin youth with an emaciated face dressed in rags, and shook his head. The boy said he would use no swords or lances but only his brain. Studying him more closely, the king saw sky-blue eyes full of fun and realised the boy was intelligent. So he asked him what he needed. A sheep and a kilo of sulphur, said the boy. Puzzled, the king gave him what he had asked for. Szewczyk killed the sheep and disembowelled it, replacing its innards with the sulphur, then sewed up its skin and placed it at night in front of the dragon's cave. It looked like a live animal grazing the riverbank. In fact this is what the dragon thought when he woke up and came out of his cave, so he crept up silently, grabbed the sheep and swallowed it in a single mouthful. But he soon began to feel thirsty. So he went down to the banks of the Vistula and began drinking. He drank so much and swallowed so much that he swelled up like a huge bladder. Withdrawing to his cave he slept for three days and nights in the hope of getting rid of all the water in his sleep. But he awoke thirstier than ever. So he went back to the river and drank and drank again, until his body became a great ball, an enormous globe full of water, and when he yawned his skin, which could not hold so much water, split and exploded. The villagers felt an enormous shock that shook the earth and frightened their livestock. When they ran to see what had happened they found the dragon blown into a thousand pieces near the cave at the foot of Wawel Hill. Who did this? they asked in astonishment. I did, said the young cobbler and everyone gazed at him in bewilderment and admiration. The king sent for his daughter, gave her to the boy in marriage and handed over half his kingdom.'

Amara smiles. 'Was it really the cobbler who did it?' she asks tenderly, remembering her father Amintore.

'An uneducated but remarkably ingenious cobbler.' There is something tender and happy in the voice of the man with the gazelles.

'Who told you this story?'

'It's an old legend. It's more important to know how to tell stories than to know how to use your fists my mother used to say, and I know now she was right.' He smiles with his lips together. His laugh is restrained and vigilant, the laugh of a man who has learned always to keep himself under control, both in joy and in pain.

An anonymous room, shabby little brown leatherette armchairs, a glass-topped table with some dog-eared magazines whose pages look as if they have been constantly turned by bored hands. A big dirty window. A cage-like structure with inside it a woman in uniform, her face soporific and gloomy. Why are police stations all over the world so similar, shabby and anonymous, never welcoming?

They have to wait, not because there's a queue, but because various officials haven't yet arrived. This the sleepy-looking official explains, indicating the little leatherette armchairs whose cushions carry the imprint of the backs and bottoms of all those who have passed hours waiting for a passport or a certificate or power of attorney.

Finally a door opens and it's their turn. The man of the gazelles talks quietly, in sophisticated and perhaps rather literary Polish. The police officer fixes him with a blank look but is nonetheless politely serious and attentive. Hans repeats what Amara has told him: 'This lady, an Italian from Florence called Maria Amara Sironi, is trying to trace a childhood friend of hers, a certain Emanuele Orenstein. We know that at one time he was living in Italy, but in 1939 the family returned to Vienna to live in a large building they owned on Schulerstrasse. In 1941 they were ejected from their apartment and sent to the Łódź ghetto. Early in 1943 something happened that Emanuele did not have time to enter in his diary. We don't know what it was, but we can imagine. He must have been loaded onto a train to Auschwitz, or so it seems. After 1942, all Jews in the Łódź ghetto were sent to Auschwitz. No more has been heard of him.'

'How do you know all this, Dr Wilkowsky?' asks the policeman, perhaps growing a little more interested in the story, seduced by Hans's beautiful voice.

'The Signora Maria Amara Sironi here present had letters from

Vienna and later from the Łódź ghetto before Emanuele vanished. His last letters are in the form of a diary written in pencil in a black exercise book hidden in a hole and discovered after the war. A simple schoolbook with pages ruled in squares for doing sums, which some charitable person, perhaps even Emanuele Orenstein himself, posted to this lady at an address written inside it. We presume he was deported to a concentration camp. The nearest was Auschwitz, so he probably ended up there. But although Signora Sironi has been to the camp and examined the archives, she could not find his name.'

'And how do you think I can help you after thirteen years?'

'At Auschwitz they told her that some of the camp documents have been transferred to police archives here. We would like permission to study them.'

'Water under the bridge, Signora Sironi. The dead are dead; let sleeping dogs lie – you know the proverb?' translates Hans reluctantly.

'Out of more than a million Jews deported to Auschwitz, six thousand survived to be liberated. Emanuele could have been among them.'

'They disposed of the children immediately. Please remind your Italian friend of that. It is unlikely any child survived.'

'But Emanuele was fifteen and seemed older than his years, and he was strong too, used to running and climbing trees. They may have kept him alive to work.'

'All things are possible. But unlikely.'

'Do you really have these documents? The lady is not only here to look for this boy. She also has to write articles for her newspaper. May we show you her press card?'

'Don't bother. I know nothing,' answers the policeman in an undertone, immediately translated by Hans who in this instance shows himself an excellent interpreter. Amara feels the policeman is lying. Why would he not want her to poke her nose into the archives of the SS? Were there secrets the authorities preferred not to reveal to the inquisitive? Or was it that they couldn't accept her as a journalist, only as a woman looking for a man, or rather a child, who vanished many years ago?

'Don't you think if he's alive he would have got in touch with you?' asks the policeman in broken German.

'That's what the man with the gazelles believes too,' says Amara and hastily corrects herself, 'that's what Dr Hans Wilkowsky also believes. If he were alive, he would have got in touch. But I believe he could be alive, but may not have tried to get in touch with me. He was a proud boy. And then … he may have assumed I'm married, as in fact I was, and that I wouldn't want to see him. He was discreet. But I really do think he could be alive and holding back and keeping silent.'

'He says go back to Auschwitz and take a closer look,' translates Hans quickly. 'Sometimes they changed their names. Or, he says, you could go to Vienna. You could find their house. And who knows, there might even be some trace of him in the ghetto at Łódź. There's nothing here to help you.'

The police officer is dismissing them. He pronounces the last words on his feet, leaning on his desk with both hands and smiling impatiently. All they can do is go.

'We should never have come near the *milicja*!' says Hans seriously, 'now we'll be followed.'

'But if we'd been spies we'd hardly have gone to them, would we? Try to be logical.'

'Logic has nothing to do with the way they do things.'

'But are we being logical?'

'We think we are. But we're just taking action. And being stupid. You by insisting on hunting for someone who vanished in '43. And I by encouraging you.'

'I never asked you to.'

'I know. But Amara, you don't understand what the cold war is. Above all it is a climate of mutual suspicion. Logic is irrelevant. What do you want to do now?'

'Let's start by taking shelter. It's begun raining again.'

The man with the gazelles and the young Italian woman whose name is the opposite of sweet walk quickly, looking for a café. But they can't find one. Hans points to some steps leading to a revolving glass door. They go up them and enter the Hotel Kazimierz. Not a soul in sight. An enormous hall, that must have known better days, welcomes them to its icy shadows. Long billiard tables are hidden under white cloths. Weak lamps hang from a high ceiling. Carpets perhaps soft and elegant in the thirties but now stained reveal their history. In one corner is an enormous piano with an abandoned air. Beyond an arch are some small round tables with egg-coloured cloths and small artificial gardenias with dusty corollas in melancholy little vases.

They sit down at a corner table and order beers. The hotel has no wine or aperitifs. Only beer and coffee. Would they like something to eat? Amara indicates no. But Hans nods. Perhaps he has had no breakfast. What would he like? The ancient waiter, dubious pinkish hair combed across his bald skull, bends over Hans as if using his hands to try and hide the brownish marks on an apron that has not been clean for a very long time. Hans asks what there is to eat. Scrambled eggs. Bread and butter. Will that do? Fine.

Not long after they have settled at their table someone sits down at the piano that dominates the area beyond the arch. Two surprisingly light and delicate hands play the theme from *The Third Man*, a film that has been filling cinemas all over the world.

For a moment Amara sees again the desolate streets of Vienna. The sensual footsteps of Alida Valli. Did she wear a raincoat and a hat?

'Who directed *The Third Man*?'

'Carol Reed,' replies Hans confidently.

'Do you like the cinema?'

'I often go to see films.'

'And who was the lead actor?'

'Orson Welles, I think.'

'And she was Alida Valli, wasn't she?'

But Hans seems disinclined to discuss the film. He concentrates on his glass of frothy beer and says quietly: 'Let's think, Amara.'

'Let's think.'

'You're still determined to find your Emanuele? How old would he be now?'

'Twenty-eight.'

'And you're certain you want to find him, dead or alive?'

'Absolutely.'

'I'll help you.'

'No need. I can manage on my own.'

'And what about the languages? Do you know Polish?'

'No.'

'And Czech?'

'No.'

'I think you need me.'

'But I warn you, I'm not going to fall in love with you. And gratitude won't make me feel obliged to sleep with you.'

'Is that what I've been asking?'

'No.'

'Don't you think I might be genuinely interested too?'

'Why?'

'Because everything to do with the Nazis disturbs me. Because by now I've learned enough to be seized by curiosity: I want to find out whether your Emanuele is alive or dead. This is a chance to understand a bit more about what happened to the few who survived. If you'll let me follow you, I'll help. And in return all I want is your friendship. Agreed?'

'Agreed.'

'But how will you manage financially? Travel, hotels?'

'I have some money saved. But what about your daughter Agnes and little Hans waiting for you in Poznań?'

'My daughter is no longer alone as I thought. She's found a companion, a Party member I frankly dislike. But at least she's got someone. They have a slightly larger house, and something to live on.'

13

Amara returns to the modest hotel named after the famous castle ,that dominates the city: the Hotel Wawel on Karmelicka Street. The young porter with red hair is sitting with his head resting on folded arms, sleeping or meditating. Amara asks for her key. He lifts his head and smiles sleepily. His face is extremely beautiful. Luminous blue eyes. A small freckled nose, a shapely mouth. A delight to look at, Amara thinks, taking the key the boy holds out to her. She goes towards the lift with a sense of peace. Can beauty give peace? Can beauty, in the very moment when you limit your-self to the pleasure of seeing, put you in harmony with the world?

Reflecting on beauty, Amara gets into the lift, presses the third-floor button and leans on the lift wall, closing her eyes. Can there be justice in beauty, or do those two truths oppose each other, each exclusive of the other? Is not beauty also equilibrium, the harmony of reason? Isn't disinterested intelligence a form of beauty? And does not thought, when generous and just, become beauty?

Her room is at the far end of a corridor of threadbare wall-to-wall carpeting. She struggles to turn the heavy key in the lock. Her room is small and smells of smoke. There is an iron bedstead against the wall, an unnecessarily high bedside locker of discol-oured wood, a naked bulb hanging from the ceiling and a handba-sin with a rusty mirror over it. The bathroom is across the corridor, some twenty metres from the bedroom. Best go there at once so as not to have to come out again in her nightdress. The doors of the wardrobe in which she puts her jacket and bag are nearly off their hinges and squeak in a sinister way. Not easy to think about beauty in such unfriendly surroundings.

The bathroom is tiled in red and yellow; a strange contrast with the insipid brown of her room. The toilet has no seat. She has to balance delicately so as not to touch the bowl that goodness knows how many guests must have used. Amara is a bit squeamish even after living through a war in which she suffered all kinds of discomforts. She remembers the house in the mountains of Tuscany where they spent a few months as evacuees. A peasants' home; its rooms oozed moisture, the beds were very high and the lavatory was outside in the yard, a stinking enclosure used by at least twenty people. You were pestered by flies by day and by ravenous mosquitoes at night. Back in Rifredi where Amintore had to return to his work as a shoemaker, they had suffered hunger, and would spend all day looking for something to put into their mouths. Often she had ventured near the hospital dump, knowing that frequently whole bags of boiled potatoes left by the patients were thrown out. She would take them home to be boiled a second time and they would eat them greedily. Just like Pinocchio with the pear skins. Before the war she hadn't dared go anywhere near the hospital dump; the mere sight of those bloodstained pieces of gauze mixed with scraps of food had disgusted her. But you could not be fastidious and pernickety when you were really hungry. She would rummage among the high piles of refuse in her rubber boots, among broken glass syringes, medicine bottles, dirty gauze and greasy rags, without so much as holding her nose.

Now sleep fogs her thoughts even though, once in bed, she can't get to sleep: what is she doing in a cheap hotel in this unfamiliar country? Is it really so important for her to find Emanuele? Thirteen years since he disappeared. Why go on struggling to find someone when she no longer knows anything about him? She could meet him in the street and not recognise him, have him before her eyes and not know it. And this man who seems so attached to her? Could that be just a trap for … for what? You're getting much too suspicious, Amara, she tells herself, half asleep, searching in her memory for the face of the man with the gazelles on his chest. His body will always now be tied to that image even though she has not since seen him wearing the jumper with gazelles running across it.

When she wakes next morning, she spends a few minutes trying to remember where she is. Her mind has emerged fresh from a vivid dream in which she has seen Emanuele up in their usual leafy tree in the garden of Villa Lorenzi, picking cherries. The bitter scent of wild fruit brushed delicately against her nostrils. She remembers spending a long time watching him climb the trunk with his grazed knees and then, agile as a monkey, move from one branch to another. Watching him she felt again the sensation she had known as a little girl. Not so much passion as a blessedly secure sense of unity. He was part of her and she was part of him. They did not need to speak to understand one another. They knew they would go on belonging to one another. They were in no hurry to make love. It was as if they were afraid of becoming adults too quickly with no chance to go back. Though they did kiss, lips locked together, rolling in each other's arms in a field. Or sitting up in the cherry tree, with leaves whisking their cheeks and threading their hair.

When Emanuele disappeared Amara had been stopped in her tracks. She had lost an arm, perhaps more, and she did not know if she could survive. She no more wanted to play, to adventure into unknown worlds, to climb trees, to laugh, or to eat. It was seven years before she had been able to take any interest in another man. This was Luca Spiga, who worked in an architects' studio and was twenty years her senior. She liked the calm, adult, discreet and perhaps rather timid way he caressed her; as she warmed to his caresses, she seemed to rediscover a body she had thought dead for ever. Luca did not press her with sexual demands. At first he just watched her, then very gently began to stroke first her hair, then her face and neck and shoulders, and his gentleness had seemed a sign of her reawakening. When he asked her to marry him she at once said yes. But she knew now that they had never shared any deep feeling, only the coming together of two chilled bodies that needed to be warmed. And once warm, they accepted the boredom of living together. By good luck they conceived no children, even though they had assumed that they would. She was sure that Luca Spiga never loved her, but he did introduce her to the cinema. He bought them a subscription to the Charlie Chaplin film club where each evening the great classics were shown: the Marx brothers' comedies, Buster Keaton, *Battleship Potemkin*, *Casablanca*, *Obsession*, *Rome Open City*, *Bicycle Thieves*. They were two good companions in adventure, not much more. When he was away, she didn't miss him. Rather, she was often happy to forget him. Then, to punish herself, she would spend two hours waiting near a public telephone for the chance to spend three minutes talking to him. Never more than three minutes; it would have cost too much. She had to watch her money and always think twice before spending any.

When her husband told her he had fallen in love with a woman younger than herself she had been hurt, but had said nothing. By now she had got to know Luca, and she knew he only required the preliminaries of love. The rest did not interest him. He liked to stroke, smell and kiss his beloved, and whisper sweet nothings into her ear. He was so convincing that women were not just deceived but trapped and fascinated. In time, thinking over his constant absences and escapes, Amara realised that the closer their relationship became, the more he needed to run away and find new bodies to caress. He was too much in love with love to dedicate himself fully to any one woman. To him, lasting commitment was unbearable imprisonment. She never understood why he had ever asked her to marry him. Perhaps for once he had believed the caresses would last. Or perhaps he had seen marriage as a way of not falling in love, so that as soon as he had felt there was a danger he might fall in love he had hurried to propose to her, just as Swann, that sophisticated creation of Proust, proposes to Odette in the firm belief that marriage will kill desire. Who knows? He was a man who knew how to listen and be tender, and he drove women mad.

The fact that she had seen through him in no way diminished the intensity of her delusion. She may never have believed in his love, but she had certainly believed in his caresses. And when his caresses were absent she dreamed of his hands. Large hands with broad, flat fingers, the balls of his thumbs sensitive, always warm, his palms dry and smooth. He knew how to caress without wanting to possess, without wanting to press on to the relief of a quick orgasm. He would start with her face: ploughing her forehead with his fingers like a tired field, smoothing and dividing her hair, letting it slip like water through his hands. Then her mouth and neck, where his thumbs would slowly search out her veins and press them lightly as if to feel the slow flow of her blood. Then her shoulders which he released from their many burdens with delicate little taps. He would fill his hands with her breasts and sometimes suck them as if to reach milk closed inside. Then he would warm her sides and belly, pressing them gently with the heat of his closed fists. He would skim lightly over her sex because the moment had not yet come for that secret nucleus of naked flesh.

Then he would pass down her back pressing as he counted each individual vertebra, in sheer wonder at the architecture of bone on which the physical equilibrium of the body depends. Then her legs and feet, first separating her toes before bringing them together again in a warm, affectionate gesture; running his knuckles over the arches of her soles, knocking against her mercurial restlessness in tribute to the grace of her walking.

His caresses were an end in themselves, possessed of an angelic sensuality. She had loved them for that. But in order to caress, Luca needed to feel a dedication that could not last. It was not his ambition to transform this ceremony of delights into a permanent habit. And practising the daily routine carelessly was not even conceivable. A perfectionist cannot be expected to turn into a slipshod repeater of predictable gestures when it comes to the adorable art of caressing.

In fact his caresses were over after barely a year of marriage. And with the end of his caresses, something changed in his character. Tenderness gave way to resentment, a subtle brutality that insinuated itself into his words and gestures. Had this been the meaning of his caresses? To use the intelligence of his hands to restrain a cruelty hidden in some part of his soul? Maybe. But he had been generous and she was grateful to him for that.

14

In the train with the man with the gazelles. On the way to Vienna. Amara had packed her suitcase in a hurry. She was happy to leave Kraków and her room at the Hotel Wawel with its brown wallpaper, the corridor with its smelly threadbare moquette, and the bathroom with its red and yellow tiles and seatless lavatory bowl. The Russian train moves slowly on its widely spaced rails. They have slept in a twin-bed compartment because the single ones were all taken. The table which folds against the wall at night is raised by day and covered with an immaculate white cloth. Hanging above is a lamp with a crimson shade surrounded by gilded pendants that tinkle lightly at each lurch of the train. The beds form a pair, not one above the other as in the trains she is used to, but side by side, with military covers and very clean sheets that smell of perfumed soap. The white curtains have a gilded trimming. An extremely ancient train perhaps once reserved for luxury passengers, but now within the reach of all.

While Amara was undressing Hans had gone out and she did the same when he took off the jumper with the flying gazelles and the white shirt he hung on a clothes-hook along with his corduroy trousers. He put his worn-out shoes side by side under his bed with his socks rolled up inside them. Amara came in to find him sitting in his pyjamas on the edge of his bunk, cigarette in hand. To avoid embarrassment they scarcely looked at each other and slept back to back. The train stopped twenty times during the night, puffing and panting, gurgling and hissing. Men's voices could be heard in the corridor exchanging information in Czech. They slept little and badly. In the morning, tired and drowsy, they reached Vienna. At last they had arrived. At six the conductor knocked on their door. Did they want coffee? They did. It turned out to be an improbable violet colour and smelled of burned sawdust. But it was hot and they drank it at a single gulp.

'Vienna is a city offended and wounded by war. There are many ruins, but some intact corners too,' says Hans. 'I can take you to a clean if humble boarding-house run by a woman I know, Frau Morgan.'

At the Pension Blumental Amara is faced with choosing between two rooms: a very noisy large one facing the road, and a smaller and more modest one that overlooks a yard and rooftops covered with pigeons. Which would Frau Sironi prefer? Amara decides on the smaller one. Silence before luxury. Frau Morgan helps her carry her luggage to her room. Soon after she knocks and places on the bedside table a small vase containing a scented rose.

'I have a garden the size of a handkerchief but it's full of flowers. I've sown mint, mallow, chives and rhubarb too. From the mint I also make liqueur, and from the rhubarb tarts. One day I'll let you taste one.'

Frau Morgan seems anxious to please. Even so, Amara leaves her suitcase open, in case Frau Morgan might like to assess her moral status from the condition of her underwear.

In the afternoon Hans takes her to the Maria Theresia Platz museum, the Kunsthistorisches gallery with its endless rooms full of masterpieces. It is not long since the great paintings were once more hung on its walls and people again began coming from all over the world to admire the ever-popular works of Rembrandt, Vermeer, Brueghel, Rubens and Dürer. Hans and Amara stop in front of one particular painting, as if under a kind of spell. The work of an unfamiliar modern artist. A large, spacious picture, in which people swarm like ants. The huge canvas depicts a day in a Nazi concentration camp. On one side an armoured train is steaming in, on the other huts are set obliquely, of a naïve yet at the same time profoundly wise design. You can make out the beds, though to describe them as beds would be an abuse of language; they are wooden shelves each holding at least five inmates, with no mattresses, covers or pillows, with nothing at all. In the foreground is a morning roll call. It is known that these took hours, with the prisoners forced to stand in the cold wearing only striped pyjamas, their bare feet in clogs. Two or three hours of torture, depending on how many inmates there were to count. In another place, right against the barbed wire, dozens of corpses lie piled up like refuse. People who died in the night and will be dragged roughly by their arms and legs to a common pit by their still living fellow prisoners.

All this is seen from a certain distance, as if the painter has been viewing the camp through binoculars from a window a hundred metres away. A lugubrious collective vision yet at the same time intense and radiant. The bodies have been painted with quick, firm lines, in which white and black alternate and run into one another. There is something very cruel yet at the same time affectionate in this presentation of a monstrous and ferocious daily existence as everyday normality. The painter seems to have had intimate knowledge of these camps. He seems to have reproduced with his eyes closed his memory of those numbed and mutilated bodies.

A bell rings. An attendant passes, rapidly waving a hand as if to indicate closing time. Hans and Amara go down the infinite stairs of the museum to a tiny eating-place, where they sit down at a table covered with a waxed cloth. They order Hungarian goulash, the cheapest thing on the menu, which is written in chalk on a blackboard hanging on the wall.

'Would you like a beer?'

'No, thank you.'

'Impressive, that picture.'

'But that's all we looked at. We missed my beloved Vermeer.'

'We'll come again.'

'Who do you think painted that camp?'

'Someone who must have known it from the inside.'

'Don't you think a painter might have imagined it and described it without having been an inmate there?'

'Not with that precision of detail.'

'So for you art is only direct reportage?'

'I think so.'

'How would you compare that to Goethe or Dante?'

'Goethe tells ominous fables. Dante invents. No one believes in his *Inferno*. It's the delirium of a catastrophical mind. What enchants is his language.'

'And Sebastopol for Tolstoy?'

'Tolstoy lived through that war; he was there, even if only as an observer.'

'What about Manzoni and the seventeenth century?'

'When a writer writes about something not experienced directly, he sets in motion the artifice of the imagination. An artifice that remains indigestible to the reader.'

'So we should throw away half the literature of the world. And nearly all modern painting.'

'The Vermeer you love so much describes his own world, his time, his spaces.'

'And Rembrandt's *Saul*?'

'Painters love mythology, but they have a trick. They make it into direct reportage by introducing their wives and children. Saskia is there in all Rembrandt's paintings. That's how he constructs his mythology. But in the long run tricks are boring.'

'So according to you no one can tell a story unless they have lived it directly.'

'No, what I'm saying is that imagination leads to fables and fables to mental regression. Nothing can have as much force as what you have lived in your own skin.'

'Then you want artists to be egocentric narcissists. With any outward-looking perspective on the world, on past times, or on faraway stories, becoming a profanation and a crime.'

'I wasn't talking of crimes. Let's leave those to Stalin who sent so many artists to their deaths because they presented a sad and contradictory reality that he disliked. But even if they had painted the optimistic and triumphalist world he wanted from them, they would still have been capable of eventually changing their minds, so he got rid of them before they even had time to regret being his friends.'

'Isn't that too reductive?'

'I remember a story once told me by a friend who was a sculptor. It seems that one day, at the celebrations at a great provincial factory in the Soviet Union that had achieved maximum productivity, a famous painter brought along a work that had been commissioned from him: he had been asked to paint the factory at work, in a happy festive atmosphere with several Stakhanovites receiving prizes. Stalin himself had been invited to the celebrations and although he had not promised to come, he arrived unexpectedly in a helicopter from Moscow, creating enthusiasm and panic. The painter was terrified of showing his enormous new canvas. Even though he had put into it everything expected of him: the workers, the machinery, the prize-giving, and even a beautiful big symbolic figure of Father Stalin with a benevolent smile on his lips.'

'The painter had agreed to do all this?'

'Not voluntarily, but he had no choice. If he'd refused, he would have risked death. That was the climate of the times.'

'And was Stalin happy?'

'He spent a long time studying the painting he'd commissioned, smiling with gratification as he noted that all his requirements had been met to the letter; he even liked the portrait of himself, something that didn't happen too often. He appreciated the fact that he had been beautified and presented as taller than he actually was, and surrounded by a halo of light that made him look almost divine. The painter, watching the dictator gradually running his gaze from one part of the picture to another and nodding with satisfaction, felt excited, almost euphoric. But suddenly he saw Stalin look surprised and worried. The great Father of his Country lifted a finger and pointed to a figure at one side, the silhouette of a worker standing with his arms folded: 'And who is this?' Everyone stared in consternation. Who was that man so obviously not working? 'Why isn't he working like all the others? Comrade, are you trying to create an incentive to strike? What do those folded arms and that self-satisfied face tell anyone who looks at the picture? You have included a saboteur in this representation of a model factory for exhibition at the Eighteenth Congress of the Communist Party of the Soviet Union!' The terrified artist stammered the reason the worker in question was just smiling and doing nothing more was because he was gazing at the great Father Stalin. But Stalin wasn't listening. Next day the painter was arrested at his house by two police officers and taken off to prison.'

'What a sad story.'

'The story of an era. And we haven't finished with it yet.'

15

'Sleep well?'

'Sickening dreams.'

'Better than lying awake.'

'What shall we do this morning?'

'What about looking for Orensteins in the phone book?'

'Done already. I found a Theodor Orenstein. Does that mean anything to you?'

'I've looked too. I found another. Name of Elisabeth.'

'I called this Theodor. He's a painter and lives in a little street near Stephansplatz, off Bäckerstrasse in the city centre.'

'Did you make an appointment?'

'He's expecting us at ten.'

Theodor Orenstein receives them in stained coloured trousers and a woollen blue and black check shirt. He seems happy to see them, even if they have clearly interrupted his work on a large painting propped against the wall that features angels flying over a huddle of reddish roofs.

The man with the gazelles offers to translate but the painter is determined to speak Italian. In fact, it really seems he wants to take the chance to practise a language grown rusty in his memory. He says he's happy to meet them, that he loves Italy, and that he would like a clearer picture of what they want from him.

He listens attentively to the story of the Emanuele Orenstein whose fate is the object of the young Italian woman's investigation. Meanwhile he offers them a glass of beer and some olives 'from Greece'. He is a man of about forty. Apparently living alone. His tiny studio flat opens onto an equally minute and lovingly cultivated garden. The room is divided by a curtain behind which can be glimpsed a bed with a red coverlet. There is little furniture: a simple shelf, a rough table covered with a confusion of brushes and small tubes of paint, a bench by the wall and two rush-seated chairs cluttered with rags. A huge radio set dominates the corner under the window. On top of the radio, stretched like a pasha on a yellow cushion, an enormous white cat follows them with its eyes without moving a muscle. Amara swallows a mouthful of beer, nibbles an olive, and asks the painter whether he has ever had a relative called Emanuele Orenstein.

The man smiles at them, blue eyes prominent in his beard-darkened face. Before answering he drains a couple of glasses of light, frothy beer. No, he has never heard the name Emanuele spoken in his family, but then there are many Orensteins in Vienna and they are all related. Can they show him a photograph? Amara brings out the familiar faded picture of Emanuele as a child from when they played together in Florence. The painter studies it in silence. Then shakes his head. The photograph rings no bell with him. His Italian is halting and slow but correct. He has visited Italy a number of times, he tells them, and is familiar with the museums of Florence and Rome. But he hasn't been back for years.

'And during the war?' Amara ventures timidly, afraid to waken painful memories.

Theodor Orenstein studies them thoughtfully, as if asking whether these strange visitors who have appeared from nowhere are worthy of hearing what he has to say. He scratches his head nervously. Then, slowly, he starts his story. His voice, initially timid and awkward, gradually gains in fluency and confidence. A soft, visionary voice that like his own painting manages gracefully to combine strange insubstantial weightless bodies with the concrete quality of roofs in a sleeping city.

When war broke out Theodor was living in Vienna with his parents in Krügerstrasse, near the State Opera. The house no longer exists. It was destroyed by bombs during the terrible raids of 1944. The building he is living in now has only recently been refurbished and belongs to the Vienna Artists'Association. He has been painting for years, and they have allotted him one room, that luckily has a handkerchief of a garden in which he has planted potatoes, courgettes and tomatoes, though these have little colour because so little sun reaches them and in winter the ground freezes.

In Krügerstrasse he and his parents had a large apartment with five rooms, in which seven people lived: father, mother and three brothers besides himself, and an old deaf aunt.

His father was a civil servant. An honest state employee who got up for the office each day at dawn, taking a tram which dropped him within a hundred metres of the Post Office.

The man with the gazelles listens attentively to the painter's tale. Amara looks from one to the other. They are so different physically, yet they resemble each other: they both have the ceremonious manner which strikes her so forcibly in Austrians. Superficially awkward, timid too perhaps because they have been taught to sublimate their feelings; slow to take fire, but once heated, capable of blazing passions. Polite and sometimes ironic if with a rather roundabout sort of irony, not always comprehensible to those who do not know them.

Another beer? Amara watches the painter pour the clear liquid, filling his own glass right to the brim. It is rather sour, this good Bavarian beer, leaving you with a dry tongue like after eating bitter fruit.

The family felt more Austrian than many who had come from elsewhere, the painter doggedly continues. They had lived in Vienna for centuries, they thought and dreamed in German; they belonged to the city, it was their way of life. Yet the day came when they were described as strangers, even condemned as enemies and shut up in a concentration camp.

His mother had always worked as a dressmaker. She went into the houses of well-off people to mend and patch, to raise or lower the hems of skirts. She earned enough to supplement her husband's meagre salary. They had closed their eyes and noses to the rising stink. A stink of racist intolerance, of cultural hatred, of persecution. In their hearts they nurtured a sacrosanct conviction that no one, for any reason whatever, would ever be able to deprive them of the right to identify themselves as Austrians, living in their own country and their own city.

But one morning a dozen SA men arrived and took over their apartment, forcing them to leave with a few personal effects in a couple of suitcases. They were forced to leave behind the expensive linen sheets with embroidered monograms that had been a wedding present to Frau Magdalena, the damask curtains inherited from grandmother Bernstein, the gold-rimmed plates, by now discoloured and chipped, given at their marriage by the Levi uncles of Linz, and the fine silver cutlery from their Vogel cousins who had emigrated to Paris in the last century.

With those two pathetic suitcases they had been loaded onto a train that took them to Poland. They were not downhearted. They were on their way to work camps, the Nazis told them, and in this belief they climbed into the wagons, almost comforted by the prospect of leaving a life that had no longer been a life since the restrictions started: confined to the house by a curfew from eight in the evening, and with no access to Aryan shops, no school, and no cinema. They were sure they would be put to work: clearing snow, digging trenches, looking after tramway crossings. They would get by.

Theodor Orenstein, meanwhile, had managed to escape before his family were deported. Being an agile and slender boy, he had hidden in a lorry full of coal that, in return for a large sum of money (the last of the family funds) had taken him far from Vienna.

He had wandered the Austrian countryside, avoiding mopping-up operations and suspicious peasants, until he came to the Polish border. There he evaded the frontier guards and, still walking, reached Darłowo on the Baltic coast. A ship was ready to take him to Sweden, but it sank and threw him up instead on the Danish island of Bornholm, which was occupied by the Germans.

'I was lucky,' he says again and again, 'I was incredibly lucky.'

In the little village of Rønne he found work mending fishing nets, and lived secretly like this till the end of the war. No one realised he was a Jew, or if they did suspect it, they kept quiet. His main worry had been the fate of his parents and little brothers: what had happened to them? Were they alive? How could he find them?

Amara watches him closely, hoping to find something of Emanuele in that shadowed face with its ingenuous eyes, that slightly emaciated body.

'Would you like some bread and cheese? I have some excellent Camembert.'

Without waiting for an answer, Theodor Orenstein goes confidently into his tiny kitchen, opens a cupboard and takes out a round loaf wrapped in a coloured cloth. He cuts it into slices and places three cubes of strong-smelling Camembert on a clean plate with a leaf of fresh mint. 'More beer?' he asks anxiously, but forgets to fetch the bottle. A little more Camembert? Amara says no, thank you, she isn't hungry. And maybe they should be on their way back to the Pension Blumental, it's getting late. But the painter Orenstein has more to say.

Don't they want to hear the story of his parents? Don't they want to hear how that ended? He can't possibly let them go so easily. It's as if he hasn't spoken for years. He is so delighted they've come that he seems to have forgotten the large painting he was working on with its angels over the roofs.

His mother and his father and the younger children, God preserve them in glory, vanished completely. Aren't they curious? Didn't they come because they wanted to know about Orensteins living in Austria? When he managed to get back to Vienna, he found their house had been bombed. The stub ends of flats were still there as if to remind the world that people had once lived in them. Shreds of greasy stained wallpaper still hung from surviving fragments of wall, with broken windows still miraculously attached to their hinges, uprooted doors and the remains of ceilings that had collapsed in a sea of rubble.

He can still remember how he sat down in the midst of those ruins, trying to remember the exact location of the house he had shared with his mother and father. 'My mother was a strong woman, able to devote herself to a hundred initiatives, but she did not understand the Nazis at all. She thought they were just trying to create a bit of order. She thought their hatred for the Jews was only a passing whim, and that they would come to have second thoughts about it. Were they not all Austrians, the SS no less than the Jews? Had they not been taught together in the same schools, Jews and non-Jews alike, and when the Kara Mustafà and his Turks had been expelled from Austria in 1683, had they not all partied and drunk together for nine days on end? Where on earth can this volcanic hatred have come from? They had forced Andrea, a neighbour who owned a shop selling exercise books and toys for children, to put a notice in her window reading: JEWS, TRAITORS! What had they betrayed and how? Those armed guards were surely only hotheads spreading terror from sheer youthful high spirits and love of power. Did they not speak of a superman with the right to distinguish the purebred from those of inferior status? But there were only a few of these people, wild and fanatical. Most of the Viennese she knew were quiet folk who asked no more than to be allowed to live and let live, to work and start families, and to look forward to a respectable old age once they had saved enough money to buy themselves a house and a small garden. That was how most people in the city thought.

'How could these good Viennese citizens, local people she knew and had always greeted, suddenly change? What had happened to make them turn away when they saw her approaching? How could they pretend they didn't know what was happening to people arrested in the street for no apparent reason? Thrown out of their shops and homes, robbed, beaten and stripped of everything they possessed?

'Many believed and repeated among themselves that this treatment was not meant for Jews in general but only for dangerous communists who wanted to abolish private property: everything you have, house and garden, a ring, a car, a book, away with it, away with the lot, give it to the working class, that's what they said, but what did everyone else have to do with the communists? People had always been on the side of law and order. Had they not conscientiously voted for Dollfuss and his Christian Social Party in 1932? Yet it had been this same trusted Dollfuss who in '33 outlawed every political party except the Patriotic Front. How could this have happened? Even so, surely someone would sort these hotheads out. They said Hitler believed in order, and that when he came to power he would deal with these fanatics and restore harmony. Why not trust him?

The mother of the painter Theodor Orenstein had believed with many other Austrian Jews that all the buffoonery would come to an end in the firm grip of a collective conscience. Someone would awake from this sleep of reason, and giving a great guffaw of laughter would shake off the stupid fanatics who were trying to ruin a country that had lived for so long at peace with itself and others.

Theodor Orenstein had devoured his piece of Camembert and went into the kitchen to find more while he continued to tell them about the reasoning of his mother, Frau Magdalena Ruthmann. Had she been an optimist? Let's just say she had been incredulous, despite what she saw happening in her beloved city where shops belonging to Jews were being systematically stoned and set on fire, where synagogues were being destroyed and the homes of the better-off were being plundered and expropriated, where employ-ees like her husband, who had nearly reached pensionable age and never missed a day's work, were peremptorily dismissed from their jobs; despite all this she believed the storm would soon pass and normality would return. But the situation got worse day by day. Naturally the subject of pensions could not even be mentioned. Could a Jew have any right to a state pension? Of course not, who knows how much money he had stolen and stuffed under his mat-tress during his lifetime! So screamed the papers; let's just get hold of that money and stop wasting everyone's time! But what Frau Magdalena von Orenstein could not accept was that her two best friends, Mitzi and Petra, had begun pretending they didn't know her. It seemed harder to put up with this than anything else. This was the really sinister aspect of the new regime which otherwise, she thought, would rapidly pass like a cyclone which, precisely because of its enormous capacity for destruction, was bound to collapse once it had swept away the city and its trees. A few people, the oldest, would be lost, but the rest would stay in place and like surviving trees would put out new leaves next spring. This was not optimism, explained the painter Theodor Orenstein as he talked of his mother, throwing into his mouth another piece of cheese, crust and all; no, this was patriotism.

Yet this brave woman, who saw herself as Austrian to the core, had been deported with thousands of other Jews simply because she belonged to another race, a race that must be exterminated. 'But when they were in the train on their way to the camp they knew nothing of this,' insists Theodor, wiping his mouth on his shirtsleeve. His teeth are stained with tobacco but the smile he turns on Amara is radiant. For him this Italian girl is directly descended from Piero della Francesca and Mantegna, two paint-ers he loves above all others and seems to see in her face with its fine chestnut hair and lively nut-brown eyes.

The trains were crammed full beyond all limits. People died of hunger and thirst. Especially those who had come from far away. It wasn't really very far from Vienna to Auschwitz. But the train would stop for hours in open country for no apparent reason. Some managed to glimpse something between the crossed planks. Many of the wagons were ordinary goods trucks without steel doors, so to prevent any contact with the outside world planks had been nailed up horizontally and vertically. But sometimes a chink had remained, and someone had clambered up on someone else's shoulders and reported back: Where were they? What could he see? Were there any guards about? Was there anyone to ask for a little water? Or who might take a bit of paper with an address on it?

But while they were discussing what to do the train would give a great jerk and continue on its way, belching out a stinking suffocating black smoke that infiltrated the chinks. Everyone was coughing. Someone swore. A child was crying. A mother tried to comfort it. Some had never left their native villages before and never been on a train. They had of course seen cattle trucks stopped at level crossings, full of the tossing silent heads of cows. Dark and peaceful yet terrified eyes peering at the outside world. Could those cows have known they were on their way to death? Of course not, though they may have sensed something. That standing crammed side by side in the dark, that mad racing without rest, light or air, was that not a sufficient sign of contempt to make them suspect a catastrophic end? But the cows passing through the crossing still seemed to be hoping for a place to graze, a little grass, a little sun. While these were men, women and children who never, no matter how vivid their imagination, could have thought they would find themselves in those same trucks, in exactly the same conditions as the cows that had staggered against one another and lowed in desperation while horseflies stung their backs and the floor became slippery from the urine flowing uncontrolled from their congested guts.

They could never have believed that one day they too would be imprisoned in those cattle trucks, crushed and desperate like the cows they had so pitied when the train had stopped near the closed barriers of a level crossing. That had been the fate of Theodor's parents. How could he know, when he had managed to escape and had never seen the inside of such a train? It was only after the end of the war that one morning he heard a survivor talking on the radio about how he had suffered on one of those freight trains where he had been thrown together with a lot of other Jews, it was only then that Theodor realised what had happened. He knew for a fact that his parents had been in those trains because the young man, presented by the radio interviewer as a miraculously unharmed extermination camp survivor, had mentioned Krügerstrasse. Theodor and his parents had lived at number 9 Krügerstrasse. The survivor himself had lived at number 17 Krügerstrasse and said that on that morning of 15 January 1944 three Jewish families had been taken away, two from number 17 and one from number 9. Number 9, the survivor continued, had a great plaque over its front door to say that Mozart, as a child, had lived a few weeks in a flat on the first floor. How strange the name of Mozart sounded in the context of that inferno of human lunacy and brutal abuse. The mere thought of Mozart jarred with that confusion of crime and persecution. What would the young wonder musician have said if he had seen with his own eyes those innocent and unsuspecting people crushed into a truck, ten, thirty or a hundred together, simply because they were Jewish? Yet now when Theodor thinks of their home at Krügerstrasse 9 he can't help feeling a sense of lightness. As though in the midst of that horror there had been one kind soul. Perhaps Mozart had never really lived in that house, perhaps it was only a myth, a grotesque boast: how could anyone ever prove the great musician had spent a few weeks in that building? He himself was not convinced, but he liked to treat the episode as historical fact. After all, who could be sure that, in some childhood letter, the adolescent Wolfgang Amadeus might not have mentioned that very building in Krügerstrasse? The mere mention of his name had been enough to prompt a smile of pleasure. Even if the smile had quickly changed to a grimace at the state of the staircase with its broken treads, the fallen and broken windows, and the main door, once embellished with decorative carvings and now reduced to a mere fragment of arch, worm-eaten and splintered. That musical name has a light liquid sound like a freshwater spring in the middle of a baked and bleak desert, insists the painter, by now in the grip of an irresistible surge of patriotic musical love. They would never have wanted to change the name of their palatial building, pretentiously known in the district as the Mozart House. Even if its forty apartments had contained more than three hundred people who hardly knew each other but had watched one another with suspicion since the passing of the anti-Semitic laws, and made accusations against each other whenever they had the chance. That name associated by everyone with familiar music and a happy collective memory, had sometimes been enough to bring a little peace to quarrels between households, to disperse persistent anger, to calm souls embittered by privation and the struggle to find a little milk or sugar. You only had to remind everyone in a loud voice, 'But ladies and gentlemen, this is the Mozart House!' and they would be struck dumb with shame and go back to their sad existence in what seemed an endless war.

The survivor had remembered the other two families deported at the same time as his own. He described them and in his portrait of a dressmaker who never stopped sewing day or night, using tablecloths and curtains torn from windows that she carried folded in a small suitcase to make shirts for men and women, Theodor had recognised his mother the seamstress, Magdalena Ruthmann, Frau Orenstein. Thus he came to know for certain that his own family had been deported that same morning as he listened eagerly to the story the survivor told.

But what exactly had the man on the radio revealed?

At this point Theodor Orenstein stops as if gripped by sudden shame. The shame of pain, the shame of words imbued with translucent beer. Shame before strangers who might misunderstand. Though he knows the man with the gazelles also lost his mother in a concentration camp.

'I did everything I could to trace that survivor, I phoned the radio, but they wouldn't give me his name and address. So I went to the Jewish community and asked them to put me in contact with the former deportee who had been interviewed on national radio, and finally I discovered his address. I went to see him and he told me about the 'dressmaker' Magdalena Ruthmann who had become famous in the camp for her sewing skills. The SS wives competed for her and she could always get something to eat. While my father, who had tried at the roll call to seem more robust than he was, had been sent out to work. Getting up at five and wearing only the regular striped uniform of an inmate and with hard cold clogs on his feet, he would go with a group of young men to move heavy frozen wooden railway sleepers from one side of a country road to the other. With no gloves and no hat. Two of his toes developed frostbite and were unceremoniously cut off in the infirmary. But the wound would not heal. Blood leaked out night and day and no rag could staunch it. My father got steadily weaker.

Then one day the weight of a sleeper made him slip and fall in the snow, and he couldn't get up again. The guard prodded him and pushed him with a stick, but it was no use. Two of his more charitable companions helped him to his feet, but he fell down in the snow again. He had no more will to fight. The guard, himself a prisoner, called to the SS man who was supervising them and who was standing apart beating his gloved hands together, wrapped in a greatcoat that reached to his feet. The SS man came over and loudly ordered the fallen man to get up. Huddling on the ground, my father knew quite well what to expect. Disobedience was not tolerated. But he could not go on, quite simply he could not go on and no longer even wanted to try. The SS man shouted at him one last time to get up, then pulled out his pistol. My father's companions went on urging him to get to his feet, but he curled up even more tightly on the ground and the officer shot him in the head.'

Such had been the fate of the father of the painter Theodor Orenstein. Or at least, this was how it had been described to him. Who knows if that man, who no longer had a name but had been reduced to a mere number shouted out at the dawn roll call, had really been the civil servant Adolf Orenstein, who once had dressed himself for the office every morning from head to foot in grey trousers with grey braces, a pearl-grey waistcoat, an iron-grey jacket, a mouse-grey tie decorated with tiny bluebells, and with a lead-grey hat on his head. Had he really been that faithful patriotic office-worker who voted for Dollfuss, the self-styled democrat who no sooner elected abolished all the political parties? Had he really been the nationalist Adolf Orenstein, who saw himself as having no religion since he practised no religion, and who had devoted all his efforts to the preservation of an Austrian state whose great traditions meant more to him than any god in the sky? Had it really been he who let himself fall in the snow, hiding his bandaged but constantly bleeding foot? The faithful husband of one single deeply-loved woman, Magdalena Ruthmann, dressmaker by profession, with whom he had shared home and bed for more than twenty years?

The painter Theodor Orenstein has no doubts. Hans seems a little puzzled, but doesn't dare speak. He knows the painter is deeply moved. How long since the last time he told the story of his father's death at Auschwitz that morning in January 1945, crushed by a railway sleeper, his foot with its two amputated toes that never stopped bleeding, his ribs so prominent in his chest that they could be counted one by one, his face hollow after his front teeth fell out one evening when he was trying to bite through a bread crust made from potato peel and, who knows, sawdust or even the plaster used to stop up holes in the huts? Who knows how long Theodor has been reliving that death, unable to come to terms with it? That useless, devastating, humiliating death. A death he has tried to forget but which rises again as if regurgitated in his throat every time he talks of his past. Perhaps he hates his visitors, thought Amara, for having forced him to remember. Will he be able to go on painting angels on roofs after being lacerated by that bloody memory? Or will he have to change the subject matter of his paintings? Why did such a painter with such memories not paint his father with his prison companions and his bandaged and bleeding foot, shifting frozen railway sleepers one morning in the snow? Amara would like to ask him but refrains. There is no room in Theodor's pale, desperate face for reasoning, only for a pain that demands respect.

16

Magdalena Ruthmann Orenstein escaped the gas chambers. He had discovered this too, but not from the survivor he had heard on the radio and later tracked down and interviewed. But rather from the diary of the widow of an SS officer who, seven years after her husband's death just before the camp was liberated, and after starving in a hovel among the ruins of Berlin, had found a publisher for her diary of the years 1944–1945. Its title was *Auschwitz*, and its subtitle *I Was There Too*. It was not the memoir of a surviving inmate, but of a woman who had lived with her SS officer husband in a little house all flowers and pretty curtains at the edge of the camp.

This woman had described how as a young bride she had lived in Bremen with her young husband who had started as an ordinary soldier in the Wehrmacht. Then with the growth of Nazism she had found herself first the wife of an SS-Hauptscharführer (Chief Squad Leader) and then of an SS-Untersturmführer (Junior Storm Leader or Second Lieutenant) and finally, transferred overnight to Berlin, the wife of an SS-Obersturmführer (Senior Storm Leader or First Lieutenant), which had made her very proud indeed. During these years three children had been born, of whom the youngest, Adolf, was a most beautiful blond child with blue eyes, just as recommended by the great Hitler. When her husband the SS-Obersturmführer received relocation orders he did not tell her where they were to live. It was only when they got there that his wife understood that they had been transferred to a work camp for Jewish prisoners. It was almost impossible for Aryan women even to pronounce the word 'Jewish' at that time. When they could not avoid it, they felt bound to add a grimace of disgust. According to the newspapers they all read, the Jews had been responsible for every kind of wickedness: as born loan-sharks they had stolen money from poor Austrians forced to struggle all day for a living, and had made secret pacts with the enemies of the fatherland, plotting to kill the Aryans and create a country in their own image. They were violent and domineering and wanted to impose communism, meaning the immediate and total confiscation of all private property, with the possible shooting of anyone who kept back anything at all for themselves, even a ramshackle old bicycle. On top of this they were usually physically ugly, with hooked noses, prominent negroid lips and greasy black hair. This was how they were depicted in caricatures; stooping, bony, hunchbacked and hostile, ready to grab any poor unsuspecting Austrian and suck his blood by sinking two canine teeth as sharp as corkscrews into his neck.

She herself, Frau Margarethe von Bjeck, had been as convinced as anyone that these Bolshevik Jews were a threat to the people of her country and that it was right that they should be interned in work camps in occupied Poland and that her husband Otto, as an SS officer, should have been sent to help run one of these camps. It was a great honour for her young SS-Obersturmführer, who ranked only below the camp commandant who was an SS-Sturmbannführer (Storm Unit Leader or Major). To have been entrusted with such a position was evidence of force of character, a powerful sense of duty and total loyalty to the Führer. Her husband had explained this to her as he opened the doors of their charming little house with its handmade wooden furniture, with little hearts carved into the backs of the chairs, armchairs upholstered in sea-blue velvet, wrought-iron beds and embroidered curtains. He had told her she must never speak to anyone except her neighbours, the wives of other SS officers, must look after the children and never ask him anything about his extremely important and highly confidential work. She had obeyed, passing her days indoors with her family or, with her husband's permission, being driven in an SS car to a nearby farm village, to buy something for herself and the children. Their daily provisions were brought every morning by a member of her husband's staff: milk, bread, meat and vegetables for the whole family.

From the windows of her little house on the edge of the camp, Margarethe could see birch trees silhouetted against the sky, and a pen full of geese whose angry and noisy squabbling could often be heard. Large geese with flat yellow beaks who produced gigantic eggs that she mixed with flour to make excellent pies, both sweet and savoury. The vegetables always came in boxes; sometimes asparagus, sometimes white cabbage, sometimes red cabbage. Sometimes she longed for a change, but she never complained.

Her husband, loyal to his country, never talked about his work at the camp. In any case, she had no curiosity and would not have wanted to go and look for herself. She stayed at home making her sweet and savoury cakes with apple or cabbage, and when she ran short of butter she sent to the camp kitchens for lard. A fat, yellow lard enclosed in tall narrow tins with red labels stuck on the top. She must never confuse them, a Polish cook once whispered in her ear as he brought her daily supply of food, with other tall narrow tins with purple labels that contained a gas in solid lumps called Zyklon B. She had gone to the trouble of remembering this but had been too lazy to think about it. Now she realised it had been an obedient sort of laziness, this not wanting to know, typical of SS wives. Better for wives to keep well away from secrets that might be dirty, even if in their hearts they believed them necessary to safeguard the fatherland. They must be shameful secrets, or they would have been discussed openly. Instead, in their identical little houses with their embroidered curtains, little drinks cabinets and cuckoo clocks, the men never spoke of what was happening in the camp. It was as if, when they came home and pulled off their boots and laid aside their stiff peaked caps, they were leaving behind disagreeable and sometimes filthy duties that could not be avoided. In those little houses with their gardens and flower beds, they ate, played with their children and made love to their young wives, as if living on islands of happiness suspended in space and time.

One day when there wasn't a single cloud in the sky, Frau Margarethe decided to go and pick some of the chicory she had seen growing luxuriantly in the fields round the camp, for the savoury pies she made with the goose eggs. She took a small knife and a basket lined with waxed paper. She put on a flowered dress that made the most of her slim waist – the bee, they had called her in the little town of Bremen – and a pair of shoes made with the orthopaedic cork heels that had taken the place of leather during the war. She felt cheerful and happy. She had made love with her husband the night before, after months when he had claimed to be too tired to touch her naked body. But last night he had kissed her again and again, and for once there had been no sign of the smell of permanganate she now so often associated with young Otto. The children had not woken her in the night and she had got up in the morning happy and well-rested, ready for the little domestic duties of the day.

While picking the chicory she had become aware of a strange smell of smoke. A smell she had never noticed in her own house, even when she opened the windows. A sweetish, feral smell, a smell which as it began to fill her nostrils seemed increasingly distasteful and disagreeable to her. She had raised her eyes, trying to make out where it was coming from, breathing the air deeply. But all round her was nothing but fields, wet grass, birches with streaky trunks and, some distance off, the walls of the camp. When the light wind that had carried the smell to her nose seemed to change direction, she had gone back to gathering chicory.

But after ten minutes or so the wind began blowing in her direction again and she had been assailed not only by the nauseous smell but by a puff of dark grey smoke that had seemed to adhere to her skin. She touched her naked arm with her hand and felt something she did not understand on her fingers. When she looked more closely, she realised it was ash. An almost imperceptible greasy ash giving off a disgusting smell.

Looking towards the camp she had noticed the chimney for the first time. It was not visible from her house, or even from her little garden. But from here, from this field where she was picking chicory, she had suddenly seen the tower in its full grandeur. It was belching out turgid grey smoke streaked with white, a bloated, greasy smoke that settled in an adhesive film.

Why did they insist on calling it a tower if it was a really a chimney? Something entered her mind like a secret, hidden memory. Suddenly she remembered words she had not understood at the time when she heard them. Words her husband Otto had spoken one evening to another officer on the telephone. Something about an oven 'that is not working as it should, two of the furnaces are out of order and what are we going to do with so many bodies waiting?' What had he been talking about, her SS officer husband Otto von Bjeck? In that moment a suspicion crossed her mind: what was the chimney for? Why did it pour out all that stinking smoke?

That evening Frau Margarethe asked her husband a question, despite the tacit agreement between them that they should never talk about life inside the camp. Despite her knowledge that he would never discuss what happened inside those walls either with her or the children. To protect his family, of course, just as sensitive people should not be exposed to the more painful images of war. But even so, after washing up and putting the children to bed, she had not been able to stop herself asking him what the chimney was for and what the foul-smelling smoke was. He did not answer, but forbade her to go out again without his permission, and above all never again to go gathering chicory in the fields round the camp. Not only that: her young husband's face, normally so serene and relaxed when he came home to his wife and children, had suddenly hardened and turned pale. The rosy lips she so loved kissing froze into an angry grimace and he said not another word all evening. Later he went out to the camp and came home blind drunk.

This was what Margarethe von Bjeck had written in her camp diary *Auschwitz: I Was There Too*, carefully preserved by the painter Theodor Orenstein. On page thirty-six she mentions the dressmaker Magdalena Ruthmann, for whom all the camp officers' wives competed because of her sewing skills. Margarethe von Bjeck sings her praises. She tells how, following her own instructions, Magdalena Ruthmann had transformed a piece of damask owned by a Jewish family whose property had been confiscated on arrival at the camp into an elegant little coat for her younger daughter. And how she had made four shirts for her husband Otto from a sheet taken from the suitcase of an elderly Dutchwoman.

The dressmaker Ruthmann, said Margarethe von Bjeck, had survived to the end, always welcome at the front doors and in the orderly and well-equipped kitchens of the SS families, not only for her skill but for her speed in transforming tablecloths and sheets into clothes for adults and children. She was always cheerful, according to the author, and always available, and the officers' wives sometimes showed her their gratitude with a goose egg or a piece of pumpkin, or at times a little bread.

According to Margarethe von Bjeck, at the liberation of the camp the dressmaker Ruthmann had been killed by a Russian soldier who had mistaken her for one of the SS. So wrote the soldier's wife who, seven years after the death of her husband, had felt a need to set down in a book her experience of the Auschwitz camp, claiming she had known nothing of what had happened there, except on the day she went to pick chicory in the fields near the camp, saw smoke rising from the chimney and remembered some incomprehensible words her husband had spoken. She had perhaps understood what was happening but had not gone to see for herself, had not tried to find out more; had kept herself to herself and only after the war had written that ambiguous book so many Austrians bought in an attempt to understand better what had happened in those camps, and how it had been possible for intelligent young women to live for several years shut up in little houses behind embroidered curtains without ever going to poke their noses into the nearby inferno.

That evening, in her bed at the pension Blumental, Amara runs over again in her mind the words of the painter Theodor and the book by the widow of the officer von Bjeck that he had showed them, its page thirty-six creased and marked where it said the dressmaker Magdalena Ruthmann had been killed by a Russian soldier who had mistaken her for one of the SS. But it did not say why she had been wrongly identified as an SS. Had she been given a Nazi uniform in return for her dressmaking work? Difficult to say. It would have been strictly forbidden for a Jewess to go anywhere near a uniform. But the author doesn't explain and the painter Theodor is consumed by doubt. The man with the gazelles suggests going together to this lady and talking to her about her memories. Theodor replies he has already thought of that, but that the author of the book is dead, or at least so he was told the day he went to look for her.

Had he himself formed any idea of how his mother might have died? He shook his head with a puzzled expression. Yet he had searched everywhere for the name of that Russian soldier who had been one of the first to reach the camp at Auschwitz. He had even been as far as Moscow in his search for this 'soldat'. He had studied lists shown him by the military authorities. He had examined the newspapers of the time, but had been unable to find any mention of the soldier who had accidentally shot his mother thinking she was an SS. So much so that he had begun to think the man was probably a figment of the imagination of von Bjeck's wife.

Were the von Bjecks a noble family? Quite likely, said the painter of angels on roofs, but a decayed one. The only noble thing they had left was their name. No property and no culture. Otto von Bjeck himself had studied little and unprofitably and enrolled in the SS because they guaranteed him a fixed salary and a house. He had met his wife at a training camp. They had married and produced four children. Then he had been sent to Auschwitz and had died there a few days before the Russians came. His wife does not say how.

His wife's book *Auschwitz: I Was There Too* was a macabre statement that had nonetheless enabled her to sell her small volume as the work of a witness not responsible for what happened. She had died after the war in the house of her mother, where she had ended up with her four small children. It was not until immediately after the war that she first understood the reality of the camp, or so she claimed. When for the first time she had pushed open that gate under the words WORK SETS YOU FREE. And seen the famous chimney tower. And the ovens in which the corpses had been thrown after they were pulled from the gas chambers.

She had passed some of the survivors, thin and dirty, chilled and enfeebled, still crowded behind the barbed wire as they waited to return home.

It was then, according to her own account, that she had begun to weep at the horror. And she had wept for the death of her young husband who, despite everything, had kissed and embraced her passionately during the dark nights in that house with embroidered curtains; she had wept for him too while she wept for those poor people who had starved to death or been gassed, and been shut up in ovens until all trace of their bodies had been destroyed, guilty because they had come from another race. That was how the widow of SS officer von Bjeck had wept, she who was to write the book *Auschwitz: I Was There Too*, and who would die of a tumour at the age of thirty-five in the house of her mother in Bremen, leaving four small orphans and a photograph of herself with her husband the Obersturmführer, both smiling with their heads pressed together.

Now the painter Theodor is resting exhausted on one of the two chairs in his humble flat, lips trembling and eyes feverish from the effort he has made. Amara smiles at him gratefully. But he has closed his eyes and seems to have nothing more to say. He is as empty as the bottle lying at his feet.

The man with the gazelles suggests it's time to go. Theodor struggles to open his eyes and focus on the people before him.

'Goodbye,' he says half-heartedly. 'And good luck with your search for Emanuele.'

He makes no effort to accompany them to the door. They leave him sitting with his legs apart, eyes dull and arms hanging loosely at his sides.

'Perhaps we should take the glasses and the plate with what's left of the cheese to the kitchen.'

'He'll look after that.'

In fact, as they close the door they see the painter struggle up from the chair and distractedly collect the glasses and the plate of Camembert and take everything behind the curtain.

'He has dazed me with his memories,' says Hans, shaking his head.

'He's been generous.'

'But not about Emanuele.'

'Do you really think he knows nothing?'

'I doubt it.'

17

One time Emanuele and Amara went on their bicycles in the direction of Monte Morello, stopping at the de' Seppi spring. Babbo Sironi who dearly loved the hills and knew everything about making expeditions, had set them up. Their rucksacks contained two omelette paninis, a bottle of water, some alcohol for use as a disinfectant, some gauze and cotton and a little merbromin antiseptic. In another much smaller box were the glue and patches they needed for their unreliable locally made tyres. They also had some milk chocolate, two apples and a map of Tuscany.

They carried pumps on their bicycle frames in case their tyres went flat as they pedalled. And they did go flat very easily. Because they were made of material produced 'by spitting', as Papà Orenstein used to say. A man both pernickety and generous. He had already been married and the father of two children when he met the beautiful Thelma Fink, who played small parts in films. He left his wife and daughters to live with a woman ten years his junior. And Thelma, who had always claimed she never wanted to tie herself down for any reason and hoped to make acting a full-time career, suddenly changed her mind: she left the cinema without suffering any obvious distress and followed her husband to Florence where he owned a toy factory. There they took a beautiful villa surrounded by greenery in the Rifredi area and produced a son whom they called Immanuel, which means 'God with us', in Italian Emanuele. In those days cows and sheep grazed the park round Villa Lorenzi, and it was amid those ample pastures that the cherry tree grew, the tree where Emanuele and the little Amara would meet and fall in love.

Amara lived with her shoemaker father and her mother in a small house some three hundred metres from the gardens of the villa, at the junction of Via Incontri and Via Alderotti. An old farmhouse with an added toilet that stuck out from the first floor.

One May morning Amara had ventured into the garden of Villa Lorenzi, whose secret passages she knew by heart, and had settled under the cherry tree book in hand, reading and imagining things. She had no idea that anyone was hidden among the branches above her head watching her. Her mind was far away in a natural harbour somewhere in the south seas, where a pioneer ship had just dropped anchor in water as transparent as glass, and where the coast was apparently empty and hospitable, but in fact full of snares for the unwary. What was Captain D to do? His ship was damaged and he needed water for his sailors.

At that point a revolving bluish-green leaf shaped like a lance came twisting down and fell on the middle of her open book. She pushed it aside without a thought. But a few seconds later another leaf, dancing and turning, landed in the same place. She brushed that away too, with a gesture of impatience. She wanted to concentrate on the bay and the ship and on the problems of Captain D and his thirsty crew

So she continued reading, but a few minutes later something hard hit her on the neck. A little red cherry that bounced off her hair and fell near her left shoe. Finally she raised her eyes from the book and bending back her head looked up to see two legs with naked sunburned feet dangling from a branch, and above them the face of a child with a blond quiff and laughing eyes. It had been her first sight of Emanuele and from then on, whenever she thought of him, she always saw that image of the free and agile body of a small boy apparently suspended in thin air, his face surprised and happy, his eyes full of the joy of life.

By the time of their bicycle expedition they had already been friends for two years. Everyone knew how close they were and no one seemed to mind. Babbo Karl Orenstein loved the little girl with the sensible and kindly air, hoping she might for a while restrain his son from the dangers he seemed so determined to throw himself headlong into. Mamma Thelma smuggled chocolate into their rucksacks whenever they set off on an expedition outside the city. Babbo Amintore Sironi was probably more cautious. Even if Mamma Stefania urged him to leave them alone; they were two children who knew perfectly well how to look after themselves. Though they were afraid of nothing they were not reckless, they were fully aware of dangers and took care to avoid them. But to Babbo Amintore they were too careless: 'There are too many delinquents about; too many crooks ready to kill just for a bicycle.' It was something they were all afraid of even if luckily so far nothing like that had happened near Rifredi. Lots of thefts yes, but no one would commit a crime just to steal a bicycle. The Orensteins were too rich to worry, protected in their villa by gardeners and guard dogs. But the Sironis, whose ancient hovel had nothing more substantial than a little wooden gate, were mistrustful, especially Amintore who as a shoemaker was used to judging people's characters from their shoes. He was extremely perspicacious and usually right. If someone was very hard on his shoes it meant he was absent-minded and often tripped or stumbled, had no sense of orientation and was always bumping into things. If he wore his shoes down on one side it must mean he was a spy with a crooked walk who backed up against walls. And as for women, he knew everything about them from the way they consumed their heels and tightened their laces, and from the polish they chose to shine the uppers of a pair of shoes finished in red Chinese lacquer, for example, or green jade or Prussian blue. Sor Amintore, as they respectfully called him in the district, trusted nobody. He had a precise and astute way of looking at them, starting with their shoes then raising his eyes up their bodies. It was an inquisitorial look and not benevolent, but he did not make mistakes. He did not trust those Orensteins from Austria, a country so quick to adopt Nazism, which he hated because to him it was obscene. Yes, he did know they were Jews, but that was the reason he approved of his daughter associating with them. He had no use at all for the rich as such. Being rich proved they must have been thieves because no one gets rich by accident. Their children might have never stolen anything themselves, but they were still perforce the children of rich thieves; and if they had inherited from rich forbears, their status depended precisely on that, and what can the rich ever know about real life? Had they ever taken a pair of holed shoes in hand to resole them? Had they ever sniffed at a pair of bootees with their laces ripped out and soles worn down from endlessly walking the pavements? Nor did he trust that Emanuele who went everywhere in bare feet, like a Zulu in Africa, and ate and slept in trees; you could smell the stink of spoilt brat from miles away. Nor did he like his daughter Amara going around with that scamp scrumping cherries from the highest branches and catching tadpoles among the stones of the Terzolle River. 'He's turning her into a wild thing,' he would say to his wife, grumbling as he carefully hammered tiny nails into a shoe. He would grumble too about the poor quality of the leather available in these times of national economic self-reliance. 'These people would palm off frogskin as calfskin,' he would say, testing with his teeth a piece of pigskin that had cost him a fortune. His mouth was his best counsellor. His mouth and teeth could tell him what to expect from a particular piece of shoe leather.

Yet it was only in the Second World War, after he had been pensioned off wounded from Ethiopia, that Sironi had started earning real money as a shoe repairer. No one could any longer afford to buy new shoes so they all went to him for new soles and laces, to have old uppers reconstructed or to have worn discoloured leather dyed. So much work of this kind came his way that he eventually took on an assistant, whom he insisted on paying well, because that was how he had started himself and he had no wish to exploit others in the way that others had exploited him.

A large photograph hanging in the back room of the shop showed the whole Sironi family: grandfather Anacleto with his well-waxed moustaches with upturned points; father Amedeo Sironi, also a shoemaker, holding in his hands the instruments of his trade, a small hammer and metal anvil. The photo dated from 1910. Next to the father and son were uncles Angelo and Anacleto, also in leather aprons with rolled-up shirtsleeves and holding shoemaker's knives. The very young Amintore was visible too, a small boy hiding behind the massive figure of his father. The photograph proclaimed the integrity and philosophy of the family: discipline, solidarity and loyalty to their trade, because that was how they saw it: theirs was an art of making and constructing, of understanding and repairing. They were faithful to a tradition of freedom and independent of everything and everyone. They nearly welcomed fascism in its heady first years when Mussolini seemed to be adopting socialist views, but when the reality became clear and the self-proclaimed socialist began associating first with the great industrialists and then with the Germans, they decided to oppose him, though cautiously because you can't mess with thugs. Amintore had done everything possible to avoid being sent to Ethiopia to fight against Africans for an empire he didn't believe in. But he had to go all the same. And had come home wounded. After that he tried to keep as low a profile as possible. He and his whole family had kept themselves to themselves, not hiding their beliefs but not parading them either. None of them joined the fascist party, not obliged to since they were not public servants. A degree of detachment was permitted to the humble self-employed. So long as it did not lead to outright denunciation of pretensions of the regime. That would bring imprisonment. They maintained a careful balance, and kept their heads down. They never wore the fez or black shirt, or joined in rallies or parades.

On one occasion Uncle Anacleto, in the photograph next to grandfather Anacleto Sironi of the thick upturned moustaches, had been stopped when going into the shop by a group of fascists who asked him why he had not raised his arm in salute and cried 'eia eia alalà' when a car passed carrying a Party leader in uniform. Terrified, Anacleto had mumbled something. The gang grabbed him by the arms and kneed him in the back, forcing open his mouth to thrust in the neck of a bottle of castor oil. When he had swallowed the lot they left him, laughing as he ran to the toilet clasping his stomach. In fact he was lucky because often, always ten against one, they would beat people with sticks or iron knuckle-dusters, kicking their unfortunate victim till he fell gasping to the ground.

There was another reason why Amintore Sironi was worried by this friendship between the rich son of a Jewish family and a humble shoemaker's daughter. It wasn't just the class difference; he believed on principle that mixtures of rank never led to anything good. What could the rich know about love and marriage? Even when they seemed kind and friendly, deep down they were still arrogant and self-satisfied. They believed their cursed money made them superior. He knew them, and he knew their shoes. And it wasn't just a matter of money, but of religion too. The Sironis weren't practising Catholics, but that was their cultural background. The Orensteins seemed not to be especially religious, but their outlook on life was certainly Jewish. What would they have done if Amara had had a son, would they have circumcised him? The very idea was more than he could take. Which was why he grumbled when she disappeared for days on end with her Emanuele.

18

That day Amara and Emanuele had headed on their bicycles for Monte Morello, despite Babbo Amintore's misgivings. They passed a yelling lorry-load of fascists returning from some nearby demonstration. The hotheads took no notice of the two children on bicycles. Perhaps they had already let off steam in some work-ingmen's club by attacking workers peacefully playing bowls, or youngsters heading for work without the compulsory fascist badge on their jackets. They knew there was an atmosphere of resistance among the factories of Rifredi. It was said that was where you'd find those treacherous communists who were plan-ning to take over everyone's house and allotment and even the women's buckles and the men's best clothes in order to national-ise them and this was not acceptable, which was why people had to be beaten up or dosed with castor oil. Fascism would bring a glorious imperial future, everybody must be clear about that. And anyone who wasn't had to be spineless, or a dangerous Jew or homosexual pervert or still worse, a Bolshevik. So the fascists threw themselves on such people in the name of their country and of the great Leader of the nation who spoke to them once a week on the radio in his fierce masculine voice from the balcony in Piazza Venezia in Rome.

Many young women were attracted to these young men with their flags and raised arms who leapt with such agility onto their lorries shouting '*eia eia alalà*' and winking at the pretty girls they met on their way and as they sang in resonant voices 'To arms! To arms! The vanguard to arms! The fascists' revenge!' They were always ready for a fight, laughing at everything and shouting 'What the hell do I care!' whenever anyone accused them of being domineering and unjust.

Amara had a cousin called Gigliola, also a shoemaker's daugh-ter, who was so in love with one of these thugs that she was always begging him to let her join his gang on their 'punitive expeditions'. But they would tease her: 'A woman coming with us? We're not ladies' men off to the drawing room, you know!' And when she insisted, they yelled in her face, 'Let's see your balls then!' and since Gigliola Sironi obviously couldn't produce any balls to order she was always left behind. She would run furiously after the lorry shouting 'Damn you, you'll be sorry for this!' No one knew whether they were supposed to be sorry they'd left her behind, or whether she was warning them that one day they would have to appear before God to account for what they had done with their clubs and their handcuffs, their flags with skulls on and their bottles of castor oil.

Gigliola often went to see Amara and battered her ears with the praises of Cosimo and his gang. To her they were a company of young gods with tanned faces and shining eyes full of hatred for the enemy, ready to punish sinners: does not the Archangel Michael use his sword to kill a dragon? And does not the Archangel Gabriel send fire and snow to strike down his enemies? Amara did not share this exalted view of these thugs her eighteen-year-old cousin Gigliola admired as avengers from heaven. To Amara they seemed nothing more than penniless boys who had learned no trade and whose way of venting their resentment on the world lay in trampling on the weakest. 'They pick fights and justify it politically,' said her father Amintore, angrily hammering nails into shoes. In the family, cousin Gigliola was dismissed as an unfortunate woman who used love to justify the violent behaviour of ruffians. Whenever she could she would go dancing with them, or to bathe with them in the Arno taking panini for everyone, or accompany them to church to ask for a blessing after some particularly ferocious action, or march with them while they sang the praises of the Duce, or motorcycle up and down the avenues with her arms clasped round the waist of her beloved Cosimo and her cheek pressed against his back. One evening when they had drunk more than usual the whole gang nearly raped her; they had been teasing her because she 'was afraid of nothing and wanted to help beat up the workers herself as if she had balls.' Luckily for her, Cosimo as their leader stopped them, not out of consideration for her but because she belonged to him so no one else could touch her.

That warm September day, Amara and Emanuele had pedalled laboriously up the Montorsoli road as far as Ceppetto church and then along the Scollini side-road until they reached the de' Seppi spring. There they tied their bicycles to the trunk of a maple with reddening pointed leaves. They walked along a path among the limes and pines, which widened at a certain point into a small but very green secluded patch of grass. There they had taken their omelette sandwiches from their rucksacks and had eaten them greedily in the shade of those pointed leaves oscillating in the sun. Mamma Thelma had been so thoughtful as to slip into her son's pack at the last minute two peeled cucumbers and a little paper twist of salt. They had devoured these too, and drunk some water from their bottles. Then they had stretched out in the sun with their heads in the shade of the dancing leaves. They did not speak or put their arms round each other. They did not even look at each other. But during those few glorious minutes they felt themselves a single being, indivisible. Their hands touched by accident and stayed clasped together while their eyes closed in bliss. Amara remembered it as a moment of absolute happiness.

Now in bed in a Viennese pension during the cold war Amara asks herself whether sex excludes love. Whether the union of two bodies brings something peremptory and immediate that tends to invade the delicate realm of feeling and brutally blast everything sky-high. How can continuity, constancy and understanding be reconciled with the lazy immediacy of sex? Why had she felt so content and happy with a deliciously full amorous happiness precisely at that moment when she and Emanuele had lain head to head on a meadow rich with new grass, under the dancing leaves of a maple fluttering in the wind of a Florentine summer? Was this the ecstasy of chaste love, as taught by the church? The kind of love St Clare and St Francis may have experienced long ago in thirteenth-century Assisi? Can it be that sexual love breeds something violent that corrupts every long-term project? Something self-satisfied that tends to use habit to destroy any exaltation of what is new? The very habit that lies at the heart of a shared life: the joy of doing the same things together, of planning the future, of feeling permanently and continuously united at every moment, day after day, hour after hour; how can that be reconciled with the satiety, with the nausea of repetition, with the need for novelty erotic love demands? Not easy to answer such questions. Also because desire had already been there, knocking impatiently for admittance to her childish belly.

Amara turns on the light. Her pillow is bunched up on one side and slithering away on the other, emaciated and flattened. She has not yet managed to get used to these Austrian beds with their concave pillows that let her head sink unsupported. She picks up the book she has been reading, *Northanger Abbey*. It was Jane Austen who gave rise to her reflections on sexuality and love. If she compares her to another woman writer more than a generation younger, Emily Brontë, she finds precisely this difference. Jane Austen always stops short of the sexual act. On the threshold of a marriage that it is assumed will be happy, though this is not investigated. But Emily Brontë does not stop outside the bedroom door. And that bedroom is the source of all the pain and suffering of a heart in love. Jane Austen is a happy, playful writer; Emily Brontë dramatic and angry. One shares the eighteenth-century grace of Mozart. The other has already passed on to the deeply felt visions of a dark romantic thinker like Beethoven.

Probably Amara would never have been here in Vienna, in the company of her eccentric travelling companion, searching for traces of Emanuele, if she had never experienced with him that love as complete in itself as an egg: radiant, perfectly formed, warm and full of life. Like the egg of Eurynome, the ancient goddess of the Pelasgians, which long nurtured inside itself all the forests of the world, all the seas, all the lakes and rivers, all the mountains and fields and birds and fish imaginable. Every living thing was enclosed in that egg, condensed into a tiny space. Only the warmth of the mother's body made the growth of the seas and the mountains possible until, as they grew, they broke the egg and spread throughout the universe, creating the Earth in all its beauty and variety.

19

Time to get up, Amara! She hurriedly pulls her legs out of the sheet which has wound itself round her waist during the night. The smell of coffee rising from lower floors urges her on. Her appointment with the man with the gazelles is at eight and she's still dreaming.

Today it's the turn of Elisabeth Orenstein, a name found in the telephone book. Could she be one of Emanuele's relatives?

Half an hour later, Amara and the man with the gazelles climb the grey stone steps to a mansion in Secession style. The great door before them has windows covered with tropical flowers and birds of paradise. A fine house still strangely intact amid the rubble of the war.

They press a button that sets off a bell worthy of a convent full of nuns. They hear hurried steps, then the handle turns and the door opens. On the threshold is a woman of average height with smiling sky-blue eyes, ruffled grey hair and hands stained with what they will later realise is glue. She already knows what they are looking for and seems happy to see them. She welcomes them into the living room and invites them to sit on small armchairs upholstered in corduroy and protected by coarse white sheets. With a quick youthful movement, she sits down cross-legged on the carpet as if used to practising yoga. Two sturdy freckled calves emerge from beneath her crumpled blue skirt.

'What can I do for you?'

Amara is about to speak, but the man with the gazelles is too quick for her. He clearly feels it his duty to smooth her path. He tells their hostess about Emanuele Orenstein, a son of Austrian Jews who lived many years in Florence before returning out of a mistaken sense of patriotism to Vienna just when the Nazis were stepping up their persecution of his race. Amara still has many letters from the little boy of that time who wrote to her almost every day. And after the war she received in the post a school exercise book containing letters he had not been able to send her. The last of these is dated May 1943 and seems to have been written in the ghetto at Łódź. His friend Maria Amara believes young Emanuele must have been transported to Auschwitz because that is what usually happened to Jews from the Łódź ghetto. That is why she is here, trying to find him alive or dead, above all because she constantly dreams that Emanuele is speaking to her, asking her to come to him. Meanwhile she would like to know if you, Elisabeth Orenstein, are related to Emanuele, and whether you ever met him or know what happened to his family.

The woman seems overwhelmed by all this information. She says yes, she did know Emanuele's parents, the engineer Karl Orenstein and his second wife Thelma Fink. But she was not related to them. She remembers hearing many discussions in the Jewish community about people who came back and she always thought their case the most striking. Others had returned from abroad during the thirties but with more reason. But that a Jewish family, however rich, should return to Vienna in the worst years of Jewish persecution had seemed exceptionally rash even to the most optimistic. Remember that most Austrian Jews, particularly the better-off ones, had already left, mostly for the United States or Palestine or Latin America. She had heard of very few travelling in the opposite direction. Though there were a few and none more striking than Karl and Thelma Orenstein. It is just possible they might be distant relatives of hers, but she has never been much interested in family relationships.

Elisabeth's mother died young. As soon as the Nazi persecutions started, her father took her with him to Holland. Just before the Nazi invasion they moved on to Palestine. There they worked hard, helping to develop the first kibbutzim. Her father, an electrotechnical engineer, applied himself to cultivating the land. Elisabeth herself collected tomatoes and drove a tractor up and down the arid furrows. They dug wells in the desert to find water for the fields. Difficult years, full of hardship but also of intense enthusiasm. Every day people arrived from all over the world and were kindly received. Everyone worked uncomplainingly in the fields as if their energy would never be exhausted. The energy of a rediscovered land, of a new nation rolling up its sleeves and building its own homes, farms, industries and schools.

Amara sympathetically watches this generous woman talking without reserve about her past. Like Emanuele's own story, a typical story of European Jews; full of variety, complexity and problems and containing both winners and losers.

'How come you didn't stay in Palestine?' asks the man with the gazelles.

'Something got spoilt with the passing of time. First constant disputes with the Palestinians whose land however legitimately we had taken away from them. The United Nations approved it and had legalised our invasion, but it was an invasion all the same and this the Palestinians were not willing to accept. On the other hand, where else could Jews who had been expelled from their homes in Europe go? Madagascar had been suggested, a project of Hitler's that came to nothing because the British navy made access to the African island impossible. And so we had to learn to use force. Militarism became stronger than the will to rebuild the land of our fathers. What had started as a wonderful duty to defend and construct turned into a senseless war against people poorer and more radically displaced than ourselves. Rather than mitigating and improving our difficult relations with the Palestinians as we had initially hoped, other Arab nations made things worse by stoking up the fire and planning to annihilate us, just like Hitler. So defending ourselves became first a necessity and then a neurosis. Who did the land belong to? To Jews with religious roots fishing in the historical waters of cities like Jerusalem and Haifa, or to the Palestinians who had cultivated it for centuries and made their homes there? And we who had lost millions of our brothers and sisters in the Nazi gas chambers, had we any right to a refuge there? We who had worked from our first arrival to transform abandoned deserts into flowering gardens, what were we to do? Let ourselves be thrown out a second time? Arms have grown daily more important, as have soldiers, generals and war heroes. My belief was that security should not start with rifles, but with the building up of a new relationship with our neighbours, with whom we needed to learn how to share the land. Ours had been a painful nomadic history, but now we wanted to settle in one place at last and cultivate our land in peace. At first this spirit of peaceful conquest and good neighbourliness did exist. Then it was somehow lost. Certainly the Arab world did nothing to encourage conciliation, but rather did everything possible to make the friction between us and the Palestinians bitterer than ever. They never raised a finger to encourage the creation of two autonomous and friendly neighbouring states. They have shouted so violently that Israel must be destroyed and the Jews eliminated that the Israeli people have come to think only in terms of defence and making preparations for war. That was not the ideal of those of us who have always been pacifists. Others wanted peace too, but they were in danger of being condemned as traitors to their own land. In short, life became difficult. Which is why we left Israel and why we are here now. In any case, German was our language and our mountains are here in central Europe; how could we ever forget our mountains?'

Elisabeth smiles as she speaks. The sky-blue eyes grow wider in her pale face. There is something sincere about her, something gentle, and yet at the same time she is clearly a fighter. She stands up and slaps her forehead with her hand. 'But where are my manners, I haven't offered you anything,' she says cheerfully, going into the kitchen, soon returning with a huge plate of fresh fruit and glasses of iced tea.

'Please try to remember something more of the family of Karl and Thelma, if you can,' presses the man with the gazelles who seems to have taken the search for Emanuele so much to heart as to have made it almost his own.

Amara bites into an apple. Her eyes follow Elisabeth's solid body as it moves lightly through her luminous house. When she let them in she had told them her work was making new bindings for antique books. In fact, spread everywhere are large volumes with newly reconstructed parchment covers, and slender books in red and brown leather covers. And jars of glue, balls of string and fine cord, bobbins of sewing-thread, rolls of paper in all colours and sheets of parchment stretched between strips of wood and presses of every size.

'Is this where you make the new bindings for your books?'

'This is the only room I have for work and receiving people. My bedroom is upstairs. Out there on the balcony I grow Italian basil and honeysuckle. This was once a great house inhabited by a Wehrmacht officer, a certain Captain Hoffman. He had fifteen rooms and I don't know how many servants. After the war it was divided into a lot of tiny apartments. I live in this one. In the other rooms there's a railwayman and his family, and a postal worker with two delightful twins who often come to see me when I'm making chocolate cake. I make it specially for them. Though it's not easy to find cocoa powder these days. And when you do find it, it's so expensive, too much for my pocket.'

The man with the gazelles keeps mentioning Emanuele but it seems Elisabeth has little more to add. 'It gets really cold here in winter. The windows don't close properly and there's no money for new ones. I have a coal stove, but the coal's in the cellar and I have to climb up and down the stairs with buckets that dirty my hands and clothes. Sometimes the water is cut off and the electricity fades and surges and blows out the bulbs. When I complain they tell me we're living in a difficult post-war period. But the war finished eleven years ago. The trouble is the city's filling with people and there isn't enough energy for everyone.'

And Emanuele? Why does she avoid mentioning him? Is there something she doesn't want to say or can't say?

Amara continues to watch the woman who has gone back to sitting on the floor, crossing her legs with remarkable agility. Now she has also taken off her shoes and is massaging her feet which are covered with white cotton socks.

'Can you really not remember anything more of this family that bears your own name? Surely people must have talked about them when they returned to the city of their ancestors in a time of total war?'

'I was in Palestine,' she answers thoughtfully. 'We knew so little about what was happening in Vienna, perhaps we didn't even want to know. Our horizons had changed completely and our problems were different. Even the books we read had changed: Tolstoy and Stefan Zweig had given way to the Bible and George Orwell. I know little or nothing of Karl and Thelma even if they may have been distant relatives. Someone even accused them of being paid German spies. It was the only explanation anyone could imagine for the choice they had made. A stupid, insane choice. It probably led to death for all of them.'

'They could also have been arrested in Italy,' Amara ventures to say. 'In October 1943 the Jews of Rome thought they were safe because they had handed over fifty kilos of gold they had struggled to collect to an SS major called Kappler in exchange for an assurance of security. The Nazis had promised that once the gold had reached them the Jews of the Rome ghetto would be left in peace. Instead early on the morning of 16 October they came with cattle trucks and collected every Jew they could lay their hands on: women, children, old people, anyone who couldn't get away. They were all deported to Auschwitz.'

'But Karl and Thelma came from Florence. Perhaps it would have been easier for them to escape the Nazis?'

'Three hundred and two were deported from Florence and the surrounding district. Does that seem little to you?'

'But do you really think they were spying for the Nazis?' persists Hans.

'I don't know. Their insistence on returning to Vienna in the midst of the deportations is too bizarre. They had a large house and expensive cars and servants. How can you explain it?'

Had she not claimed to know nothing about them? That she had been in Palestine? How did she know that they had a large house and a lot of servants? But neither the man with the gazelles nor Amara dares to contradict her. She seems so sure of herself. Clearly she believes Emanuele's family sold themselves to the Nazis. But in return for what? In return for safety for themselves? How could they have trusted the Nazis? But could they have survived even if they had?

'I have no more to tell you, dear Amara, dear Hans. I really do hope they weren't spies because it would be a black mark against us all. How could they have joined the Nazis who had set themselves so ruthlessly to wipe us all out? To ensure safety for themselves? One or two did that, but they paid dearly for it. You couldn't negotiate with the Nazis, you could only fight them. If they sweet-talked you it was only to squash you more effectively a moment later. Everyone knew that. Perhaps, having been living in Florence, they had never really known what the Nazis and their imitators, the fascists, were capable of.'

'What would you advise us to do next in our search for traces of Emanuele? Who in any case can't be held responsible for the decision his parents made.'

'I'm sorry about little Emanuele. He'd be a handsome young man today.'

Amara starts. How can this woman know if he was handsome or ugly? Or is she saying this just for the sake of saying anything? Looked at more closely, she seems more enigmatic and impenetrable than she appeared at first. There is a shadow in her eyes that Amara cannot interpret. But she can guess from the contradictions and enigmatic silences that something is being left unsaid.

'You could go and see their house. I have an old telephone book from the forties I kept merely from curiosity. I'll get it for you. Have a look. If the building wasn't bombed, someone there might remember Karl and Thelma and little Emanuele better than I can. Maybe they were seen leaving in lorries like so many others, or in a limousine, as would be fitting for those who were rich and respected.'

'We know where they lived, in Schulerstrasse.'

'There you are then,' concludes Elisabeth with a kindly smile.

There seems nothing more to say. She watches them with generous eyes that nevertheless contain a hint of farewell. The man with the gazelles senses what is about to follow, and after ceremoniously kissing the hand of the binder of antique books he heads for the stairs.

Back at the Pension Blumental Amara finds a letter waiting for her. Who can have written to her in Vienna, at the address of a pension she has told no one about? She hurriedly opens the envelope. The handwriting at once brings to mind her ex-husband. It is in fact from him.

Dear Amara. I got your address from the newspaper. I don't want to disturb you, I know you're on a work assignment, but I'm in hospital and would like to talk to you. Before I go I'd like to say a few things. Forgive me for interrupting your journey. But it's only because I'm in such bad shape that I'm doing it. I shall probably not leave this hospital alive. I've read some of your articles from Poland. Congratulations. I need to see you one last time, please do as I ask, here's some money for the journey, I hope no one steals it, I've put it between two sheets of paper so no one can see it. Waiting anxiously for you, your Luca.

Amara opens the windows of her room, which smells stuffy, and thinks of the beautiful slim body of Luca Spiga. In hospital? How can she have known nothing about it? Logic tells her he's probably blackmailing her, but a gut feeling is urgently pressing her to rush to the sick man's bedside. Before she has even had time to wash her hands she finds herself thinking how to change the ticket she had already reserved and what to put in her suitcase. She will come back, she knows she must do that, but how long will she have to be away? Reason tells her to wait, to think things over, to find out more before leaving. But instinct has already made her pull down her case from on top of the large wardrobe, and open drawers large and small to start collecting together her things.

20

Three p.m. The train to Italy. With a bag bought at the last minute, into which she has hastily thrust her nightdress, some underclothes, the exercise book in which she drafts her articles and two books. She has left her father Amintore's suitcase with her jumpers, skirts, blouses and shoes in the care of Frau Morgan. It was not easy to tell the man with the gazelles that she was about to rush away.

'If you are separated from your husband why hurry to him the moment he calls for you?'

'He's ill, in hospital. He wants to see me before he dies. I'd be a monster not to go.'

'I think you're making a mistake, just when we've discovered something definite.'

'There's nothing definite, Hans. We're all at sea.'

'We were about to go and see where Emanuele lived. I've already phoned the woman who is caretaker there. The building survived, it wasn't destroyed by the bombs. They were expecting us tomorrow morning.'

'Well, tell them we'll come next week. I'm going and coming back, but I can't just not go.'

'And who's paying for this trip?'

'Luca sent me money for my ticket.'

'So it's serious.'

'I really think it is.'

'But haven't you always said he's a man who would rather forget?'

'Well, goodnight Hans. You go back to your daughter in Poznań, and I'll send you a telegram the minute I'm free to come back. I promise we will go on with our researches together.'

The man with the gazelles looks at her, discouraged. But he stops insisting. He senses her determination. Will he wait for her?

When she sees him turn and move away with his usual swinging step, shoulders slightly rounded, his fine bold neck bent forward, she is seized by apprehension and pain. 'I'll be back soon, I promise!' she shouts at his back. She sees him turn slowly. Even at a distance, she can see his eyes shining with joy. 'I'm counting on it!' he calls and disappears round the corner.

The train is a mobile home that favours more intimate thoughts. Amara has found a window seat. The air is full of that atmosphere of sweaty socks, apples and cigarettes typical of third-class carriages, but in compensation she has the compartment to herself. She is free to shut herself into her corner and bury herself in her book.

When the future captain climbs the stairs of the navigation office in London he finds himself faced with two women knitting. Conrad doesn't say it in so many words but describes them as though they were the Fates intent on spinning the thread of life. The captain stops for a moment dumbfounded. What are those two women doing in his path? Is it a presentiment of disaster? But he is a young man and tosses fear aside with a bold gesture. He will accept command of that ship, even if he knows she is old and in poor condition. He will go to Africa. Something tells him it will be a trip to hell, that it will teach him the horror human beings are capable of. But this will not stop him. He will go on to the end. Because this voyage is his destiny. And the reason he has eyes in his head is to watch and observe. To understand? Perhaps not even that. But to watch, certainly, and to bear witness to that horror. Halfway through the chapter she lifts her eyes from the printed words of the book to the window streaming with water. Outside, a dense landscape of trees. The train seems to be entering an unending forest. The branches beyond the wet panes are green with a touch of blue and then of red. Her thoughts go to Emanuele whom she feels she is betraying with this sudden abandonment. Emanuele whom death has transformed into an eternal small boy with a seductive face: a lock of blond hair perpetually falling across his broad brow, a little strong-willed nose, bright brown eyes and a sarcastic, rebellious smile sometimes shot through with pure tenderness. Those the gods love die young. Can she be sure she is not pursuing a ghost? Only ghosts can always stay themselves, always equally lovable and ready to appear at every turn of the eyes. And Luca Spiga, the man of the caresses, the man who though twenty years her senior once enchanted her with his soft, low voice and his abstention from any abrupt, angry or even irritable gesture; why does he now present himself in such a dominant way to her memory? She thought she had forgotten him. And instead, there he is, tender and precise as in the first year they lived together. Only later, only when he was beginning to get bored, did he change into an absent husband. Was that a ghost too? Who is it calling to her from his deathbed, the first Luca or the second?

Now the forest changes to a cupola or tunnel, with a dark interior. A darkness made up of curious watching eyes. Predatory eyes that penetrate the dim carriage, searching for prey. Eyes with a suspicious look. This is the cold war, this is the cold war. The terrified words of the man with the gazelles. Who should she listen to? For now she will go where the most basic duty takes her: to open the door to anyone who knocks.

At the border: another long wait. Armed guards taking away people's passports, two men smoking as they chat in the corridor. Amara can't distinguish their words but the sound of their voices reminds her of the light rumble of thunder among clouds heavy with rain. Now the train has emerged from its tunnel of trees. It stops at a station sheltered by badly lit roofs. She can hear the piston rhythms of the engine. Memory mixes personal experience with images from films seen with Luca in the little auditorium of the Charlie Chaplin Cineclub at Rifredi. Maybe Jean Cocteau's *Orphée* or Carol Reed's *The Third Man*. A figure in a long white raincoat is standing stiffly on the pavement watching her as rain falls on him. Then unexpectedly he smiles, takes off his hat and makes her a light bow. Could it be Humphrey Bogart?

Better to return to Marlow and his Congo River, over which the sails of the ivory-traders lightly float. Why is the young captain so insistent in his search for that Kurz who is believed to know more than any other European about blacks and elephants? Who is it forcing him to follow that unscrupulous man who has put down roots in a world of slaves where each head is worth less than a piece of ivory? Where the darkness grows ever more dense and complex and at the bottom of which nothing can be found except the horror of a heart of darkness? Is Marlow a ghost too? Is it not too early, at twenty-six, for her to be chasing shadows rather than real live people? But her mind sees little difference. In the village square at the centre of her thoughts people who have really existed, imagined people, living people and dead people all walk and talk absolutely naturally. Even if she can tell them apart, she does not want to use a tape measure to establish who belongs on the one side and who on the other, who is worthy of her attention and who not. It is perhaps war, privation, fear, the absolute throw-of-the-dice chance of places and refuges, even of life itself, that have taught her this: to welcome the dead and the living with equal joy. In fact here is little Emanuele who, she now sees, is opening the sliding door of the compartment and, terribly serious, comes to sit facing her on one of the empty seats. He has a book in his hands. He opens it. He buries himself in his reading. He has the same dry, agile body as when he was eleven, the same dark eyes, the same quick, nervous hands. Only his quiff of hair is now grey. A child grown prematurely old.

'Emanuele!' calls Amara, barely trusting her voice.

He slowly lifts his head with an interrogative look as if wondering whether he knows her. But the answer seems to be no. He doesn't recognise her.

'Where are you going?' she asks softly.

He doesn't answer. His mind is elsewhere. Anxious to return to his book. But what is he reading? No matter how she stretches her neck, she can't manage to read the title on the cover. She can just recognise a word or two in German.

'Emanuele!' she calls again. They are alone in the empty compartment; the last passengers got off at Milan. There's a more festive atmosphere now. From the corridor she hears the voice of a woman selling panini and pop: 'Sparkling fizzy drinks!'

When Amara turns again to look at the seat opposite, the boy Emanuele has vanished. Only the book is still there, open face-down on the seat. Amara picks it up and reads the title: *Pinocchio*. In a German translation. She wants to laugh. When she and Emanuele used to read together, the books they found in his father's library were never in German. When can he have changed one language for another? Though that very book in German seems to be there to remind her that a language now divides her from their common past. German, a language she doesn't know well, has snatched him away from her and projected him into that distant future for which she is fishing among the roots of the past.

Amara gently replaces the upturned book on the empty seat and goes back to reading about the voyages of Captain Marlow.

21

The empty house has a stuffy smell. Amara opens all the windows. Late September, but it's still hot.

She decides not to unpack her things but to go straight to the hospital. But to which department? Which ward? She phones Luca's sister Susanna, known as Suzy, even though they have had no contact for years. Surely urgency will justify her!

'Is it true Luca's in hospital?'

'He is.'

'How is he?'

'Had a minor heart attack. But now he's better. No chance of that killing him!' She can hear Suzy laughing at the other end of the line. A strange woman, her sister-in-law. Wild red hair, face puffy with drink, trembling hands. Intelligent, ironic eyes.

'He's written to say he wants to talk to me before he dies.'

'Dies my foot! He's in better health than I am.'

'People can die of heart attacks.'

'Not always. He's had a fright … That's true enough.' She laughs again. She likes to seem more cynical than she really is. Though she usually likes to shrug her shoulders at anything in her own life that hasn't worked out as she would have liked. Three men – one of them Indian – two miscarriages and a sickly son. She once said, 'I'm a failure, Amara, and I boast about it.' But who knows what she meant by 'failure'? And why should she be proud of it? Just to be seen to be brave? Obstinate and fearless? Yet she and Luca both knew how to fascinate others. They were both more loved than loving. Even to the extent of causing a suicide: a twenty-year-old girl who when she felt rejected by the man of the caresses, pulled a plastic bag over her head and tied it tightly round her neck. Both were good at stimulating the senses of others, if unable to carry through any relationship, whether of love or friendship.

'Can you tell me where to find him? Which ward is he on?'

'Cardiology department. Ward 16. You'll see a gardenia on the wall. Each ward is named for a particular flower. He's on Gardenia. But it smells of disinfectant.' She laughs again. Amara can almost see her red curls shaking.

'That's where I'll go, then.'

'He'll probably have nothing to say to you. All he likes is being cuddled. You know him, don't you.'

'He sent me a desperate letter.'

'His last flame has left him, he's feeling lonely.'

'What's that to do with me?'

'You're still his wife.'

'We split up two years ago.'

'But he still thinks of you as his wife. Perhaps the only woman he can rely on in the midst of all the coming and going of those little flushing devices he's been having.'

'Flushing devices!?'

'Well, yes, little beach girls, all plunging necklines and make-up. It's reached a point where real beauties avoid him. He's getting old, Amara dear. No longer so easy for him to find ladies to deceive.'

'You're hard on your brother, Suzy.'

'He's hard on me. Do you think he gave me any help when Vannino was in hospital and seemed to be dying? Or when I had to move house? Do you think he's ever been there for me when I needed someone to complain to? I know he can't stand people who grumble, but when your husband leaves you in the lurch with a disabled son and you find yourself on your own with no job at forty, what use is a brother who can't lend you a helping hand?'

'Listen, I'm off now. I could call you again this evening.'

'Why not come to supper? I've made pasta al forno and I'm on my own. Do come, it'll be nice to see you. Years since we last met. Let me remind you of the address: Via Guelfa 3, remember? Near Piazza di Crocifisso. Will you come?'

'Well, thank you … Actually I've only just arrived and haven't yet …'

'Alone, aren't you? I didn't suppose you'd be with a man. Well then. No need to worry about anyone. I'll expect you at eight-thirty. Anyway, they'll throw you out of the hospital at seven. Ciao.'

'Shall I bring anything?'

'A bottle of wine, red, ciao.'

The hospital. Splintery floors, windows that won't close. Despite the flowers on the doors, an aggressive stench of disinfectant, sick bodies, sour breath and foul air. She recognises the ward from the painted and framed gardenia on the door of Room 16.

She can make out three beds in the half-light. It's difficult to tell them apart, but an arm rises from the bed at the far end, near the window. She too lifts a hand. She goes over. The man she had married, Luca Spiga, is stretched on crumpled sheets in pyjamas, with red socks on his feet, hair stuck to his cheeks, eyes swollen and face unshaven. Where's that beautiful Luca, once so full of seductive caresses? He's developed a little round stomach, like a craving for pregnancy. His long beard gives him an unkempt and sickly air. But he's not as pale as she had imagined he would be; two red knobs on his cheeks give him the look of a farm worker who has been hoeing in the sun.

'Well, you look fine.'

'I've been near death, Amara. I've been waiting for you.'

'What was it you wanted to tell me?'

'I can't talk here just like that in front of everybody.'

'Whisper in my ear. I've come here especially from Vienna.'

'You've really come especially to see me?'

'Yes, especially for you.'

'Good lord, what an honour!'

It's obvious he has nothing in particular to say, as his sister rightly guessed. All he wanted was attention and a little affection. Taking an iron chair, Amara sits down beside him and prepares herself to be patient. As always, his eyes caress sweetly, like his soft persuasive voice.

'Your sister says you've made me come here for nothing.'

'Suzy hates me.'

'Maybe she knows you better than I do.'

'She's always written me off as a good-for-nothing.'

'How's work?'

'Going badly. I don't feel at home in this architectural studio. But I have to work.'

'Can't you set up on your own?'

'Too much to worry about, too many arguments, I couldn't face it. Perhaps better to be paid a monthly salary, even a small one, than to spend my Saturdays and Sundays drawing up little plans for horrible apartments to pay the taxman and the rent. I don't want trouble.'

'You never change. All you want is freedom without responsibility.'

'Have you come here to criticise me?'

'I've come because you said it was urgent, that you needed to talk to me.'

'And who says that's not the truth!?'

'All right. Talk to me when you feel up to it. How are you feeling? I haven't even asked you that. What bad manners.'

'Not so much bad-mannered as slipping off. There's something else on your mind. Have you got a man?'

'No.'

'I'm glad.'

'On the contrary, you ought to be sorry I haven't got a man to travel with me and make love to me.'

'You know what I think, Amara ...' but the sentence stays unfinished. Silence descends between their two tense bodies.

'What did you want to tell me, Luca?' Amara asks after a long pause during which he takes her hand and squeezes it between his own.

'I wanted to say we should come together again, you and me. You need a man to love and look after. I need a woman ...'

'To look after you, I know. Luca, you're too explicit. You can't even lie elegantly.'

'You were born to look after people, you were. You're a failed mother.'

'Failed? I intend to marry again and have at least two children.'

'You never will, Amara, you're too fond of dreaming. Dreaming and caring for people.'

'Dreaming and caring for people? Wrong. I shall find myself a husband, as I say, and start a family.'

As she speaks she can feel the warmth of those hands she has loved: large, smooth and tender. She closes her eyes. A moment of reckoning. This man who caresses really does know how to caress. It's as if he's pulling her by the arm along a very smooth chute or slide towards an obscure garden of delights. She pulls back her hand with an abrupt gesture that irritates her ex-husband.

'Your hands are as wonderful as ever, but stop trying to seduce me. It won't work.'

'Are you sure?'

'Very sure.'

'Then listen: you shall have complete liberty. I'm not thinking of a typical husband and wife situation, but an agreement between equals. You in your part of the house, I in mine. You can even have lovers; I shan't say a word. You'll be free to do whatever you like. In exchange all I ask of you is your company. Just a bit of company. A presence. Eating together and chatting about this and that. To touch your hand, that's all I ask of you, every now and then maybe to make love; d'you remember we used to be rather good at that, us two? I don't think it's too much to ask. What do you say?'

'I'd like to remind you that it was you who told me you'd fallen in love with another woman, even younger than me.'

'I know, I know. But then you went away. We could so easily have gone on living together without making love. But now everything's different, I've discovered how weak I am and how fragile my body is, that I need rest and good company. I've had enough of sex. Can you believe that? It nauseates me. I want to dedicate myself to painting, you know I've always been a painter.'

'All this because you've had a minor heart attack and it's scared you.'

'Nature has given me a warning. And I want to stop drinking, stop smoking and stop searching for young bodies. My life will change completely, in fact it has already changed, do you believe me?'

'No.'

'Why are you so distrustful?'

'I've heard you talk like this before. I'm not saying you don't mean what you say. But then you forget. The problem is, I don't love you any more. I'm no longer interested in descending to pacts.'

'I thought you had another man and were hiding that from me. Can you understand that it offends me that you no longer think me worthy of your confidence?'

'The simple fact is I don't love you. Does that seem so absurd?'

'I may be a megalomaniac but I need to feel the women I've loved can never forget me. I shall put it even more strongly: I know you still love me. I'm certain of it or you wouldn't have hurried so quickly to my side.'

'Haven't you just told me that I'm motivated by dreams and a need to care for others? Well, this need to care for others is what brought me here. A need that I accept is archaic and profoundly unfashionable.'

'But the point is: you are here. That's all that matters now. I don't want to argue. Please give me your hand again, I shan't ask anything more of you. Not even to come back tomorrow. When are you leaving?'

'I thought you were dying.'

'Not yet. Aren't you pleased?'

'Let's just say you deceived me with that urgent letter.'

'Okay, let's say I deceived you. So what? I wanted to see you, that's the point. I believe I still love you, very much. And do you know something? Love is contagious. When you love someone, you end up infecting the other person like with an illness.'

'I shall stay three days. Time to see you out of hospital. Then I'm going back to Vienna.'

'But what on earth can there be for you to do in Vienna, that ugly half-dead city?'

'You could say Florence is half-dead too. But it isn't.'

'I'm jealous. Are you in love with an Austrian?'

'I'm looking for a child.'

'A child?'

'A child who disappeared in 1943.'

22

Suzy comes to the door dressed in black, carrot-coloured curls round her neck and forehead. Amara can't remember her looking so beautiful and vivacious before. Her radiant eyes are the colour of cocoa. She's in high-heels, her manicured nails varnished with oxblood. They embrace. Suzy hands her a mauve-coloured aperitif with an olive in it and invites her to sit down at table. She hurries into the kitchen and immediately reappears, holding high in gloved hands a blue ceramic baking-dish that she places carefully on the tablecloth, but not before slipping a wicker mat under it. The promised pasta al forno.

'This is all there is, help yourself.'

She smiles with satisfaction. Amara notices two of her front teeth have been rebuilt. Seen close to, her eyes look tired and slightly drunk.

'Vannino?'

'With his father. Every so often he agrees to do his duty and take him for a day or two. Then he brings him back worn out.'

'So the two of you are on good terms?'

'Every month he forgets to pay the maintenance he owes. I have to write, phone him, insist the boy is also his. He delays and delays and sometimes misses a whole month. Children need a father as well as a mother, don't you think? Luckily, even in the worst moments, I've never spoken badly of his father to Vannino. I'm not stupid. The child's growing up nicely, well-balanced if a bit sickly but that's not my fault. He was born at seven months and has never fully made up for the two months he lost. But what did that madman Luca tell you?'

'He wants me to go back to him.'

'A sensible idea at last. And you?'

'I said no.'

'No, absolutely no?'

'No.'

'Wouldn't you like him to give you a child? He'd be an excellent father.'

'I don't want that.'

'Pity. I would have liked to keep you in the family. You know I like you.'

'I like you too.'

'But we'll stay sisters-in-law?'

'Of course.'

'Have you found a new love?'

'Is it impossible even for you to understand that a woman might want to live on her own?'

'At twenty-six you should be thinking of the future. Are you going back to Vienna?'

'In three days.'

'What on earth can there be for you to do in that half-dead city?'

'You and Luca seem to think with one brain. You say the same things.'

'I bet you're chasing a man. A blond?'

'I'm chasing a child who disappeared in 1943.'

'I can't believe that.'

'I'm also writing articles for the papers. It's my job.'

'Do they pay much?'

'Very little.'

Amara is fed up with repeating the same things. The pasta al forno is excellent. The sauce contains a touch of fried aubergine and salted capers. Amara tells Suzy she cooks really well. Suzy smiles with satisfaction. She has always liked messing about with pans.

In the street afterwards it strikes Amara her visit has been pointless. In the end they had little to say to one another. And Suzy seemed to be under pressure from her brother Luca to win her over. Amara is not sure about this but it could be possible.

Walking through a Florence in the throes of reconstruction disturbs her a bit. The old shops on Via dei Calzaioli do not seem happy with the gigantic new machines pushing, excavating and levelling the city and filling it with cement. She loves the scent of fresh coffee boldly mixed with a light smell of cat's piss, fresh straw, hanging melon and cut leather that lingers in the little streets of the centre. The smell of her childhood. The time when holding the hand of her mother, the beautiful Stefania, she would go out to look for something to eat in a Florence darkened by war. Sometimes they had to queue for hours to buy a bag of flour or a packet of lard. To make a pudding, Stefania would soak hard bread in milk and cook it over the fire with a little sugar. All very precious ingredients that could only occasionally be found, and when they were there would always be a party. Her father's bicycle was very important to him and he would carry it up and down the stairs rather than leave it in the street. Everyone knew a bicycle could disappear in the time it took to go through the front door even if it had been chained and elaborately locked up. The bicycle thieves were so quick and skilful that no one ever managed to catch them. So if he did not want to lose his bicycle he virtually had to glue himself to it and even carry it into his shop and home, never leaving it unattended for a minute.

Two young parents: Stefania famous for her beauty and elegant walk, her long legs, narrow waist, flexible neck, light shining hair, gentle eyes and kindly smile. Amintore, known as the ferret for his small strong agile climber's body, his high cheekbones, powerful and extremely white teeth, neat little moustache and lively, inquisitive eyes. Stefania would often tell how he had won her with the obstinacy of a mule, no matter how hard she had tried to reject him. When they met, she had been teaching at a school run by nuns while he had been working as a shoemaker in his father's shop. Then, in an impulse of independence, Amintore had escaped from his shoemaking family and found work in a bakery. This involved staying up all night to control the rising of the bread and sleeping when he could in the morning, while his two fellow-workers took the round loaves out of the oven and carried them by bicycle all round the district stacked in baskets and protected by a check cloth. Stefania had been engaged to a certain Mario, a collector of patents, an unusual job that took him far afield. But his work must have been well paid because he was one of the few in the district to own a red Lambda that went like a rocket and was held in awe by everybody. Stefania had many admirers in Rifredi and even further afield. Her bold beauty and couldn't-care-less walk made men want to 'grab her and dominate her' as one sarcastic youngster put it. But, ever fresh and fragrant, she would move on with a great toss of her nut-brown shoulder-length hair. People said she washed her hair with flower-water and went up into the hills to gather wild roses and buttercups which she would steep in a basin of water. But these were just stories. In Florence, in those hard times, if you picked flowers it was to eat them, not to perfume your hair. You would brown them, stalks and all. 'You can even eat paper if you fry it,' her grandmother would say, then still working as a washerwoman.

Stefania would go out early in the morning to buy fresh bread at the bakery. Then, holding it close to her chest, she would meet her fiancé Mario on the shingle by the Terzolle River. He would bring a thermos of barley coffee and she her bread baton. After they had gone down the steps to the shingle, they would follow a prickly path till they reached a clearing among the brambles. There, under the leafy branches of a stunted acacia, Mario would spread his raincoat on the arid, fissured earth and make her comfortable, so they could both enjoy consuming that exquisite chewy freshly made bread. Then they would kiss and cuddle. They never did more than that, partly because someone might have seen them, and partly because she had made it clear from the beginning that she wanted to come to her wedding a virgin and would rather die than change her mind. He had accepted this condition and they would spend hours kissing with great gusto. But only on holidays, because on weekdays, after kissing Mario, Stefania had to run quickly to school.

Amintore the baker was already in love and would make eyes at her. But she never even looked at him. She knew he was in love with her, but the short, thin boy always covered with flour, with his starched cotton cap and little Latin-lover's moustache, was not to her taste. If anything, if she had had to leave her Mario who hunted all over Italy for patents, she would have gone to Muzio, a tall, polite young man who sometimes took her to the cinema. Mario made jealous scenes about this Muzio. Who is he? What does he want? Why do you go out alone with him? But she didn't care. She was determined to be free and no one could give her orders. This is how it is, and if you don't like it you know what you can do! So he put up with it. Even if he occasionally threatened her with extreme punishments that had to remain unspecified, since she was not afraid of losing him, and if he had dared to hit her she would never have looked at him again.

One day Stefania found Amintore was spying on her. She noticed him pretending to be passing by chance as she left the cinema. He was neat and clean, in a dark obviously new suit with his moustache quivering like a cat's whiskers. He looked at her in such despair that she burst out laughing. And perhaps felt a touch of curiosity for the short sturdy young man suffering for her in silence. But she continued her usual routine, every morning passing the bakery where he would be ready shaven in a clean shirt, keeping awake to serve her freshly baked batons and following her with his eyes as she set off, proud and self-assured, for the shingle by the Terzolle.

Amintore had told all this to his daughter Maria Amara during the years when he used to walk her to school, carrying in a jute bag the tin that held her bread-and-omelette snack lunch. She asked him how he had got to know mother and how they came to get married. She had been a child with the curiosity of a sleuth, 'almost like a police officer', he would laugh with a mixture of admiration and disapproval. It was not good for little girls to be too inquisitive. There were many things it was not suitable for them to know. But nothing could put her off. She was nothing like as proud and self-assured as the untameable Stefania, and to tell the truth less beautiful and so less sure of herself, more closed and introspective, but in no way less obstinate than her mother.

Even when Stefania died just after the end of the war from poorly treated typhus, Amara had persisted in asking her father about their young days, and about how it happened that her mother, who had turned so many heads, finally chose him.

There was a part of that story that Amintore had been reluctant to tell Amara. He had always changed the subject when he reached a certain point in the love triangle. But Amara had been so persistent that finally one day he told her everything.

23

'Well, Papà, how come Mamma picked you? Wouldn't that Mario who collected patents have been more suitable?'

'You don't even know what patents are, what are you chattering about.'

'I do though, they're a sort of stamp of ownership when you invent something.'

'Good girl! He collected them to offer them to the industries that were coming into existence in Tuscany at that time.'

'A special sort of corkscrew, a cork-and-wood machine for making coffee, a kind of soap made with sand and lard ...'

'How d'you know that?'

'Aunt Miriam told me.'

'Yes, that's just how it was. He was a strange type, that Mario. I never liked him.'

'Of course not, you were jealous. If he had married Mamma, what would I have been like? Taller and more beautiful?'

'You're very beautiful as you are.'

'Tell me about Muzio who used to take her to the cinema. Were you jealous of him too?'

'I always followed her. Even if I was so exhausted I was half-dead, I would slip into the cinema after them and sit at the back and see some film that didn't interest me at all. Perhaps I even came to develop a special taste in films from watching American ones. Stefania liked Marlene Dietrich, she really adored her. She knew by heart the names of her lovers, who in any case were her directors or those who worked with her: the great von Sternberg, Billy Wilder, Orson Welles, Gary Cooper, Jean Gabin, Burt Lancaster. See, I remember them perfectly. In her room Stefania had photos of Marlene in every possible pose. I can see them to this day. In one Marlene was standing, arrogant and utterly beautiful in a black tailcoat, with a top hat on her head and a white carnation in her buttonhole. In another she was the exact opposite, very feminine, her body barely hidden by transparent voile crossed by silver branches that glittered in the lights of the set, a white mink stole over one shoulder and a very long cigarette-holder in her black-gloved hand. What a vision! Even I sometimes stood there bewitched, admiring those photographs. I don't know where Stefania got them. She had so many and had pasted them up on the wall above her bed.

'Sitting in the cinema I would often drop off because I had so little time for sleep. Sometimes I'd wake up to find myself alone in an empty auditorium. I would get up stiffly and go out to look for them. I might catch a distant glimpse of them saying goodbye outside her home in Piazza Dalmazia. My heart would stop as I waited to see if they would kiss. She would hold out her hand. He would seem to touch her hair with his lips, then casually go off. I would hide. I had become a real idiot for love.'

'But why did she choose you if she wasn't attracted to you?'

'Things went on like this for nearly a year. With Mario taking her to the shingle by the Terzolle in the mornings and Muzio taking her to the cinema in the evenings. There was another one too, one I hated because he was twice her age and I thought him repulsive. A businessman, always smart, always wearing a tie. He would wait at the entrance of the school where she worked in Via di Casa Murata, and take her to the Cascine for a cup of cream with wafers. I could have killed him. She flirted with him, laughing shamelessly, but he was of no importance to her. I would watch her from far off eating that cream as voraciously as if she was gobbling up the man himself.'

'And you were there all the time spying, Papà?'

'Well, I was trying to understand. But the more I watched the less I understood. One day I saw them shut up together in a car having an argument, her and the businessman, at the corner of Piazza Dalmazia. He was waving his hands about and shaking his head again and again; his red cheeks really annoyed me. She was quiet and didn't move. Now and then she would shake out her hair which was lying loose on her shoulders. She was so beautiful that even from a distance I was utterly overwhelmed. I thought: now I'll go and save her from that brute, now I'll go. But I was afraid she might turn on me. And what could I have done if she had stopped coming to the bakery?'

'But what were they arguing about? Did Mamma tell you later?'

'Yes, she told me. The tapir was trying to get her to marry him. She said no, she was engaged to Mario. But he went on and on. He said he wanted to marry her before the new fascist law taxing singles became operative. He even wanted to give her a child.'

'And in the meantime she fell in love with you?'

'Oh no, not at all. She wanted to marry Mario, the one with the patents, and she very nearly did.'

'But why didn't she then?'

'Now that you're a big girl I can tell you. Something happened so terrible that your mother never recovered from it.'

'Tell me, Papà.'

'If I tell you will you promise to forget what I say as soon as I've said it?'

'How can I make promises if I don't even know what you're talking about?'

'Just promise.'

'I'll try. But what happened?'

'What happened was that Mario once saw her kissing Muzio and was so angry he went to ask a friend of his, a certain Nanni, to help him take revenge. Nanni was a fanatical fascist and one of a gang of thugs. He was very happy to get such a job. He said: Just leave it to me! Mario said, don't hurt her too much; it would be enough if they tied her to a tree in the country and left her there for the night. That was what he wanted and his friend promised to do it. So a couple of mornings later, Nanni took some of his friends to wait for Stefania outside the Madonna del Bambino elementary school where she worked as a teacher. They pushed her into a car and drove her into the country where they tied her to a large oak tree. Stefania was confused, she didn't understand. She asked in the shameless manner so typical of her: who are you? who sent you? And despite the fact that Mario had begged them not to mention his name, they blurted it out: your fiancé sent us because he saw you kissing another man. And they laughed as if they were doing a noble deed. She was furious and began showing her contempt for them, telling them they were cowards: four men against one woman, you disgust me! First they teased her, then they got angry. One of Nanni's friends, a great fat boy who was always with them, thinking to impress his leader, slapped her face so hard her nose started bleeding. Despite the blood and the lamp-black from her eyebrows mixing with her tears, Stefania refused to give in to fear and went on shouting at them that they would regret it, and that she would hunt them down and kill them one by one with her father's rifle.

'At first, Nanni watched her with a certain admiration, then something in him snapped. Her furious face, cheeks red with tears and blood and eyes glaring with hate, made him determined to humiliate her once and for all, stamping on her boldness and forcing her to scream for mercy! But even when he started punching her, she went on attacking him. So you want the whole works, do you, said Nanni, you want to be fucked! And he jumped on her like a fury, ripping off her skirt and knickers. His companions stood watching, uncertain whether they could join in this feast of violence, or whether they must leave this victim to their leader. Meanwhile they got ready to unbutton their flies. Stefania was still struggling to free her hands from the rope. Then she bit Nanni's arm hard, and the pain, far from stopping him, spurred him on. But before he could go any further he couldn't stop himself ejaculating and let go, spitting and swearing and calling her a tart. Giving her a final kick in the belly he moved off with his companions, singing loudly: *Show stone to the enemies before you, Keep your heart whole for your friends. Let your eye be bold, and your step be quick, And loud your cry of valour!* Nanni felt he had now matured from a young boy into a real fascist and that this vulgar act had made a man of him in the eyes of the gang.

'Stefania was discovered by a farm worker, a man called Passeri, who had been on his way home with his donkey. He stopped when he noticed something bright among the trees. Stefania's white woollen socks that Aunt Miriam had crocheted for her. She still had them on even though she had lost shoes, skirt and knickers. The socks were as white as the moon if stained on one side with blood. Passeri was a charitable man and he untied her hands and feet and helped her to clean off the blood disfiguring her face and legs. He carried her on his donkey all the way to the hospital. Next day she lodged an accusation.

'Mario meanwhile had heard about the rape and grabbed his hair in his hands. This was not what he'd wanted. He hurried to the hospital to ask Stefania's pardon but she spat in his face and

told him if he came again she would denounce him as the insti-
gator of the disgusting act. He went away with his tail between
his legs. He continued to apologise, sending her flowers picked on
the banks of the Terzolle, and love letters which she always tore
up unread. After many months of this she sent him a final letter
telling him never to write to her or come near her again: to her it
was as if he'd never been born and had never even had a name.'

'Are you crying, Papà?'

'It was all complicated by politics, my dear. Maybe I shouldn't
have told you about the rape of your mother, but I wanted you to
know about it. Nanni went on to be a big fish. He's a Member
of Parliament now. It's right you should know this. It's the way
our country works. Instead of punishing bullies, it celebrates them
and pays them a salary. He's managed to stay afloat. He's rich now.
He never discusses his past. But he has lots of ideas for the future.
Haven't you heard his voice on the radio?'

'No, Papà.'

'Your mother, who never had a political idea in her head,
became a sworn enemy of the regime. All her previous admirers
vanished, whether because of fear or contempt no one knows. A
woman carries the violence she suffers on her own shoulders like a
sackful of rocks, you know. Even Muzio disappeared, tall, elegant,
handsome Muzio. I was the only admirer left. A little later my
father died leaving me the shoemaking business so I had to give up
the bakery and go back to the profession of my ancestors.'

'So she chose you because she had no one else?' Amara liked
teasing her father. And she wanted to lighten the atmosphere after
the grim story of the rape.

'I think she began to think better of me when she found I wasn't
a paid-up member of the fascist party, and that I kept away from
their rallies and never made the Roman salute or wore the badge
or sang anthems in honour of the Duce. One Sunday we made love
behind the shop among sacks of flour and bowls of yeast. That's
when you were conceived, Amara, in tenderness and consolation. I
don't think beautiful Stefania ever really loved me. I was too small
and dark. She liked tall, lanky, elegant, blond types like Muzio
and Mario, with blue eyes and smooth hands, Daddy's boys complete with car and dégagé air. That was her type. Instead she got
me with my wild hair, eyes like a desperate oriental khan and the

ridiculous pomaded moustache she teased me about, and with no car, only a bicycle; I was a total disaster. But she was grateful and fond of me.'

'Did she never take a lover, Papà?'

'She didn't have much time to, Amara dear, even if she'd wanted to. As you well know, she was still very young when she fell ill. It seemed just a slight fever, a mere nothing, but it turned out to be typhus, and the idiot of a doctor treated her for flu. By the time they realised it was typhus it was too late. She died beside me, at night, without a sound. And while she was dying you were sleeping the sleep of the blessed and I hadn't the courage to wake you. She went so quickly, Amara darling.'

'Was it she who gave me this stupid name, Amara?'

'She would have preferred Marlene, like Marlene Dietrich in *The Blue Angel*, a film that came out the year you were born. One of the films I saw from the back row in that ramshackle cinema with wooden seats that made such a noise every time you got up or sat down.'

'Wasn't I named after a little bear born in a circus near our home? That's what you once told me.'

'Yes, maybe. Perhaps. I can't really remember. But there was a bitter taste in my mouth from what was happening in this country. The increasing arrogance and bullying, the shortage of work, the new laws that made it almost impossible for anyone to breathe. Not surprising we were bitter, don't you think? Then you arrived bitter, in fact very bitter, considering the times you were born in.'

'But why did you never marry again, Papà?'

'I never found anyone as good as your mother Stefania.'

'But she's dead now and you're still alive.'

'I talk to her. I go to her grave and tell her what I've been doing. I talk to her about you and about myself. And in her own way, she answers.'

'How?'

'She doesn't need words. Thoughts travel faster than words. I can see her and hear her. She's wiser now she's dead. Not so haughty as she was. But she can still smile.'

24

This morning the hospital is flooded with sunlight. The broken shutters, the flaking walls, the old iron beds, don't seem so gloomy and decrepit. The polished floor shines beneath the nurses' coarse shoes. Medicine bottles tinkle as the trolleys go backwards and forwards.

There's a party atmosphere and a great crowd of relatives in shirtsleeves with shopping bags over their arms on their way to see the patients. Three children are playing with a toy tractor on the floor. There's even a sad-looking cat with bald patches in his fur, crouched on the sill before an open window.

Luca greets her from a distance. He is walking in the corridor with a pretty young nurse with long blonde hair and a white cap worn sideways. Thank goodness he's found a distraction, thinks Amara, cheerfully approaching him. She is carrying a paper bag containing doughnuts that are still hot. She bought them in the street from a little boy with a squint who was struggling to keep off the flies with a homemade fan made from chicken feathers.

Luca hurriedly dismisses the young nurse and advances with unsteady steps. Now he seems more like the Luca she used to know: tall, suave, seductive and unpunished.

'How are you?' she asks, offering the sugared doughnuts.

'I can't eat those, Amara, but thanks all the same. Have you thought about my suggestion?'

'I have, and my answer is no.'

'Will you go back to Vienna?'

'I'm staying here three days; I shall go and see my father, then I'm off.'

'Three days from today? Let's say four not counting yesterday. Why attach so much importance to that child who must have been dead for years?'

'I don't even know why myself. I like to think he could be still alive.'

'You've always been one to chase after dreams. Here am I with my living body and you go running after someone who's dead.'

'I want to know if Emanuele made it.'

'You're raving mad.'

'Tell me about your last flame, as Suzy calls her.'

'I don't feel like it.'

'Was she a blonde or a brunette?'

'You know I have a weakness for blondes.'

'How much younger than you?'

'What does it matter? She treated me as if we were the same age. We did all sorts of things together: journeys, expeditions, planning the future. We'd already paid the deposit on a new home on Viale Michelangelo.'

'How much did that cost?'

'A tiny flat. Where the gardener of a villa used to live. Falling to bits but just what we needed.'

'So you've lost the deposit, have you?'

'I've lost it, yes.'

'Why did your blonde leave you?'

'Who knows? You women are unpredictable and strange. You can never be trusted.'

'What did you do to her?'

'Nothing.'

'I bet you started fooling around with the maid. Or something of the sort.'

'A neighbour. Actually the owner. A very elegant little woman. But I wasn't short-changing my partner. I was head-over-heels in love.'

'You were head-over-heels in love with your partner but you were caressing another woman.'

'Well, you know how it is with me. Faced with a beautiful woman, I can't resist. But I was doing nothing wrong. Just a little flirtation on the side. Neither of us took it seriously.'

'But as luck would have it your flame … what's her name?'

'Angelica.'

'As luck would have it, Angelica took it badly and left you.'

'Too jealous. But I wouldn't have stood for that in any case.'

'Has it never occurred to you that exclusiveness might be essential for love?'

'Seems a vulgar idea to me.'

'Vulgar it may be, but it must have some foundation in reality since most people think it an absolute necessity.'

'Exactly, absolute. I'm against everything absolute.'

'You'd even be capable of flirting with death himself, you would.'

'And would that make life jealous?'

'Life would have good reason to be, don't you think? If you're really flirting with death, you have to be irrevocably abandoning life. Like with your little heart attack.'

'Well, the metaphor's spot on.' He laughs, becoming once again the Luca of long ago whose smile bewitched so many women.

'Have you never been jealous yourself?'

'I don't want to own anyone, you know that. For me it's enough to caresss another body and feel it respond to my caresses. What need is there for exclusivity?'

'If you ever really did fall in love you might even get jealous.'

'I believe in the peaceful sharing of property. Exclusive property doesn't tempt me. I'm a real democrat.'

'But when women fall in love they assume you'll be faithful to them. At least during the short time when you tell them you love them.'

'They get that wrong. I make no claims on exclusivity but I don't guarantee it either. I'm a free man.'

'A free man, with the freedom of a tree in a desert.'

'I'm not afraid of being alone.'

'Liar! When all you do is ask me to keep you company.'

'The contradictions of a fearless spirit like my own. I'm not afraid of being alone but I enjoy company, especially the company of young women like you.'

'Goodbye, Luca. I'm off to see my father. We'll meet again tomorrow.'

25

Amara opens the French window to the little balcony overlooking Via Alderotti.

The roses have withered and their leaves are yellow. Despite the fact that she stuck two full bottles of water upside down in the vase. And covered it with fine river-gravel left to soften in water beforehand for two days. But it has been hot and the plants have dried up. With her fingers she detaches a dead rose, straightens a bent corolla, agitates the parched soil and gives the little plants a lot of water while a gecko shoots between her feet and goes into hiding under the edge of a saucer that holds a vase.

Go back to Luca? Why not? asks an insistent little voice. But it would be like reliving something already known and experienced. Perhaps he is right to call preferring a ghost to a living body perversion. Yet Emanuele's head continues to present itself persistently to her imagination. God is with us, that's what the name Immanuel means. But is Immanuel with us?

She must find out whether he is dead or alive before she can decide anything. She wishes she was already back in Vienna. She has sent in four articles from the city of Mozart. And her boss has seemed satisfied. It's not easy to describe the cold war. Perhaps it's best to start from particular moments, from insignificant details that reveal a common feeling, a smell or a climate. And to expand from there all the way to reflections on history. But she doesn't always succeed. Sometimes it feels like trying to grind water in a mortar. She has told her readers about her train journey, about the Pension Blumental, about Frau Morgan. She has described Kraków and Auschwitz. She must do some interviews that lie outside her inquiries about Emanuele. Her longing to return to Vienna gets more intense every day. She hasn't finished her work as a witness to what has happened in that country numbed and impoverished by Nazism and the war. But at the same time she will resume her search for Emanuele. The man with the gazelles is waiting and there is nothing to keep her here in Florence. Her father? Yes of course, the sick Amintore shut up in the care home run by the Ursuline nuns of Villa Cisterna. I must go and see him, she tells herself, steeping a black teabag in a cup of boiling water.

She eats a biscuit sitting on a rush-seated chair in the small single room into which have been crammed a bed, a cooker fixed to the wall on a bracket, a basin that also serves as a bath and, hidden by a curtain, a toilet. How is it possible to inhabit just ten square metres? By using the kitchen table as a writing desk and adding books to the shelves full of food and pans. The house in Via Alderotti that once belonged to grandfather Sironi and later to her father, and is now divided into four flats for the children of her Aunt Miriam. An extra toilet projects from the outside wall like a fungus. All Italy is poor, even if noisy reconstruction work disturbs the sleep of those who have other things to think about.

At night Amara settles happily into the solitary bed where she has so often let her mind wander. She quickly falls asleep from accumulated exhaustion. No sooner are her eyes closed than she sees Emanuele reaching out a hand to her from the cherry tree. Come up, he says, come up because bombs are on the way. Here we'll be safe.

Next morning she hurriedly washes and dresses to go to the Ursulines where her father has been living for nearly two years now, victim of a degenerative illness. The streets are empty. A fresh breeze is blowing from the north. Sister Adele greets her with an abrupt nod, considerate but uncommunicative.

'How is my father?'

The nun doesn't answer immediately. Perhaps she hasn't heard; she heads into the damp entrance hall with its smell of soup for the poor.

'How is my father?' Amara repeats, struggling to keep up on the steep stone stairs.

'You'll find him a good deal changed.'

'How changed?'

'Not really with us.'

'Is he very ill?'

'No, he's well enough, but his mind tends to wander. Sometimes

I hear him singing to himself. He hammers in imaginary nails and beats time by clicking his tongue. He was a shoemaker, wasn't he?'

'Yes.'

'He thinks he's still in his shop.'

Turning a corner, she sees him. Amintore Sironi, in a wheelchair, at the end of the loggia. His illness has bent and stiffened him. He has a rug over his knees, and a yellow and black check beret pulled down on his head. She goes up to him and smiles. But he looks at her as if he does not know who she is. When she bends to kiss him he explodes angrily:

'So you've come at last after all this time!'

'How are you feeling, Papà?'

'I've been waiting for you.'

Amara takes his hand in both hers and lifts it to her cheek. She is suddenly stricken by guilt; he was waiting for me, she tells herself, and there was I busy far away, wasting time when he needed me.

'Isn't my Stefania beautiful?' he says, turning to the nun who nods compassionately.

So he's mistaken her for her mother. And now what? Go along with it or correct him? She watches him a moment in bewilderment. She feels her father's strong fingers squeeze her wrist, then slip into her closed fist with a lascivious gesture. The smiling nun moves away. She has other things to do. She leaves Amara alone with her father who thinks she is his wife.

'Papà,' starts Amara timidly, 'I've brought you some fresh doughnuts. Do you like doughnuts?'

But he seems not to hear her, perhaps he isn't even listening. There's a radiant smile on his pale dry lips. He holds her hand tightly and begins humming.

'What are you singing, Papà?' Amara bends over him and tries to catch the notes from the mouth of a sick man who has lost his memory. But perhaps no, perhaps he hasn't really lost his memory, perhaps it would be more accurate to say that his memory has overcome his conscience. A fragile man at the mercy of a powerful memory. Now she thinks she recognises the tune. A song of the Alpine troops, from the time when he was a National Service recruit in the Cadore Mountains: 'Down in the valley there's a tavern, And fun and fun, Down in the valley there's a tavern, Where we Alpine soldiers love to be ... And if I'm a girl pale as

a rhinestone, A winestone a winestone, and bottles of wine!'
He's singing a cheerful hit-song about wine, ignoring the war, the
wounds and the fear.

'I've been waiting for you, Stefania,' he says now in a smooth
clear voice. Not like his humming a moment ago, when he was
muddling the notes. He squeezes her hand so hard it hurts. 'I'm
always alone. Why do you always leave me alone? But I knew
you'd come. So I put up with the nuns, and with all these idiots
round me. And that nurse Lucia who keeps telling me you're dead
and buried. Dead my foot! I know you're alive. And here you are
at last. Isn't this a live hand? And a live arm? Do the dead wear
clothes? What lovely material you're wearing! So soft, so soft. Silk
is it? Or percale perhaps? I've always liked percale, it reminds me
of those white flowers, what are they called? You know, the ones
that seem to be ceramic, with a single yellow pistil and a strange
smell of dry figs and hydrolyte. Do you remember when I used to
add hydrolyte to the water and you would say: more, Amintore,
more! And I would put in the powder and then the water would
sting the tongue like bicarbonate … In my opinion, hydrolyte is
just bicarbonate … Do the dead wear shoes? I can see them, you
know, the little red shoes you're wearing, really beautiful, you
could even dance in them, couldn't you? We should go dancing
more often. It's years since we last went dancing, Stefania darling.
Now let me take off this cap which stinks of sickness and wash my
hands and we'll go out together. Here they always force me to eat
the same stuff: potatoes and cabbage, cabbage and potatoes. They
say there's a war on but that's just talk. The war ended years ago,
I know that. Sometimes they give me a boiled egg, but what can
I do with a boiled egg? What I need is a nice chicken. Next time
you come will you bring me a nice little chicken? Do the dead wear
silk stockings, eh? Do the dead wear knickers? I can feel them,
you know, I can even feel them through your skirt, I can feel the
elastic on your knickers. Are you wearing the ones I like? Those
black ones with a little ruff round your thighs, is that what you're
wearing? Show me, Stefania!'

Amara pulls abruptly away from her father as he touches her
legs and her sex.

'Papà, it's me, Amara!' she says more loudly, angrily. But he
doesn't hear. He gives her a dark look and reaches out to draw her

closer again. 'Where are you?' he shouts, worried now. 'Why are you moving away?'

'Papà, I'm Amara, your daughter, I'm Amara!'

At last he seems to understand and releases his grip. His eyes fill with tears. With his mouth open he turns a more comprehending look on her, but seems unable to find words.

'What did you come for? To make fun of me?'

'I came to see you, Papà. Such a long time since we met.'

'You've always been rather plain and dull. Are you trying to pass yourself off as your mother who was far more beautiful and intelligent than you could ever be?'

'No, no, Papà, I just wanted to say hello.'

'I don't need you or your visits,' her father says harshly, holding her eye. 'You're coming to spy on my death, I know.'

Suddenly Sister Adele is there to help, swift and silent as if she has sprung from a hole in the ground. Who knows where she has been or whether she followed the whole scene? She seems to have been prepared for what would happen. And now here she is, solicitous and maternal. She picks up the rug which Amara's father had flung away in a fit of rage, and wipes the saliva dribbling from his mouth. She says a few affectionate and reassuring words to him, then takes in both hands the bar at the back of his chair and pushes it, still talking softly to him, towards the end of the loggia. Amara follows sadly. She is not sure whether this is the end of the conversation, or just a brief interruption.

They come into a great hall with high windows reaching up to the ceiling. In it are other wheelchairs and other nuns. In the middle a long table with a flowered cloth. Metal plates with rough edges and metal beakers. A powerful smell of cooking fat and unwashed hair. Two young nuns come and go from the kitchen with steaming cauldrons.

Sister Adele pushes the wheelchair up to the table and arranges the furious Amintore in front of a full plate. She hands him a large spoon made from bright metal and moves away. Perhaps I should go now, Amara tells herself. But something keeps her in that distressing place that reminds her of the year she spent with Ursuline nuns at a convent at Calenzano when she was a little girl. The same brusque, essential gestures, efficient and sometimes even a bit brutal. Yet she had loved Sister Carmela. She had asked her to be her mother and she had agreed, always with the same no-nonsense efficiency, but not without humour. 'I'm not really your mother, remember that,' she had said with a laugh. Her soft eyes had a slight squint; you could never tell where they were looking. Her cheeks, red as two apples, and her smile overcrowded with teeth gave her a slightly clownish look. But Amara became very fond of her. She got her to wash her hair and mend her socks, and ran to throw her arms round her waist when she felt anyone had been treating her badly. Strangely, Sister Carmela, so ready to cut her nails or sew a patch on her jumper, became touchy and sharp when Amara tried to learn more about her life. 'I was abandoned in a basket on the Nile,' she would say, giggling. 'Why the Nile?' Sister Carmela wouldn't answer. Or else in a very low voice she would murmur, 'Les jardins du Nil.' 'You know French, Sister Carmelina?' 'I know nothing, I'm tired,' the nun would say brusquely, and send her about her business. Then at table she would make sure Amara got a double helping of tomato jam. Amara didn't at all like the tomato jam the sisters were so proud of. She would end up swapping it for a piece of hard bread or half a glass of milk.

When her father came to take her home again, Amara cried for days. She could not forget the apron with its good smell of basil that Sister Carmela wore over her habit, or the patient hands that lingered over her hair, pulling but never hurting, to loosen the knots. She couldn't forget Sister Carmela's raucous, almost aphonic voice. Or how once, when she had a high temperature, Sister Carmela had held ice against her head and stayed up with her all night as she sweated in delirium.

She had looked for Sister Carmela when she returned to the school in the early fifties, but they told her she had gone away, and they didn't know where or didn't want to tell her. The Sisters were not allowed to form affectionate relationships with pupils. She had gone back to see the bed where she had slept and the window from which a hundred times she had looked out at the far-off fields and the pile of sheaves that had grown smaller day by day and the low-flying swallows, and where she had smelt the fragrance of field balm and hay. Her life seemed marked by absences: her mother Stefania, Sister Carmelina, and then her Emanuele, always intent on climbing the cherry tree.

As she lies stretched out trying to fall asleep she tries to imagine

Sister Carmelina on a farm looking after the chickens. She remembers hearing her say that her people had a farm in Friuli. Who knows what she told her beloved hens in that raucous voice of hers? Or perhaps she ended up in Africa looking after lepers. That too was something Amara had heard her say: 'When I leave here I shall go and look after lepers.' It had been hard to understand at the time how she could plan to dedicate her life to looking after lepers. But now it was different; Amara seemed to understand it had not just been an ideological project, but an imaginative choice. Fantasising about a hospital required in the middle of the desert, where children die of hunger and women give birth standing up surrounded by mud, where water is precious and life not worth a cent; a way of feeling alive and somehow useful. But at the same time Amara shuddered to realise that she might have done nothing but bend over wounds watching them ooze pus and search for disinfectant and bandages where none could be found, and try to bring a little unpolluted water to the lips of a dying man. The power of a ravenous and distant God found expression through the humble Sister Carmelina. But it was precisely because of that voracious appetite for souls and that distance characteristic of all omnipotent beings, that the nuns allotted Carmela/Carmelina her personal destiny and personal suffering with such extravagant generosity. There is something senseless and yet magnificent in self-sacrifice, and that is what Sister Carmelina was looking for: a sign to make her life precious rather than superfluous.

Amara has unconsciously if timidly camouflaged herself against a curtain at the far end of the hall and unnoticed watches the scene: the nuns are helping the chronic sick to take their places round the roughly laid table. There is water in gigantic opaque glass jugs. Bread, weighed out and cut into equal slices, stands before each place. Fishing in the steaming cauldrons with ladles, the nuns serve the boiling soup onto the metal plates. But why metal, as if they are prisoners? So they can't break them, perhaps? To make them last longer? Or perhaps to humiliate them like prisoners, to make it clear that no one trusts their hands or their movements?

The old people have eyes only for their soup. They count the beans floating amid the islands of fat, and the pieces of carrot and potato that slither through the boiling broth. The elderly women are wearing ankle-length dark wool skirts, with blue, grey or brown cardigans buttoned at the front. Some have a white blouse with a coloured lace collar under their cardigans, and some a rolled scarf round their necks. Nearly all the men are in slippers and walk badly. A bustling nun gets them to take off their hats and stick their napkins into their shirt-collars. They obey with bad grace.

Sister Adele stands and reads a passage from the Gospels: 'Blessed are the poor in spirit: for theirs is the kingdom of heaven. Blessed are they that mourn: for they shall be comforted. Blessed are the meek: for they shall inherit the earth. Blessed are they which do hunger and thirst after righteousness: for they shall be filled. Blessed are the merciful: for they shall obtain mercy. Blessed are the pure in heart: for they shall see God. Blessed are the peace-makers: for they shall be called the children of God. Blessed are they which are persecuted for righteousness' sake: for theirs is the kingdom of heaven. This is the Sermon on the Mount, as reported in the Gospel of the Apostle Matthew, amen.'

The sick people half-listen, fiddling with their bread and crumbling it on the tablecloth. They wait impatiently, not daring to move their faces any nearer to their plates. Finally a nun with a sharp voice proclaims from the kitchen door: '*Ora pro nobis, amen*! You may start eating!' And suddenly all the spoons dive into the soup to re-emerge full and head for trembling, greedy, clumsy mouths.

Amara watches little Amintore who, even if his head is not entirely under control, behaves with dignity and a certain astute courtesy. He inserts his spoon in his soup nonchalantly as if at the very moment when the others are betraying impatience and greed, he himself has lost his appetite. Then, with a slow movement of the wrist, he dips his spoon into the soup again, fills it and waits for it to cool a little; then lifts it first to his nostrils to breathe in the warm, greasy aroma of the broth, and only then to his lips which he opens slowly and gracefully. With nearly all the others, the rising and falling of the spoon causes a little broth to fall on the table and the cloth, or worse still on trousers or skirt, but Amintore doesn't lose a drop. With calm, slow movements he bends forward and sucks again and again without ever letting his elbow slip, his little finger raised like that of a minor prince at a royal table. He never lifts his eyes from his plate, a slight smile on his unmarked face.

As she is about to leave, Amara sees him lift his head with a sly flash of mischief and fix his eyes on her as if he had known she was there all the time and had deliberately ignored her. His smile spreads affectionately. Putting down his spoon he waves. 'Ciao, Stefania!' he calls loudly, then turns back to his soup without giving her another look.

26

Who knows why the train is such a familiar friend. It carries her, enfolds her and protects her. Imposes a rhythm on her thoughts. Never a discordant rhythm, thinks Amara, sucking the end of her pencil as she turns the pages of Conrad. The sliding door opened and Lev Nikolayevich Myshkin came in. A young man dressed entirely in black, his tight jacket making him look thinner than he really is. His ravaged yet naïve smile pushing him towards the precipices of the world. How familiar that man has been to her! Perhaps more familiar than Nastasya Filippovna or even Aglaya. The splendour of meekness. The inexpressible wonder of idiocy and compassion. Is not that the reason she has followed him step by step? For the way Myshkin, the idiot, runs into his future almost by chance and is marked for life by it. He sees Nastasya for the first time in a portrait, as happens with fateful premonitions. A portrait that has fallen into his hands by chance. When she herself enters headlong, throwing open one door and pushing another, the idiot can't summon up the courage to speak to her. She doesn't even notice him. She takes him for a servant and throws her fur to him, running off at high speed. In that running, in that careless indifference, the whole relationship between Myshkin and Nastasya is outlined. A relationship composed of cruelty on one side and silent expectation on the other. A relationship that will make them into friends and enemies, mutual slaves and unhappy lovers. Leading them to the murderous night in which the idiot finds himself once again with Rogozhin, the man who has killed the woman he loves, and they discuss absurd things at the bedside of the little dead woman. Only the little marble foot looking on from under the sheet reminds us that someone has murdered an innocent and perverse girl. They talk and talk, all night long. Is this what friendship between men is? Myshkin, inspired by absolute and thus irrational compassion, utterly pure and therefore splendid, considers Rogozhin even more his friend, despite the delicate corpse of the infatuated girl lying there between them as proof of the irrationality of love.

The train makes every reflection serpentine, humble, wise. Thought assumes the cadence of the wheels and rhythmically works through ideas as if kilometres of reflections must be traversed. Indeed, the train may carry the idea of dragging or pulling away, *traîner* as the French say. Is that where the word 'train' comes from? She immediately gets out the little etymological dictionary she always carries with her. The word is from the Late Latin 'trenum', a cart for transporting things. But the most astonishing thing is that 'trenum' derives in its turn from the Greek word 'threnos' meaning 'funeral chant'. Which comes first, the cart carrying the provisions for the army or lamentation for the death of a hero? It would be logical to start with war and the impedimenta and provisions and weapons necessary for the soldiers and go on later to funeral lamentations for the deaths of so many young men. But no, the Greek word comes before the Latin one. The contradictions of a language with so many ancestors, all different. She likes to think the train recalls supplies for war but at the same time also carries an ability to console and sing songs for the dead. In the end, every train moves towards the realm of the dead, bearing ideas and meditations that feed on themselves. This is how she likes to think of it, this smoky train travelling through fields still full of land mines and through bombed cities and woods that have given refuge to desperate fugitives, as it heads slowly for Vienna.

Her father Amintore loved trains. Although he travelled very little himself, on Sundays he would set out on the floor a complicated system of rails and make miniature trains run on them, perfect copies of trains from various past periods, accurately copied from old rolling-stock and from old locomotives with fine long snouts, even with make-believe steam puffing from their chimneys.

Amintore had never liked real travel. After military service as an Alpinist in the Cadore Mountains, he had been sent to 'civilise' black people in Ethiopia, coming home wounded. That had been enough. No, for their honeymoon he took her mother Stefania to Venice. After that horrible act of violence she had insisted on getting married immediately. She couldn't bear to live alone any longer. Her parents had died young. She was alone in the great house in Piazza Dalmazia. They could have lived together in her parents' apartment, but Stefania had preferred to adapt herself to the little house in Via Alderotti, near Villa Lorenzi and the park where one day the little Amara would spend so much time running and playing with Emanuele.

How often Amintore had told her about that trip to Venice! The idea of streets of water had made a profound impression on him. 'You wear shoes and walk on asphalt, but in fact you're surrounded by water. You go up on a little bridge and see greenish waves forming beneath you, you go down stairs and see water following you, you get into a boat and the current of liquid goes with you. It was as if I was made of water myself too, liquefied, without a skeleton, moving like a stream.'

They had been to see a glass factory at Murano. Astonished and delighted like a child, her father Amintore, open-mouthed and wide-eyed, had witnessed the transformation of a huge drop of liquid glass into a solid bulbous vase. He had learned something from that wonderful metamorphosis: was it not the same with their own bodies that started almost liquid and then grew solid, at first shining new only to grow gradually more cracked and fragmentary, to end up broken and thrown away? Even human thoughts, at their birth, often have a miraculous transparency, a luminous liquidity that gradually becomes more opaque and worn out. This is true of religions too, and even of nations. Perhaps even his love for the lovely Stefania would undergo the same transformation; from a limpid and joyous liquid to something familiar and opaque, unrecognisable? So he sadly asked himself, carrying in his mind the image of that glass melting and running and slithering, dissolving only to coagulate like a precious memory as soon as it was held away from the fire. It was an image of the power and fragility of the universe. He had talked about this to his daughter, often, remembering that trip to Venice that had been one of the few memorable events in his humble life as a cobbler. He had discovered the consistency of water outside a bottle or bucket. He had joyfully followed things that run, that silently modify themselves in the purity of matter. And he had thought of his own spirit as having become a broken glass. He had so much longed for a strong young hand to grab it with tongs and put it back in the fire to make it liquid again, mobile and ready to take on new shapes. Why do we stay in a predictable form, always the same? he had asked his little daughter, certain she would not understand, but hoping she might remember something of his words.

The memory of all those Sundays sitting on the floor with her father Amintore, busy with his model trains, return to her memory as the train draws her towards the future. Perhaps it is from this, from the imaginary journeys her father took, that she derives her love of trains. Who knows! With a few rapid movements the young Amintore would move aside the two shabby armchairs and the bench that stood round the table. He would close the table's gate-legs and push it against the wall, clearing a space for his trains to run. He claimed it was for her that he set out his railway, but he himself was the real enthusiast. Hurrying to buy new model engines as soon as they came out. Spending hours coupling carriages to make up trains. Learning the name of every steam or electric locomotive in the world.

How often he had dragged her when she was little to the railway museum near the station, where obsolete rolling-stock was preserved! He had hoisted her up into one of those ancient steam engines that looked like something from a Buster Keaton film, especially his most famous one, *The General*. A film her father told her about and which she saw many years later with Luca at the Chaplin Club. An adventurous and indomitable train hurling itself over mined bridges and racing like a maddened horse past fields and meadows and cities, staking out a road between forests and mountains.

Did these mobile toys represent journeys Amintore could have made but never did make? There would have been enough money for occasional expeditions across the border. But something always stopped him. Perhaps the ugly experience of 1935 in Ethiopia, where he discovered poverty and sickness and was forced to shoot at people for whom he felt no dislike. Sometimes Amara would find him bending over a map, busily planning a journey that would have taken them far away. He would apply for passports, set aside money for their tickets and choose what clothes to take, but at the last moment something always stopped him. Their suitcases, standing ready, would remain mysteriously empty. He preferred familiar local expeditions to Monte Morello and its peaks: Poggio dell'Aia which reached 950 metres amid pines, oaks and silver firs; Poggio Casaccia, and Poggio della Cornachiaccia which he loved best of all, for its view of the Vaglia valley.

27

She sees him from a distance raising his hand. And there are the gazelles, running across his chest. This cheers her up. She had asked him to wear the same sweater as when they met on the first journey, from Vienna to Kraków. Coming near him, she meets the bergamot fragrance he has put on for her. He has a blissful smile and a little bunch of wild flowers in his hand.

'Your husband?'

'He's fine.'

'So he just wanted you back for love.'

'I don't know about love, but he certainly wanted attention.'

'So he wasn't ill at all?'

'No, in hospital but not at the point of death as he'd led me to believe.'

'I bet he asked you to go back and live with him again.'

'How do you know?'

'I can guess.'

'That was it, exactly.'

'And you said no?'

'Did you guess that too?'

'I imagine you wouldn't want to.'

'What do you think I want?'

'I don't know. Nor do you, for that matter. Or rather: you want to find your Emanuele. That's clear enough. But more mysteriously, you're after something else.'

'What?'

'I'm not sure. Maybe an Amara you don't know.'

'And what have you been doing these last few days?'

'Gone on with the search.'

'And?'

'I went to have a look at the Schulerstrasse house where the Orensteins lived. A family of ex-Nazis live there now. Not bad from an anthropological point of view. Then I went to ferret about in the city archives. I found another Orenstein. Name of Peter. I've made an appointment with him for tomorrow. Can you come?'

'That's what I came back for.'

'I had hoped you came back for me.'

'I returned to go on with the search.'

'I take that back, I'm sorry.'

'Well, where shall we start?'

'With Peter Orenstein. Our appointment's for tomorrow at ten. Okay?'

Returning to Pension Blumental, Amara finds Frau Morgan cleaning the stairs. She has tied her ample skirts at the ankle with elastic as though about to mount a bicycle. She is extremely polite but somehow inscrutable. Difficult to know what she's thinking. She puts on a professional smile, then forgets herself and seems to become a child again. The expression in her big nut-brown eyes is at the same time disconcerted and bored, as if she's surprised by the world and its peculiarities but forcing herself to accept it for what it is. Amara wonders what she did during the war. She uses her unavoidable entry into the reception area to sign the guestbook and try to get Frau Morgan to talk. Her eye falls on the framed photograph of a handsome man in military uniform.

'My husband Franz,' says Frau Morgan, following Amara's gaze. Her smile freezes on her lips.

'Is he dead?'

'Killed in the war, like so many others. Shall I help you to your room with your suitcase?'

'No thank you, I'll manage on my own.'

Frau Morgan dries her hands on the dark green apron over her skirt. She's wearing comic Turkish-style slippers with turned-up toes.

'Have any letters arrived for me?'

'No post for Signora Sironi.'

She says this in Italian as if to show that she too loves the land of sun and knows a word or two of its language. She stands stock-still, not daring to dismiss Amara.

'D'you mind if I sit here a moment before I go up to my room?'

'Not at all, please do. Would you like some coffee?'

'That would be nice.'

Amara sits down and looks around. Rather a wretched home: two rooms with a half-window overlooking the street. Yet everything is in its place and as genteel as possible with doilies, little white cushions, lilac wallpaper with tulips on it, glass ornaments and fake carnations. A huge radio set is enthroned on a chest of drawers, and from the centre light with its yellow lace shade hangs a spiral of sticky paper covered with little black flies.

'A good thing this building survived the bombs.'

'It was damaged. But we fixed it.'

'Have you always lived here?'

'Yes, my husband inherited it.'

'He was a handsome man, I can tell from the photo. Which year did he die?'

'Right at the beginning of the war. Shot down as a pilot in October '39.'

'Unlucky.'

'Twenty-five years old.'

'Children?'

'None.'

'And you never married again?'

'Where would I find a husband? All the men died in the war, Frau Sironi. Only us women were left.'

Amara looks at her curiously. After the first few hostile moments, Frau Morgan seems to have relaxed a little. Perhaps she doesn't mind talking about herself, being asked questions. She is always alone. It occurs to Amara she could start an article for her paper with Frau Morgan's statement 'All the men are dead'. What happened to the widows, daughters and sisters of those soldiers killed in the war?

'How have you managed to survive?'

'I divided the rooms up and started a pension. Only four rooms but it's enough to keep me going.'

'Did you ever hear anything about the concentration camps?'

'Certainly not. I knew the Jews were shut up in ghettos.'

'But a time came when the ghettos were evacuated and destroyed. Didn't you ever ask yourself what happened to all those Jews?'

'I had other things to think about, Frau Sironi. I had to find something to eat, survive the bombing and search for water because all the mains in the district had been blown up.'

'And when did you discover that the Jews in the camps had been gassed?'

'After the war. A disgrace. It was no accident the Nazis went into hiding. Luckily my Franz was in the Luftwaffe. He was never in the SS.'

'Can you remember anything of the time when the cities were overrun by gangs of thugs? When slogans denouncing the Jews went up in the shops?'

'It's all different now, but at that time there was an enthusiasm, a confidence, a joy in being alive that made all these little things though admittedly dissonant seem unimportant.'

'Dissonance unimportant? If a singer sings out of tune with the orchestra, the audience boos and whistles.'

'It was a country in love with a new era, you understand … no, you wouldn't understand … a country on fire with a new pride and boldness after a long history of humiliation. We were all drunk. And when you're drunk you don't see the details, you see everything wholesale, you're exultant, ready to do anything for the idol of the moment.'

'Drunk with hatred for a people whose only fault was to exist?'

'We believed the Jews did business, speculated, stole, wanted to destroy our country. Hitler said they wanted a world war so they could eliminate the Aryan race. That's what was in all the newspapers and they kept on repeating it again and again.'

'Did you never think it might be propaganda?'

'Drunks are happy to drink bad wine too. They can't tell the difference between that and good wine.'

'Was that how your husband Franz thought as well?'

'We all thought like that. It was a common attitude. And if you didn't think like that you were in trouble.'

'So there were a few people who didn't think like that?'

'Just a few but they were thought mad. Love is exclusive and looks for absolutes.'

'Do you think Nazism was born out of love?'

'A sick love that soon turned into tyranny. I know that from my own experience. What could have persuaded a little girl like me to cram herself into a uniform covered with buttons and run to rallies and raise my arm rhythmically in honour of Hitler? How could they convince me to march with thousands of other students, sticking our legs straight up in the air? Love, only love and pride in our country. And the voice of the Führer had more power than any whip, a powerful spirit that burned our throats and made the blood race in our veins.'

'So you were a committed Nazi!'

'I can admit that now it's all in the past.'

'The binge is over. And then?'

'You wake up and say: how could I ever have believed all that? How could I? Even if I, Dorothea Morgan, never did anything, but let others do it all, that's sometimes even worse. How could I never have seen the abyss we were hurling ourselves into?'

'So all those dead, tormented people were simply the result of an enormous obscene collective binge?'

'When you're drunk you don't know what you're doing. We were blind drunk and in love with a criminal. That can happen, you know, just ask any psychologist. People of good family who would never hurt a fly, people who care about their country and the future of their children, can be blinded by love for a man, ready to surrender their own will to his, out of admiration for a word that exalts and seduces. To surrender their own future, even life itself, to an assassin to do what he likes with. That's how it was with me, but I assure you with millions of others it was just the same. Millions of poor people who had nothing to gain from Nazism. It wasn't fear, indignation or greed that pushed them towards racism, even if many did enrich themselves shamefully by grabbing everything from those poor families who went to the extermination camps. But we didn't know that then. We thought they'd been taken away to do forced labour. Most people didn't speculate or steal, they just saw themselves as taking part in a great moment of history. We'd gone to war against people who threatened Austria and the Germanic peoples. Who wanted to crush us totally and kill us, and we were fighting them. It was no more than self-defence.'

'But who was it who wanted to destroy the Germanic nations? Communists? Homosexuals? Gypsies? Jews? The sick? The crippled? Who was it precisely?'

'In war people die. You can't mourn every death, every casualty. I could have been killed myself from one moment to the next. Like my Franz. I cried for days and days. Then one morning I said: Dorothea, this weeping means nothing, it's egoistical. You're crying because of a personal insult, when the country is triumphantly raising its head to face the whole world and demand respect, love, and obedience.'

'And when did you become aware that all this was an aberration, Frau Morgan?'

'Just after the war, when the newspapers began saying how things really were and we saw the photographs. Who could have imagined they gassed those poor children and threw them into crematorium ovens? It was monstrous.'

'There are some who say you didn't want to know the truth.'

'Italy also had a tyrant, and he was loved and followed too. When did you find out how things really were?'

'I was a child. I was in love with Emanuele Orenstein, not with any tyrant. Then he left for Vienna with his family and I never saw him again. I'm here to find out whether he died in a camp or survived.'

'This is why you're here, Frau Sironi? I hope you find him.'

'Please forgive me if I've upset you with all my questions. But I'm inquisitive and trying to understand.'

'It's so long since I last spoke of those times. It needed a foreigner to come here and call up distant feelings we're perhaps ashamed of. As if we'd woken after a massive binge and vowed never to drink again.'

'Do you think the people of Austria have vaccinated themselves against every form of Nazism?'

'For myself I would say yes. But you never know. Perhaps more should be said about it. Discussion in the schools.'

'Is it shame that stops people discussing it, or are they afraid of meeting ghosts too depressing to face?'

'There's nothing worse than coming to your senses after a mistaken love. For the first time you see the person as he really is and ask yourself how you could ever have trusted such a person, how you could ever have put your future in his hands. Now we see him as a monster with an ugly voice, the eyes of a lunatic and the gestures of a madman. But at the time we even thought him beautiful! Even kind! Even fascinating! We were all in love with him.'

'Titania falls in love with the head of an ass. Just because Puck has squirted a little magic juice in her eyes! Is that how you think love comes about, Frau Morgan?'

'For me, yes. Love is utterly blind and incapable of reasoning. Do you know why we fall in love with a particular person?'

'Preferably because we like the way he thinks and reasons, how he speaks and moves, and for his smell and his voice and his hands and his eyes.'

'Well, to me Hitler had beautiful hands, shining eyes and profound thoughts and moved like a cherub. I don't know about his smell because I never got near enough to find out. But let's say that sometimes a scent of roses and violets came from far off that surprised even me. The smell of my country celebrating, of my country victorious.'

'I imagine the smell of defeat must have swept away the smell of roses and violets.'

'Defeat smells of putrid flesh.'

Amara sees Frau Morgan suddenly sit down with her hands in her lap, breathing heavily as if from running up the stairs. But she does not seem unhappy, only tired.

28

At ten in the morning the man with the gazelles and Amara are at Peter Orenstein's door ringing a bell whose hoarse sound echoes through an apparently empty house.

No one comes to open, not even after they ring a second and a third time.

'But he arranged to see us at ten,' says Hans.

'What shall we do? Shall we wait?'

'Let's wait a little longer.'

After ringing several more times, Amara and Hans sit down outside on the top step waiting for any sign of life. Perhaps the master of the house has gone out and will be back soon. Perhaps he's fallen asleep. Or changed his mind. All they can do is wait patiently.

This morning the man with the gazelles has a nice smell of carnation-scented soap. In her mind Amara goes back over what Frau Morgan said. How important is the smell of a person close to you? Frau Morgan was aware of the Führer's smell of roses and violets from kilometres away. To what extent do we invent smells?

Hans talks of his mother, the resolute Hanna Paduk, a Hungarian Jew who died in the Treblinka camp. She wore her long curly blonde hair in braids round her head. 'She was funny, she walked like a young goose because of flat feet. But her voice was not that of a goose, it was the most beautiful and expressive voice I've ever heard. When I was little she used to sing me to sleep with folk songs: *Schlaf, Kindlein, schlaf! Dein Vater ist ein Schaf, Die Mutter ist im Pommerland, Pommerland ist abgebrannt, Schlaf, Kindlein, schlaf.* Do you know what that means? *Sleep baby sleep, Your father's just a sheep, Your mother's in Pomerania-land, Pomerania's all burned down, Sleep baby sleep.*

'Her voice bewitched me. I would force myself to stay awake so I could go on listening. But she would be in a hurry to get away. I would hold her hand tight and beg her: sing more! And she would sing, soft and low close to my ear so as not to disturb the others. Her breath smelled of onions. I don't know why my poor mother always ate onions. Perhaps they were the only vegetables available in the market at that time. I ate boiled onions too, and I have to say they were excellent. But I couldn't smell my own breath. I could smell hers. It was sourish and sweet at the same time. Onions and words, onions and fluent notes. I would have happily lived like that for ever. There's something perverse about growing up, developing strong teeth, hairs on one's chest, a moustache, corns on one's feet. Why do we grow? It's so stupid.'

Hans is no longer looking at her. He is speaking as if alone, eyes half closed, barely moving his lips. Telling of his mother, the sweet Hanna rejected by her own kitchen. The marvellous singing bird, who faced with her oven had no idea what to do. She would forget to stir the stew, add too much salt or too much pepper and over-cook the vegetables; in her hands rice became food for chickens and the meat was always scorched. She didn't even know how to buy at the market. During the war, when food was rationed but you could buy on the black market, she would return home happily to her husband after tracking down two sausages which then turned out to be full of worms, or place on the table a fine melon that was rotten inside. One day she brought some extremely green pears, so hard that neither teeth nor the blade of a knife could penetrate them. Let's put them on the window ledge till they're ripe, she said in her soft, musical voice. So they were spread on the balcony and watched. But those spiteful pears, so unerringly chosen by clumsy Hanna, quietly turned from wooden to rotten with nothing in between. Not only that, but they began to leak a stinking liquid and had to be thrown in the dustbin, where not even stray dogs would give them a glance.

Hanna read a lot and her husband Tadeusz teased her for liking modern novels. He himself was a musician of great distinction who for 'major historical reasons', in his own words, had failed even before beginning his career as an orchestral conductor. At most he was occasionally allowed to conduct an orchestra of young students at the Vienna Academy. But one morning while they were rehearsing the alarm sounded. He continued conduct-ing as if it was nothing; there were far too many alarms, and in his candid opinion the people who controlled the sirens overdid things. Perplexed, the musicians looked at each other and went on playing. But when they heard hissing sounds followed by explosions, they grabbed their instruments and headed for the shelters. Tadeusz was left alone – well, not entirely alone, because the principal violin stayed with him, a very tall young man with curls on his collar and clear, smiling eyes. They began discussing music: 'My father has always remembered that morning and that conversation. He says he never talked with more passion, more freedom or more joy with any of his musicians. They scarcely noticed that a bomb had destroyed half the building. But the hall of the Academy had miraculously survived and they had gone on talking about music until someone came in, injured and covered with dust, searching for refuge in the only part of the building that was still intact. Some other musicians were carried in on stretchers, and the entrance hall of the Academy rapidly became an improvised hospital with stretcher-bearers running from one side to the other. The wounded were settled on the floor on the red padded carpets that served for sound insulation during rehearsals, while the dead were piled in the corridor next to the area where the violins, double basses, horns and flutes were stored. Nearly all the musicians who had taken refuge underground were injured. Two were dead: the pianist, a father of three small children, and the timpanist, a sturdy athletic young man whose muscles and ready smile had been envied by all. The others were lying there on the floor, one with a broken arm, one with shattered legs, one with bleeding ears, moaning quietly in childish voices. The conductor, Tadeusz, and the principal violin, Ferenc Bruman, became instant nurses, helping to strip off the orchestra's clothes and holding them while their injuries were disinfected and bandaged, and helping them to swallow pills administered by medical students who had run over from the nearby School of Medicine after the explosion and collapse of the shelter. These were mere boys who applied to the letter what they had learned from books in their first months at the School: that splints were needed for broken bones, alcohol for wounds that must first be cleaned with soap and water, and stitches made with needle and suture thread for superficial wounds. But where could they find splints and needles and thread for sutures?

Hans is so engrossed in his story that he doesn't notice the door behind them beginning to open. Amara jumps up, terrified. Hans goes on talking about his father the conductor and his mother Hanna who died of want in Treblinka concentration camp in 1944. Meanwhile a long head with sparse grey hair looks out and watches them, eyes wide with surprise.

'Who are you?'

At last Hans is aware of the man. He leaps up and gives an automatic military salute, for no apparent reason clicking his heels and lifting his hand to the peak of his cap.

'We're looking for Peter Orenstein.'

'I am he. What do you want?'

The man doesn't ask them in. On the contrary, he closes the door behind himself, and looks suspiciously at them. His eyes are puffy and his eyelids wrinkled, and he has one cheek disfigured by a deep hole as if someone has excavated it with a knife; his mouth is drawn tight by mean lips that barely cover little false teeth.

'What do you want from Peter Orenstein?'

'The lady you see beside me,' starts the man with the gazelles in his usual formal manner, putting himself at something of a disadvantage, 'is an Italian lady, a Signora Maria Amara Sironi, and she has come to Vienna to look for traces of a childhood friend, called Orenstein like yourself.'

'Emanuele Orenstein,' adds Amara, looking the man straight in the eye as if to emphasise that they haven't come to swindle or rob him, but only to find out what they can from someone who might be a relative. But Peter Orenstein seems not to understand. Perhaps he has been asleep. He rolls up his eyes and knits his brows crossly.

'I know no Emanuele Orenstein,' he says finally, trying to control a shrill voice that tends to pepper what he says with nervous little cries.

'Very well, we've obviously made a mistake. I'm sorry. Please forgive us for disturbing you.'

'But why are you trying to find this Emanuele Orenstein?' says the man, who no longer seems so anxious to get rid of them. Has he grown curious?

'He was a childhood friend. We used to play together.'

'Where?' asks the man, screwing up his eyes.

'In Florence, Via Alderotti; does Villa Lorenzi mean anything to you?'

'Come in.'

The man pulls out his keys and opens the door again. Who knows what made him change his mind? He seems more trusting now. He stands aside and welcomes them in. Indoors, there's a smell of horses. All the windows are fast shut. The house is dark and full of dark heavy furniture. As if made for a larger house then brought here and pushed against the walls so as not to take up too much room. Two faded yellow velvet curtains hang from the high windows of the sitting room, the only light things in that dark house. The sofas may once have been yellow too, but they are now grey and stained.

'Come in, please sit down,' says the man in a conciliatory voice, going into the kitchen to find something to drink. He comes back balancing a bottle of liqueur and three mismatched glasses on a small tray.

'Well, what happened to this Emanuele Orenstein?' says the man, pouring sticky liqueur into the glasses. Goodness knows how long since that bottle was last touched; its glass neck is encrusted with deposits of whitish sugar.

'In 1939 the Orenstein family decided to return to Vienna. This is what Signora Sironi finds difficult to understand and it makes no sense to me either. There is no logic in what they did. Letters reached Amara from Vienna. She can show you one if you like. She always carries them with her. First the Orensteins lived in a large house they owned, on Schulerstrasse. Then they were thrown out and taken to the ghetto in Łódź together with other Jewish families. A few more letters reached Signora Sironi from the ghetto; the post still seems to have been working to begin with. Then nothing. But after the war she was sent an exercise book containing other letters written in the ghetto when Emanuele still had a pencil but no more envelopes or money for stamps.'

'Why not let the lady speak for herself?' says Peter Orenstein crossly.

'Her German is not very good. I'm here to help her.'

'I understand Italian.'

The man fixes his gaze on Amara, smiling mysteriously. The story seems to interest him.

'The lady suspects Emanuele Orenstein must have been transported to Auschwitz because many of those who were in the Łódź ghetto ended up there,' persists the man with the gazelles with a regretful smile.

'And has she been to Auschwitz to check the registers?'

'Yes, I've been there. But I didn't find anything.'

'And you think he might still be alive?'

'Possibly. I hope so.'

'Another drop of gentian liqueur? I made it myself.'

Amara says, no, thank you. It's too sweet for her. And there's something stale about it that she doesn't like. Now the man behaves strangely, rubbing his hands together and opening his eyes wide. He fills his own glass, gulps the liqueur down and pours some more. He licks up the last drops, hanging his tongue out of his mouth like a dog. He obviously knows something, but what?

'May I see that letter, Frau Sironi?'

Amara pulls the letters from her bag. By now they are crumpled and fading but still carefully preserved in a large envelope wrapped in transparent cellophane. She extracts one from the envelope and hands it to the man who takes it with trembling hands. He lifts it to his eyes and reads greedily.

In the semi-darkness, Amara detects a glitter. Tears are rolling down his cheeks.

'I was that child,' he says, lifting a wet face to Amara. The man with the gazelles starts in his chair. Amara sits as if turned to stone. Not only from the revelation, but because this man claiming to be her childhood friend is so utterly unrecognisable. How can there be nothing, absolutely nothing, in him of the Emanuele she once knew? Where is the smooth blond hair? The kind smile? The lively, affectionate eyes? The man facing her is like an angry owl, staring at her with obvious distaste, as he moves his dead lips like a horse over his false teeth.

'I don't recognise you ...' says Amara in embarrassment. Her only thought is to run away from this house and this man who is clearly fooling her, she has no idea why but he is clearly fooling her.

'Let's leave it at that. I'm tired,' says the self-proclaimed Emanuele, changing his tone.

'But why do you call yourself Peter?' asks Amara.

'It's a long story. I don't feel like going into it at the moment. Anyway, I've closed the door on that past. Now please go away. Go!'

29

That evening, sitting at a table at the Figlmüller beerhouse, the man with the gazelles and Amara ask themselves about that strange meeting with Peter Orenstein who claimed to be Emanuele Orenstein. But if he doesn't resemble Emanuele in any way? And in any case, he must be much older than twenty-eight; he looks at least forty-five. Amara lifts to her lips the good draught beer an elderly waiter has placed before her, but she doesn't feel like drinking.

After claiming to be the Emanuele they are looking for, the man to all intents and purposes threw them out of the house. Amara had no time to ask him the questions on the tip of her tongue. She had no chance to clarify, understand or ask anything. Still weeping and panting, the man had taken them to the door saying he wanted to be alone. Out of tact, dazed and perplexed, they left without asking anything more, and without even retrieving the letter that Amara always liked to have with her.

'We must go back for the letter.'

'And to ask more questions. He can't get away with it like that, leaving everything in doubt.'

'We need to find out why he's pretending to be what he isn't.'

'But the furniture was very much like the Orenstein family furniture. Fake sixteenth-century, with small carvings in dark wood. Expensive items from Florence, made for a large house with plenty of room in it.'

'But how can he have aged so much? He looked at least fifty.'

'With the face of a hungry wolf.'

'He must be an impostor who wants to get something out of passing himself off as somebody else.'

'That hole in his cheek ...'

'We don't look like rich people. What can he hope to gain?'

'But those tears, Hans, they seemed real enough.'

'If what he says is true, your Emanuele has turned into a monster. Either that or the man's a speculator. A clever actor.'

'Could a concentration camp reduce a young man to such a state?'

'Anything can happen, even to the extent of turning a child into an old man.'

'But did you notice his hair? Almost bald and what's left of it was white. How can a man of twenty-eight have a head like that? The war ended eleven years ago. There's been time enough to get over it.'

'It is strange.'

'I don't understand a thing, Hans. What shall we do?'

'We must go back. He's got to explain his name to us and much more.'

'And we must get that letter back.'

'The letter, yes.'

They look at each other. Amara bursts out laughing, but it is sad, nervous laughter. Hans lifts the tankard of fresh beer to his lips and drinks, closing his eyes and throwing back his head. Amara drinks too. Everything is getting complicated if also a little grotesque.

'But if it really does turn out to be him, what will you do, Amara?'

'I've no idea.'

'Do you think you would still love him?'

'Yes of course, but not what we met.'

'You must have realised he would be different from the person you remembered.'

'Different but not unrecognisable. This is a different person, Hans, someone else. It frightens me. He even has a different name. It can't be him.'

'Anyone who escaped from the concentration camps has to be different from other people ... as if he had died and risen again.'

'Died and risen again?'

'That friend of my father's I was talking about, the principal violin of the Budapest Academy who was engaged for a series of concerts in Vienna: Ferenc Bruman. He spent two years in Africa with his father who was a diplomat. He used to tell a strange story about how they once ran into a tribe from the north of the Ivory

Coast. Hunters who went naked apart from a cache-sexe of leaves, with a knife in their belts and a long spear always in their hands. When the two came into these people's village, a man had just died. Next morning all the village elders gathered in the shade of a large mango tree. They had placed the dead man, all washed and clothed, against the tree and all crouched round him. Then one of the men started questioning him: Why have you died? What killed you? Who will you leave your spear to? And so on. At each question the elder pulled the dead man by the sleeve, and they understood his reply from the way his head moved, and everyone knew what he was trying to say. Well, I think Emanuele Orenstein is dead and we're questioning a substitute according to some archaic magic rite. We need to understand what this dead man is trying to tell us, like the Africans in the northern Ivory Coast.'

'I don't believe he's trying to tell us anything. More likely trying to hide something from us, Hans. But what?'

'I wish I could discuss it with my father. He has an extraordinary eye for people and never gets things wrong.'

'Your father's still alive?'

'Seventy-six, but like a young man. He lives in Budapest. I'd like you to meet him. A wise, lucid man. He chops the firewood for his stove every day.'

'Did he never marry again after your mother's death?'

'He lived a couple of years with a girl my age. But she got bored and left him. Now he lives on his own. No, to be honest, with a friend, the principal violin of the Budapest Academy orchestra, Ferenc Bruman, the one I've just been telling you about, remember? The man who was saved with him the time they talked about music on the day of the great bombing raid on Vienna. The afternoon the Academy collapsed and they survived unscathed while everyone else was killed or wounded. Now he teaches music and earns enough to buy his daily food and fill his evening pipe. They're like a married couple, him and Ferenc, they quarrel a lot but get on well enough. They've had a small flat assigned to them in Budapest, right in the centre, near the Corvin cinema, in Magdolna utca. I'd love to introduce you to them both: Ferenc, an excellent violinist, and Tadeusz, a man of great talent, generous and cultured. I'd really like you to meet them. After the raid they'd survived by talking about music they disappeared, then met again a few years after the war. Ferenc was playing the violin in the street. My father could no longer find an orchestra to take him on as its conductor, so he started teaching. They decided to set up house together. First with the girl I was telling you about, Odette. She was a bit on the plump side but had a pretty face and they both liked her. Best of all she was cheerful, with a sort of open, child-like cheerfulness that did the two old men good. I'm not exactly sure but I think she probably shared her favours between them. In return they let her have a fine room and a huge bed with a flow-ered chintz cover, bought her a rather bald rabbit fur, lit a stove every day to keep her warm and made sure she didn't go short of food. She thanked them by doing the ironing and looking after the housework. Ferenc did the cooking and my father chopped the wood. I think it was a good life for all three. I hardly ever went to see them, but when I did I found them cheerful, active and full of ideas. My father got it into his head to teach Odette opera. He said she had a good voice and got her to practice every day. In my opinion she couldn't sing in tune, but it was lovely to see them doing things together; they played together and she sang. Natu-rally the piano was aborted before it could even be born. Odette got bored with vocal exercises, found a young man who wanted to marry her and disappeared one morning without a word.'

'And the two men have stayed together?'

'They've gone on in the same way, but without the domestic cheerfulness that had made for such a happy atmosphere; they are perhaps quieter and more peaceful now. They've learned to buy non-iron shirts and fast foods. My father still chops wood and Ferenc still looks after the kitchen. Most recently they've bought a motorcycle with a sidecar and go roaring about the place, all kitted out in goggles and airmen's helmets.'

30

Amara is still sleeping when Frau Morgan climbs the stairs and calls: 'A phone call for you, Frau Sironi.' Amara puts on her slippers and goes downstairs yawning. The telephone on the wall is cleaned every morning with huge wads of cotton wool steeped in alcohol by the hard-working Frau Morgan. Amara recognises the voice at once. Hans, the man with the gazelles. In her mind that's how she sees him, as though the gazelles are stamped on his chest and, even without his sweater, are leaping and running towards the future. Hans tells her breathlessly he has just read in the paper about an archive discovered in an underground SS shelter near the camp at Auschwitz. Why not go and study these new lists? They contain a large number of names, written up by hand complete with days of arrival and everything.

'We have to go there, Amara. I'll go and buy tickets. I'll pass by to pick up your passport for the visas towards ten, okay?'

Amara says yes. She turns to see Frau Morgan with a cup of coffee especially for her. By now she has developed a taste for their investigations and addresses her lodger in a conspiratorial tone.

'News, Frau Sironi?'

Amara would like to tell her about the man passing himself off as Emanuele but who doesn't resemble him in the least and is in any case much too old. But she makes no mention of that meeting which still seems unreal. Instead she tells her about the new lists discovered in the SS shelter and of the trip they are going to make to Poland as soon as they have the necessary visas.

But the police are getting suspicious. What are these two up to going backwards and forwards between Vienna and Kraków? They are interrogated separately. Amara has to spend hours and hours waiting on a bench while they interrogate Hans, then it is her turn to face the usual questions to which she replies wearily, trying not to let it get on her nerves too much. But the police hold all possible or imaginable cards in their hands. Since the two are not commercial travellers, no one can understand why they are constantly asking permission to cross the border. Amara being a journalist doesn't make things any better. What does she want to write? What is the ideological line of her paper? Et cetera, et cetera.

'Come back in two days.'

'But in two days we'll have lost our train reservation.'

'You can make another.'

Amara tries to explain that she has been sent by an independent Italian newspaper to write about the countries of Eastern Europe. She pulls out permits, her journalist's card, her passport. But the police are inflexible.

'Come back in two days.'

For Hans it's even worse. What is he really after, this half-Jewish, half-Hungarian, half-Austrian man, half journalist and half not, half music teacher and half student, wanting permission to travel to Poland? Does he not understand that we're in the middle of a full-scale cold war? That the border is closed? That urgent, important reasons are needed for anyone to be allowed to travel? That the reasons they are giving seem to make no sense? That rubber-stamps and visas issued by the government of Austria are not valid for Poland, or even for Hungary and Czechoslovakia, the countries they want to pass through in order to reach Kraków? The fact that his mother was Hungarian and died in a Nazi concentration camp is irrelevant. So is the fact that his father is a musician living in Budapest. How can it possibly be of any interest to the frontier administration that the young lady is travelling with him – and is she married or not? – if married, where is her husband? Or is she separated? And where does she want to go?

There is simply no end to the questions, and every time a new official appears they have to start again at the beginning. Hours and days pass like this. They spend the first night with the police, sitting on a bench. At about four in the morning a kind and very young policeman, moved by pity, brings them hot tea and a blanket. At nine the interrogation begins again. Then, at one, an officer in a torn uniform tells Amara she can go back to the pension, but that the man, Hans Wilkowsky, must stay with the police.

'But why?'

'Madam, please go. You're lucky we aren't repatriating you to Italy. As soon as we have all the information we need we'll release you. If we get it. If we're satisfied with it. Meanwhile please go back to the Pension Blumental. We'll be in touch.'

So she was dismissed. She left the police with her clothes crumpled and her hair stuck to her cheeks after a night sleeping against the dirty wall of the waiting room, with her feet gone numb inside her shoes.

Frau Morgan greeted her with an enigmatic smile.

Amara went up to her room and stretched on her bed trying to read a book and forget all that wasted time. Next morning there was a knock on her door.

'You're wanted on the phone, Frau Sironi.'

She ran down the stairs, hoping anxiously that it was Hans. She felt lost in Vienna without him.

'They've withheld my passport.'

'Then what can we do?'

'They've only given me a permit to Kraków and back, passing through Budapest. That should be enough to reach Auschwitz.'

'And our time-expired tickets?'

'I managed to change them. It cost a bit. See you at Figlmüller's in an hour?'

Figlmüller's, once just a beer cellar, now a fourth-class restaurant, is full of smoke. The menu for the day is nailed to the wall on a piece of cardboard. Pork crackling with beans, sauerkraut and sweet-cooked potato.

Amara has sat down by a window marked with greasy fingerprints and traces of long-dried rain. Outside there's a boy playing in the middle of the square with a dog, making it jump and run round in circles. He picks up a stone and throws it to the far end of the square. The dog rushes off, picks up the stone in its mouth and brings it back wagging its tail at the child, who wipes his nose on the sleeve of a patched and faded red sports shirt. The dog drops the stone right in front of the boy's down-at-heel shoes; the boy bends to pick it up and solemnly throws it again towards the flower beds at the far end of the square. The dog shoots off like an arrow, runs around with its nose to the ground, finds the stone, picks it up and runs back, leaping over obstacles like a hare. Enchanted, Amara watches this game that could go on for ever. A game of sudden loss and rediscovery, of going away and returning. Who knows why it gives so much pleasure to both boy and dog? The repetition of a familiar action? The freedom of a chase that leads nowhere and is thus entirely gratuitous and pointless? The joy of two creatures acting in unison on opposite sides of the square? The sheer pleasure of being able to flex one's muscles? There's something insane about repetition. But it can also bring great peace. Aren't lullabies based on repetition? And magic spells and prayers? The more often one repeats a gesture the less one understands it. And in that failure to understand lies the mystery of a game that imitates the mysteries of the universe.

But look, there's a tall figure crossing the square between the boy and the dog with rapid, joyful steps. Hans. A man who is winning, it occurs to her. But winning over what? Certainly not over poverty. Over the cold? No. Over love? Not that either. Over life? Perhaps; over the meagre, angry life of the post-war years that promises so little for the future. He has on his usual sweater with the running gazelles. His elderly boy's head sits firmly on his thin neck. His light-brown hair with its occasional streak of grey is slipping softly across his broad brow. A sudden surge of affection drives her to wave a hand timidly in his direction. But Hans doesn't notice her through the dirty glass. Entering with firm steps he looks round; sees her sitting in the corner, smiles and goes over to her.

He's wearing motorcyclist's gauntlets even though he sold his motorcycle years ago. On top of the gazelles he has a waterproof jacket slung over one shoulder.

'What can a citizen of the West want in a city of the East? Why can't Mr Hans Wilkowsky stay at home? What is all this coming and going? What can he hope to find in the camp at Auschwitz? And why is he taking with him Mrs Maria Amara Sironi Spiga, an Italian from Florence? I explained it a hundred times,' says Hans, sipping a large cup of milky coffee, 'but they seem incapable of understanding.'

Amara has propped her elbows on the little table cut from a single piece of wood, and is listening with a worried expression.

'My transparency alarms them. They asked me so many questions that by now they know everything there is to know about my life. But nothing satisfies them. They're as suspicious as monkeys. Just wait and see, they'll interrogate Frau Morgan. And we can expect a visit to your room in the Pension Blumental. They'll go through everything then put it all back as it was. Their conscience isn't clear. I told them repeatedly that we're searching for traces of a child who disappeared in '43. And that you are also writing articles for an Italian paper. Who knows what they think can be hidden behind that. They're probably following us now. Listening to every word we say. But why should we care?'

'Do you really mean they could be spying on us at this very moment?'

'Possibly. How could all those guards and secret service agents make a living, if not from the existence of people like you and me who refuse to stay quietly at home but insist on travelling from city to city in pursuit of a child now grown up, who just possibly may have survived the war?'

'And my permit?'

'You'll have to wait. They won't say anything definite. Maybe two days, maybe five. There are things they have to check. I expect they'll have phoned the police in Florence about you. And they'll have rummaged through the whole of my past to find out who I am and what I want. For a bureaucrat it's difficult to understand that anything can ever exist for no particular reason. There's no obvious reason why I should come with you on your search for Emanuele Orenstein, there's no obvious reason at all for your search, and there's no reason they can understand for why you should want to go to Auschwitz again.'

'Well, there is a reason. We're going to study the new lists of arrivals at the camp.'

'But that makes no sense to them. Too vague, too sentimental. It has to be a front for something else.'

'What on earth can they suspect? They won't find anything and in the end they'll get tired.'

'Let's hope so.'

'Shouldn't you be writing for your paper? Make the most of the chance. I'll take you to see the Belvedere Gardens.'

'No, no gardens. I want to write about Vienna and the cold war. How the people are living and what they're thinking.'

'I'll help you if you like.'

'Have you no work of your own you should be getting on with, Hans?'

'I did. But I've lost it. I'll manage, though.'

'How?'

'Well, for example, by being a father to brides at the altar. So many men have died and someone has to take their place. I can perform. I have my own tailcoat. And I know how to smile nicely. People always say: you seem too young to be her father, but it's wonderful how you and your daughter are as alike as two peas in a pod!'

He laughs, throwing back his head. Amara notices two gaps between his side teeth. Seeing her looking at his mouth, he shyly cups his hand under his nose.

When an hour later Amara returns to the Pension Blumental, Frau Morgan, red in the face, stops her before she can go upstairs. 'You have caused me to suffer two hours of interrogation this morning.'

Amara apologises. But what can they have been asking? Frau Morgan looks askance, uncertain what, if anything, to say. All the fear caused by the war and the Nazi terror is coming to the surface again. We must all keep our mouths shut, Frau Morgan seems to be saying with her slightly squinting eyes that are looking simultaneously above and to one side of Amara's face. Always mind your own business and keep clear of other people's. Especially foreigners; you always have to keep them at arm's length, because they only bring trouble.

'They turned your room upside down, I warn you,' adds Frau Morgan brusquely, heading for the stairs.

'Never mind. I'll sort that out.'

'I've done it already. I just left a few papers on the floor because I wasn't sure where to put them.'

'I have no secrets, Frau Morgan. There's nothing hidden in my room.'

'But they don't believe that. If only you know how many questions they asked me. And then they accused me of civil disobedience for taking two hours to report your name to the police.'

'It's the cold war, Frau Morgan.'

'If I was you, I'd be furious. And they took away a packet of letters.'

'They'll find it very difficult to decipher them, and they'll discover they're only letters from my father, written down by Sister

Adele. And from my husband Luca Spiga, who wants us to start living together again. Not very interesting, don't you think?'

'I don't like the police and I don't want them in my house, Frau Sironi. I'm very sorry but I must ask you to pack your bags. I don't want them suspecting me. I have a boarding-house to run, you understand, and my good name to protect.'

'As soon as my visas for Kraków and Budapest come through I'll be on my way. I promise. But please can I stay two more days? You won't see the police again, they'll be too busy trying to decipher all those letters written in Italian. Just two days, all right? Then I'll go.'

Frau Morgan half-closes her eyes, thinking things over. Her lips grow stiff and thin. She is clearly torn between sympathy for the young Italian who has always paid so promptly for her room, and fear of the police and what the neighbours may say when they realise she is herself being investigated. Then she bows her head in a less than enthusiastic gesture of assent.

31

The library should open at nine but today things are not as they should be. The doors are closed, and even when Amara and the man with the gazelles knock, nobody answers. They sit down on the steps that lead up to the great door decorated with historical scenes, and share a bunch of September grapes.

He is wearing a green shirt and beneath its gaudy collar the sweater with the running gazelles can be seen. She has on a light-blue raincoat and pink beret that give her the look of a high-school student.

They stand in silence watching the people pass. There's still a lot of poverty around. Many people are wrapped in heavy patched coats, either too long or too short, with sweaters in dark colours so as not to show the dirt. Anyway, who has access to hot water? And soap is too expensive. Tired early-morning faces, resentful from having slept badly and too briefly, and knowing they must now face an exhausting and humiliating day. The young run; they have cheap clothes and second-hand army boots. The old move slowly in long handmade scarves and synthetic cloth caps.

'How can this man and his gazelles make a living just by leading young brides to the altar as if they were his daughters, playing at being their father?' asks Amara, pointing at the herd of gazelles running in orderly procession towards the future.

Hans turns his suntanned face towards her. The light-brown lock of hair slips over his brow. He screws up his ash-grey eyes with the patient gesture of one who must explain the inexplicable.

'The house I live in is my own, my grandfather left it to me. I give music lessons, like my father. To his pupils. I inherited them with the house' – when he smiles he takes on the malicious look of a child embarrassed by having to talk to others and planning to distract their attention with cunning little stratagems – 'with that and the weddings I get by.'

'I'm lucky too. I write for a provincial paper. It doesn't have masses of readers but the few it does have think about what they read. They pay me on the nail. And I can write what I like.'

'Do you keep a diary?'

'No.'

'I do.'

'Will you let me read it one day?'

'Maybe.'

Looking up Amara sees an elderly man advancing on them: he is extremely thin with long legs. His violet-coloured jacket hangs from his shoulders, his black trousers are covered with stains and he has two folders under his arm. He climbs the steps slowly. His trousers are too short. They ride up at each step exposing thin ankles lined with thick blue veins that stand out in relief, his two long broad feet confined in rubber sandals. His fine, modest face is surrounded by white hair, balding yet also thick, that forms a halo round his skeletal head. He is like a tired, perplexed Old Testament prophet laboriously climbing the steps to paradise, but not worried about getting there quickly.

Amara and the man with the gazelles get up and follow him up the steps. Finding his keys, he pushes open the great dark wooden door; they follow him in.

The spacious entrance hall smells of mould.

'Sir and madam would like?'

'Can we visit the library?'

'It opens at ten.'

'It says nine outside.'

'I arrive at ten. The secretary comes when she feels like it. She's supposed to be here at nine but at the moment she's off work.'

'Well, it's nearly ten. Can we come in?'

'Write your names here. Show me your papers. Leave your umbrellas and bags, if you have any.'

The old man sits down exhausted after pushing towards them a large exercise book with scuffed pages.

It's a venerable local library with tall windows, long worm-eaten tables and uniform wooden chairs, though some have broken backs and stuffing coming out of their seats in tufts.

Amara and Hans go to the catalogue. Not much on the concentration camps, as if there could be nothing to say about facts so near in time and so inexplicable. On the other hand, not even the library's readers seem anxious to know more. The books standing upright side by side seem never to have been touched, opened or consulted. They are chilly to the touch and their pages uncut. Undoubtedly there are more documents to be found in the libraries of the camps.

Amara reads their titles, pulls out a volume or two, puts them back in their places. More than anything, they are historical explanations. Few accounts by witnesses. Few novels or stories of the camps.

She sees Hans crouched on the floor, deep in what looks like a new volume.

'What are you reading?'

'Witness accounts of the siege of Stalingrad.'

Amara too crouches down and tries to read by pushing her head over his shoulder. It is clear the book was printed quite recently on wartime paper, coarse and fragile, and it is shabby.

'Dear Magda, Miraculously I'm still alive, I can't think how,' translates Hans aloud into refined and precise Italian. 'All my mates are dead. The Russians surrounded us and began firing from all sides. I lost my shoes, but I took a pair from a soldier who died at my side. Out of the five hundred Hungarians with me, only three are still alive. I never saw such fierce crossfire. I was hit too. I fell and lost consciousness. I thought I was dead but then, with the coming of night and silence, I found I was still alive, still breathing. But I couldn't move. I must be completely shattered, I thought, even if I couldn't feel any pain. Then I realised that though still alive I was crushed under two dead bodies. I didn't even know where my companions had gone. Then I found them by chance, behind a group of Finns and Romanians pulling a cart full of wounded. I don't know if you'll ever get this letter. It'll be best if I bring it to you myself in my pocket if I manage to get home, if we manage to overcome the Russians who are wearing us down. Or it may reach you with my corpse, though that's not likely since no one collects the dead here. There's no time to bury them. The wounded are barely rescued, and even then often die in the field hospitals because there are no more dressings or medicines, or even doctors: they are dead too. Goodbye darling sister, I really hope to see you again not in paradise but in our own lovely Budapest, your brother Oskar Horvath.'

'What was a Hungarian doing with the Germans?'

'It was the famous Operation Barbarossa, haven't you heard of that?'

Amara admits she knows nothing, and asks Hans to tell her about it. She likes it when he reconstructs history for her. It excites her and her eyes light up.

'Operation Barbarossa was invented by Hitler. Having swallowed at a single gulp Poland, Denmark and Norway, not to mention the Netherlands, the whole of Belgium and half of France, and after signing a non-aggression pact with Russia, he decided, scoundrel that he was, to attack his Russian ally without warning so as to disarm him and grab his oil and mineral resources.'

'So the soldier Horvath would have been with Hitler in Russia as an invader even though he didn't want to be?'

'Naturally. Horthy's Hungary had allied itself with Hitler who forced it to join his tripartite alliance with Italy and Japan. The Führer called up the various Horvaths and placed them under the command of his colonels. So they had no alternative but to follow him when he treacherously decided to invade the USSR, forcing his unwilling allies to go with him, as well as the willing ones like Italy, who of course wasn't doing it for nothing, but was looking forward to her own share of the oil. That was the origin of the Italian Army in Russia or ARMIR, which was sent in with the worst possible equipment and arms. Hitler was desperate to get everything done before the winter, which had been so disastrous for other invaders of Russia; remember Napoleon.'

'So the soldier Horvath would have followed the Nazis to Russia and written from there to his sister?'

'On the night of 21 June 1941 Hitler's troops crossed the border into Russia and after only thirteen days had arrived within twenty-two kilometres of Moscow. They besieged Leningrad and took Kiev and Odessa. Out of 128 Soviet divisions they immediately immobilised twenty-eight, treacherously, without so much as a declaration of war. Hitler cared nothing about pacts and didn't believe in subtlety, he was a predator and acted accordingly. Among other things, he ordered his soldiers to ignore the rules of war. Prisoners were to be killed with a bullet to the head, even generals. He didn't give a damn for the Geneva Convention. He just wanted to spread terror and make it clear who was in charge.

The Red Army chiefs who until a few days before had been his allies were all killed, shot without trial. Meanwhile he pushed his remaining divisions towards Stalingrad, the gateway to the Caucasus where the Russian oil was to be found.'

'But the Russians fought back, both in Leningrad and in Stalingrad, I do know that. But how did the Nazis manage to lose when they were so much better prepared and armed, stronger and utterly unscrupulous?'

'The Krauts advanced into Soviet territory with a boldness and presumption that took the wind out of the sails of those facing them. Hitler was used to winning by gambling, tricks and violence; he had the mentality of a bandit and cared nothing for his own soldiers who were dying in thousands, or his generals who were advising him to stop and change tactics; all he understood was murderous fury.'

'So it went badly for him ...'

'It went badly for him, but not immediately. He was able to cause terrible military disasters. He had prepared on the grand scale. Do you know how many men he sent to the Russian front? Three million, I mean three million soldiers, with three thousand tanks and three thousand planes. No small matter.'

'And how many Italians were there in the ARMIR?'

'Nearly sixty thousand, commanded by General Messe. At that time it was still known as the CSIR, or "Italian Expeditionary Corps in Russia". But Messe left because he disagreed with Mussolini's decision to send in six more divisions. And I think he was right. He was replaced by General Italo Gariboldo and the Expeditionary Corps became the ARMIR, or Italian Army in Russia.'

'"They were three hundred, Young and strong, And they are dead,"' quoted Amara.

'Many more than that, sadly. There are also some letters from Italian soldiers in this book. I'll read you one if you like. Very few were saved. Nothing more was ever heard about most of the men, not even whether they lived or died.'

'And then?'

'In the first months Hitler's method of aggression and burned earth, of running ahead of everything and everybody, of hitting hard and using surprise, brought success, as it had elsewhere. His orders were strict: keep captured soldiers alive only so long as they can be used as forced labour, otherwise kill them! Which was against all the rules of war. But Nazi thinking was basic and lethal: the Russian NCOs came from barbarous and inferior races, so they must be instantly eliminated, regardless of whether they fought or surrendered. This was the order. And show no respect for civilians: strip them of everything; feel free to plunder and kill anyone getting in the way, including women, children and the old. That was Hitler's philosophy of war. And it clearly created panic. The population hid and fled; they were terrified. But with Moscow threatened and Leningrad on the point of collapse, something snapped in the Russian people and they decided to resist to the last drop of blood, regardless of the cost. And they were truly extraordinary. We must give them credit for that. If they'd let the Nazis occupy Moscow and destroy Leningrad and Stalingrad, I don't believe you and I would be here talking like this in this peaceful library in Vienna.'

Amara watches him attentively. This man with his passion for history astonishes her. What lies behind his prodigious memory? And how does he manage to remember so many languages and read them as if each was his mother tongue?

Meanwhile the Old Testament prophet has come close and is regarding them with an air of disapproval. Why are they sitting on the floor with an open book in their hands? But he doesn't question them or otherwise disturb them. Perhaps he too has been infected by Hans's passion and Amara's curiosity and eagerness to learn. He watches them and listens with increasing attention.

32

'Well?'

Amara knows more or less how things went, but she loves listening as the excited yet serene voice of Hans explains, remembers and considers, extracting from his extraordinary memory dates, statistics and descriptions.

'From the Russian point of view, by autumn 1941 the war seemed to have been lost. The Baltic states, Belarus, the northern Crimea and a good part of the Ukraine had been occupied by Hitler. One and a half million members of the Red Army ended up as prisoners in Nazi camps, or working in German factories.'

'But what could have changed the fortunes of war? How could Hitler's method of speed and aggression, betrayal and murder, surprise and burned earth, ever fail when it had worked so well till then in Poland and Holland and even in France?'

'There are probably many reasons. In July 1942 the Nazi Sixth Army attacked on the line of the Don, about a hundred kilometres from Stalingrad. The idea was that once the city had fallen, they would have free hands in the south of the Soviet Union, and from there could join up with the Japanese army which had meanwhile occupied Malaya, the Philippines, Singapore and Burma. The tactic was always the same: surprise, brutality, rapid aggression and the systematic assassination of enemies, particulary military ones, and particularly the most senior of them, without hesitation or pity. On the other hand the Red Army had a fine commander in Marshal Zhukov. And Zhukov decided the tactic of defence and waiting was mistaken, rather it was essential to attack and hit hard.'

'But how was Zhukov able to pass from defence to attack, I mean, how was he able to convince Stalin who was controlling everything from above?'

'The first thing was to stop leaving all choices of time and place to the Nazis. Zhukov knew his only chance of winning was to take the initiative himself, and for him to decide times and places and thus be able to work out manoeuvres of encirclement. It seemed impossible but in the end it worked. Meanwhile Hitler, aware that his troops were not advancing as he expected them to, sent in three more divisions: the Seventeenth and Eleventh Infantry, plus the Fourth Panzer Army. Zhukov, faced with such an array of forces, was forced to retreat. But slowly and methodically he continued the encirclement, preventing the Nazis from advancing more than two kilometres a day. In a month they only managed to gain sixty kilometres.'

'But winter was approaching, as the history books tell us about Napoleon. Do you think Hitler was aware of that?'

'He was certainly aware that Russia in autumn would be treacherous. He knew how it had been for Napoleon. So he began to press harder. But he got stuck, unable either to advance or retreat. The people of Stalingrad knew the outcome of the war now depended entirely on them and they fought to the last gasp. Boys, old men, women, everyone, made themselves available to help the soldiers against the Germans, joining the 62nd and 64th armies or helping as porters and postmen. It is said that more than sixty thousand civilians, including men over fifty and boys of thirteen and fourteen years of age, took up arms to defend the city.'

'But meanwhile people were still dying.'

'The Germans died in huge numbers. The situation took them by surprise, they were so used to winning. They lost twenty-four thousand men outside Stalingrad, and five hundred tanks as well.'

'Then finally winter came.'

'It was on 17 November 1942, according to reports, that it began to snow, making things even more difficult for the German armies. Facing them was a city up in arms on all sides. Snipers were firing on them from roofs and windows, while hand grenades were blowing up tanks. The first unit to yield was the Romanian Kletskaya Army, which enabled Zhukov to close the circle and imprison the Germans in a vice. General von Paulus had no idea what to do. He had repeatedly begged Hitler to let him withdraw from the quagmire so as to gain time and reorganise, but the only answer he received was "A German soldier must continue to stand where he has planted his foot."'

'Couldn't he disobey Hitler?'

'Of course. But he was too used to obedience. An honourable man who had given his word. In fact, a whole series of considerations made him powerless in the face of the Red Army which had caught him in a noose, squeezing his shoulders and sides.'

'Was he killed?'

'On 8 January 1943 the Russian command suggested to the Germans, by now surrounded and deprived of supplies, that they should surrender with honour. That meant leaving them in uniform, respecting the code of war and treating those they took prisoner, both officers and men, with consideration. They had two days to decide. Von Paulus communicated the terms to Hitler. Hitler, proud and stupid as always, turned them down, inflicting a terrible price on his forces. According to his twisted logic all that was left to them was to 'conquer or die', when it was already clear that victory was impossible so that he was in effect sending them all to be slaughtered.'

'Did they all die?'

'They were still a powerful force. But on 10 January Soviet artillery and planes began to bombard them incessantly day and night, while Soviet tanks advanced. The surrounded German soldiers, their supplies and munitions cut off and deprived of food and cover, surrendered en masse.'

'If they had agreed to capitulate, would they have had better conditions and fewer losses?'

'Between 27 and 29 January 1943 the Russians captured more than fifteen thousand German and allied soldiers. On 31 January Von Paulus was made a prisoner.'

'Did they kill him?'

'They asked him why he hadn't escaped by air as he could have done and he answered that he had to remain with his men, and this earned him the esteem of the Russians who treated him with a certain respect.'

'A gentleman of the old school.'

'Probably, judging by his aristocratic name. Even so, the Battle of Stalingrad remains one of the biggest and most ferocious battles in human history. The Axis lost a million and a half men, three thousand five hundred tanks, twelve thousand cannon and mortars and three thousand planes. Who knows how the Normandy landings of June 1944 would have gone if the greater part of the German forces had not been encircled in Russia.'

'And the Italian ARMIR?'

'It suffered disastrously from the lunatic ambitions of Hitler and Mussolini. Yet the boys of the ARMIR fought with great courage. For a whole month the Vicenza division managed to make headway against the Russians who were ten times more numerous and hidden in frozen holes in the steppes. And the Julia division held its position north of Stalingrad. Even if on 26 January '43 they were finally defeated and dispersed.'

'You promised to read me an Italian letter.'

'Of course, here's one: "*Dear Amelia. It's thirty degrees below today. Many of our men have frozen feet. I keep mine moving, the way Grandpa taught me. It's a great advantage to have been born and lived in the Friuli Mountains. Grandpa used to say: Never give way to the cold; fight back, jump, shout, leap about, but if you don't keep moving you're fucked. The trouble is our weapons freeze. They jam like a solid block of ice. How can we fire them? Yesterday we fought a battle for a place called Nikolayevka. We fought from twelve to three. I don't know how many died. You couldn't even walk there were so many bodies on the ground. I never stopped moving and this saved me from freezing to death. It was terrible seeing Giovanni crying because he could not walk any more and his tears turning to ice on his face. I hope I'll get home again, love Giacomo ...*"'

'Did Giacomo get home?'

'I don't know. It doesn't say here. But it's been calculated that among the Italians there were twenty-six thousand dead, forty-three thousand wounded and nearly seventy thousand missing.'

'How many did come home?'

'After the war the Soviet Union repatriated ten thousand Italian prisoners of war. Two hundred and twenty-nine thousand had left Italy and what with those repatriated, wounded and frostbitten, twenty-nine thousand six hundred and ninety came back. Wholesale butchery. It has been said the only corps that can regard itself as having been undefeated on Russian soil is the Italian Alpine Army Corps. No one knows who said it. But they were certainly heroic.'

'Which contributed more to the defeat of Hitler, Stalingrad or the Normandy landings?'

'The one couldn't have happened without the other. Remember Hitler had invaded the whole of Europe and had decided beforehand to occupy Britain, as well as Russia of course. Europe was at his feet and this made him ever more sure of himself and increasingly bold and irrational. I don't know if he understood when he lost the Battle of Stalingrad, where he had been crushed as if by a boa constrictor, that he was on his way to total defeat. I've no idea. But he had been totally convinced he could conquer everything and everybody.'

'But these letters from the front; did they reach their destinations? And who read them?'

'Someone collected them to make a memorial volume.'

At that moment the Old Testament prophet, the elderly librarian with enormous feet and a halo of white hair, came up to them smiling.

'I am the soldier called Horvath,' he says in a small voice. He seems moved. 'It was I who collected these letters from fellow soldiers to preserve the memory of the horror.'

The man with the gazelles looks at him with surprise and curiosity.

'Were you actually at Stalingrad? Are you Hungarian?'

'My father was from Pécs and my mother from Klagenfurt. I was born in Budapest.'

'How old were you when you were called up?'

'Forty-five. But by then everyone was involved. In my heart I was against the Hitler regime, but I couldn't admit it. I was sent with many other reservists who like me had served in the First World War, to the Russian front. They needed fresh forces there. In those days I was still tough, not like now when a puff of wind could blow me away. I was young and strong and had a full head of dark hair. My hair went white in '43 after forty-eight consecutive hours in the midst of a monstrous battle with shells whistling from all sides. People died without a cry or a word, our eyes blinded by fog. The sky rained down bombs. It was 28 January. I was oiling my rifle when the storm began; they fired at us from all sides. We no longer had any rearguard and even if we'd wanted to we couldn't have retreated. All we could do was hold up our hands and surrender, hoping our enemies wouldn't kill us. I grabbed a white rag and went up to a Soviet tank. I'd been wounded by a grenade which didn't quite miss me but stripped off my clothes, singeing my hair and neck. A soldier stuck his head out of the tank and roared with laughter. He said something to his friends in a dialect I didn't understand and pointed at me. I couldn't see what was so funny, being almost naked, though I still had my socks round my ankles; I was singed black all over including my head and neck, with my few remaining hairs standing on end. The man must have felt sorry for me because he said 'Get in,' so I did. Among other things I told him I was a Hungarian who had been forced to fight with the Germans. I spoke to him in Russian but he just went on and on laughing. That's how I survived. Then they put me in a camp for Axis prisoners. It wasn't too bad. They gave us clothes and food. Shirts from dead men, but so what, better than nothing. They treated our wounds. And fed us once a day, potatoes boiled in broth. And powdered fish dissolved in the water that made a grey scum, but it was hot and we liked it. Like manna from heaven to us.'

'And when did you get home?'

'Three years later, at the end of the war. My hair had gone completely white and I was full of parasites. I had to delouse myself very thoroughly. But like all the poor I had parasites in my stomach: a bulging belly full of voracious worms that devoured everything I ate. But by now I was less exhausted and skeletal and was even beginning to put on weight. When I got back to my village they said, 'Hi, Horvath, welcome home! We thought you were dead.' And when they saw I was putting on weight they said, 'We can see it's not quite true that you starved at Stalingrad!' No one realised that three years had passed since those horrors. But that didn't matter to me. That was for the others. And that's how I got the idea of collecting letters sent home by soldiers who didn't survive. I went to see people and gathered together a large number of letters. I wrote letters to people myself and went to a lot of trouble. Then the library here helped me to publish the book. I'm glad it interested you. I'll give you a copy. I've got heaps of them. Not many people want them. It seems the voices of the dead are of no interest. I deliberately put it up there in full view in the hope people might look at it. But no one touches it. You're the first to have opened it and read it. For this I'd like to offer you a coffee. Come with me to my den.'

33

Moving with agility on his long thin legs, the elderly Horvath leads them to a little room almost too small to contain three people.

'My kitchen, my living room, my lumber room, my study and my thinking corner. Please make yourselves at home.'

But where? There's only one chair and it's occupied by a pile of books. The table is piled with papers and magazines. But Horvath will not admit defeat; he runs out, opens the head librarian's office and returns with two wooden folding chairs.

'In any case the head librarian never appears. The secretary has just had a baby so it stands to reason she's off work. Busy breast-feeding. But I can't understand how the head librarian ever got his job. Anyway, he's only interested in politicking. Hardly anyone ever comes to the library and I look after everything.'

As he speaks, he pulls down from a shelf three ceramic mugs with hook-shaped handles. Lighting a gas ring, he puts on a small pan filled with water from the tap. He opens an American army tin of soluble coffee, puts a spoonful in each mug and when the water boils he pours it into the cups. The coffee foams and spatters.

'A little milk too?'

Amara and Hans say no. But he still extracts a tube of con-densed milk from a shelf full of books and squirts it like tooth-paste into the boiling coffee.

'All done. Unfortunately there's no sugar. But the milk is sweet. It's the only way I have of sweetening coffee.' He laughs. His teeth are broken and stained.

'But what are you two doing here, what are your names?'

Amara and Hans tell him. And as they sip the bitterish coffee flavoured by the ancient pan that has boiled everything from onions to cabbage, potatoes and the occasional pork chop, they tell him their experiences. Horvath, who seemed so annoyed to have had to open the door to them that morning, is now cheerful and sociable. He presses them to have more coffee and tells his own story, without excessive modesty.

'I toured half Europe collecting these Stalingrad letters. You will say: how can you have toured Europe when you haven't a penny to your name? But I'm good at chatting to people, I get them involved and they invite me to lunch or dinner, they ask me to spend the night at their homes. Even a railwayman became so passionately interested in the idea of the book that he let me travel free in his cab, pretending I was a railwayman too.'

'How many had you collected by the time you finished?'

'A hundred or so, I think, I've never counted them. Every now and then another reaches me, even now. The word has got around. Someone may remember the bombardment of 10 January. Someone else that of 31 January when the Russians captured more than fifteen thousand Germans. Then somebody might want to describe in detail how he managed to get home and how it took him a year, perhaps, wandering about, stopping to work for this person or that, taking cows to pasture to earn a pittance and then continuing his travels, always on foot, with the aim of reaching his own village.'

'So you never went back to Hungary?'

'I did go back. But the house had fallen down and my people were all dead. There was no place for me. I decided to come here to Austria, and worked for five months on a farm near the border. But they wouldn't let me across the frontier without a permit and I had no papers; I'd lost everything when I was wounded. All those hours under two dead bodies. I always remember them with gratitude; they saved my life. One night I had to go out because a cow was in labour and I couldn't find the vet. She mooed and mooed and couldn't get the calf out. So I started pulling its legs and while I pulled I talked gently to the cow who was nervous, until she quietened down and I finally got her offspring out. I was covered in blood but the calf was born and the mother was safe and sound. Look, you should have been an obstetrician, I said to myself, you have the right hands for it. My boss was so pleased he gave me some money, enough for me to be able to buy myself a passage across the border. I was quickly taken past the barbed wire at night and into the snow-covered mountain forest. Which way should I go? I asked my guide, but he held out his hand: first you pay. I paid him. And he immediately turned his back on me without even saying goodbye. Which way? I asked in desperation and he said, Go down to the valley. And so I did but after the first valley there was another then yet another. And I didn't know whether I was going straight or crooked or where I was. I walked for a night and a day through a snowstorm with nothing to eat or drink. Then I saw a cave and slipped inside and found some wolves who looked at me as though I was a creature from another planet. I must have looked strange with my torn and dirty trousers, two blankets round my shoulders, enormous sandals made from a couple of American tyres, and white hair standing on end. The wolves gave me a wide berth and let me sleep; I couldn't go any further. Next day I started walking again. There was no visible horizon; it was snowing continuously with a blizzard blowing. I had no idea where I was or where I was heading. Finally I came on a hovel and knocked, terrified that I'd find a forest ranger or police officer who would want to send me back to Hungary. Instead I found a countrywoman who was helping a she-goat to give birth. She made room for me at her side. Strange, don't you think? From a calf to a kid. My life was hanging on a thread of maternity. Two corpses had saved me from being killed and two newborn animals saved me from freezing to death. The kindly countrywoman gave me a little milk from the she-goat and I was so unbelievably happy that I fell asleep there beside her. I stayed for three days and nights in that hut with no idea where I was, delirious with a high fever. The peasant woman, whose name was Herta, visited me and brought me milk. I was exhausted and my fever got worse but I was not about to die, I did know that. On the fifth day I felt better. This time when Herta brought me milk she kissed me and unbuttoned my flies and said, Look how well you are, you're ready for love. So that's what we did, there among the little goats. Herta seemed happy and so was I. I asked her rather carefully where we were. She spoke a strange dialect I could barely understand, but she explained, with the help of marks on the ground, that we were in Hungary, in the woods near Répcelak. I believed her; I had no reason not to. But it wasn't true. The fact was that all the local men were dead and my Herta thought herself a queen because she had found a man for herself. She wanted to keep me. That was why she lied. In fact I was already in Austria, in the mountains round Sopron, near the Neusiedler See and the Hungarian border. She knew I wanted to get to Austria, so kept me isolated, promising that as soon as I was strong enough she would help me across the border herself. So I stayed in that freezing hovel, kept warm by the goats, for more than three months. I knew I depended on her. I didn't know the area which was all forest and on my own I would have been lost. I was afraid they'd stop me at the frontier and I believed the Hungarian guide had tricked me. Instead it was the woman who was fooling me. But she was sweet, my Herta. Methodical and reliable. She would bring me food: bread, an egg, a piece of fresh cheese. We would kiss till our lips were sore. We would make love, then she would leave again. Have you got a husband? I asked her once. She shook her head. If she'd had one he was dead. Any children? She gave an inscrutable smile. I would have liked to go to her home and meet her family, but she didn't want that. She wanted me entirely for herself, hidden in that hovel in the woods with the goats. But after three months I was bored and felt trapped, and told her with some force I was not prepared to go on living like a mouse. She nodded very seriously. That evening she brought me a knapsack with fresh bread, dried meat, a piece of cheese and a small bottle of brandy. We kissed as we always did and made love more passionately than ever. Then she left and I never saw her again. I had no idea which way to go. But I could see a village in the distance in the forest, clinging to a steep hillside. I headed for it assuming it must be a Hungarian village. I was afraid and walked slowly, thinking things over in my mind. On the road I met a peasant and when I spoke to him I understood at once that my Herta had deceived me. We were in Austria, no doubt about it. I burst out laughing; the peasant didn't understand. I laughed and laughed and he looked at me strangely. I asked him whether he had any work for me. I told him I was a vet, that I was good at helping cows to give birth. He took me with him and gave me fresh clothes and something to eat. He understood I was someone who had escaped but that didn't matter to him. A free vet was more interesting. So I used the tiny library in the village and started studying books on medicine. And eventually I made it. I've learned so much from books. For that I love them and will always love them.'

'But how did you come to be a librarian?'

'I spent so much time in the village library that I became everybody's friend and when the old librarian died I asked if I could take his place. I was satisfied with very little and was good with the archives. They accepted me. They could see I was a serious worker and after a few years I was transferred to Vienna to restore this old library which had been bombed.'

'I'd like a copy of your book,' says Hans who has brought the book with him and is turning it in his hands.

'I'll make you a present of it. I'm sorry I can't offer you an armchair so you can read more comfortably. The city has been almost entirely rebuilt but libraries are last on the list; what does it matter if part of the building is in a state of collapse, if there is no room for any more books or if there is no heating? Not many people want to read when they have to spend their days trying to find a little coal, or something to put into their mouths. And the few who do come in never stay precisely because it is so cold and we are short of chairs.'

Finally, half-closing his eyes, he asks them in a humble voice as if afraid of being indiscreet, what they are looking for in Vienna.

Hans explains. Horvath looks at them in wonder.

'It's extraordinary, this fidelity to memory,' he says with a mixture of admiration and disquiet. 'I realise it's difficult ... even if the Nazis did keep registers, in the end they destroyed them all. Or nearly all of them. You say some new ones have been found?'

'It seems so.'

'Then why have the allies not appropriated them?'

'That's just what we want to find out. We're waiting for our visas.'

'You'll have to wait a long time. Unless I come with you. I need to look for some books in Kraków. It's easier for a librarian to get a visa for a short trip to look for books. You can come with me.'

Amara looks at him apprehensively. How to curb his enthusiasm? And how can such a journey by a Hungarian, an Austrian and an Italian to the kingdom of the dead be organised?

'You'll see, I can be useful to you,' he says, with a smile on his lips that suddenly makes him young and beautiful.

'But ... and the library? Who will look after it while you're away?'

'It's time the secretary came back to work. She's already been off for months on maternity leave. I'll put everything in her hands and take a few days off. I haven't had a holiday for years.'

34

Such a strange trio. Horvath, Hans and Amara, on the train to Kraków. But at the last moment they decide to go via Hungary. Hans has written to tell his father he would like to pay him a visit. And his father has answered happily that he's looking forward to it. And Horvath would like to put a flower on his sister's grave and see if anything is left of the house where he lived as a child.

At Hegyeshalom, at the border, the engine shuts down completely. It will be a long wait, which was predictable. Many get out to look for a coffee at the bar which has already been stripped bare by the previous train; it has nothing left to offer except little bags of camomile from the Ukraine, loose powdered sweets that look as if they have been sitting in their glass jar since before the war, and Russian cigarettes, the 'papiroskas' the soldiers despise partly because they are Russian but also because they consist almost entirely of paper, and what little tobacco there is in them stinks of sawdust.

The frontier guards search the carriages. They stop suspiciously in front of the foreigners. Hans particularly alarms them: his origins are too heterogeneous, his journeys up and down Eastern Europe excite mistrust. Amara's papers are in order but what is an Italian woman doing on a ramshackle train from Vienna to Kraków via Budapest? Luckily Horvath is there, with his ascetic air and ability to speak both excellent Hungarian and German. He is even able to speak polished Russian to the Soviet supervisors who are always present at the frontiers. With Olympian calm and a permanent smile, Horvath explains slowly and simply who they are and where they are going. To look for books for a new library in Vienna. Hungarian books for Hungarian readers living in Austria. The guards are dumbfounded. Who is this old man with such an authoritative air who travels for days to go and look for books? There's certainly something about him to instil respect. And they withdraw without comment.

The three are taken to the station offices and searched by the gloved hands of inscrutable guards. Their passports are taken away. Their bags are opened, rummaged in and examined with comic pedantry. A small bottle of water scented with Parma violets that Amara has in her bag is uncorked and sniffed by first one soldier then another, then by yet a third. The little bottle is passed from hand to hand almost as if it might contain liquid explosive. But in the end Amara realises that these young guards, two of whom are women, are motivated less by suspicion than by a morbid curiosity about the products of the West; they finger the underclothes and open the blouses and shake out the skirts as if to say: just look at the bourgeois pretensions of the West. But when all's said and done, what's it all about? Nothing to speak of.

The three friends are hungry. But there is nothing to eat. They have spent a whole day in the train, and consumed the provisions they prudently brought with them. They never imagined there would be so many stops, so much waiting, and so many obstacles before they reached Budapest.

In the evening the train starts again. A fragment of moon is hanging like an icicle over a potato-shaped mountain. Dogs are barking far away. Horvath is cold. He pulls a chequered blanket from his cardboard suitcase and drapes it round his shoulders.

'Aren't you hungry?'

'Cold.'

'I'm hungry.'

'Me too.'

'Shall I see if I can find something?'

'You won't find anything. The train's full of starving people.'

At Győr the carriages fill with Hungarian soldiers from Czechoslovakia who laugh, eat and fool around. Apart from one who is weeping in a corner because he has lost his best friend. But not in war, as Horvath will report later with his mania for getting into conversation with everybody. A soldier called Bilo has died of typhus after drinking contaminated water. The happy brigade is on its way from East Germany to Szeged. They have been at work on frontier defences. 'War? Rubbish,' says one boy, stuffing an enormous omelette roll into his mouth. 'There are no more wars in the world, and there never will be any more. All wars are over. And that's a fact.' The youngsters cheer. One pulls from his knapsack a flat bottle in a lovingly crafted red wool cover and lifts it to his mouth. Someone shouts and reaches out a hand. The boy passes the bottle. Pálinka, the commonest form of plum brandy. Others open their own knapsacks and take out bottles of every shape. All neatly covered in coloured covers crocheted by solicitous mothers and wives. 'To warm you when you feel cold,' they will have said as they dressed the little glass bottle or aluminium or pewter flask.

But in no time at all the carriage is an encampment of shouting and singing drunks. One vomits out of the window. Another gets a friend to start delousing him.

'Couldn't we move to another carriage?' suggests Amara tentatively.

'But where? Can't you see the whole train's full? There are people stretched out in the corridors.'

The train stops several times in open countryside. Peasant women in flowered cotton headscarves approach the carriages, at first shyly then more and more shamelessly, to sell hard-boiled eggs, dried figs and little wild apples. And the young soldiers stretch out their arms to bargain and shout, finally buying an egg for eight or a basket of plums for twenty. The women haggle too from below, but more softly. They are afraid of rebukes or fines from the railway police.

Now the soldiers doze, lulled by the slow regular rhythm of the wheels. One snores with his head propped on a companion's shoulder. They have thrown their rifles onto the netting racks that hang above their wooden benches. It isn't easy to sleep. The seats are hard and hunger is gnawing at them. Amara watches the countryside fill with shadows beyond the dirty window. A delicate bluish mist descends on the landscape, hiding trees and fields and even a little river running beside the track punctuated by black and white stones. The moon is closer now and has become more human, hinting at an unfocused smile. Through the dirty window Amara can make out the small figure of woman walking fast. Strange: either the train has slowed down, or the woman is running or rather flying. She tries to see the woman's face but it is hidden by a cascade of nut-brown hair leaping and dancing in time with her steps. There is something familiar about the woman. Her strong, rapid step, her rebellious head, her long muscular arms are those of ... there can be no doubt about it, her mother Stefania! How can it have taken Amara so long to realise it? The beautiful young Stefania, long dead but now more alive and active than ever. Where are you going? asks Amara with her mouth closed. Stefania doesn't turn to look at her but seems delighted simply to be running beside the train. She is completely engrossed in her flight as if in some childhood contest. Amara timidly reaches out a hand to knock on the glass window with her knuckles. Finally Stefania lifts her head. She has the most beautiful big eyes but they do not see Amara. She can't recognise me because the glass is so dirty, Amara tells herself. She goes on knocking discreetly on the window. Stefania smiles, but more to herself than to Amara. Where are you going, Mamma? Stop a moment, sit down with me. But in that instant her mother vanishes, leaving only her smile. The smile of the moon hanging there in the dark. You always cheat me, Mamma, you always have cheated me, like the Cheshire Cat in *Alice in Wonderland*. You slip off without speaking to me, not a single word, stop, say something to me! She tries to remember how it was when her mother bent over her when she was a child and hummed the tune of the wordless chorus from *Madam Butterfly*. Her mother was so beautiful that it hurt Amara's eyes to look at her. And her voice rose from her throat like a tender breath of air. Why did you go away so soon? Then she sees her, covered with soil and blood, being raped by that friend of the lover who wanted to punish her. Papà has told me about it but don't be ashamed, it wasn't your fault. She sees Stefania move her hand to her bleeding legs and spit with rage. She sees her run towards a stream and crouch to wash the blood off her thighs. This is not what I wanted, says a well-dressed young man watching from behind a tree. I didn't want it to end like this. I only wanted a light punishment, not a massacre. But Stefania turns her back and walks off, determined never to see him again. Will you go and report him? Do that, Mamma Stefania, please do that! But at that moment a whistle pierces her ear and she feels a hand on her shoulder.

'Budapest, Amara, wake up!'

Outside, the intermittent light of yellow street lamps and a voice booming from a loudspeaker. The engine snorts, ready to start again. Horvath is lifting her luggage down from the rack.

'Thanks.'

Hans pulls on the sweater with the running gazelles. His fingers rake the hair back from his brow. More than ever he looks like a child grown old before his time, with grey stubble on his cheeks, and a mouth pouting with sleep and hunger.

'Where are all the soldiers?'

'Got off before us.'

'Did you pick up the book that slipped down on the seat beside me?'

'I've got everything. Let's go.'

In her state halfway between sleep and waking everything seems new and astonishing: why are those girls in white shirts with badges on their hats standing to attention before the train? Singing in melancholy voices to welcome some bigwig. And whose are those suitcases that shine like gold in the early morning sun, piled up in the station entrance hall? And where is that exquisite smell of freshly made coffee coming from, and that mixed smell of apple tart and dirty latrines?

'I'd like some coffee'

'Me too.'

'The shutters are still down on the bars. D'you know what time it is?'

'Seven?'

'No, five.'

'Then where can that smell of coffee be coming from?'

'Some private house.'

The three set off, gloomily stretching themselves, lugging their large and small bags along the platform among the cigarette ends.

'Look, the river!'

A great dark serpent that unwinds slow and powerful before them. It has a majestic air. Above them stands Vajdahunyad Castle, grey stone glowing in the early sun, beautiful and proud.

'Your father isn't meeting us?'

'I told him not to. We'll take a taxi. But first let's find some coffee.'

The first place they find open is a milk shop. A tall sturdy woman is rolling up the blind. She switches on the light and watches them come in weighed down by their luggage, faces contorted. She smiles with amusement, and moves quickly behind the counter to put some milk on to heat.

35

Hans's father has generously decided to put all three of them up. The man with the gazelles and Horvath are to sleep in the living room and Amara in the kitchen; while Hans's father Tadeusz and Ferenc Bruman share the main bedroom.

Tadeusz Wilkowsky has a talent for making cakes. He has set aside some hard bread and combined with pieces of apple and raisins and lard bought in the Sunday market, he has concocted an excellent strudel which crumbles the moment you touch it, though not the smallest bit is wasted. His friend Ferenc, after the dessert and a small glass of homemade apple brandy, delights them on this first evening, when he takes up his violin to play Bach's *Chaconne*, as though filling the house with an austere song of welcome.

Everyone has his or her own story to tell. Horvath talks about his experience at Stalingrad and his work as a librarian in Vienna, Hans describes his curious activities as a surrogate father for brides, and Amara remembers little Emanuele who she is sure is still alive and whom she will sooner or later find. She is unable to stop herself reading one of the boy's letters aloud. The men smoke in silence thinking of who knows what. They would like to help her, they say. But how? Each proposes a different plan: go back to Auschwitz and check the new lists. Or make a thorough search of his home in the Łódź ghetto even if there can't possibly be anything left of it after the long allied bombardment. Why not study the newspapers of the time? Or ask special permission to rummage in the SS archives. And what about that Peter Orenstein who claims to be the Emanuele they are looking for?

'In my opinion he's a swindler.'

'I think so too.'

No one has any confidence in the self-proclaimed Emanuele Orenstein. Particularly Amara whose senses refuse in the most categorical manner possible to recognise him. It isn't him, she says firmly, it absolutely can't be him. A person may change, but only up to a certain point. Something must always remain of what he was before, even if he was a child then and is now a man.

Yet she still harbours a doubt and every now and then wakes in the night with her heart in her mouth, thinking she has got it all wrong. What if it really is Emanuele? And if he is hiding simply because he is afraid he will not be accepted? Can affection depend so much on appearances? What if someone can be so completely transformed by painful experiences that they even destroy the memory of the person they once were? Is it a particular body one loves, or a being undergoing transformation?

They argue it out, four men and one woman, in that tiny apartment in Budapest, unaware of the deadly wave about to burst on their heads. The city sleeps and wakes again with steady, laborious rhythms. Everything seems calm. Their home on Magdolna utca is certainly a mess but friendly and peaceful; it only becomes noisy when all five sit round the table to eat a dish concocted by Tadeusz. They see themselves as part of an unchanging story, in the mysterious epoch that has followed an atrocious war, struggling with the same shortages as all the other inhabitants of this sad and subdued city.

Instead, without suspecting it in the least, they are on the lid of a boiling saucepan. A pan about to explode as day by day they wait for visas for Poland, write articles on the tedium and restrictions of communism, cook pork and potato pies, down tankards of Soproni beer and chatter about this and that, while they think up unrealistic schemes for discovering a child swallowed up by history.

'There's an electric atmosphere in the city,' repeats old Tadeusz. But no one is listening.

'What did you find at the market today,' Horvath asks him.

'Some nuts. Some rice. A hectogram of butter for eighty-three forints. I even found a piece of soap and that's a miracle because for months there's been no soap anywhere in Budapest.'

'Bread?'

'No bread. Hard-tack biscuits.'

'What, like yesterday? They're disgusting.'

'That's all there is.'

'You should have got to the market earlier.'

'Then why don't you go? It's always me that has to do the searching.'

'I can't, you know that.'

'Because you're asleep, that's why.'

'Stop squabbling, Father. Did you buy a paper?'

'No one buys newspapers here. Just to read the voice of the Party always saying the same things? It's not worth a penny.'

'There must be something about the Twentieth Congress of the Communist Party of the Soviet Union.'

'Not a thing. All secret.'

'But it was on the radio: the secret text of Khruschev's speech has even been published in the *New York Times*.'

'Nonsense. When the Russians say secret, they mean secret. They have a sort of diabolical, maniacal, obsessive passion for secrets. So many secrets they don't even know what they think themselves because they've lost the key to their own thoughts.'

'A secret mother who gives birth to a secret son who in his turn marries a very secret bride, who after nine months gives birth to a top secret son, and so on.'

'But this time something has leaked out. The secret has gone into circulation and flown all the way to New York. Isn't that extraordinary?'

'If true, it would be the beginning of the end for communism. You can't have communism without secrets.'

'Enough secrets to make a tomb.'

'Enough tombs to make a cemetery.'

The men laugh. Amara watches them tenderly. She asks herself how she can have ended up in this strange city, in the sole company of men, in a foreign country, in such a tiny home that they constantly stumble over one another. Yet they get on well, despite the scarce food cooked in the most extraordinary ways because of the lack of butter and oil, listening to the radio in a language of which she is only now beginning to understand an occasional word.

'We must get hold of a copy of the American paper.'

'It's the only thing they were talking about yesterday at the Petőfi Circle.'

'You went to the Petőfi Circle without telling me.'

'Just happened to be passing by.'

'What were they saying?'

'The place was packed as tight as an egg. You couldn't even stand against the walls.'

'Were they discussing the Khrushchev report?'

'The Khrushchev report, just that. Which according to the Party should have remained secret. And instead, there it was all over the biggest of the capitalist newspapers, completely mad!'

'But what does this report say? Anything we don't already know?'

'Perhaps we did know, but when one of them says it, it all adds up.'

'Meaning?'

'Meaning that Stalin falsified the trials, that he forced his enemies to make confessions under torture, that he had them shot for no reason. First his opponents, then his friends and collaborators, and on and on, the friends of his friends and those who collaborated with his collaborators.'

'But they can't say such things about our great and valiant father Stalin,' says Tadeusz, pretending to wipe away tears. A pantomime. The others laugh.

'And what are they saying about Hungary?'

'That the country's dead.'

'The Petőfi Circle doesn't seem in the least bit dead. You should have heard them!'

'Were they shouting?'

'No, not in the least. But you could have cut the atmosphere with a knife. And some were saying straight out it's time we declared our independence.'

'Well, today there's to be a demonstration at the university. Let's go there.'

'To look for trouble?'

'I'm going.'

'Me too.'

'And me.'

'And me.'

36

A hall with long windows at the university. The doors have been thrown open, but it is impossible to get in or out because so many people are crowded together there. Even on the stone balustrades there are youngsters crouching to listen with their heads thrust through the iron grilles. But it is difficult to hear much. There are no microphones, and even though the speakers are shouting, their voices are easily lost in the mass of bodies. Yet poorly dressed girls and boys, wearing high boots for protection from the universal mud on this day of autumnal rain, are listening with great seriousness to whoever gets up to speak on the platform. Some voices penetrate the hum of the crowd, others don't. Confusion. Meanwhile more people crowd in from the surrounding streets, from Baross, from József körút, from Üllői.

At last a megaphone is passed from hand to hand over the heads of the assembled students and citizens to reach the platform. Now, amplified by the megaphone, the clear and resonant voice of a young man manages to reach even beyond the large crowded hall.

'Soviets out of Hungary!' he yells to universal applause. Some whistle, but happily. Some stamp their feet and raise both arms in a gesture of defiance. 'Soviets out of Hungary!' The shout spreads round the hall. Meanwhile there is movement near the door. The crowd squeezes up silently to make room for a boy to move forward dragging his feet in shoes that are too big for him. He holds a flag on a heavy pole resting on his narrow shoulder. Everyone turns towards the flag; there is something new and amazing about it. In place of the red star and hammer and sickle it has a hole in it through which the frescoed ceiling of the hall can be seen. Never before has the Hungarian flag been stripped of a symbol so cumbersome yet at the same time in everyone's view so lethal.

The effect of this mutilated symbol is extraordinary. Some

cheer. Some shout and raise their hands towards the flag. Others weep openly, without shame.

'But aren't those two policemen?' asks Tadeusz, turning to his son's friends. Hans sees two police officers standing quietly smiling as they watch the crowd yelling against the Soviets. Something unthinkable before. What has happened to the Brother Party and the Father Country and all their pretensions and crude suggestions?

Now the man with the gazelles translates the speaker's words for Amara: 'One: Autonomy for Our Country. Two: Free Elections. Three: Restoration of political parties. Four: Formation of a new government under Comrade Imre Nagy. Five: Exit from the Warsaw Pact. Six: Revision of the economic and political relations between Hungary and the Soviet Union. Seven: Freedom for all political prisoners. Eight: Abolition of the ÁVH secret police. Nine: Restoration of free trade. Ten: All criminal officials of the Stalin and Rákosi eras to face a tribunal. Eleven: An end to compulsory kolkhozisation …'

The voice ends in a shout. Someone else snatches the megaphone and yells something incomprehensible. Many people whistle. Some raise their hands and shout 'Go, go.' Others form a chorus that chants: 'One, Autonomy. Two, Free Elections. Three, Free Franchise. Four, Nagy and New Government. Five, Out of Warsaw Pact. Six, Public Trial for ÁVH officials …'

'What's the ÁVH?' asks Amara.

'Rákosi's secret police. Terrible. Ferocious. Spying on people every moment of their lives. Anyone could be denounced at any moment, thrown into jail for nothing. Tortured, executed by shooting. Dissidents sent to concentration camps to die of privation. Rákosi worked through them too. He introduced Stalin's pronouncements in the schools. Even saying the word liberty became treason.'

A rapid movement in the crush of bodies forces them back dangerously towards the wall. A group of students is trying to leave the hall, pushing back all those standing in the doorway, forming a wave that hurls the latest arrivals down the stairs, among them Amara and Hans. Where's Horvath? asks Hans. He's vanished; goodness knows where he is. But Tadeusz and the violinist have disappeared too, thrust aside by the overflowing crowd.

Hans takes Amara's hand to pull her away from the mob. The streets have become crowded. A spontaneous demonstration is spreading from Múzeum körút, led by women in coats with head-scarves tied under their chins. Followed by men in hats and rain-coats with threadbare elbows. An air of dignified poverty and a powerful will to protest. All are holding up their with two fingers extended and the others folded down. V for victory? Amara moves close to Hans. The crowd frightens her a little. She is afraid of being squashed at any moment. But the bodies have a miraculous capacity to move very close, as if glued together, without getting hurt. They carry the smell of their homes wherever they go. A smell of pickled cabbage and of cheap meat boiled many times to make it tender and extract a broth to last a week, of onions cooked in ashes, of lye, of cheap cigarettes, of unwashed hair because there is no shampoo or soap, of rotten teeth, garlic and paprika. 'The smell of freedom,' says Hans, sniffing the air, 'I have not smelled it for such a long time.'

Hans and Amara let the crowd, noisy and compact, carry them on. Who could have imagined this the morning they first arrived in the muffled and stifling silence of a city that seemed asleep! Who could have known that these people were just waiting for a sign to come into the streets! At Kálvin Square where the crowd divides before joining together again in Üllői utca. A bustling group of young men are carrying hammers, saws, chisels and picks. Some ten of them have a long ladder which they lean up against a wall. Then, very quickly, a child in a red hat runs up it with a hammer and defaces the Soviet emblem, a plaster hammer and sickle over the main entrance to a building. People collect the pieces of plaster that fly off and throw them happily into the air as if playing a game. Further on some men in ties and long coats are smashing the window of a shop that sells Soviet records and books. A young man with fine gipsy features squeezes into the shop through the broken glass and brings out armfuls of records and books. He throws them to his friends outside who pile them on the ground where someone has already started a bonfire. The young man goes in and out of the hole in the window and throws out records with the official symbol on their sleeves and books whose covers pro-claim in gold letters Stalin, Stalin, Lenin, Stalin, and so on. More people swell the crowd. Two boys head for a grocer's shop only to be immediately warned: 'No looting! No stealing! There'll be trouble if you take anything!'

'Let's go,' murmurs Amara, afraid of the mob. Still holding her wrist, Hans pulls her towards Jòzsef körút. But wherever they go they still find snaking crowds of seemingly aimless people on the move; pushing, shouting, raising their hands and waving flags. By now nearly all the flags have a hole in the middle. Hungarian flags minus the red star.

Now the crowd pushes them towards Erzsébet körút and from there along Andrássy ut as far as György dózsa, towards Felvonulasi Square. Exhausted, they arrive with the great snake right under the flight of steps leading to the gigantic statue of Stalin. But by the time they reach the square the statue has already been torn down. All that remains to cast defiance at the sky are its two empty dark bronze boots. Into one of them someone has thrust the pole of a Hungarian flag with a hole in it.

'The dictator's gone. But he's left his boots behind. A bad sign. It shows he means to come back.'

'Where have they taken the statue?'

'To the centre, to Blaha Lujza Square,' answers a voice from the crowd.

'Shall we go there?' says a woman with a child in her arms.

'I don't give a damn about Stalin. He's dead and buried,' says a man with a cigarette glued to his lips, as he sucks in smoke and blows it out again without using his fingers.

'Where then?'

'Why not Party headquarters? I'd like to see what they're up to there!'

37

'But where are they running?'

'No idea.'

Some people are moving rapidly in one direction, while others are hurrying in the opposite direction. Here and there a crowd forms. A bonfire has been lit in front of Communist Party headquarters, where the door has been broken down and burned. On the fire have been thrown cardboard portraits of the hated 'comrade' Rákosi. In Köztársaság Square a young man with a worried expression leans out from a first-floor balcony to throw into the street some rolled-up red flags. Two girls with short hair collect them and throw them with theatrical gestures onto a pyre that has just been lit. The red flags burn quickly. A lad with trousers held up by a string round his waist and no coat tries to keep the fire burning by stirring up the dying flames with a long pole of uncertain origin. A man in a blue hat, legs wide apart, is taking a stream of photographs with a large camera. Two soldiers in ankle-length greatcoats and high belts pose for their picture. A child is crying desperately. To comfort him his mother hoists him up on her bicycle which she is holding by the handlebars. The child, no longer obstructed by long coats, looks around in astonishment. His mother strokes his head with a smoke-stained hand.

Suddenly shots are heard. Amara starts. Hans pulls her towards the wall. The shots continue but luckily move further off. People are running. 'What's happening?' shouts a woman hurrying behind a group of youngsters. No one answers. But two girls appear, pushing through the crowd in the opposite direction, their faces distraught and one of them weeping desperately. 'The ÁVH are firing at unarmed people.' 'Where?' 'At the occupied radio station.' 'Shooting at demonstrators in the street.' 'My brother,' cries the weeping girl, 'they've hit my brother.' Her friend pulls her in the direction of the nearby hospital. The crowd seems less eager to head for the radio. Some stop in small groups to argue vigorously. Others decide despite everything to press on. A man advances down the middle of the road brandishing a pole with a card nailed at the top. Hans translates: 'Nagy will address the Hungarian people, nine p.m., in front of parliament.'

'But it's half-past nine already,' says Amara looking at her watch. Is it possible they've already been so long on the move!

'Let's run. Maybe he's still speaking.'

Others, like them, hurry after the man with the placard in the direction of Kossuth tér. It's difficult to understand what's happening in the city. A turmoil of actions succeeding one another in rapid improvisation from Buda to Pest. Someone reports furious shooting from the area of the Kilian barracks. Someone else says Russian tanks have been called in, and someone else that Mikoyan and Suslov have passed in a diplomatic car with darkened windows, while yet another person swears that Khrushchev himself has been seen peeping out of an enormous silver limousine. But no one believes this. There is laughter. Even so, things are getting serious.

'Let's hurry. I can hear the loudspeaker! He's definitely still there.'

But when they come within sight of parliament, Nagy has gone. Thousands of people are slowly dispersing down the side streets.

'Well then?'

'Shall we go home?'

Amara is getting very hungry. But where to find anything to eat? The bars are closed. The shops bolted shut. Every Hungarian is out in the street this day of 23 October 1956. Ignoring the cold, the fierce wind that fans the fires and the continual threat of rain. Flags with a hole cut in the middle are everywhere, like the one at the university.

Suddenly Amara flinches with shock. A few metres in front of her is a man in dark clothes, boots and a black jacket, tied by the waist to a lamp post with his head hanging down.

'An ÁVH man,' whispers Hans in her ear. Amara looks with disgust at the purplish blood leaking from the corpse's nostrils. The light of the street lamps flickering in the wind makes shadows dance on his face so that he seems to be moving and breathing.

'He's still alive. We must untie him!'

'Dead as a doornail. Anyway, someone he'd tortured must have recognised him and killed him. They spied for the Russians and were brutally cruel to poor innocent people. He's not worth your pity.'

'But it does upset me,' insists Amara, unable to tear her eyes away from the white face of the young man with his smart moustache, and highly polished boots, the showy watch on his wrist and the dark blood draining from his dead nostrils. She wishes she could staunch his wounds. But Hans takes her elbow and pulls her far away from Party headquarters, along Luther Street.

Now the crowd opens and divides. Before them, in the greyness of a square strewn with papers and stones and dimly lit by weak street lamps, a Soviet tank appears. Hans guides Amara by the arm towards a side street. But astonishingly the tank has lost its usual air of menace, and about thirty young men are standing on it, prancing about and shouting and holding up a Hungarian flag.

'Look, they've hijacked the tank! They've hijacked it. How can it go forward with all those people on top of it.' Hans laughs happily. Even he is surprised. A Soviet tank reduced to a people-carrier for partygoers celebrating a rather easily achieved freedom.

'Don't you think it's time to go home?'

'Why?'

'We don't know anything about the others. What if Horvath got hurt?'

'He'll be as happy as a sandboy. This is a great day, Amara. We must make the most of it. After years of submission, of obedience, fear, terror and repressed hatred, here we are living a day when people are saying no, breaking their silence, joyfully being themselves without pretence, loving their own country and at last feeling independent without being spied on, controlled and obstructed ... A great day, Amara, and I'm so happy I've been able to live it on the streets together with the Hungarian people.'

'Who's that?'

Hans turns and sees a man standing near them. Not tall but majestic in manner. A loaded bandolier over one shoulder, hat pulled down low on his forehead and a loaded rifle in his hand. But the most surprising thing is that under his trousers, instead of an ankle one leg is a piece of wood that ends on the stone pavement like a broken branch.

'János Mesz, the man with the wooden leg. Everyone knows him. Famous for his courage.'

But the man, who looks as if he has been posing for a photograph in the ardour of his courage, now limps off quickly towards Corvin Lane.

'Let's go and see what's happening,' says Hans, still gripping Amara's wrist.

Round the corner are the hospital gardens. They see Tadeusz approaching with the violinist, and behind them Horvath too. Tadeusz has an ancient rifle on his shoulder. Ferenc is busily munching a perec or pretzel, a twisted ring-shaped roll encrusted with salt. Horvath follows, paler than ever. He has lost his beret and seems tired, but is smiling happily.

'We meet again at last. Where have you come from?'

'The Corvin cinema. That's where the hardliners are. They've formed a group. And captured two armoured cars. They're saying the Russians are coming. That seems unlikely to me. But we're arming ourselves for all eventualities.'

'Did they give you that rifle?'

'Can we go on letting ourselves be shot at like unprotected pigeons? The ÁVH have been firing into the crowd, hundreds are dead.'

'And we've forced open the doors of the arms depots.'

'Who's "we"?'

'Us, them, the citizens.'

'And now they're handing everyone rifles.'

'Even to those who don't know how to fire them?'

'Even to them.'

'I've never fired a gun in my life,' says Tadeusz, 'but if I have to …' He laughs, snatching a piece of perec from Ferenc, who protests.

'Would you like one too?'

'I don't know how to shoot.'

'Nor me.'

They laugh. They pass pieces of perec among themselves, breaking in many pieces the circular salt-encrusted bread, the only thing to be found in the streets today. 'There's a woman with an enormous backside selling them by the kilo in Kisfaludy utca. Shall I go and get two more?'

A smiling girl goes up to a man who is leaning against a main entrance right beside them. She has a bandage on her forehead, and two bandoliers full of bullets over her chest. She has wound a black scarf three times round her neck. She talks intimately to the man and laughs. Then they kiss, unaware of everything and everyone else. A kiss right in the middle of a popular uprising. A deliberate exhibition? Someone claps. But the two still cling together. They go on kissing as if they were alone. Four children are unscrewing the wheels of what must have been an ÁVH car: it is large and shiny and has a dozen hammers and sickles stuck on its windows. A woman walking down the middle of the road is kicking an empty tin that is making a hellish noise. Someone shouts 'Stop that, you cow!' but she takes no notice and goes on kicking the blackened empty tin. An elegant man in a cream-coloured raincoat is sketching a coat of arms on the side of a lorry with a small brush dipped in white paint.

'The republican arms of Kossuth,' explains Tadeusz.

Now they have reached József Boulevard, and sit down on the entrance steps to a large closed building to rest their tired and muddy feet.

A man in a tattered shirt passes clasping two loaves of French bread.

'Where did you get those?'

'They're distributing them at the Corvin cinema. If you hurry you might be in time to get some.'

'But I thought they were handing out arms?'

'The arms are finished. Now they're giving out bread.'

So the friends make their way to the Corvin cinema, a large circular building with its doors open to hungry people going in and out with armfuls of white French loaves.

'Where are you from?'

To pass the time as they queue, Amara studies two posters on the wall by the cinema entrance. The title of the first film, displayed in huge letters, is *In Perfect Rhythm*. A very handsome worker bends over an assembly line brandishing a monkey wrench, while the haloed head of Stalin smiles paternally behind him. As Amara gazes at this enormous poster an egg flies past and smashes on the face of the Great Father. Turning quickly, she just manages to dodge a second egg that cracks against an immense photograph advertising a Romanian film called *Life Always Wins*, on which two female peasants with round faces rise up to indicate with outstretched arms the horizon from which a red ball is approaching. The two women have bunches of carrots under their arms. Their mouths embellished with gold teeth are stretched in smiles that are presumably intended to be reassuring but are in fact menacing. It might not be a bad idea to sit there in the dark resting your eyes on one of those films the posters are promoting.

The Corvin cinema is very crowded. Its seats have been removed. In the dark auditorium young people are handing out bottles of milk by gaslight. A blackened coal-basket contains oval forms that from a distance look like dirty bundles. In fact they are a kind of bread. On the stage a mime leaps about portraying the Soviets arriving and the Hungarians resisting them. He does everything himself: first he is a Soviet soldier in full uniform climbing out of a tank, then suddenly he is a Hungarian rebel firing at the tank and then climbing up on top of it. Then he mimes a dog pissing on the tank's caterpillar tracks oblivious of the soldier's cries of protest. Then a little boy playing football with his friends. Then he rises up on his legs to become a dead soldier opening his wings to fly to paradise. But what does he find in paradise? A little Hungarian tribunal that interrogates him on his actions. From behind, lanky and exhausted, comes the massive moustachioed figure of Stalin who furtively steals the soldier's wings and runs off sneering.

Hans comes up, looking worried.

'Our own government has called in the Soviet tanks,' he says. 'Fortunately the ones in question are part of the standing army already here. There aren't many of them and they know us. But they could still do a lot of damage. Let's go.'

38

That evening, over a soup of water in which an onion has been boiled and pieces of potato float, the five talk about what they have seen during the day in the city. But what is happening? asks Horvath, who seems to have come down that moment from the moon like Monsieur Candide. Tadeusz maintains they've landed by chance in the eye of the cyclone. A historical cyclone. Nothing else had happened since 1948 when, after victory over the Nazis, they had set themselves with cheerful enthusiasm to reconstruct their country: 'Discussions went on all night. Philosophy was mixed with politics and art and theatre with economics. We were convinced we were bringing to birth a new society, without injustice or violence.'

'You're forgetting the arrest of Béla Kovacs on Stalin's orders. An alarm bell none of us took any notice of,' says Tadeusz.

'And how long did this enthusiasm last, my friend?'

'Long enough to regenerate a life.'

'You forget how Zdanov and his criticisms landed on all our heads like a bucket of cold water.'

'I'm not forgetting that. What I'm saying is that 1948 was a year of great dreams. Which we woke from with a sore arse.'

'You are forgetting the trial of Rajk and the purges that followed, utterly unjust and brutal.'

'Well, what about now, then?'

At this point the voices start interrupting each other. Everyone has his own opinion, while outside the sound of shooting intensifies. But who's doing the shooting? Hans runs to the window but can't see anything. Tadeusz fiddles with the huge radio set, an Orion with a striped face, which is sitting on a primitive icebox covered with a blue cloth. The icebox is empty. It is two days since they last saw the young boy who normally tours the district from morning to night on his bicycle with its large carrier full of ice.

Tadeusz twiddles the knob producing whistles, wheezes and

crackles. Finally a contemptuous stentorian voice comes through clearly. 'That's Gerö,' Tadeusz recognises it at once as that of the Party secretary, the most hated of the Stalinist bureaucrats.

'Citizens, don't be deceived!' says the cutting voice. 'Go back to your homes and listen to the directives of the glorious Hungarian Communist Party. Those at this moment putting the city to fire and sword are enemies of communism, enemies of Hungary, enemies of the People. They are in the pay of agents of the secret police of enemy countries. Their aim is to destroy everything the People have achieved in recent years, to reintroduce capitalism in our country. Citizens, don't let yourselves be deceived. Budapest has fallen into the hands of a small group of lawless counter-revolutionaries. Stay at home, show your dissent from these hysterical criminals who hope to damage everything we hold most sacred in our country. Citiz– ' The voice is interrupted by the violent whirling of a *csárdás* dance.

Tadeusz looks at the radio in perplexity. The others too look up as if wondering what's going on.

'This is Radio Kossuth, Radio Freedom!' shouts a youthful voice. The *csárdás* fades and the room fills with a rapid excited chatter. Horvath stands spoon in hand before the radio with his mouth open as if paralysed. The violinist bursts out laughing. Hans goes closer to the loudspeaker with his ears pricked.

'They've taken the radio, they've taken the radio, boys!'
'Shall we go and see?'
'Wait a minute!'
'Let me hear what he's saying. Let me listen!'

The excited voice is shouting into the microphone as if it were a megaphone: 'Budapest is in the hands of insurgents. We are no counter-revolutionaries. We are the citizens of this city, of this country; people who have had enough of Soviet bullying, who will stand no more servility from our own leaders, who have had enough of spies, arbitrary arrests, meaningless trials, torture and executions; enough of the single Party and censorship of everything and everyone. For once we, the citizens of Budapest, say No, whatever the cost. We demand the immediate withdrawal of our country from the Warsaw Pact. We demand immediate free elections and the abolition of the ÁVH secret service and its chief

Gerö. We demand the right of a free vote for all, and the right of a free press and free speech. We demand …'

But the young man is interrupted by other voices. A girl with a voice like a child declaims in an inspired tone a poem by Gyula Illyés often heard at this time:

Where there's tyranny, there's tyranny
Not only in the rifle
not only in the prison, not only in the torture chamber
not only in the voice of the guard at night
not only in the obscure language of denunciation,
or in Morse code tapped on prison walls
not only in confessions
or the judge's verdict of guilty without right of appeal!
Tyranny is everywhere
even in the nurturing warmth of schools and in fatherly advice
in a mother's smile
in goodbye kisses
… in the face of the woman you love
that suddenly turns to stone
yes, tyranny is there too
in words of love
in words of ecstasy
like a small fly in the wine
tyranny is there
because you can never be alone
not even in your dreams
not even when you embrace
and even before that, when you feel desire
and wherever tyranny is
nothing has any meaning
not even the most faithful word
not even what I write myself
because from the very beginning
tyranny supervises your grave,
tyranny decides who you have been
who you are now and who you will be
even your ashes will still serve
tyranny…'

But the child is interrupted: everyone wants to speak, to say what they have to say. Someone is laughing in the background. Soon after more shots are heard. Moments of silence. The radio seems struck dumb. Then the music is back, and in that tiny kitchen in a small Budapest flat, in the midst of the smell of cabbage and unwashed clothes, four men start dancing to the rhythm of the *csárdás*. Amara watches astounded, incredulous. Then Hans takes her hand to show her the dance: right step, left step, a twirl, a hop. The two chairs and the pallet where Amara sleeps are moved to the far end of the little kitchen, the table is folded against the wall and the men wave their arms and leap and turn while on the radio the *csárdás* gets louder and louder.

But very soon the music is brutally silenced. 'It is 23.30 hours on 23 October 1956,' says an agitated voice, 'we must give you the facts, comrades, before those damned people falsify them. The ÁVH opened fire on the crowd after several of them were hit by stones thrown from below. They have killed about a hundred people. Many are still lying wounded in the road. They are being taken to hospital though there is little light or water there. One boy has just died from loss of blood, we've brought him here to the radio so everyone can see him. If you have a camera, please come and take a photograph. His first name is László, surname unknown. He was fifteen years old. Hit in the head by a Soviet bullet. The government says it never ordered the ÁVH to fire on the crowd. But they did it nevertheless, encouraged and supported by Soviet troops. They must be held accountable for this ...'

More shots are heard. The radio goes silent. A cry rips the air followed by desperate weeping. But what's happening? The loud-speaker pours out an avalanche of song: a Red Army chorus.

The five sit in a circle round the ancient Orion waiting for more news. But the music continues with no human voice to explain what is happening at the Hungarian National Radio.

The friends start arguing again. Tadeusz lights a cigarette. Hans pours a little homemade brandy into a dirty glass and offers it round. Each takes a sip and passes the glass on. They know how much that brandy is worth and how little is left.

A voice at last! Attention switches to the big Orion standing on its iceless icebox. 'This is Radio Budapest. Here is an announce-ment by the Government of the Hungarian People's Republic.

fascist and reactionary elements have attacked public buildings and assaulted troops and the police. In order to re-establish order and promote eventual initiatives designed to re-introduce the rule of law, from this moment all assemblies and demonstrations are forbidden. The army has orders to apply every measure consistent with the law to all who do not obey these orders.'

A long silence follows. The radio seems to have gone dumb. Then the calm voice resumes: 'Dear listeners, a special announcement. At today's meeting of the Politburo the date of the next session of the Central Committee has been fixed for 31 October. On the agenda will be the present situation and the duties of the Party in this connection. Report by Comrade Gerö.' An old-fashioned version of the Soviet national anthem follows.

Horvath looks around in astonishment. 'So it's all over, then?'

'Nothing is over. They've recaptured the radio. That's all. They want to persuade the Hungarian people that those who come out into the street are enemy agents, hired criminals. To give the real situation, they would have to admit that everybody is in the street, starting with the workers, who are all signed-up members of the Communist Party, together with students, professors, housewives, shopkeepers, craftsmen, writers and artists; all there to protest. They can't either admit this or deny it.'

The radio splutters and crackles but recovers, after an attempt at more Soviet choruses. 'Dear listeners. The Politburo has requested the Central Committee to announce an immediate meeting to discuss the present situation and the duty that faces us.' Band music follows.

'And now we shall tell you about a film soon to be shown in cinemas throughout the land,' announces a peaceful female voice. Shots can be heard in the background, some quite near at hand. The male voice returns and interrupts the publicity for the film: 'Dear listeners. The recent announcement about a meeting of the Central Committee was based on mistaken information. The Central Committee will meet again in a few days.'

General laughter. 'They really don't know what to say.'

The shots continue.

'I think we should go and have a look.'

'When can we sleep? I'm tired.'

'You think this is a night for sleeping? All bedlam has broken loose and all you can think of is going to sleep.'

'But I'm so sleepy.'

'Stay here then. We'll go, okay, Amara?'

Amara looks at them in confusion. She is tired, but she realises this is an exceptional night and not for sleeping. She must send a report to her paper and she wonders if the phone lines to Italy are working.

Meanwhile the carefully modulated voice of the presenter has resumed: 'This is Radio Budapest: a special announcement. The armed attacks carried out during the night by sinister counter-revolutionary gangs have created an extremely grave situation.' A short silence. Cries are heard in the background. A dry shot. Then the music begins again at full volume.

'See, they're admitting it, now they're admitting it!' shouts Horvath.

'Quiet, let's hear what comes next!'

'The outlaws have forcibly entered factories and public buildings and killed many civilians, members of the national armed forces and State security agents,' announces the voice, forcibly keeping itself under control.

'What the hell do you mean, outlaws!' shouts Tadeusz, aiming punches at the radio. 'Have you been out in the street yourself, you bastard, have you been out? Where are these outlaws, you fucker!'

'Quiet, I want to listen.'

'The government has been taken off guard by such a violent and ruthless attack,' continues the voice, rapid and breathless, 'and for this reason, bearing in mind the provisions of the Warsaw Pact, it has asked for support from units of the Soviet services stationed in Hungary.'

A cry of rage in the room. Meanwhile the voice continues undaunted: 'The government expects that Soviet units will participate in the restoration of order. We ask citizens to keep calm and support the Soviet and Hungarian troops in carrying out their mission.'

Hans rushes to get his jacket. But Tadeusz stops him, his face tired and desolate. 'Don't go out now. You can do nothing to help. And you could get a bullet in your head for your pains.'

'The city is about to be invaded by the Soviets and you expect me to stay at home and sleep!'

'It isn't about to be invaded. The troops they are talking about are already stationed here. Everything is still to be decided. Till now nearly all those Russians have fraternised with us. Didn't you see the tanks passing with university students on top of them?'

'I want to see it all with my own eyes.'

'It's late, better to go to bed and get some sleep. After all, they have to sleep too. We'll have a tough day before us tomorrow.'

'Do you think they'll bring in their real tanks, the ones from outside Hungary?'

'I don't know. If Europe helps us ... If the United Nations recognise our neutrality ... If they're afraid of the masses and trust Nagy ... If someone makes a move, perhaps Tito ... we may be able to establish a different Hungary.'

'I'm going, Father. I'll be back soon.'

'But leave Amara here.'

'She can decide for herself.'

'She's an Italian. What has all this got to do with her?'

'We're up to our necks in it.'

'Goodbye, everybody. If you don't see me tomorrow morning, come and bury me.'

'Don't be so melodramatic,' says Horvath. 'And be sure to keep us in the picture!'

Amara decides at the last minute not to go. The need for sleep has given her a violent pain in the nape of the neck. She needs to lie down for a bit. I'll join him later, she tells herself. But she falls asleep at once.

39

It's almost morning when something wakes her. A sense of suffocation. Amara gets up and opens the window. Outside, at last, it is silent. The cold hits her in the face. She goes back to bed, but cannot get to sleep. In the dark her fingers reach like thieves for Emanuele's black exercise book which she keeps under her pillow. Her eyes begin to read again the familiar words that seem perpetually new.

The Ghetto, Łódź. 18 April '42

For several days now we've been tormented by swarms of fleas that get everywhere. They are obsessive and tenacious. The more you kill the more they reproduce themselves from one night to the next, thousands of them, and they invade beds and clothes. We've tried putting petroleum under each foot of the bed. Though Mamma believes in talcum powder. She says fleas hate talcum powder. But it makes you laugh that in the whole ghetto there's not a pinch of talcum powder to be found. We've taken to boiling everything: clothes, sheets. It's only when we boil cloth that the damn things die. But there are others hidden in cracks in the floor, clefts in wood and the interstices of tiles, and the minute you spread clean sheets on the bed you're attacked again. You should see the water in the pan after it's been boiling clothes for a while: black with fleas. You can cream them off with a skimmer, like fat.

Łódź. 22 April '42

Amara darling, I'm afraid I shan't ever get out of here. I'm covered with chilblains and you can count my ribs, I weigh forty kilos, I may have tuberculosis. I've spat blood a number of times, but I don't want to go to the ghetto hospital because they conduct constant rounding-up operations and if you are really ill they jot down your name on a list and at the next deportation they throw you onto a lorry and off you go. I don't want to end up in Auschwitz or Chełmno. Even if what they say of those places isn't true, even if they really are just labour camps, I don't trust them. Here at least we're together and can survive somehow. Mamma says I'm too distrustful; if it was down to her she would leave at once, convinced she was heading for a better place. We'd get a bit more to eat then, she says. But deep down I don't think even she has any confidence. Here at least we do have a home of our own, even if it consists of only one room. There, it seems they throw everyone together in a kind of hen-coop. There's talk of dead bodies piled in ditches, of a foul-smelling smoke constantly pouring from the camp chimneys. The smoke of burned bodies. Can we trust them? Nobody knows how things really are. Some say it's just rumours. Others insist it's all true. I'm still working, even if they only pay me forty Reichsmarks a month. It's the only reason they don't take me away: if I work I'm productive and if I'm productive I'm helping the war effort. Twelve or thirteen hours a day for a handful of Reichsmarks. They don't talk about złotys any more now, only marks. Which is like saying that the cost of goods in the ghetto has doubled without any increase in our pay. A kilo of sugar costs eighteen RM. And who can allow themselves that! Even Mamma, weakened as she is, gets up at five to go to the factory. Even she has realised that so long as she can work she won't be deported. Her optimism keeps her alive. She believes in a benign future. We'll get out of here, she says, I feel it, the allies will come, they'll liberate us, you'll see, we'll start living again, eating and sleeping. We'll even get back to Florence, to Amara. Yes. Mutti, we'll get out of here. But when?

Time to sleep, Amara, time to sleep, says a sensible voice inside a dark room that she persists in regarding as the place of internal tribunals. But there's an echo and her words return to her doubled. People seem different in that empty room. But who can be there other than that tiresome pain in the arse, her maltreated conscience?

Her fingers, of their own free will, open, run and give signals and her eyes follow, drowsy but attentive. All she can do is return to Emanuele's words that spring to life again in those pencil markings, if sometimes so weak and faint as to be almost invisible.

Łódź. 15 May '42

This morning on my way to work I saw a woman crouched on the dry mud selling early cherries. I went up to her thinking to buy a few, but had a severe shock.

Three marks each. I took one in my hand just to smell it, but the woman made a scene. If you eat it I'll force you to spit it out, she said, either you pay or nothing, don't touch it! I abused her in a loud voice, calling her a thief, and she answered in verse: Filthy boy, can't you see yourself? Got no hair and covered with scabs! Go and piss somewhere else! But if she's selling those cherries it must mean someone is buying them. There are distinctions even here in the ghetto, where some Jews have rights and others don't, rich Jews and poor Jews. Only rich in a manner of speaking, of course, but a little less stricken than we who were once seriously rich and are now the lowest of the low.

Łódź. 3 June '42

Papà has been arrested. He was on a list of workers of low productivity. They took him away. We've heard nothing of him for days. Mamma in her invincible optimism says they'll have sent him home. But I don't believe it. I'm afraid they've deported him, like Uncle Eduard who disappeared into the void after he was thrown onto a lorry at five in the morning. There's no longer talk of shootings, only of goods trains leaving for Chełmno or Auschwitz or even Dachau. We don't really know what goes on inside the camps. The Germans call them labour camps. But there's a rumour doing the rounds that anyone who can't work is shut in a large room and suffocated with gas. That's what's being said. By voices overheard by the sharp ears of people who know German well and work in the SS kitchens or barber shop.

Łódź. 6 June '42

This morning on Zidowska Street I saw three girls with scarves on their heads and stars on their chests running away. Two German soldiers were after them. They ran quickly, leaping over any obstacles: buckets, shovels, dead bodies. Then one of the soldiers shouted 'Stop, or I'll shoot!' All three went on running so both soldiers fired together. The girls fell, first the one at the back, striking her face on the pavement; then the second, dressed in black, who curled up on the ground and shook as if with St Vitus' Dance. The third, though hit, continued to run. The stronger of the soldiers shouted and chased her. The other stopped to make sure the two fallen girls were dead. The wounded girl had nearly reached the corner of the street when the SS man reached her, knocked her down with the butt of his rifle and shot her in the head.

Despite the hunger that torments me, but perhaps precisely so as not to think about it, I slipped into the theatre on Krawiecka Street where on Saturdays they put on concerts or funny plays to raise morale. It seems strange to have theatre performances in a besieged ghetto. But it's the only thing they can do. That's what they say. The hall was packed. There was a strong smell of feet. But also intense concentration. One comedian mimicked the wretches in the camp. Another set to music all the things he would have liked to eat. Two girls danced like bears. Everyone laughed. At the end they went round with a small plate. Some people gave two pfennigs, some half a pfennig. I was ashamed: I had nothing in my pocket, nothing at all. The hand holding the plate was trembling. I pulled out the slice of bread I had kept for my supper and gave that. She thanked me with a click of the tongue.

9 June '42

Papà has been found dead with his chest ripped open by bayonet thrusts. A woman working at same textile factory as Mamma found him, thrown down near the wall of the ghetto. Mutti tried to drag him away to bury him, but two guards came at once with rifles cocked and sent her back to work. We recited the Kaddish at home at night in memory of him. Two neighbours joined us, Kasimir and Maximilian, boys who have lost their father and mother and work with me at the carpentry shop. They are from Vienna too. They brought some barley coffee, a great luxury these days, and we sat on the floor to talk. Max is extremely well informed. It seems he is friends with a young SS girl who supervises the ghetto hospital. Every now and then she gives him something to eat in exchange for a little sex. That's what his brother says but there may be a touch of malice in it because they always go out together but Kasimir comes home with empty hands, while Max always has something in his pocket: half an apple, a slice of bread, a potato. Max says they are emptying the hospital. They have already taken away the old and ill and no one knows where to. Certainly not to work, so it must be to the cemetery. But now it seems they want to take away the children too. But to send them where?

It's my birthday today, Amara. But I'm so tired I can hardly write. Even so I will write, so long as there's anything left of my pencil. Because I want what's happening in this place to be known. Max, who is so well nourished that I think Kasimir must be right to say Max is ready to sell himself for a bowl of soup, has told me the Nazis are winning on all fronts. He doesn't seem desperate when he says it; he has a mocking smile I don't like. He says Sebastopol has fallen and the Führer's armies have reached the Don district. He says that in the Chełmno and Auschwitz camps children are being shut in gas chambers and, once dead, are burned in cremation ovens. But who tells you all these horrible things? objects Mamma who as always wants to look on the bright side. She doesn't believe the rumours but thinks they are poison spread by the SS to terrorise the Jews. Shut your nasty mouth, Max, she says angrily, but Max just looks her up and down with a cold, ironic stare that brings shudders to the spine.

Łódź. 5 September '42

Today I went out of the carpentry shop to get some planks and stayed sitting in the sun for a few minutes. The last warmth on my back before a winter of cold. The 'Black Man', as we call the foreman, came and beat me up. I dragged myself home where I found my mother furious. Read this, she said, just read it; though I could hardly stand. She disinfected the cuts and bruises on my back with a little lukewarm water and soap. Read it! she repeated. An announcement from Rumkowski that had been hung up in her factory, among other places. I'll copy it here because I believe everyone should know it in its true atrocity. 'A terrible blow has struck the ghetto. We are being asked to give up our most precious possession – our old people and children. I have been judged unworthy of having a child of my own and thus have dedicated the best years of my life to the children of others. I have lived and breathed with the little ones and I could never have imagined I would be forced to sacrifice them at the altar with my own hands. But in my old age I have to reach out my hand and implore you: Brothers and sisters! Pass them to me! Fathers and mothers! Give me your children!' My mother says she will go and spit in his face. I begged her to calm down. Max sniggered when I got him to read the announcement. Don't you realise this will save us, you and me and other young people strong enough to work? The children, poor things, are too little to understand and serve no purpose. As for the old, they haven't much time left anyway. You should thank our leader instead of criticising him, you're as stupid as my brother Kasimir.

15 September '42

The ghetto has entrusted its children and old people to the loving hands of our leader Rumkowski: may they depart in peace.

20 October '42

Only four potatoes left. I'm still spitting blood. A neighbour of seventy died of hunger last night. My legs are swelling up. I'm scared, Amara. Why don't the allies come? Why don't they bombard the Łódź ghetto? Why does no one in the world do anything for us?

24 December '42

The SS choirs and the Christian chapel can be heard celebrating on the other side of the wall. Tonight we'll go and search for scraps.

25 December '42

Found some potato peel. And a fish's head. Also a piece of dessert but so mixed with soil it was impossible to put it in my mouth. Max made me a present of a segment of orange. Who knows where it came from! Perhaps the officers' mess.

31 December '42

They've distributed an extra ration of bread to everybody and a spoonful of jam. Mamma gave her portion to me. She said she never liked jam! In return she told me that the women workers sometimes agree for one of them to distract the foreman while the others damage the machinery so it can't continue producing uniforms for the army. I told her the sentence for sabotage is shooting or hanging. She shrugged her shoulders.

Twenty below zero. Can't write anything. My mule-headed mother is coping better than me. I'm dying, Amara, I can't go on.

With a mouthful of blood stained on my shirt, my mother took me to Wesola Street, all that's left of the ghetto hospital. I've started a cure. The Jewish doctors are kind. They get a little more to eat than us. But there aren't many of them and they work all night. Am I going to get better, doctor? I asked. Of course — as soon as the war is over, he answered with a smile.

Max says all hell has been let loose in the Warsaw ghetto. With the help of the Polish Resistance, the men hid arms they had bought at an exorbitant price. On the agreed day they pulled out these ancient revolvers and hunting rifles and started firing at their Nazi jailers. But how did it finish, Max? Well, how would you expect? With the victory of the forces of law and order. What law? The existing law, that's the only one. The law of the SS? Jawohl! You're a pig! I just see what the rest of you don't see. You'll all die. But I shall save myself. I have been promised that by Willy, who knows a thing or two. Hitler's going to win, Willy will become a general and I shall enter Berlin with him in an open car under a torrent of flowers. You believe that swine? In any case you haven't long to live, in the state you've been reduced to, poor Emanuele! Damn you, Max, I don't want to talk to you any more, you're a beast! But he just laughs; the rest of us get thinner but he puts on weight.

Mamma arrested. I went to look for her in Czarnieckiego Street, in the ghetto prisons. They told me there was no Thelma Fink or Thelma Orenstein there. But I caught a glimpse of her behind a door that opened and closed rapidly. She was tied up and her face was all swollen from blows. I had to go back to the carpentry shop. Where Max was quick to put me in the picture: your tart of a mother formed a small group of female saboteurs. They put four machines out of action. The work of the factory was halted. Technicians were called in. The defects were discovered. Someone turned spy. She was the leader. She'll certainly be sent to Auschwitz. And you with her, you can count on it.

30 April '43

Thelma Fink, once famous variety star, a woman of unquenchable fortitude, owner of a thousand furs, wife of the toy-manufacturer industrialist Karl Orenstein, Florentine by adoption, worker no. 52899 at the textile factory of the Third Reich in the ghetto of Łódź, mother of one Emanuele Orenstein who works there in the carpentry shop, has been hanged in the Basarowa Street marketplace at the end of Lutomierska Street, the place nowadays preferred by Rumkowski for his addresses to the population of the ghetto whom he calls his beloved children.

6 May '43

I wake to the sound of Mamma's footsteps as she puts away plates in the kitchen. There's nothing to eat, Mutti! But she continues regardless. She puts water on to boil. She strikes a match a thousand times but it won't light and repeatedly turns the knob of the gas ring but it produces no gas. Mamma, please, go to sleep, I'll see to it. But she won't speak. She's mute, diligent, insufferable. Why can't you leave me in peace, Mutti? I told Rumkowski I'm the daughter of an officer in the Austrian army, and that my father won a medal for military valour, which was pinned to his chest by the emperor in person. Mamma, please stop it, you're giving me a headache. But she laughs and goes on fussing over the pans. She's driving me mad. Please let me sleep because tomorrow I must be at the carpenter's at six. Mamma, you're dead, can't you understand that? But she takes no notice and goes on shifting pans and plates.

20 May '43

Yesterday at dawn they took away all the people in the house next door. Among them Kasimir and Max. I saw them from the window, being dragged onto the lorry with the others, furious. Max was dumbfounded. Who knows what his protector will say!

Now I must get ready because they will certainly come tomorrow for the people in our building. I shall hide this exercise book in the hole in the wall. In the hope, God help me! that the building will not collapse and that someone will find it. The last lot have all been sent to Auschwitz. It seems there isn't even room for another fly at Chełmno. But at Auschwitz they are building new accommodation. Max said so. Goodbye, Amara. I send you a last kiss. Your Emanuele.

40

At eight in the morning Hans reappears with a loaf of bread under his arm and a bag of dried figs. 'I've also got some instant coffee in my pocket.' He's radiant. He says the city has by no means been pacified. The whole country, not only Budapest, is in revolt against the Rákosi government. There has been shooting between the ÁVH and the workers.

'But best of all, Nagy has been chosen to head the government. And Maléter, the officer who refused to open fire on the insurgents, is now Minister of Defence,' he adds, putting the bread down on the table. 'Councils of workers are being formed in all the factories, on the model of the first one at Miskolc. They are working towards a general strike. The Russians seem to have got the point. Probably they don't want to be seen as jailers by the whole world. Khrushchev is not Stalin.'

Amara fills the small pan with tap water that tastes of chlorine and contains a little rust. She lights the gas which luckily has not been cut off, and puts the water on to heat.

Horvath is still asleep. When he comes into the kitchen in his pyjamas, a blanket round his shoulders, bony white ankles sticking out and his skin a maze of blue veins, the friends receive him with applause. His floating white hair is like a halo and his blue eyes are shining.

Amara pours the coffee into the glasses which she has rinsed with the help of a fragment of soap discovered under the sink. She slices the bread and puts it on the only clean plate in the house.

Horvath claims he isn't hungry but swallows his slice of bread in huge mouthfuls and scalds his tongue on his boiling-hot coffee. Ferenc, at the smell of the coffee, also appears in his pyjamas. With his violin stuck under his ear he plays them a Paganini *Scherzo*. Tadeusz watches him, smiling tenderly.

Hans, glass of coffee in hand, goes to switch on the radio.

'They told me that in one single night any number of new free broadcasters have come onto the air. Who knows if we'll be able to hear them on this old set!'

He places his powerful hands on the ugly great Orion with its light-coloured wooden sides and oblong glass window lit by mysterious lights. A brown cloth grille stretches between four chipped knobs. The loudspeaker blows, whistles and puffs like an old steam engine. But finally a radiant if agitated voice emerges to tell them: 'This is Radio Borsod. We announce the dissolution of the local ÁVH and that Soviet troops stationed in the area have not intervened. Factory Councils have been meeting all night to draw up a list of proposals to present to the new Nagy government, including recognition of political parties, free elections and the expulsion of all Soviet troops from the Republic.'

The five gather once more, cold but with their glasses steaming in their hands, round the big Orion. Hans translates quickly and concisely. A happy female voice announces, 'Gerö and his Stalinist friends have left the country! They are joining Rákosi in exile in the USSR. Let's hope they don't ever dare to come back!' A triumphal march by Verdi follows.

'All this music!' shouts Tadeusz. 'We want to hear how things are going!'

'Why are you twiddling that knob?'

'I want to hear better!'

'You'll lose the station it took me so much trouble to find!'

'We'll find another!'

Tadeusz continues turning the knob. Eventually he finds a third free station. Crowding close, the friends make out a young female voice above the crackling and hissing: 'Radio Győr-Sopron. The world is watching us, comrades. Everyone's eyes are on us. Radio France has announced that Hungarian workers are successfully attacking the forces of the communist police. Radio Monaco has broadcast live the voice of comrade Zoltán Frei who was present at the shoot-out in front of parliament in Budapest. He has given evidence that the police fired at a crowd armed with nothing but stones. A rumour is circulating that we are fascists. But we declare with pride that we are socialists. If attacked we shall defend our country and our liberties with weapons ... The latest news: in Italy 101 communist intellectuals have signed an appeal for solidarity with the Hungarian revolution. And students in Rome, Milan and

Naples are demonstrating in our support. Thank you, Italy!'

Now the five seem more cheerful. They have drunk hot coffee and eaten bread and dried figs, and now they smoke a cigarette with a satisfied air, even if their eyes never leave the radio for a moment. Tadeusz continues manipulating the knob, brilliantly capturing every word that leaps out from unofficial sources. But every now and then they are chilled by the cold and presumptuous voice of the official Radio, recaptured since yesterday, angrily commanding citizens not to leave their homes. 'From every part of the land telegrams are reaching the Central Committee of the Hungarian Workers' Party, expressing the indignation of the nations' workers at the criminal actions of the counter-revolutionaries, and assuring the Party and Government of their determination to defend the socialist order from attack by any enemy.'

'Twiddle the knob, Tadeusz, no more of that stuff!'

Tadeusz shrugs his shoulders, mortified. 'We need to hear what the official Radio is saying too!'

But here are strident, excited voices, clearly recorded in the street: 'Me and my sister Olga left home to go to work. After a few metres, at the corner of the ring road and Rudas László utca, near where the hairdresser's used to be, we saw a big hole in the middle of the street. We had to go back.' Suddenly a male voice interrupts: 'We were lined up in front of the Astoria Hotel, workers and others, and we shouted "Soviets out of Hungary!" and "An end to martial law!" The locally-stationed Soviet tanks didn't fire on us. We explained to the Russian soldiers that we're not counter-revolutionaries, we're independent socialists who want a better socialism ... Some of them embraced us. I think they'd had orders not to fire on us, and they left their weapons hanging from their shoulders. We thrust the Hungarian flag into the mouths of the cannons. They invited us on board and took us where we wanted to go. I tell you, my friends, the Russian soldiers are on our side.'

'It really seems impossible,' broods Hans, chewing his nails.

'Well, are we going to make it then?' says Tadeusz.

Horvath has taken the blanket off his shoulders. Underneath he is fully clothed. He is holding a book in his hand and reading aloud from Pascal: 'Imagine a great number of men in chains, all condemned to death, with some every day having their throats cut in full view of the others, so that the survivors see their own future in the fate of those like them and, looking at each other in sorrow and without hope, await their turn. That is the human condition.'

'What on earth are you talking about, Horvath!'

'Pascal said that, not me!'

'Who cares a fig about your Pascal, keep him to yourself!' says Tadeusz angrily, twiddling the knob.

'Is this the time for that sort of stuff?' says Hans reproachfully.

But Horvath is no way put out. Entirely serious, he opens at random another page of the *Pensées*: 'To make sure passion cannot harm us, let us live as if we only had eight days of life left.'

'Please stop!'

'If we must make a present of eight days of our lives, we might just as well make a present of a hundred years.'

'Well said! But that'll do now. Let's listen to the voices from the city.'

'Or from the whole nation.'

Horvath lifts his eyes from the book and studies the others with compassion. He fearlessly opens another page and reads on, ignoring their protests: 'When I consider the brevity of my life, absorbed in the eternity that has gone before it and will follow after it, and the tiny space I fill and am scarcely even aware of, buried in the infinite immensity of a universe I do not know and that does not know me, I am terrified and wonder at the fact that I am here rather than there, now rather than later. Who put me here?'

'Horvath, you horror!'

'Can't you stop being a librarian even for a minute?'

But Horvath is unrelenting, and while the radio continues to crackle and spit, he remorselessly continues to read Pascal's words: 'Are you less of a slave because your master loves you and flatters you? Lucky slave! Your master may flatter you now, but he'll be beating you soon enough.'

'Well said, Pascal! There you have those slaves of Rákosi and Gerö who think their Soviet master's their friend because he gives them a slap on the back.'

'We are fools to entrust ourselves to the company of those who are like ourselves: as miserable as we are, as impotent as we are, they will never be able to help us; we shall die alone,' continues the Old Testament prophet, lifting the page close under his nose.

'That's enough, Horvath, you're making me nervous.'

'Just be careful. If you don't stop I shall throw your book out of the window,' adds Tadeusz, raising his voice.

The violinist is playing Paganini again. A little ray of sunlight comes in from the kitchen window. On such a grey damp day it seems a miracle. Everyone watches it light up a dancing whirl of dust.

Horvath sighs and closes his book. But he can't resist repeating the last Pascal aphorism that he has just read: 'It is horrible to feel everything you possess is failing. Amen.'

'Throw that book away! Come here and listen,' urges Tadeusz, still searching out new voices on the radio.

'Well, here we are with comrade Dudás and his bodyguards, and the hundred and fifty men with him who have occupied the editorial offices of the Party paper *Szabad Nep*. What are your plans, comrade Dudás?'

A sound of chairs being moved and heavy breathing. Then the voice of Dudás, raucous and determined: 'We are already printing a hundred thousand copies of a new paper to be called *Magyar Fuggetlenseg*. Our response to the concept of the single party.'

The sound of a rotary press can be heard.

'When will the first number be ready?'

'This very day,' shouts Dudás happily.

'We must get a copy of this new paper,' says Hans.

'For news?'

'As a souvenir.'

'Comrades, comrades,' cries the radio. The five fall silent. The voice has managed to grab their attention despite Horvath's Pascal, Ferenc's violin and shots fired in the street.

'Comrades, here is the speech Nagy made in front of parliament. Unfortunately we did not manage to record it because our batteries were flat. He said he recognises the national and democratic character of the insurrection. Those were his exact words. He announced that the Soviet troops will withdraw and the ÁVH will be dissolved, and that Gerö has already left for Moscow to join Rákosi. Comrades, we are free!'

Tadeusz starts leaping about the room. Horvath watches him with pity. Ferenc strikes up a jig. Tadeusz begins going round in circles. After a bit even Horvath is infected by the euphoria and joins the others in the middle of the kitchen with huge ungainly capers.

41

Horvath has developed a high temperature and is treating himself
with powdered aspirin that Hans has procured at considerable
expense. The serving of the medicine on a Eucharistic host found
in Ferenc's cupboard (which is full of the most unlikely objects),
has become a ceremony in which everyone takes part. Hans spreads
what is supposed to be half a gram of aspirin on the middle of the
host which Ferenc holds open with three fingers, seeing that the
soft little disc has a tendency to roll itself up. Tadeusz adds a drop
of water and the host is then closed by the wise hands of Hans who
folds it carefully and lifts it on high. At this point Horvath closes
his eyes like a child and sticks out a long tongue red with fever, on
which Hans places the host. Immediately after this Horvath pro-
trudes his lips and tries to swallow the medicine with the help of a
mouthful of tap water.

The coffee is finished and no more can be found anywhere. In its
place there has arrived on the market a tea from China with very
dark curled leaves that tastes like sundried straw. It seems Khrushchev has paid a visit to Mao and the two have decided to increase
their trade links to include tea, poultry, lard and soya beans, which
reach Hungary via the Soviet Union.

It's even difficult to find bread. There are the usual perecs which
Hans calls pretzels and eats with gusto even though they are made
from potato flour and stick to your teeth. 'They're supposed to be
crisp,' says Hans, 'but hunger is hunger.' The great Orion on top
of the iceless icebox is kept permanently on. Radio Kossuth and
Radio Petőfi transmit classical music, most frequently Shostakovi-
ch's Fifth Symphony, Borodin's D Major Quartet, Rimsky-Korsa-
kov's *Shéhérazade*, Kodály's *Galánta Dances* and Khachaturian's
Sabre Dance. Every so often the music is interrupted by an appeal
for calm. And above all, an insistence that people should hand in
their arms. 'All weapons, even the smallest, must be handed in to

the government.' But judging by the continued insistence, it seems reasonable to conclude that the arms are not being given up.

Every now and then they pick up the voice of a free radio station, but these tend to be no sooner born than they die again. Young voices that tell of a great longing for change. They announce that new workers' councils are being formed spontaneously in factories throughout the land. Some discuss the concept of the dictatorship of the proletariat. Others go back to Trotsky's theories of permanent revolution, while others again refer directly to the young Marx, and many invoke the free market. In fact, huge confusion. There is only one thing they all agree on: Soviets out of Hungary! And immediate free elections!

Shoot-outs are constantly denounced in various parts of the country, above all battles between the ÁVH and the insurgents. The Soviets take little part preferring to leave things to Rákosi's old military police, the most hated force in the whole country.

The five get some hot soup inside them, made from the broth of a few meatless chicken bones, lots of margarine, half an onion and two rather soft potatoes. Suddenly an unusual voice comes over the radio. A tender woman's voice singing in English. Something really unexpected.

'But that's Doris Day!' says Ferenc, lifting his head.

They all listen. It really does seem to be Doris Day, the blonde girl with shining eyes who draws crowds to the cinemas throughout the world. Except in the self-styled socialist countries where she can only circulate in clandestine form in a few smoky film clubs frequented by youthful film lovers and only tolerated by the censorship because they appeal to such small audiences.

'What's Doris Day doing on Hungarian radio?'

'Someone must have recorded the song secretly after picking it up on long wave, and is now broadcasting it from one of the free radio stations.'

The clear voice of the young mother trying to save her son from kidnappers in Hitchcock's film penetrates the tiny apartment. '*Que sera sera, Whatever will be will be, The future's not ours to see, Que sera sera …*' Horvath laughs, but his laugh turns into an insistent hollow cough that nearly makes his eyes start from their sockets.

'I'll get the thermometer,' says Tadeusz.

But Horvath holds up his hand as if to ward it off.

'I really don't want to know if I have a temperature or not. In any case, I won't take anything except aspirin.'

'Okay, but if it's bronchitis, we're going to the hospital.'

'For heaven's sake!'

In fact, no one thinks it's a good idea to go to the hospital in such a wind. It's late October. The cold has become intense. The city is in the hands of insurgents, and there is a shortage of basic necessities.

'"The Nagy government,"' reads Hans in a newspaper just printed and being distributed free in the street, '"the new government that contains communists, social democrats, members of the National Peasants' Party and small proprietors, seems to have been accepted by the Soviets and to be taking its first steps towards normalisation. Cardinal Mindszenty has been freed after many years in prison. The secret police, the ÁVH, has been abolished. Its place will be taken by a National Guard. Maléter has been promoted to general and made Minister of Defence. Free trade unions and cultural associations are being born again ..."'

'So all is well, damn it, everything is perfect, but in that case why is the city so uneasy and why is so much shooting still to be heard? And why can't we find any food?'

Tadeusz has another newspaper in his hand, the *Independence*, which is launching a fierce attack on the new government. 'These people aren't satisfied,' says Tadeusz, reading huge headlines printed in an ink that stains the tips of their fingers: '"We don't recognise the Nagy government which is showing weakness towards the Soviet Union. We should not and cannot bargain. We no longer want the Soviets here. They have been occupying our country for eleven years. We don't want them on our territory any more; we don't want them shaping our politics for us, choosing our leaders, deciding our agrarian policies, our military investments, the products we manufacture, or planning our towns. Above all we don't want their censorship. No more denunciations, disappearances, concentration camps, farcical trials and tribunals whose only aim is to suppress those who do not see things the way they do!"'

'It's not as if they were speaking straight out!' remarks Ferenc, walking about violin in hand without ever finding time to play it.

But Tadeusz intervenes: 'This is no time for music, Ferenc. Go and find some meat for our supper.' But the voice of Doris Day has moved them all. Like the voice of freedom.

'"Let us ask the United Nations for military assistance in liberating a country that has spent too many years under the Soviet yoke. We demand a neutral Hungary. We insist on leaving the Warsaw Pact immediately. We want all Russian troops out of the country. Asylum and Hungarian citizenship, if they want it, can be granted only to soldiers who have fraternised with the insurgents,"' reads Hans, smiling.

'All this is extremely naïve.'

'But it's the truth.'

'What truth, you fool?'

'What the people are thinking, idiot, can't you understand that?'

'"Don't touch anything in the shops, even if the windows are shattered!"' Hans reads on, nodding. '"Let no one accuse us of being bandits! Even if you're dying of hunger, don't touch what doesn't belong to you! We are in the process of organising points for the free distribution of bread and milk. Come and find us at the Corvin cinema or the newspaper offices, there will always be something for you. Signed József Dudás."'

'You know what, I'm going at once.'

'Wait, I'll come too.'

Amara and Hans start down the stairs. Outside it's drizzling. Amara ties a scarf round her head. Hans puts on a Russian sailor's cap, made of a limp waterproof material, with a little rigid peak from which a small red star has been ripped.

42

Amara and Hans come out of Magdolna, take Baross utca to
Kálvin tér, from there pass along a section of Múzeum körút
and head for Dohány utca. They run into a long queue of people
waiting their turn to get a little bread. A woman wrapped in two
coats, one longer than the other, is selling perecs from a pile on
top of a chest of drawers dragged goodness knows how to that
place. But they are of such poor quality and so mouldy that no
one stops to buy. A group of students pass them at speed, singing
the 'Marseillaise': *Allons enfants de la patrie, le jour de gloire est
arrivé, contre nous de la tirannie, l'étendard sanglant est levé …*

Hans sings with them, moved. Amara watches silently. How
much that music brings back to her! Amintore repeating the forbidden words in a low voice after checking that no one was listening. Her mother running to close the windows before joining in,
mangling the words: *Aux armes citoyens, formez vos bataillons.
Marchons, marchons! qu'un sand impur abreuve nos sillons!*

At every step there's someone giving out leaflets. Hans takes
them all and thrusts them into his pocket.

'What do they say?'

'I don't know, we'll look later.'

'There, that's the Kilian barracks,' Hans points with his finger
and stops in consternation. Nothing is left of the barracks but
walls riddled with holes. Its roof has collapsed, its doors have been
broken down, its windows are black cavities. In front, covered
with chalk, is a line of dead bodies. Russian soldiers and Hungarian citizens lying side by side close to the road. They look the same
under the layer of lime someone has strewn on them. Twisted
statues like the dead recovered from the ash of Vesuvius and preserved in the museums of Naples, caught in a moment of confusion when trying to escape. Very young boys, their uncovered faces
stained with blood and their eyes wide open as if in an attempt

to understand the mystery of this defining journey. Poor quality clothes and boots smeared with mud.

A lorry backs up slowly. Two men in uniform, their red stars replaced by ribbons in the national colours, start dragging the bodies towards the lorry. Two others, sub-machine guns slung over their shoulders, lift them up to the level of the lorry, almost making them fly through the air.

Amara is deeply upset. In spite of herself her eyes fill with stinging tears.

'Let's go away!' says Hans, for whom the excitement of the 'Marseillaise' has been replaced by depression and angry brooding. But Amara plants her feet like a mule and goes on staring at those bodies almost playfully lifted with an undulating movement before being unceremoniously thrown onto the lorry.

'Wait a moment, I'll ask what's been happening,' says Hans, going up to a man who is leaning against a tree smoking. He too has his rifle over his shoulder and seems lost in contemplation of the dead.

The two talk for a while. The man stays leaning on his tree. Hans presses him with questions. Then, after a quick salute, returns to Amara.

'Colonel Pál Maléter was ordered to recapture the Kilian barracks from the insurgents. They gave him five tanks and the men of the Esztergom armoured division, plus a hundred officer cadets from the Kossuth Academy. But by the time he reached the Kilian on the morning of the 24th he had only one tank left. The others had stopped on the way, seized by armed citizens. The officer cadets refused to fire on civilians. So Colonel Maléter, instead of attacking the occupants of the barracks, decided to negotiate a ceasefire with them thus clearly putting himself on the side of the insurgents. Then the Hungarian military authorities called in the Soviets who arrived and began bombarding the barracks. A full-scale battle followed. Men were killed on both sides. Let's go.'

Amara moves on reluctantly. They pass in front of a hotel with two armed guards outside it. The old name, Hotel Britannia, has been erased and replaced by BÉKE in cardboard block capitals.

'Shall we go in and get something hot?'

Amara nods. The thick carpet adorning the floor has been covered by coloured rags on which the muddy prints of boots can be seen. The hotel bar is crowded. All eyes turn to the newcomers. Someone greets them in French. 'The Western journalists' favourite hotel,' says Hans, ordering a draught beer. The table they lean their elbows on is sticky.

'What would you like to drink?'

'Tea.'

The waitress is wearing an ankle-length coat, though it's not particularly cold inside. Then Amara notices that every opening of the door brings in a gust of cold air. The windows of the kitchen have been blown out and all the waiters are going in and out in thick coats.

The tea turns out to be hot water darkened by some leaf without taste or smell but as sweet as treacle. Amara takes her cup in both hands.

'At least it's hot.'

'Have we got the money to pay for it?'

Hans nods. He drinks his beer at a single draught and wipes his mouth on the sleeve of his sweater. Meanwhile a fat bald man has come to their table.

'Journalists?'

'Yes and no,' says Hans.

'You need visas?'

'Just waiting for them.'

'Italians? How many of you?'

'The lady is Italian. Maria Amara Sironi. I'm a mixture, part Hungarian and part Austrian … And you?'

'Call me Alain. I can't remember my surname. I've crossed too many borders. But anyway, if you need visas I can get you two. Not more.'

'We want to get to Poland.'

'Poland? What for?'

'To look for a child, or rather a man.'

'I don't think you'll be able to get to Poland just now. I can get you into Austria, nothing more.'

'How much?'

'Eight hundred forints each.'

'I think we'll wait.'

'Could take a long time. I don't think the Soviets are going to give way.'

'In what sense?'

'They may invade in the grand manner. Hundreds of tanks and thousands of men. Make a clean sweep of everything. Maybe even bomb the city.'

'Are you advising us to get out?'

'It would seem logical. There are people prepared to pay a thousand forints just to get to the Andau Bridge. It could soon be too late.'

'Well, we're in no hurry,' says Hans casually. But then he adds, 'Can you give me your phone number? In case of need, I could call you.'

The bald man looks pityingly at them.

'The telephones are tapped. And in any case, they don't work. They've cut the lines. If you want me, you'll find me here.'

With this he gets up, takes Amara's white hand in both his own and kisses it in an extremely theatrical manner before leaving them with a cunning conspiratorial smile.

'Might be useful.'

'But could we trust him? Anyway, who's got eight hundred forints?'

On the way out they notice on a little table in a corner of the lounge a metal radio set with aerodynamic lines and a long aerial; a lot of people are sitting round it listening.

Amara and Hans go closer. The voice is speaking in English. It says a Hungarian delegation is on the point of leaving for the United Nations to attract the attention of delegates to the problem of their country. 'A massive intervention by the Soviet Union is feared,' comments the speaker. 'The Hungarians remember that the Warsaw Pact states that allies may intervene in the case of external aggression against a member country, but this is not the case in Hungary at present.' The journalist also states that President Eisenhower has made a statement in New York deploring in advance any aggression whatever by the Soviet Union against a people fighting for their freedom, adding the exact words: 'America is on the side of the Hungarians with all her heart. The students and workers fighting on the streets of Hungarian cities are subject to the rights of man, as expressly guaranteed to the Hungarian people by the peace treaty signed by the Hungarian leadership and their associated allied powers, including the Soviet Union and the United States.'

'In short, we can count on the United States. Great news!'

43

Yet another bonfire. They're burning a mountain of Soviet flags. A man in a padded jacket is taking photographs, down on one knee on the wet stone pavement. 'Pedrazzini of *Paris Match*,' says someone, pointing at him. A group of young people are walking hand in hand. The usual woman with the enormous bottom is selling perecs at the corner of Dohány utca, next to a cart. Pieces of coal are smoking in a rusty tin drum; every so often she stirs them with a stick. A strange ambulance passes in the form of a cart pulled by a bicycle. A small boy with bound head is pedalling. Behind, black hair tied back with string, is a girl steadying a rolled-up stretcher. Both have white shirts. Over the girl's knees is a white flag with a red cross glued to it. The pair clank rapidly down the potholed street.

Amara and Hans hurry towards the Corvin cinema. There is always the risk of a sniper firing from a high window or balcony. An ÁVH officer avenging dead friends. The streets are covered with mud. Small handwritten posters have been stuck on the walls. But they do not stop to read. They are in a hurry. They must find bread for their friends. It's already no mean thing that Tadeusz and Ferenc have agreed to put them up in that tiny apartment. And now, on top of that, Horvath is ill. They must find coffee and milk. In front of the cinema is a Soviet tank captured by the rebels. On it are a dozen youths with machine guns. A bareheaded boy well wrapped in a long black coat stops them to ask for identification. Hans pulls out his papers. The boy studies them carefully. He seems unconvinced.

'Austrian?'

'Yes, my mother was Hungarian.'

'And what are you doing here?'

'Visiting my father.'

'Occupation?'

Hans doesn't know what to say. He glances at Amara who gestures with her head. Can he tell them his job is taking brides to the altar?

Amara answers for him: 'He's a journalist,' she says in French.

The young man in the long coat, now joined by a boy in a red beret with a red scarf round his neck, gives them a puzzled look.

'You are Italian?'

'Yes.'

'What are you doing here?'

Amara turns to Hans. She doesn't understand.

'Will she write that we are counter-revolutionaries?'

'She will tell what she has seen. That everyone is out in the streets, workers and students, housewives and employees. She will write that there's a festive atmosphere that does the heart good.'

The young man in the long coat gives them a slap on the back and lets them pass. In front of the Corvin cinema there's a crush of people. People on the steps, in the entrance and in the foyer, pushing, muttering and chattering.

They join the queue. Hans lights a cigarette. Some women come out with bread batons under their arms.

'Is there any milk?'

'Yes, but I don't know for how much longer. It's a long queue.'

A woman with a small baby slung on her back appears. People move to let her pass. A short sturdy man is singing in a low voice 'Que sera sera ...' Doris Day's song broadcast by a radio station and immediately copied by other improvised radio stations. None of these people can have seen the film in which a mother uses that very song to save her son! But everyone knows what's involved. The Hitchcock film has become an unexpected symbol of resistance. Someone else launches into Que sera sera ... and a dissonant little chorus is born. A woman weeps. A man caresses her head. 'They say the Russians are leaving.' 'But can you believe they'll let go as easily as that?' 'I saw them heading north with my own eyes.' 'That's true, I saw it too.' 'No, you fool. They're just withdrawing to their base at Tököl. They won't let anyone near there. They say Suslov and Mikoyan have slipped in secretly by air to check the situation on behalf of Khruschchev.' 'But we have the Nagy government, which is what the absolute majority of the Hungarian people want. I'd like to see what they can do against a government legitimised by the people.' 'Don't push, you idiot!' 'Let's hope they won't run out of bread!' 'Stop pushing, you fucker!'

An hour has already passed and they have only advanced a few steps towards the inside of the cinema. Now it's raining harder. People are protecting their heads with newspapers. Everyone is pushing towards the sheltering roof of the cinema. Two children of about eight pass in the street in ankle-length military raincoats. They are proudly holding Hungarian flags in their hands. Behind them the crowd is moving slowly. A group of workers are in a hurry to reach the parliament with a petition from a bus factory at Borsod. They make no effort to shelter from the rain. A few have caps; the rest nothing, their wet hair glued to their brows and necks.

An hour later they are still outside the cinema. By now it's dark. Hans has finished his cigarettes. Their feet are beginning to freeze; they are tired of standing in the cold.

'Amara, you go home. I'll wait. No point in us both staying here.'

'The queue's moving more quickly now.'

It's true. Now one knows why, but people have begun to come out more quickly. And no more are arriving to add to the crush. Finlly Amara and Hans manage to get into the auditorium, which smells strongly of wet shoes and fresh bread. When they reach the place of distribution the smell is still there, fragrant and inviting, but there is no bread left. A man with his machine gun over his shoulder makes a desolate gesture. He offers them a bag of flour and a tin of Romanian condensed milk. There is nothing else left.

All they can do now is go home. With the flour and the milk under their arms.

Outside the rain has become heavier and more aggressive, with icy blasts of wind. Amara and Hans press on close to the walls, making the most of the projecting roofs. Many of the street lamps have been broken. It isn't easy to see. After a bit they realise they are lost. What to do? Hans asks the way from a small boy passing on a bicycle, who brakes abruptly. He looks pityingly at them, and indicates they must retrace their steps to find Magdolna.

Frozen, they rapidly go back they way they've come. Suddenly they are in front of a lighted window, with a brown notice stuck on it saying CAFÉ.

'Shall we go in?' says Hans. 'They might have something hot.'

Amara follows him through a revolving door and down a dark corridor until a double door with a lining admits them to an absurd interior: inside a sort of alcove dug out of the wall, surrounded by red candles, a woman with a head piled with ash-blonde hair and a mouth painted in the shape of a heart is sitting singing and playing at an upright piano. The room is empty. The woman smiles at the new arrivals from under her towering hair. She has two gold front teeth, and a big white bosom wobbling inside a dress of evanescent lace. A vision from another age.

Amara and Hans sit down in two comfortable armchairs uphostered in red velvet. In front of them is a little round table with a linen cloth.

'Where on earth have we come to?' whispers Hans.

'We've made a leap in time. Nothing happened in Budapest today.'

Meanwhile an elderly waiter appears. It is obvious from the extremely cautious way he moves his feet and rolls his peering eyes that he can't see very well. His tailcoat is threadbare and dirty. These people are like extras in a very poor film projecting images of a bygone age in an empty cinema.

'What can I bring you?'

'Something hot, please.'

'A punch?'

'Have you no hot coffee? Perhaps with a little milk?'

'Coffee's off, sir. But we do have tea.'

'That Chinese stuff with rolled-up leaves? No thanks.' Amara laughs and Hans laughs with her.

'It's Russian tea, aromatic,' protests the waiter.

'No, thanks,' says Hans, looking at him to gauge any reaction. But the other doesn't bat an eyelid.

'Please bring the punch.'

'And for madame?'

'She will have punch too.'

The waiter moves away, walking with care. Now the woman at the piano starts singing again and surprises them. '*Que sera sera, Whatever will be will be, The future's not ours to see, Que sera sera ...*'

'Doris Day's song.'

'Incredible.'

But there is something provocative in that song. Something passionate in the shrill voice of this woman past her first youth, with her gold-toothed smile, ash-blonde hair marked by the curling iron, and gentle, languid heavily made-up eyes.

'Well, Amara, what now?'

'In what sense?'

'No, I mean, we've stopped in Budapest for me to say hello to my father and his violinist friend and been caught up in something unexpected and magnificent. I'm happy about that. But what about our plan to go to Poland and check those new lists of deported people? I'm afraid we're going to have to go back to Vienna.'

'I've written two articles but I can't get through to the paper on the phone.'

'They'll put them on the front page!'

'I have to dictate them first.'

'You've pulled off a real scoop.'

'I hope they've got some good photos.'

'We ought to go back to Béke and ask. That's where all the journalists are. They'll know about sending articles and photos.'

'Yes, we must really go there …'

'Then we'll also be able to see the fat man with the permits again.'

'And pay him eight hundred forints each?'

'How can we ever find sixteen hundred forints!'

'I could sell the amber necklace my mother left me.'

'I doubt you'd get sixteen hundred for that.'

'I've got a gold ring too.'

'We'll never make it.'

'We can try offering them to the bald man.'

'I bet you haven't been thinking so much about Emanuele Orenstein for the last day or two.'

'I dream of him at night. But by day I've had other things to think about, it's true.'

'Is he always up in the tree when you dream of him?'

'Yes.'

'Always in the cherry tree asking you to climb up and join him?'

'More or less.'

'You should get down from that tree, Amara.'

'Why?'

'Because it's down here on the ground that life happens, not up in trees with an invisible boy who makes too many claims on his status as a ghost.'

'We did come to an agreement, Hans.'

'I know, and I'll stick to it. But what would you like to do now?'

'I'm worried about Horvath and his fever. We haven't even found any aspirin. Let's go back home.'

'OK.'

44

There's no one at home. Not even the feverish Horvath. But the door is locked and nothing has been disturbed. A note must have been left somewhere. In the kitchen perhaps? Or the bathroom? But no matter how hard they search, they find nothing written. Hans lifts the phone, but it is silent. All they can do is wait. Amara, just for something to do, empties the flour onto the kitchen table and starts mixing it with a little water. She has no yeast but never mind, it will be unleavened bread but no less nourishing for that.

Meanwhile Hans has gone to turn on the radio. It takes a little while for the old Orion to warm up. Then the croaks and cracks and whistles begin.

'It's like being in a fish-and-chip shop.'

Finally, amid the great noise of spluttering frying pans, an excited male voice, distorted and intermittent, emerges from the background speaking French: 'The Cairo aerodrome at Abu Ghilla has been bombed by planes of RAF Bomber Command, taking off in a constant stream from the British aircraft-carriers Eagle, Albion and Bulwark. Also from the French carriers Lafayette and Arromanches. In reply Nasser has sunk forty ships in the Suez Canal. The Israelis have invaded the Gaza Strip and the Sinai Peninsula, moving their troops ever nearer to the Canal. The USSR is threatening to intervene on the side of Egypt to defend its own rights. Colonel Nasser has warned that he will send his warplanes over London and Paris if the blitz on Egypt continues.'

A key can be heard in the lock. Tadeusz enters wrapped like a sausage in his long padded coat. He takes off his beret and throws it on the floor.

'What's going on?'

'Horvath has pneumonia. We've left him at the hospital. They're out of penicillin, though they're expecting more supplies.'

'And Ferenc?'

'He's stayed with him.'

'Let's go and see him.'

'I must finish the bread.'

'All right, we'll go. You come and join us later.'

'Where is the hospital?'

'On Baross utca. You can't miss it, go straight towards the river nearly as far as Kalvin Square, then turn into Maria utca and you'll find it.'

Tadeusz and Hans go out leaving the door open. The French radio station transmitting from goodness knows where is now describing the antecedents of the Suez war. Amara listens as she kneads the flour.

'The Suez Canal was opened in 1869, financed by France and the government of Egypt. In 1875 the British government bought Egypt's share, ceding partial control of the Canal in exchange. In 1882, during a foreign invasion of Egypt, the United Kingdom assumed de facto control of the Canal. Clearly, the Canal has always had great strategic importance as the link between Great Britain and her empire in India, as became clear during both world wars. During the first war it was closed to all ships not belonging to allies of the French and British. During the second it was fiercely defended during the North Africa campaign. In 1948 the founding of the State of Israel was immediately followed by an Arab-Israeli conflict that established the independence of Israel.'

The voice is suddenly swallowed up in incomprehensible gurgles. From the street the sound of machine gun and rifles can be heard. Amara, hands covered in soft sticky dough, goes to the window. She sees a shocking sight: a bus stops in the middle of the road with its step backwards, lifeless. Curiosity gets the better of her fear. Softly the cannon does not fire. She takes an instinctive step backwards, life. Curiosity gets the better of her fear. Softly approaching the window again, she sees the cannon has swung round and is now trained on the windows of the building on the opposite side of the road. But still it does not fire. It seems to be trying to find a target to shoot at. What should she do? Run down the stairs and escape through the yard or wait, hiding under the part of the wall that carries the room's supporting beam? Ten minutes pass, a quarter of an hour. Nothing. Ever so slowly, Amara goes back to look out of the window. Now the street is

— 249 —

empty. The tank has disappeared. She draws a sigh of relief. Turning back to the table, she finds the flour has hardened and cracked. Flour of the worst quality, she tells herself cleaning her encrusted fingers. Adding a little warm water, she begins kneading again. Dreaming over the housework, as Luca put it. Is that all she's capable of? She should be at the Béke trying to send off her reports. Instead here she is making bread for her travelling companions.

Emanuele comes powerfully back into her mind. Where can he be now? Why has she stopped trying to find him? But she hasn't stopped trying to find him, she says in her own defence; she has been pinned down in this foreign city by an extraordinary situation she could never have foreseen or imagined possible. But why is she not doing everything possible to get to Poland, to the camp at Auschwitz, where he must have been interned? She has already accepted Hans's suggestion that they should go back to Vienna. Is not that a journey? She remembers the final words in the black exercise book someone posted to her after the war.

Now I must get ready because tomorrow they're certain to come for everyone who lives in this building. I'll hide this notebook in the hole in the wall. In the hope, God help me, that the building doesn't collapse, and that someone finds it. The last people to leave have all been headed for Auschwitz. It seems there's not even room for another fly at Chełmno. Whereas at Auschwitz they're putting up new buildings. That's what Max said. Goodbye, Amara. I send you a last kiss. Your Emanuele.

Meanwhile the radio has ... her surprise ... come a hymn of freedom. voice of Doris Day singing whatever surprise. ... become a hymn of freedom. Que sera sera, Whatever will be, will be, the future's not ours to see, Que sera sera ... A song whose words suggest an obscure fatalism, but which in fact with its music arouses a sort of communal enthusiasm inspiring resistance. In the film freedom is achieved through the courage of a mother who has known how to investigate, discover and be patient. Like Hungary?

She tries to remember Emanuele's kiss. Thin and slightly sweaty lips and fragrant breath. The nostalgia of those kisses takes her breath away.

She tries to hear his voice again, but her ears cannot take in

— 250 —

anything except sounds of the present: shots in the street, the squeaking of a cart, a horse's hoofs on the flagstones, and the voice on the radio which has returned to set out arguments in support of the Egyptians against the British and French who today are bombarding Egypt and distracting attention from little Hungary's appeal for help in asserting her independence.

She closes her eyes, searching her memory for that face she loved so much. The lock of hair that constantly fell across his brow. Those nut-coloured eyes so deep and serious even when they laughed. Those arms so powerful when he clung to branches, those broad hands reaching out their long fingers towards her. Come on, climb! But it is her own voice saying the words. His image eludes her and cannot speak. Her head is an empty room echoing with sinister sounds.

The key turns in the door. Hans is out of breath. He has run up the stairs two at a time.

'How's Horvath?'

'Better. He'll be fine in a few days. They found some penicillin. Finished kneading the bread?'

'I've put it in the oven.'

'How have you been getting on here all on your own?'

'I was terrified to see a tank pointing its gun straight at our window. But then it slowly turned to face the other way and eventually disappeared.'

'The Russian soldiers are leaving,' breaks in a voice from the radio, trying to sound confident but with something tragically interrogative about it. So much so that Hans looks at the ancient Orion as if to say: explain yourself properly, my boy!

'They're vacating their base at Tököl,' the voice continues. 'We've won! We've won! Everyone out into Parliament Square!

'The Nagy government has announced that we are entering a thorough process of reorganisation. The power of the police has passed from the ÁVH to the National Guards. Parliament is already full of new parties. The people's representatives are negotiating with the Soviets the withdrawal of all their soldiers and tanks from Hungarian soil. Kádár and Nagy are united and hurrying things forward. The Soviets seem to be in agreement. We have sent a delegation to the United Nations asking them to accept our request for neutral status.'

'They really do seem to be leaving,' comments Hans after translating the young man's agitated words. 'Negotiations have reached a good point. Hungary is going to be neutral, do you realise that? She will leave the Warsaw Pact. She'll have her own autonomous parliament. It seems incredible that the Russians have accepted this. But it really does seem to be so. Perhaps Khrushchev really does represent a new trend in politics. Or, to be more sarcastic, he must be asking the opinion of his allies.'

Hans is sitting astride the chair while she looks into the oven. The bread is beginning to brown, but not rising.

'I've never before made bread without yeast. Who knows how it'll turn out.'

'Unleavened bread.'

'Yes.'

'With your bare arms and rolled-up sleeves, and your floury hands grasping a knife, you remind me of Judith in the Old Testament, ready to cut off the head of the infidel leader to save her own people.'

'I'm not interested in cutting off heads, I'd rather fasten them in place. The knife is for slicing the last onion in the house. Let's hope Tadeusz will bring us something we can eat.'

The door opens and it is indeed Tadeusz that comes in. His shoes are muddy and his face looks tired.

Behind him is Ferenc, violin-case in hand.

'Been playing at the hospital?'

'I keep weapons in it. And a pistol they gave me at the Corvin. Even if I've never used it. I don't think I'd even know how to use it. But today there's something else. Two apples I pinched at the hospital.'

'You've been stealing food from the sick!'

'They were next to a dead man.'

'I wish you hadn't said that.'

'But the apples aren't dead. Look how beautiful they are! They look as if they've been painted, they're so red and shiny.'

'Maybe they're fake ...'

'He was lying there with his mouth open and his eyes closed. I don't know what he died of. The apples were on his bedside locker.'

'And you took them.'

'I don't think the dead need apples.'

'Bilateral negotiations are continuing,' says the radio, and they all crowd round to listen.

'The Minister of Defence, General Maléter, is negotiating with the Soviets the waithdrawal of all their troops from this country, whether permanently stationed here or not. The delegation for the United Nations left this morning. Prime Minister Nagy has confirmed the exit of Hungary from the Warsaw Pact.'

Amara pulls the bread out of the oven. It resembles nothing so much as a flat, dry pizza. But it's hot and smells of spices.

'Did you put in any cinnamon?'

'I found a little at the bottom of a jar.'

'It's like a cake,'

The four sit down round the only table. Two sit on the chairs and the other two on the bench Amara sleeps on at night. On the table is the flat bread perfumed with cinnamon straight from the oven, a ratatouille of potatoes and onion, and some slightly rusty tap water. They tuck in with gusto.

45

The windows of the hospital are broken, patched with cardboard clumsily stuck down at the corners with sticking plaster. The building is crowded with beds to trip over: along the disintegrating floors of the corridors, in the waiting rooms. In the wards twenty patients are crammed into a space that would normally hold three.

Horvath is stretched out, his long feet with their pale blue veins sticking out from under a too-short cover. His eyes are bluer than usual, his smile animated.

Amara sits down on the bed and takes his hand. It is still very hot; the fever is still on him.

'I'm perfectly well, but these shits won't let me go.'

Amara squeezes his burning hand. It's not true that he's perfectly well. But the fever seems to be over-exciting him in a way that causes him constantly to move his feet, grimace, laugh meaninglessly and roll his eyes.

'Last night three people died in here. They no longer even put up screens. They lift the dead by the arms and feet and carry them away. No idea where. The morgue I suppose. Maybe they cover them with lime, like with those who die in the street. D'you remember that terribly young soldier with a hole in his forehead and his face masked by white lead as if he was about to make an entry on the stage? I'm sure he died without feeling anything. Better so. Must have been sixteen years old. Got out of a tank to escape being burned alive and they shot him instantly. It must have been the man with the wooden leg.'

'What's his name?'

'Said to be an infallible marksman. Never misses. But that soldier was a child. Maybe they'd taken him from one of their subject nations: Ukraine, Estonia, Armenia. They must have said: put on this uniform, take this rifle, get in and come with us. And he obeyed. Without knowing it he'd been thrust into a tank to go and kill the boys of a subject nation just like his own. He can have had no idea that they would throw a can of petrol to set fire to the tank, forcing him to get out to avoid being burned alive, and that he would be shot by an infallible marksman like the man with the wooden leg. But what's his name?'

'János Mesz.'

'You remember everything, Tadeusz.'

'It's not a big city. Lots of us know each other.'

'Now please go because we must apply medication,' says a nurse in a white coat stained with blood. Two doctors with masks over their mouths approach the bed of a boy who has had both legs amputated.

Amara, Hans and Tadeusz go out into the corridor but find themselves crushed between one bed and the next, in the midst of a coming and going of nurses and volunteers carrying pans of urine, syringes dancing on tin trays and small dishes of soup for anyone who can eat.

The boy with the amputated legs cries out when they touch his raw flesh. Then he quietens down, facing his medication with courage. Amara hears the nurse say, 'Bravo Pál, bravo Pál, just a minute more, just one minute, then we'll leave you in peace.'

'But will I be able to walk?'

'Of course you will, with crutches,' answers the girl frankly, before going on to another bed containing an old man at the point of death.

'We've finished now. You can come back in,' says the nurse, carrying away a bundle of dirty dressings.

The three come close to Horvath's bed. He is so pale his blood seems to be no longer circulating. He's clearly doing everything he can not to cough. He swallows. Jerks. Presses his throat with his hand. Then suddenly loses control and the cough shakes his chest, shoulders, neck and head.

Amara again takes his hand in both of hers. He is not so fiercely hot any more. Perhaps his temperature is going down following his injection. He seems calmer. They don't know what to say to one another. Hans is standing by the window. Tadeusz is leaning on the bars of the bed as if to rest his tired legs. Amara looks round. The old man who just now was in his death throes has stopped breathing. The boy with the amputated legs is moaning softly. Tears are drying round his eyes and on his round cheeks.

Horvath starts coughing again. Amara bends over him, trying to reassure him that he'll soon be well again and be able to leave this horrible overcrowded place, that they'll come and fetch him as soon as his fever is gone.

'Have you been writing about what's happening in Budapest?'

'Yes, but I can't reach Italy by phone.'

'Did you know the *Paris Match* photographer was fatally wounded in the street? The nurses told me, you must write that.'

'How can I?'

'Send it all by telegram.'

'A telegram several pages long? How much would that cost?'

'Never mind the cost; it would be worth it, wouldn't it? People need to know what's happening here.'

'We have to go, it's getting late,' says Hans, coming back to Horvath and stroking his head. 'We'll meet again tomorrow.'

But Horvath doesn't want to let them go. He grabs Amara's arm and squeezes it between his terribly thin fingers. She sits down on his bed again. There are no chairs anywhere near, and standing up she can't speak privately to him.

'Amara,' he says, his mouth close to her ear, 'if I die, don't leave me here in the hospital. Take me away.'

'You're not dying, Horvath. We're all going to go back to Vienna. You have work to do with your books.'

'If I get better, fine, I'll come with you. But if I die I'd rather be burned in the street than left in some icy morgue and used for experiments.'

'What are you saying!'

'Do you promise me?'

'I promise you.'

'You know, my mother died of pneumonia too.'

'What was your mother like?'

'Very small and thin, but with a smile everyone liked. I can still remember her hair reaching down to her bony shoulders. She never grew up. Perhaps that's why she died young. She was a schoolgirl all her life, the sort you meet in the street with books under her arm. Always reading. She would burn the soup because she was buried in a novel, she would forget everything. Even me: once when I was five, she set me on a seat in a tram and started reading. When we reached our stop she got out with the book still under her nose, leaving me on the seat. I went round and round the tram route. Till finally it got dark and someone took me to the police. That's what my mother was like. And I've inherited a bit of her absent-mindedness.'

'You are extremely absent-minded, Horvath. But come to that, so am I.'

Horvath laughs for them both. Now he is no longer grasping her arm with tense, spasmodic fingers, but caressing the back of her hand.

'You know, I loved my mother and her hair so much I've never been able to love any other woman.'

'A bit like me with Emanuele,' says Amara, wanting to draw away from his rough, feverish hand. But out of kindness, she doesn't.

'Tell me more about your mother,' she says.

'She never ate much. So little, in fact, that my father would say: remember you're not a little bird, you're a woman. And she would laugh. She just wasn't hungry. But I knew if there were any pickled gherkins in the house they would vanish in a flash. She had a passion for gherkins in vinegar. They weren't often to be seen in our house, they were too expensive. But occasionally someone would give us a jar. And she would eat the lot. 'You haven't left even one for me,' my father would grumble. And she would shake her hair, mortified. I myself didn't like pickled gherkins at all. Once for her birthday I bought her a kilo of them from a very fashionable delicatessen in the city centre. I wrapped them and tied the packet with a red bow. Do you know, that evening she ate them all, every single one. Of course she was ill in the night. She had stomach pains and threw up all the gherkins. My father made her a camomile tisane. Then she fell asleep with her head on his shoulder, on the sofa. He didn't dare move for fear of waking her. I think they loved each other very much. Or perhaps not. But it seemed like it to me. When my mother died my father wasn't there. She was in hospital with pneumonia and asked for her husband but he was far away at work and didn't think her illness was serious enough for him to come back. Then, only a year after she died my father married again, a stupid woman full of airs I could never stand.'

Horvath would have liked to say more, but the nurse interrupts them because it's time for supper. Broth made from a cube with a little semolina in it. Which the patients consume avidly. They aren't given so much as a slice of bread. Bread is for the healthy, for those who have to shoot and organise, to run from one end of the city to the other.

Meanwhile the boy with amputated legs has died from loss of blood. They couldn't stop the bleeding. It is still dripping through the mattress forming a pool that is growing darker and darker. Amara tries not to look at the boy, who has died in silence, but with his face contracted by the strain of fighting the pain. His neck muscles are tense cords and his closed fists lie abandoned by his sides.

Horvath has swallowed his soup. He asks if there's anything else. But that's all the supper the hospital can allow the sick.

Time to go. Soon they'll be closing the doors. Even if the closing is merely symbolic because at all hours of the night ambulances arrive, and even tricycles like the one she saw in Corvin Lane, unloading the more or less severely wounded.

'I really am hungry,' says Horvath in her ear when she bends down to kiss him goodnight.

'Tomorrow I'll bring you some bread I've made myself. It's a bit flat, but edible even so.'

'Will you bring me a little sugar too? Here they give us tea without sugar.'

'If I can find any.'

'I'm afraid you won't. In the whole of Budapest there's no more than a teaspoonful of the stuff. In my opinion the Russkies are trying to make the point that without them we're screwed.'

At that moment the door opens and two elderly women come in dragging by the arms a Russian soldier with his uniform in rags. Blood is draining from his nose and mouth. His head is thrown back. His hair is short and blond like ears of corn and his head is that of a child.

'What's this one doing here,' shouts the nurse György, known to all for his rough manners, 'we haven't enough room for our own people. Take him back where you found him!'

'But he's only a little boy! He needs help!'

'I'll never treat a Soviet soldier. Just let him die.'

'Don't be such a swine, György. Have pity!' says one of the

women, drying hands wet with blood on the corners of the big squared scarf that covers her head.

'Do they have any pity for us when they go shooting in our houses? Do they have pity when they occupy our streets with their damned tanks?'

'It's not his fault! He's only a child and God knows where he comes from!'

'Just leave him there and I'll have a look in a minute.'

46

Next morning Horvath unexpectedly returns to the flat. Amara opens the door and sees him before her. The same ankle-length trousers, the same dark-blue beret, the same sparse white hair over neck and shoulders.

'But you have to be cured then!'

'They needed the bed. Sent me away.'

'We'll look after you. Considering what they gave you …'

'I'm sorry. But I really didn't know where to go.'

Tadeusz teases him, affectionately draping the blanket round his shoulders and making him a cup of dark and tasteless Chinese tea. Ferenc has been lucky enough to find half a kilo of sugar.

'Please put in plenty.'

'How many spoonfuls – two, three, four?'

'Ten. I've seen too many people die in the last few days. Let me console myself with a little sugar, I seem to have cemeteries for eyes.'

Although old Tadeusz says nothing and is as polite as ever, Amara feels communal life is getting strenuous for the two owners of the flat. It is getting more difficult daily to find enough food for everyone. The house is always messy and dirty. It's impossible to find wood for the stove. Coal is expensive and it's getting colder. Ferenc has had the idea of stopping the draughts pouring in through the rickety old windows by forcing rolls of cotton wool into the cracks. Effective, but it means you can't open the windows. The result is a stuffy stagnant smell that hits you when you come in from outside. How can five people live in such a tiny space?

Amara discusses it with Hans who agrees they should leave. But how can they without permits?

'How about trying again with that bald man at the Béke hotel?'

'Eight hundred forints for a permit is crazy. Do you know how much a worker earns in a month? Four or five hundred. And in any case we haven't the money.'

'Couldn't your father lend it to us?'

'He's already helped me so often in the past. I don't want to exploit him. And then everyone's afraid of the future. What's going to happen? No one can say. Anyone with a little money or a bit of gold keeps tight hold of it.'

'We'll find a way. Meantime I must try and get some articles to my paper.'

'All right, let's go.'

They run down the stairs two at a time. Outside the air is freezing, but there is an infectious sense of excitement. People are dancing round improvised fires in the middle of the streets. Men and women are out for a walk, even at night, smoking and chattering but without ever putting down rifle or machine gun or or taking off the bandoliers slung round their shoulders. Not wanting to appear too menacing they wear a flower in their hats or a coloured scarf round their necks. Everyone says the Soviet tanks are pulling back. In fact fewer and fewer are to be seen around. There is widespread belief in the delegation that has left for the United Nations. Surely they won't be able to resist the will of an entire nation that has demonstrated with so many sacrifices its new and irresistible longing for freedom.

At the Béke hotel there is no one to be seen. Where have the few foreign journalists who live there gone? Are they all out trying to understand what is happening? The fat bald man can't be found. Though three waitresses dressed in black with immaculate aprons are going about with trays loaded with glasses and plates. But the glasses and plates are empty.

Amara asks if the telephones are working. The sulky receptionist advises her to go down to the basement where the telephone girls are. Hans and Amara go downstairs. In a small badly lit room three girls are sitting at a switchboard, their temples gripped by steel-sprung headphones, pushing and pulling plugs with worn wires. Perhaps lines to the outside world are working again.

One of the telephonists signs to them to wait. Amara and Hans sit down on a bench covered by a velvet cloth with a gilded fringe. Inside the cubicles, each marked by an enormous silver letter B, people can be seen with receivers that are obviously not working properly.

They go on waiting. Every so often someone emerges from a

cubicle shaking his head. The telephone girls are agitated, angrily pulling out plugs, talking in bursts and shouting into microphones that show no sign of life.

'I'm going for a little walk,' says Hans, getting to his feet. 'Maybe I'll run into the bald man. You stay and wait for a free cubicle and a line to Florence. Let's hope we get through before one o'clock.'

He moves away. Amara picks up her articles to check though them before dictating. So difficult to give life to what one has seen! To go from living to writing needs a leap which may look short and easy from a distance, but seen close up is revealed as an almost impassable gully with steep smooth sides. Yet the gap must be bridged. There is no knowing if one will reach the other side alive or dead. If she could only manage to tell just a little of what is happening in this country, if she could convey the expectation, the hopes, the fears, the sacrifices, the joys of these days of liberation from a blind and violent regime, she would be happy. But will she ever be able to do it?

A bell rings repeatedly. Rapid voices. An imperious gesture, and it's her turn. She runs to cubicle 4. She grasps the receiver. At the other end of the line there is no call-corder but a metallic voice that repeats: 'Hello, Italy? Italy?'

'Hello? I'm speaking from Budapest, who's there?' But the voice at the other end disappears. Now she can only hear the voice of the operator: 'Hello, Italy? Italy?'

'Florence, speak now!'

'I'm here, but I can't hear anyone at the other end. Nobody.'

'Speak now!'

A storm of whistles hits her ear, then what sounds like a toad singing, nothing intelligible, then more crackles and prolonged whistles.

'No line to Italy, no line to Florence, sorry Miss Sironi, maybe tomorrow.'

Amara puts her articles, handwritten in a school exercise book, back into her shoulder bag and goes back up the stairs to the foyer. No sign of Hans. But now more people can be seen going in and out through the revolving door. She sits down in a wide, comfortable armchair with huge arms covered in blue velvet. And waits.

In front of her two English people are murmuring in low voices as they study a map spread out on the table before them. A woman and a man of medium height: he is fair-haired and stocky, wearing a black leather jacket; she is slim, indeed very thin, a brunette wrapped in a purple raincoat. They are excited and unaware that someone is watching them curiously.

'Have you heard anything new?' asks Amara timidly, plucking up courage.

The two look up, annoyed at the interruption but polite and willing to reply.

'Are you a journalist too?'

'Trying to be.'

'Did you manage to get through on the phone?'

'No.'

'Nor did we.'

'Any news?' insists Amara.

'Nothing much. But there are rumours of a massive movement of Soviet tanks from the north.'

'The usual tanks stationed in Hungary?'

'Apparently something different, but nothing is certain.'

The two turn back to their map, forgetting Amara who opens her exercise book to scribble down another article to send to Florence. She must try a telegram, as Horvath said, but she needs Hans for the Hungarian language.

And here he is, quick and confident as always, the gazelles running across his chest. He has a small bag in his hand.

'Perecs?'

'No, sausages. Some for everyone.'

'And potatoes?'

'We'll try and find some.'

47

Tadeusz and Hans are always out looking for something to eat.
But also trying to find news of what's happening in and around the
city. Ferenc has started playing his violin again. Amara, without
anyone asking it of her, is staying close to old Horvath to look
after him and keep him company. Hans never goes out without
the rifle given him by the boys at the Corvin cinema. He probably
doesn't know how to fire it, but carries it all the same. 'I shan't try
unless the Russians come with their tanks,' he says firmly. Every
now and then Tadeusz and his son bring back a bread baton, a
couple of eggs, a tin of powdered milk or some aspirins.

Horvath has decided that in daytime he prefers the kitchen. He
lies stretched on Amara's camp bed reading, sleeping, chattering, listening to the radio. He is happy if she stays near him, and
together they bend over the table where she spreads rice to clean
it of little stones and mouse excrement, or to separate good dried
beans from mouldy ones, or to peel potatoes.

The old Orion seems to have calmed down. No more excited
voices crowding each other out, but announcements preceded by
specially chosen music: Mozart, Paganini, Scriabin and Bartók,
alternating with songs of the moment: *Lili Marlene*, *When the
saints go marching in*, *Egy mondat a zsdrnokagrol*.

'One senses a desire for peace in the country,' says Ferenc. 'Less
anarchy and more organisation, this is the order of the day and I'd
say that the Hungarians are adapting themseleves sensibly to it.
You can even see this in the distribution centres which are no longer
being run on a primitive private basis, but by the government which
is replacing the self-proclaimed revolutionary armed guards with
a proper corps of National Guards; haven't the rest of you noticed
that too? They're only boys, but they have a serious and responsible look about them. I've watched them mounting guard over the
most important institutions in the city: parliament, the Ministry

of Defence, the Post Office, the prisons. We should embrace them and thank them for their dedication, don't you think?'

Every now and then the old Orion brings a voice telling of new students' or workers' initiatives in and around Budapest. Horvath turns the radio up: 'We're gathered in the great hall. Plenty of seats but no one is sitting down. We are standing in front of the platform. The students all gathered here with their colourful clothes and books under their arms. Immediately afterwards the professors came in, rejoicing as if at a festival. Many had red, white and green rosettes on their jacket lapels. Dead comrades were remembered. Then those professors who had touched the hearts of the students stepped forward. The oldest, Professor Karely, spoke of slaves who submit for ages but finally explode, like Spartacus when he recognised the longing for liberty in so many thousands of men.'

'But he didn't say they all ended up crucified,' remarks Horvath sarcastically.

'Professor Erderly, in his turn, maintained that the Magyars have always been forced to submit to lords and masters, but have always fought tenaciously to get rid of them. Now we are showing ourselves equally couragious in rebuilding a sadly rundown country with no functioning economy, a country forced by its allied masters to concentrate everything on arms rather than the development of agriculture, and on heavy industry rather than on the services necessary to improve the condition of human life. But we are not interested in a policy of power. We want peace and neutrality …'

'They always repeat the same things,' remarks Horvath, 'but they are right. They are perfectly right. I too repeat the same things about my fever, about my pneumonia. A sick people repeats itself ad nauseam until it regains its health.'

Now a female voice recites in slow, soft cadences a poem by Nâzım Hikmet:

They were sad, my love
they were happy, full of hope
they were courageous and heroic
your words,
they were men.

Horvath loves poetry. You need only remember that his modest luggage contains two volumes of poetry, Rilke and Walt Whitman.

'Under Rákosi, that stuff would have landed you straight in prison,' remarks Ferenc, before withdrawing to play his violin.

Horvath is wearing some knee socks Hans found for him on a stall. They are well worn and faded, but warm. When the man with the gazelles brought them, wrapped in a piece of newspaper, Horvath jumped for joy. But then, when he opened the parcel and took a good look at them, it was obvious they were so threadbare on the heels as to be useless. Amara darned them for him with wool of a different colour, but what matter? – the important thing was to keep warm. Thanks to the bottomless contents of Ferenc's cupboard, which even contained needles of every possible size and several balls of wool.

'Will you tell me something about your Emanuele?' says Horvath suddenly, turning down the radio which was now playing nothing but trivial little marches.

'I've told you about him so often, Horvath, you must be bored with the subject.'

'We are here for him, Amara.'

'The real reason we're here is to see Hans's father and his violinist friend Ferenc.'

'In passing, on the way to Auschwitz. Remember?'

'Of course I remember.'

'I know, it's not our fault Budapest was struck by an earthquake the moment we arrived.'

'What d'you want to know?'

'Why you have loved him so much and kept this love alive for so many years.'

'I don't know what to tell you, Horvath. Why do we love someone? I don't know. And the more you love the less you know why. Have you never loved anyone?'

'Oh yes. But I've always been rejected. I've never known reciprocated love.'

'But you were a handsome boy. And you're still a handsome man, Horvath.'

'Don't be silly, Amara. I'm an old wreck.'

'I know some very ugly men who have been much loved. But why do you think your love was never returned?'

'I don't know. Maybe I was afraid. If a woman fell in love with me, I ran off.'

'So you were the one who didn't want reciprocated love.'

'It could be. I wanted something more every time. A more beautiful woman, or a more intelligent or more sensitive one. The one I had seemed dull and boring. I made love to her for a few months, then got bored.'

'A sort of Don Giovanni, then?'

'I never found a woman I was completely happy with. As soon as I got to know her better, my arms dropped to my sides.'

'So you never fell in love.'

'Yes, but only for a month, or at most two. I had loves that struck me like lightning. That warmed my heart. Then they came to an end, but the warmth stayed with me. Maybe that's how it is. I like living in the warmth of memory. The actual person gets in the way of my dedicating myself to that warmth. You and I probably resemble one another more than you think, Amara. You too live on memories and your heart is still warm from a fire that died years ago. Like the stars we can still see in the sky even though they exploded and expired millennia ago. It's the light that travels on. And we live in that light.'

'Yes, perhaps we are alike, Horvath.'

'That's why I asked you to tell me about him.'

'Would you like me to read you his letters?'

'You've already read them to me many times. And I don't want to hear about the ghetto at Łódź and people dying of hunger. Tell me something about Rifredi and life when you were children.'

'One morning we went out together with our bicycles. We went up into the hills. Took a narrow country road. And pedalled energetically up slopes covered with rocks. The Florence countryside was so beautiful. There were broad beans in flower, and potatoes with rich green leaves, in among hundreds of poppies of an unbelievable red. And on we went, flying ahead on those bicycles, scattering the stones, hurling ourselves into the valleys, climbing the hills beyond, it was a huge joy. Suddenly, round a curve, we came on an enormous cow. Calm and extremely beautiful, and with no intention of moving. Our brakes, you know, weren't very effective. I threw myself into the beans to the right and Emanuele into the dried-up bed of a sort of stream to the left. The cow raised her head and looked at us in surprise. We got up all covered with scratches and bumps. Emanuele had hurt his thigh and torn the left shoulder of his shirt. I had taken the skin off both my knees which were bleeding badly, and hurt my temple; I had ridden slap into a large sharp rock. But do you know what Emanuele did instead of swearing at the cow? He sat down beside me and licked the wound on my forehead, saying saliva was a disinfectant. I closed my eyes and left him to it. His tongue was so large and rough that I convinced myself it was the cow. Even today I think I must have really been stunned and unaware of the cow coming up to me and licking the gash on my forehead, as dogs sometimes do when they have a wound.'

'Was it Emanuele or the cow?'

'I don't know. It could have been him.'

'Did you make love?'

'We never did, Horvath. We were too young. And also very prudish and easily embarrassed. We thought sexual love was something for grown-ups.'

'And even now you still live in the memory of that cow's tongue on the wound on your forehead. Amara, frankly, I think you're in a worse state than I am.'

Amara and Horvath laugh together. At that moment the man with the gazelles comes in, carrying his father, like Anchises, on his back.

'What's happened?'

'He got hit by a bullet in his side.'

Hans lays his father down on Amara's camp bed in the kitchen and starts taking off his sweater. Under that he finds another pullover, and under that yet another.

'But how many pullovers are you wearing, Father?'

Tadeusz laughs. Hans laughs too. Ferenc has noticed nothing. He goes on playing the violin shut up in the bedroom. Amara bundles up the pullovers for the wash. On Tadeusz's white skin is a hole with a black border. No blood. But there is something sinister about that hole in his flesh.

'It's nothing. Could you get some alcohol please, Amara, it's in Ferenc's cupboard.'

At that moment Ferenc comes into the room with his violin on his arm. He sees the wound and throws himself onto Tadeusz, embracing him as if he were dying.

'It's nothing, Ferenc, just a bullet that needs to be removed.'

'We'll get you to the hospital.'

'Wait. Call János. Let's try him before going near that hell of a hospital.'

48

Tadeusz's doctor friend, János Szabó, comes. He tries to extract the bullet, but fails. It seems to have penetrated deeply. 'We'll need more instruments to get that out,' says Szabó. 'But we'll try again.' An X-ray would be useful, but at the moment the radiography machines in the hospitals aren't working. He disinfects the wound and takes the patient's temperature, giving him an injection of penicillin, the last that he has. If the bullet stays where it is, Tadeusz will heal in a few days, the doctor says.

Hans has made him some of that Chinese tea that tastes like straw. Amara has scraped the sugar jar to sweeten it. The doctor appreciates the hot drink, knowing how hard it is to find provisions in these days of readjustment. This is the word everyone is using, 'the readjustment of the country'. People are talking about it everywhere. The shops are still shut, but they are 'readjusting' before opening again to the public. The schools are closed, to readjust their windows and clean their classrooms of the plaster debris caused by the aggression of the Russian tanks stationed in Hungary. Those same tanks that they have watched departing in line ahead, bound for the frontier. But there were not that many of them and only a few turned their guns on buildings. The Post Office has reopened even though its doors have been broken down and its windows have been replaced by pieces of cardboard glued in place. The national radio has 'readjusted' its machinery, has recalled its technicians and is now working and faithfully transmitting what is happening in the country, with one eye on the Nagy government which really is moving in the direction most Hungarians want.

Tadeusz's doctor friend János tells them that a few days ago he met an unusual procession of cars in the street. 'I looked into them. D'you know who was in the first car? Cardinal Mindszenty.'

The others look at him in surprise.

'Where was he going?'

'Have they released him from prison?'

'A brave dog,' remarks János. 'He was condemned in 1944 by the Nazis for hiding opponents of Hitler, remember? He never watched his tongue, that Christlike man; one day, I remember, he said on the radio that everyone knew what the T4 programme involved: it had forced the SS doctors to kill seven hundred thousand handicapped people, psychopaths, mongols, and the mad, both children and adults. That's what he said and nobody believed him. Then came the war and the post-war period. Do you think he had the least intention of controlling his awkward tongue? Once the Nazis were finished he started criticising the communists: he said in public that their elections were a fraud, a total fraud, that they wanted to gag the church and get rid of parish priests. They arrested him in 1948, as if to show that ... and packed him off like a parcel to the little village of Felsőpetény. But the funniest thing happened when a group of ÁVH officers went to fetch him and move him to secure accommodation. They were terrified he might be set free. Meanwhile a delegation from a revolutionary council arrived in the village with the same aim of taking the cardinal to secure accommodation. But that was not all. Immediately afterwards a third delegation arrived consisting of National Guard, commanded by Antal Pálinkás, also with the intention of making the cardinal safe. A hilarious situation, with some pulling the cardinal one way and some another. And he himself? He decided on the official group led by Major Antal Pálinkás, alias Pallavicini. As an Italian you should know that a branch of the Pallavicini family came to Budapest in 1700 and settled here. Did you know that?'

'No,' admits Amara, amused.

'Prince Antonio, born in Budapest, speaks the roughest urban dialect, can you believe it, he didn't even know where Italy was, he considered himself a Magyar, but like a real aristocrat he was ashamed of his princely name and so decided to call himself Antal Pálinkás, a distinctly proletarian name. A huge joke. But that name has brought him luck since, as a proletarian Magyar fighting the Soviets, he has been promoted to colonel by Nagy who sent him to rescue the cardinal, for which the Church will be eternally grateful to him.'

Dr János has a fine proud head, smooth thick brown hair that slips over his ears, light-blue eyes, and an impressive nose with a bump in the middle that lends him an air of strength and decisiveness. But his smile is that of a sad little boy.

The old Orion is now broadcasting Verdi's *Requiem* which explodes in the Wilkowsky kitchen with majestic power. The liberation of the cardinal brings in its wake vaguely religious music and even prayers, inconceivable up to a few days earlier.

'The political prisoners have been set free!' a cheerful voice announces breathlessly, 'the political prisoners have been set free!'

'Who knows how many will now pass themselves off as political prisoners,' remarks Dr Szabó sourly.

Amara asks him if he would like to stay to lunch. Ferenc has found a packet of pasta in his miraculous cupboard and Amara has offered to serve it according to a special recipe of her own. Difficult, because they have no oil or butter and only a little lard, no tinned tomatoes and only a few old peppers. Can you make sauce for spaghetti from just lard and peppers?

Dr Szabó decides to stay. Tempted by the spaghetti which reminds him of a journey to Italy many years ago. He was a child, he explains, and his mother, a pianist, forced him to sit long hours at the piano. Meanwhile he secretly spied on his father, a doctor. One day, without letting his mother see him, he followed his father to the hospital and saw him go down to the basement where dead bodies were kept. He climbed up on a low wall to be able to see through a small window and watched his father, sheathed in white with two pairs of green gloves, bending over the naked body of a boy and dissecting it. Instead of putting him off medicine for life, the sight of this lugubrious operation thrilled him, and the next day he firmly told his mother that he had no intention of being a pianist as she wanted, but would follow his father and be a doctor.

And so it happened. And he was satisfied, even if he suffered a good deal. In the war he'd had to care for hundreds of wounded men, watching them die before his eyes. Among other things he too had been hit, in the calf. He pulls up his mud-splashed trouser leg to show the friends an ugly scar cutting across the middle of his right leg. He smiles contentedly. And asks for another cigarette, but there aren't any more in the house.

'Then give me those dog-ends,' he says, eyeing an ashtray with a number of twisted stumps in it.

With his skilful hairy white hands he opens the cigarette ends, lays aside the lacerated paper and with the balls of his thumbs gathers together the remaining tobacco. Then he pulls a steel cigarette case from an internal jacket pocket, snaps it open and extracts some small white rectangles. He smooths one out, pours on the scorched tobacco, rolls it with consummate mastery and wraps it, finally closing the paper with a touch of his tongue.

'Done,' he says with satisfaction.

Hans reaches him a burning wax vesta. He draws in a good mouthful, half-closing his eyes, then passes the long dry cigarette to the others. Each in turn grasps the slender paper cylinder, luxuriously inhaling the acrid smoke. All except Amara who has never smoked. In fact, she thinks these miasmas in the tiny kitchen with its hermetically sealed windows will make her eyes weep. But what can she do?

The spaghetti is ready and everyone looks for somewhere to sit. Three find room on Amara's camp bed, two take a chair each and one makes do with the bathroom stool.

The spaghetti with lard and pepper sauce is excellent. The friends eat eagerly and happily. Ferenc has found a bottle of white wine in his miraculous cupboard. It has no labels and its colour, something between topaz and verdegris, is rather disquieting. But Hans pours it liberally; a dense wine with a strong flavour of sulphur.

'From the vineyards along the Tisza River, a Tokay that must be at least five years old.'

The table is cheerful, despite the bullet in Tadeusz's side, despite Horvath's cavernous cough, despite the uncertainties of the future. No more shooting is heard from the street. And the radio announces the good news that the schools will open again in a few days. The shops will be full of new stock. The delegation to the United Nations has been received with all the respect it deserves. Will Hungary's request for neutrality be accepted? The world is looking on. That is what everyone is saying.

'A little country like Hungary, who could ever have thought it! Hurling itself like David against Goliath,' says Tadeusz, knocking back a mouthful of that cold wine with its taste of resin.

'We've done it, all credit to this cussed population with its hard horns,' says Hans, drumming his fingertips on the table.

'It could never have happened in Stalin's time, I can tell you. He would have squashed us like lice. But now, after Khrushchev's speech to the Twentieth Congress, they've become more careful. They've drawn in their claws like cats when they want to be cuddled.' So says Dr János Szabó, using his fingers to help get his mouth round the spaghetti which is escaping in all directions, covering his hands and cheeks with grease.

'No doubt Khrushchev is still consulting his socialist friends. And Mao? Do you think he will find the words to ask him straight out: where is it written that one socialist country may attack another socialist country? And Tito? That wily fellow would never publicly approve of an act of repression, since everyone has been able to establish, even from the work of international photographers, that it's not a mere question of half a dozen fascists in the square, but of the whole Magyar people, headed by the very workers that all these people hold in such veneration? But Tito will intrigue in secret; I don't trust his tail, I don't trust his teeth, and I don't trust the claws he's learned to sharpen out of sight of those other nasty cats hunting for mice to swallow at a single gulp.'

'Don't forget, the workers and peasants are the angriest. How can they set themselves against people who hold them in the palm of their hands?'

'What about the writers and musicians, the film makers and painters?'

'No one gives a damn about them.'

'But there are others: general employees, housewives, doctors, nurses, teachers; haven't you seen them on the streets?'

'They can't possibly set themselves against everybody!'

'But I'm sure Tito will discourage that dwarfish Russian from taking despotic initiatives. He will have told him, "You've denounced Stalin for his authoritarian policies, and now you want to behave in the same way".'

'If you denounce the cynical policies of a tyrant, you can't yourself play the same game.'

'But even the French workers have gone on strike dozens of times in our support!'

'And even the Italians … well, some of the Italians, have taken our side.'

'Togliatti.'

'He's not on our side.'

'Togliatti always sides with the Communist Party of the Soviet Union.'

'Yet they've seen and heard what's happening. There are wonderful photographs.'

'The world wants peace. There has been too much war; now it's time for peace and peace there will be.'

'So you trust that scum?'

'Who d'you mean?'

'Who? Who? Those who've been holding us under water without letting us breathe for all these years.'

'Don't forget, they freed us from the Nazis.'

'How extraordinary it was to see them emerging from the mists one morning in 1945. Huge, creaking and powerful. They came to free a people brutalised by the Nazis. How we'd longed for them. They advanced with their red flags that we all trusted. Just imagine what a vision!'

'And now they're ready to crush us in the name of communism.'

'But what do we really want, that's the point?'

'We all want our voices to be heard, not just one voice, that seems clear to me.'

'The dictatorship of the proletariat, does anyone still believe in that?'

'Not me.'

'Nor me.'

'Well, then?'

'The single party. Do you believe in that?'

'I don't, no.'

'Nor me.'

'And the great leader whose portrait peers at you from every wall and whose statue stands in every square ... Do you believe in him?'

'Powerful leaders usually begin with enthusiasm and generosity, but end up as fools, often even mad, neurotic and suspicious.'

'Power corrupts, but absolute power corrupts absolutely ... who said that?'

'It must have been your Pascal.'

'No, no, not Pascal!'

'Was Stalin mad?'

'What can you expect of a man, who shoots his best generals at the height of a war? Who has his best friends tortured till they confess to being spies? Who has all his country's best doctors strangled because they have the temerity to protest about the neglect of the hospitals; you can't say such a man wasn't mad!'

'All dreams! You're all dreaming, dear friends, you've forgotten partition. They've divided the world: one part on this side, the other on that. We are on this side and cannot be on that side. Can't you see that neither the United Nations, nor the whole of America headed by the United States, can do anything to save us from the clutches of the Soviets?'

They all turn towards Dr Szabó, thinking that perhaps, after all, he is right. But may we not hope for once?

'And now, Tadeusz, let's have another look at your wound.'

Tadeusz lifts his sweater. The wound is still open. János takes a close look. He makes a grimace. He says he'll pass by tomorrow with more suitable instruments and they'll eject that damn bullet from the hole where it has hidden itself.

'Now get some sleep, we'll talk about it tomorrow. It's getting colder. The streets are going to freeze. Maybe it'll even snow a bit.'

Dr Szabó explains in his melodious voice that he likes snow because it refines everything. But of course it soon turns to slush and becomes slippery and sticks to things. Well, now he really is going. He says goodbye to everyone and thanks them for the delicious spaghetti. He advises Horvath to stay indoors. Goodnight, all. He moves towards the front door with slow steps. A last goodnight, a smile, and he's gone.

49

At five in the morning Amara wakes thinking, oh God, an earth-quake! Her camp bed is shaking, and so are the windows and the whole building. She gets up, terrified. Going towards the front door she runs into Hans, who is quickly pulling his sweater over his pyjamas.

'An earthquake?'

'No, tanks.'

'Tanks?'

'Look out of the window. But don't let yourself be seen. Turn off the light. Wake Horvath, wake Tadeusz. They're invading the city.'

From outside comes a dull continuous rumbling roar, as if an avalanche is falling on the streets of the centre. Even a suddenly broken dyke emptying tons of water and mud on the poor sleeping city would not produce a comparable sound, dull and terrible, making the pavements shake and windows rattle. From the window Amara sees a line of tanks advancing down Baross utca, their guns pointing straight up at windows on a level with their own.

Horvath is behind her, hair on end, struggling for breath, watching the street in astonishment. He daren't even cough. A moment later Ferenc comes too, his violin clutched to his chest and his eyes puffy with sleep and fear. Then Tadeusz, holding his side, pale and silent.

Hans runs to switch on the radio. 'Attention, attention. This is your Prime Minister, Imre Nagy. At dawn today the Soviet army launched an attack on the capital with the obvious aim of overturning the legal Hungarian democratic government. Our troops are fighting back, and the government is at its post. I want the Hungarian people and the whole world to know this.' A disturbing silence follows, as if the radio has been struck dumb. Hans twiddles the knob repeatedly but there is nothing else to be heard, no signals or voices or music. A minute later Nagy's desperate plea is repeated in French, English, Russian, Polish, Czech and German.

Outside it is still dark. The friends look at each other, disconsolate. What can they do? 'Stay indoors!' Now the radio is speaking again, but it is not clear whose voice they are hearing. 'Don't move. Don't shoot. Let's shed no blood!' The *Sabre Dance* follows. But only briefly; the music is interrupted by a solemn voice: 'This is Free Radio Kossuth. Don't surrender to the tanks. Try to set them on fire. A rag soaked in petrol thrown from your window will do. We must not surrender! We shall sell our bodies dear!' The sound of cannons firing can be heard in the background. The voice continues undaunted. 'A representative of the Union of Writers has just joined us, out of breath. He would like to read out an appeal just formulated by the Petőfi Circle: "To every writer, every scholar, every Academy and Scientific Society, and to the intellectuals of the whole world: there isn't a moment to lose. Today, 4 November, Soviet tanks have invaded the centre of Budapest. Tell the whole world that they are destroying us. Help Hungary!"'

'I have to go and see,' says Hans, heading for the door. Tadeusz grabs his elbow.

'You're not leaving here.'

'I must see what's happening, Father.'

'Isn't it enough for you that I've been hit?'

'By some damned ÁVH sniper.'

'Whoever it was, the bullet's still there.'

'Does it hurt a lot?'

'No, just a twinge.'

'Well, I want to have a look. I'll be back.'

'Please don't go!'

But Hans is obstinate, and once he gets something into his head it's not easy to stop him. Watching him go, Tadeusz sits down abruptly on a chair with a kind of sob. Amara knows he is more ill than he wants people to believe. She tries to get him to lie down on her camp bed. But no one wants to sit, let alone lie. Horvath is walking backwards and forwards with the usual blanket over his shoulders and his feet bare again even though Amara has carefully darned his stockings. Indomitable feet that can never be confined within ordinary shoes. Ferenc is holding his violin against his chest as if it were a child he must save. Tadeusz, at the window, is watching what is happening outside in the street.

The line of tanks is endless, their menacing cannons pointing upwards. Aimed at closed windows. Slow and sinister they advance, shaking the streets. Enormous blunt steel brutes, hermetically sealed, heading across town for the heart of the city.

A free radio voice shouts out their progress: 'They are advancing from Váci Street, from Andrássy, from Üllői, from Baross, from Rákozi, from Lenin, from Pater, from Soroksari, moving towards the centre, thousands of them, citizens beware!'

Amara is about to prepare some hot food when the shooting begins. The tanks bombard buildings indiscriminately to right and left, to create panic and terror. But incredibly, there is a lively response from roofs and windows. The rattling of Kalashnikovs can be heard. The dull thump of mortars echoes from every street. Every now and then a tank is hit by a stone wrapped in a burning rag soaked in petrol. Most of these improvised bombs slide off the sides of the iron beasts and end up on the wet pavement. But one or two manage to hit the engine and start a fire. The tank burns, and no sooner does the driver try to get out than he is seen from the roofs and hit with precision by a marksman. The other tanks reply by firing at the high windows. Plaster flies, amid an explosion of windows and screech of broken hinges.

The only thing to do is to run to earth in Tadeusz's bedroom which overlooks the courtyard and wait there for it to end. Shooting can be heard from the outskirts where the big factories are, and from the centre: from Parliament Square, from the Corvin cinema which has been an assembly point for the insurgents, and from Party headquarters in Köztársaság Square, scene of the fiercest fighting. Cannons and howitzers, perhaps hand grenades too. There seems no end to the deafening, obscene noise.

But a voice that seems familiar calls them back to the kitchen, to the great Orion that is now speaking with a different note, the voice of the victor.

'Calling the Hungarian people: the Revolutionary Government of workers and peasants has now been re-established. The movement that exploded on 23 October had the noble aim of eliminating the last vestiges of the crimes committed against Party and People by Rákosi and his friends and of defending the independence and sovereign power of the nation. The weakness of the Nagy regime and the growth of counter-revolutionary elements infiltrating the popular movement were endangering our socialist accomplishments, our People's State, the power of our workers and peasants and the very existence of our country.'

The friends look at each other aghast. The voice shows such self-confidence and arrogance in asserting the reverse of the truth as to leave them breathless.

'How can they turn the facts upside down in this obscene manner?' Tadeusz asks himself darkly, translating into French for Amara.

But the voice goes on, with the calm of one who knows he has the power of arms behind him.

'Reactionaries have raised their hand against our democratic regime. Their aim is to restore the factories and the means of production to the capitalists and the land to the great proprietors. They have already mobilised Horthy's militia, those representatives of a despotic and exploitative order, with the aim of placing the people under their yoke. If they had won, they would have calmly established slavery, poverty, unemployment and pitiless aristocratic oppression in place of liberty, welfare and democracy.'

'See how they are trying to flatter the young.'

'These honest patriots have only wished to make our society, our politics and our economy more democratic ... So it is unjust and illegitimate to accuse them of subversion. Nevertheless we must not lose sight of the fact that, due to the weakness of the Nagy regime, counter-revolutionary forces in our country have in recent days been assassinating, robbing and despoiling the Hungarian people ... Today we observe with great sadness and a heavy heart the alarming situation in which our dear country has been placed by these counter-revolutionary elements, and also because of certain elements of goodwill which respect progress, but have allowed themselves to be seduced into serving reaction. Hungarians, brothers, soldiers, citizens. We must flush out these counter-revolutionaries, identify them, set them in the pillory and render them harmless.'

'Wait for the best bit!'

In fact the climax emerges unexpectedly, the bitter medicine good Hungarians now have to swallow: 'In the interests of the people and of the whole working class, the new government now led by Comrade Kádár has asked the Soviet army to assist the Hungarian people in their attempt to annihilate the dark forces of reaction and help us as we re-establish order and tranquillity in our country.'

'There, now they've shown the claws they were keeping hidden, see? If they had not been called in, the Soviets would not have been able to come into our country. Without a formal request from a government legitimised by the people it would have been an invasion pure and simple, wouldn't it?'

Tadeusz is in tears; Ferenc is stroking his head to comfort him. A louder than usual explosion throws them all to the ground. The neighbouring building must have been hit. They go into the next room and hope the whole building does not collapse.

'During the war we used to go down to the cellars. But then they closed them.'

'What are the other people who live here doing?'

'There's not a soul on the stairs. They've all shut themselves in and are keeping quiet like us. Anyway, what can anyone do against all those tanks?'

'We could go up on the roof and throw down grenades.'

'And where would we get grenades?'

Ferenc, amid the general despair, sticks his violin under his chin and begins Bach's *Chaconne*. Perhaps the only thing that makes any sense. Only those elegant, geometrical, rational notes are capable of imposing meaningful thought on chaos, death, arrogance and bullying.

A loud knocking on the outside door. A moment of panic. Horvath, blanket round his shoulders, calloused feet naked and face twisted, goes to peer through the spyhole. He opens the door. There on the threshold is the man with the gazelles. Amara runs and throws her arms round him. Tadeusz weeps with joy. Ferenc, never far from his violin, quickly plays a *Romanian Dance* by Béla Bartók to celebrate the return of their friend.

'We thought you were dead.'

'And here I am.'

'But it's two days since you went out saying you would be back directly. What happened?'

'I had to hide. The first night I slept in the back room of a shop, taking refuge with others from a round-up. The second night I slept on a sofa at the Hotel Béke. I took a few risks, but not too many. The Soviets are so impressed by the grand scale of their own invasion that they don't notice details.'

'But what did you do?'

'Have you any news?'

'The Corvin cinema has been virtually destroyed. The parliament is as full of holes as a shovel used for target practice. The Király barracks has been smashed to pieces. The national army headquarters has been besieged. General Gyula Varadi has been arrested and taken away by the Russians.'

'And Nagy?'

'Taken refuge with other members of his government in the Yugoslav Embassy.'

'And Maléter?'

'Arrested.'

'And Dudás?'

'Arrested.'

'And the delegation to the United Nations and all the promises they made us?'

'As far as words go, they're a hundred per cent with us. But no one dares touch the internal affairs of the Warsaw Pact.'

'And Kádár, who was with Nagy? Is he with the rebels? Or is it true he's betrayed us, the swine? I can't believe it, wasn't it he who a few days ago declared in favour of the great new workers' revolution?'

'He's changed his mind.'

'So was it his voice we heard on the radio, asking the Soviet armed forces to intervene in the name of the Hungarian people? But what does it all mean?'

'At one point Kádár disappeared, remember? No one could find him anywhere. It seems they flew him to Moscow and told him either you're with us or against us. One or the other. In short, if he agreed to ask officially for armed assistance they'd spare him and he could join the new government. If not he would disappear into some Russian prison and later be shot for high treason. So he made up his mind.'

'But we've heard firing. A lot of sub-machine guns against the uproar of heavy artillery. There must have been some resistance.'

'A great deal. From every roof in Budapest. Against thousands of tanks. The Corvin cinema and its garrison resisted for two days, firing and throwing grenades. At the Hay Market they kept the Soviet tanks at bay for twenty-four hours. They were nearly all killed. Including the man with the wooden leg, d'you remember him? The man we saw our first day in Budapest.'

'It's hopeless to try and resist tanks. It can never be done.'

'D'you know how many Soviet tanks there are here now? Five thousand. More than Hitler threw at Russia in 1941. They're talking of fifteen thousand dead and fifty thousand Hungarian wounded. Our people seem to have managed to burn nearly a hundred Soviet tanks and kill nearly a thousand Russian soldiers.'

'Who told you all this?'

'The foreign journalists at the Béke are always well informed.'

'And what about phone lines to the outside world?'.

'They function intermittently. But many of the journalists have private radio transmitters. That's how they communicate.'

'But what did you see yourself?'

'Trams overturned. Houses smashed to pieces. Huge numbers of dead lying in the streets. I saw a group of students loaded onto a lorry. I went to look for the woman who always used to sell perecs at the corner of Dohány utca, d'you remember? But she's vanished. I wanted to bring home a little sugar and some bread, but everything's closed and locked up. A general strike has been announced. Not a single worker has gone back to his workplace. They want to take the city by famine. Outside the metallurgical factories on Csepel Island, I saw a barricade built against a crowd of Soviet tanks. The Russians have arrived in their thousands, marching in orderly ranks and firing in all directions. And they've been answered with cannons. I don't know where they got them from, but they managed to destroy at least ten Soviet tanks with them. The Russian artillery even climbed to the top of Gellért Hill to fire down onto the Csepel workers. At one point when they sent a plane to bomb the factory, the workers managed to hit it with a rudimentary missile and smash it into a thousand pieces. Everyone cheered. They seemed invincible, our metal workers at Csepel. But the Soviets brought in a dozen planes from an hour away that dropped hundreds of bombs and Csepel vanished, destroyed. Hundreds were killed. I saw people queueing for bread in defiance of the bullets raining down on them from all sides. There's a general strike in progress but our people have organised distribution posts that move according to where the tanks go. The Russians have set fire to the reserves of petrol at the port, sending stinking black smoke soaring into the sky. In the midst of all this some citizens have concerned themselves with stopping thieves, the profiteers who loot the smashed houses. I saw one boy throw a hand grenade from a window. It blew a tank into the air. He looked out again to gauge the effect and another tank fired at him. I saw his head fall from his body into the road. Other tanks gathered in front of his home, leaving only a fragment of wall standing. Many have died, buried in the ruins. Some came out into the road to attack the tanks, hurling petrol and burning faggots. Then they hid behind the hospital. The Russians, furious, set fire to the hospital. And when the doctors and nurses fled with their patients, planes flew low over them to shoot them one by one. I threw myself to the ground with the rest. I saw mud thrown up from the pavement by the shells right next to my head. But I think I must be protected by the gods because I wasn't hit. But I saw many die at my side. Though nothing can stop the Magyar boys running like madmen among the tanks, zigzagging so as not to be hit. Then turning suddenly to throw a grenade or a burning bottle. Even boys of fifteen or sixteen. A group of about thirty were surrounded and captured. Half of them, the ones with weapons, were immediately killed with a bullet to the head; the others were piled into a lorry which set off at speed for the base at Koliko. I was told they were students from a mathematical college. Many people are heading for the borders. They have no intention of staying under a new Soviet dictatorship. Large numbers of them. But before they go, some stop to bury the dead. I've seen improvised graves dug at the roadside: a little pile of earth, a few flowers, a wooden cross with a light stuck on top. I met long lines of people with bundles on their shoulders heading for Austria. Back at the Hotel Béke I looked for the bald man selling visas. But I couldn't find him. I was stopped twice by Russian soldiers and twice by insurgents. Luckily I'd got rid of my rifle. I spoke Russian to the first lot, Hungarian to the second. They let me pass.'

A wheezing sound is heard. They all turn. Tadeusz is lying on the floor, apparently struggling for breath. Hans leans over him.

'Let's take him to the hospital immediately,' says Ferenc.

'The hospital's been burned down, I saw it with my own eyes.'

'Let's call János.'

'All the telephone lines have been cut.'

'I'll go and look for him,' Ferenc suggests.

'It's dangerous. Wait!'

But Ferenc won't wait, and still holding his violin he goes to the door in his slippers, beside himself, weeping.

'Put on your shoes! And leave your violin behind!'

Ferenc quickly puts on his shoes but goes out with the violin clutched to his chest. A moment later he returns out of breath, puts his violin down by the door and sets off again, coat inside out and beret pulled down over his eyes.

51

Dr János Szabó comes but all he can do is confirm that Tadeusz has died, from internal haemorrhage.

'We should have taken him to hospital two days ago.'

'The hospital's been burned down, Hans.'

'Even so, we should have taken him. Tried everything possible.'

'How can we not have realised how ill he was?'

'He said he was all right.'

'You mean he hid what he was feeling so as not to scare us?'

Dr Szabó maintains that the bullet, instead of staying in one place, started moving about and burst a vein, and that it was this that killed him.

Hans blames him for not having said how dangerous the wound was. But Dr Szabó spreads his arms.

'Without the right instruments I couldn't tell. Sometimes bullets stop where they are and stay fixed in the flesh. But obviously this one had no intention of keeping still and moved about until it touched a vital spot. But without instruments there was nothing I could do.'

With his long, delicate fingers Dr Szabó combs the dead man's hair, closes his eyes and crosses his arms on his chest.

At the same moment a burst of artillery shatters all the windows on the side facing the road. A very near miss. The violence of the blow bursts a pipe in two places. Water begins to spurt in both kitchen and bathroom. Hans runs to stop the kitchen leak while Ferenc wraps rags round the hole in the bathroom. He asks Amara for more and more rags, my God, we're being inundated here! Big tears roll down his cheeks and he makes no attempt to wipe them away. Horvath follows, barefoot, trying to help. Amara searches everywhere for rags, string, laces, anything to stop the water gushing over the floor.

'Find the master tap, you fools!' shouts Hans.

'I know there is one, I know it, but I can't remember where it is,' says Ferenc, going round in circles. 'It was Tadeusz who looked after these things.'

Now the friends start searching for the mains lever, even going as far as the landing. But no master tap can be found. In the meantime the floor has become slippery, and in some places the water has risen several centimetres. They need more rags, but where can they find any? Amara takes some of Tadeusz's clothes to block the pipes. Ferenc tears them from her hands.

'Not these!' he says angrily, lifting his nose in the air.

But a little later, with the water round his ankles, he changes his mind and takes Tadeusz's clothes to the burst pipe.

'He won't be needing them again, anyway,' he says, giving Amara a wry smile.

The broken windows let in the cold but disturbing noises too: the cries of a child looking for its mother. The crackle of machine guns from round the corner, the incessant sound of the caterpillar treads of the tanks as they continue to tour the city even though it is now two days since the fateful 4 November. The old Orion transmits peremptory commands. 'Hand in your weapons!' 'Go back to work!' cries the arrogant voice of the new authority but no one hands in any weapons or goes back to work. The general strike has begun, and the aim is for it to continue as long as possible. In the Wilkowsky home they have at last managed to find the master tap and and stop the water. But now they have nothing to drink or wash with. Tadeusz lies on his bed with arms crossed and a serene expression on his face; eyes are closed as if he is sleeping. The big bloodstain on his side has been covered by a folded sheet. Ferenc has dressed him in a fine navy jumper and new trousers.

Dr János Szabó says that now his duty is done and he must go. Ferenc stops him, crying that he can't go until the ceremonies have been completed. They all stand by the bed. Hans is the only one who can't keep still, moving his hands constantly to keep himself under control. Now he is wrestling with two candle-ends he wants to light and place on the wooden headboard. The hot wax runs over his fingers but he ignores it, focusing all his attention on trying to make the candles stick to the edge of the wood and not fall. Then he mumbles that they need a flower, but where to find one when the whole city is carpeted in snow. Ferenc lifts his violin to his shoulder and strikes up Fauré's *Elégie*. Soft music whose undulating motion slowly penetrates every mind. Amara sees Tadeusz alive again: his tireless cheerfulness, his need to bring everyone pleasure, his fine intelligent forehead, his strong arms. She remembers his voice, a little hoarse from smoking, his nicotine-stained fingers, his ash-grey eyes, his courage and his restlessness.

It would be nice if you and Hans could stay here with me, he had said to Amara one day. And she had been thinking he was fed up with them! I'd like it if you stayed in this house. The horror will pass, good days will return; I'll do the cooking, you know I like cooking. And he had kissed her on the mouth. Not a sensual kiss, but it had surprised her all the same. A kiss to make her feel she had become one of them, perhaps even a member of the family.

At last Hans stops fiddling with the candles. He strokes his father's pale brow, then speaks in a low, emotional voice.

'Tadeusz was a just man. I don't know if he was a good father: he always treated me more like a friend than a son and it may be that sons need a father more than a friend. But he did it from generosity, from a feeling for democracy. He believed in people being equals. It was the same with his wife, my mother: he was more interested in being her companion than her husband. The Nazis cut short this illusion which otherwise might have lasted very much longer. He was a splendid musician, even if his timings and rhythms were never in step with those of his contemporaries. As an orchestral conductor he missed more than one opportunity. But I rate highly a man who attached more importance to his pride than his ambition. I'm glad chance brought me to Budapest at this terrible devastating time. I was determined to come and see him even though I knew he was in fine shape. Perhaps it was a presentiment. And these days have given me the chance to know a different father, courageous and daring. I'm happy I was able to share with him the last days of his life, fighting a common enemy. Just as he once hated the Nazism that killed his wife, so now he could not accept Stalinism, which has taken away his own life. I'm so proud I was able to stand at his side in this last battle for freedom. Goodbye, Father. Be careful when you reach paradise because that too is bound to be divided into two hostile camps. The cold war isn't over. Beware of stray shots. I shall always love you.'

One by one, they all bend to kiss Tadeusz's cold white forehead.

He seems to be sleeping peacefully. Ferenc starts playing again after drying his tears on a sodden, screwed-up handkerchief. Accompanied by the deafening rumble of tank tracks, continuous rifle fire and the intermittent thud of cannons. Now the dead man must be buried. Then they must somehow seal the windows with cardboard and finish fixing the burst water pipes.

52

The train for Vienna. The man with the gazelles is sitting opposite Amara. Horvath is reading with his nose in his book. The engine is whistling and puffing. It is an old steam goods train, adapted for passenger use: its steel floor lined with linoleum, the seats wooden, heavy and very uncomfortable. Above their heads netting racks bulging with bundles of various sizes.

Amara has a book open in front of her. But her eyes refuse to stay on the page, constantly lifting to look at the dirty windows, behind which the countryside slowly passes, sometimes hidden by clouds of black smoke. Birches, snow-covered firs, more birches, beeches, oaks with heavy white branches. The wide fields seem so light as to be suspended in mid-air. The eye sweeps across a whiteness that unites earth and sky. The outside world has assumed contours as smooth, delicate and soft as a child's skin.

The last days in Budapest were feverish. Dr János Szabó, perhaps feeling guilty for having been unable to save his friend Tadeusz, took charge of the burial. The cemetery was in chaos; no one any longer knew anything of graves and plots. So he had the great idea of digging a ditch in the Gyal forest some twenty kilometres from Budapest. They borrowed a van and loaded it with the body wrapped in a sheet, together with spades and shovels.

They took it in turns to dig, starting with Ferenc. To grasp the shovel, he put down his violin, shut in its black case, beside him on the snow. Hans rolled up his sleeves and despite the cold opened the buttons of his plush-lined cotton shirt. Horvath, wearing in honour of the occasion the now darned and hence multicoloured stockings Tadeusz had given him, was as usual in sandals made from strips of leather, like an innocent blue-eyed St Francis ready to talk to the birds. Amara too, squeezed into her little blue coat, her red beret on her head and in dark blue woollen gloves, struck the frozen soil with the pick. The deeper they dug, the softer the earth became. Finally Hans jumped into the grave to shovel out the mud, piling it on top of the snow.

They even found some flowers. Or rather, Ferenc did, paying a 'fortune' as he put it to a florist who had reopened his shop 'to survive'. Goodness knows where those giant tulips had come from, their red petals seeming to tremble in the cold on that freshly dug grave filled in with earth and snow.

By midday they were back at home. They drank some wine that Ferenc had kept for special occasions. In honour of Tadeusz, he said through his tears. A good fermented wine straight from Italy, he guaranteed, in fact from Sicily. But the label was in Polish. They smoked ill-smelling cigarettes made from shag sold in the street at half a forint per gram. They devoured some ginger biscuits, also from Ferenc's mysterious cupboard which was always kept locked. But Dr Szabó didn't stay with them to enjoy the Sicilian wine. He said goodbye to everyone, and as he was leaving Ferenc gave him a cap that had belonged to Tadeusz. 'You wear it, he won't need it any more. It's good quality wool.' Dr Szabó took the cap and turned it round in both hands, sniffing it as if searching for the smell of his dead friend. Then he slowly pressed it down on his head and went out without another word.

The burst water pipes were repaired by Hans who borrowed a blow lamp and some solder. But nothing could be done about the windows because they had no glass. They blocked them as best they could with waxed cloth while Ferenc stuck his rolls of cotton wool into the corners to shut out draughts.

It was clear to them all that they couldn't go on staying in the building. Ferenc talked about going to Miskolc where he had a sister. Horvath wanted to go back to Vienna. The man with the gazelles and Amara too saw Vienna as a refuge. But without visas it would be difficult for them to leave.

For days on end they lived on peaches in syrup, the only thing to be found in the State shops which had opened their doors again. These shops also sold horrible ash-coloured shoes, sweaters as full of thorns as a blackberry bush, soap that dissolved too rapidly in water, and tubes of toothpaste which were somehow already half empty. They had plenty of second-hand army greatcoats, and strange crocheted berets from China, their brother country, with whom Russia and therefore Hungary also had been having a tempestuous relationship but with whom the new government, following Mao's visit and Khrushchev's revelation of his hostility to Stalin, was doing business. It was said that Mao had been one of those to insist on the Soviet repression of Hungary. As had Tito who had seemed to support Nagy in the first days of the revolt. This had also been the attitude of Togliatti, representative of the biggest and most prestigious Communist Party in Europe; in fact it was said among other things that he had been most ferocious in his condemnation of the 'counter-revolutionary' Hungarian insurgents, who in his view must be 'squashed without pity'.

Neither the State shops nor the reorganised ordinary shops had any bread or fresh milk. Only cans of condensed milk stamped with large words in Czech, and dried meat in the form of the twisted batons given to soldiers in the trenches. And great quantities of peaches in syrup from Yugoslavia, a sign of new brotherly relations with a country that until a month ago had been their fiercest enemy.

Hans and Amara made their way every day to the Hotel Béke, he to search for the bald man who had offered them permits for Austria, she to try to dictate 'live' articles to Italy. But the bald man could not be found and the telephone lines only worked in fits and starts. Even so Amara did manage to dictate two long articles, if with the interruptions it must have taken her three hours. All the same she was late and the paper had already had the news from international agencies.

They had opened Tadeusz's will; he had left two thousand forints to his son Hans, and to Ferenc his furniture, books and maps and a valuable drawing by Munch that he had himself inherited from his father. Hans ran to the Hotel Béke and this time did find the bald Alain who in exchange for two thousand forints gave him three tickets and three permits for Vienna.

So here they are now. Horvath has completely recovered from his pneumonia despite the cold and lack of medicines and the general discomforts of the time. He walks happily through the train chattering to people of all kinds. He is no longer wearing the long darned socks but has reverted to his friar's sandals and the half-mast trousers that leave uncovered his extremely thin ankles and their network of bluish veins. Only one innovation: he has cut his white hair which was getting in his way. His eyes shine on either side of his long nose. Even Hans seems younger. The death of his father sobered him. But in compensation, the responsibility of looking after the house and the effort of going out in the cold to look for firewood and of touring the whole city on foot, has made him dry and tough. The light-brown lock of hair still falls over his brow,

At this moment he is relaxed, smiling at Amara as if newly recovered from a serious illness. His face is pale but confident. He too is happy to have escaped from the trap of Budapest, to be able once more to face a normal life. After all, it is still not long since the end of the war, and to land in the midst of another war was an almost unbearable surprise.

The morning of the day before, the two of them had sat down together at the little table. Hans had taken hold of her hands and asked her what she planned to do. She thought for a bit. Then answered perhaps a little too firmly: 'I want to go on searching for Emanuele ...'

'All right. Let's do that. But it'll be harder to go back to Auschwitz now. They've got more strict about the borders. They won't even let you through as an Italian.'

'Then let's search in Vienna. His family lived there for years. There must be somebody there who knows what happened.'

Hans stretches out on the seat with his eyes closed. Perhaps he's planning to go to sleep but the seats are too uncomfortable.

Horvath comes down the corridor with a paper bag in his hand.

'Like some?'

'Let's have a look.'

Hans peers into the bag. Dried bananas. He sticks in two fingers and pulls out a sticky black pointed tongue of banana and lifts it to his mouth. He chews slowly.

'Not bad,' he remarks, 'where did you find them?'

'At the far end of the train, bought them from a man from Prague. He deals in dried fruit. I'd have rather had figs, but he had none left. His apples were all finished too, and his dates. All he had left were these little slices of banana.'

'How much did you pay for them?'

'More than they were worth. But we have to eat something before we get to Vienna.'

Hans watches him, chewing another small piece of burned-looking banana. Horvath offers the bag to Amara and she too pushes a sticky little strip into her mouth and chews it blissfully. Hunger can make any food delicious. True, a hot coffee or even a crunchy pretzel would be better than these sticky dried bananas, but that's all that's available to fill their stomachs.

'I've had a word with the conductor. He's says there's been a warning of mines on the track. We'll probably have to stop for a bit.'

In fact, less than a minute later, the train brakes. The pistons can be heard slowing down while the engine whistles and puffs, struggles along a little way then stops, gasping, on the frozen rails, in the middle of a field of snow. The sun has broken through the dark clouds like an egg yolk, bright and brilliant. Reflections on the snow have transformed the countryside into pure silver. In the sky a pale half-moon is hanging too like an electric bulb of frosted glass.

Hans pulls down the window. They breathe in fresh, pungent air. In the distance some women in long dark coats are hurrying towards the train, each with something in her hand. When they are near enough they lift their hands to show what they have to sell: a basket of hard-boiled eggs, some salt-encrusted perecs, a bowl of pickled gherkins. Hans buys what will fit into one of Amara's headscarfs: six boiled eggs, six pretzels and three pickled gherkins. But is there nothing to drink? He indicates thirst, throwing back his head and pointing his thumb at his open mouth. The woman laughs, revealing an absence of front teeth. She sticks two fingers in her mouth and gives a loud whistle. A small boy runs up with under his arm an enormous metal thermos from which he pours a sugared black tea that he sells at ten centimes a mug. Amara drinks greedily, burning her tongue, and passes the mug to Hans who has it refilled and passes it on to Horvath. Lastly he drinks himself. No one cares that the mug has been through the mouths of heaven knows how many people. When the thermos is empty the small boy runs to have it filled again by a man wrapped in an ancient heavily patched army greatcoat, perhaps his father, who is sitting in the snow with a metal can between his legs. The child hands over the money which the man pockets before slowly opening the large lid of the can to pour the boiling liquid into the thermos. Then the child runs off to pour more tea for other thirsty and frozen passengers.

53

Frau Morgan hugs Amara as soon as she sees her. She seems to have no hard feelings, and is ready to take her back at the Pension Blumental despite the trouble caused her by the police. Amara drags her father's old suitcase up the stairs. The only thing Frau Morgan asks is that she should take off her muddy shoes first. So she leaves them at the entrance, near the stove, and climbs the steep stairs in her stockinged feet. A little ashamed of her stockings, dirty and full of holes. But in Budapest she had no chance to change them.

She has her old room again: small, with two windows overlooking the yard and the roofs. Opening the windows she can see the little wooden tables in the restaurant that overlooks the courtyard, each with its lamp under a tiny reddish shade. Every time its door is thrown open the clash of plates and smell of salty fried food reaches up to the top floor. From the other window overlooking the roofs, she is sometimes involved in a squabble between pigeons fighting over a worm or midge, who knows. They too are going hungry in such a difficult year as 1956.

The high bed is as clean as ever; its immaculate sheet smelling of laundry and its quilt, folded back as is the custom in this part of the world, sheathed in a white cover with yellow stripes. The pillow is the kind she hates, into which you sink till your ears and even your eyes are covered.

Before she went up Frau Morgan handed her a card from Susanna: *Where are you? Give some sign of life. Lots of love and best wishes!* As though she hasn't been in Italy for years. As though she has been crossing a desert in the dark. 'A shadow insatiable of splendid appearances, of frightful realities; a shadow darker than the shadow of the night,' as Conrad puts it. No one would believe her. Now that she has returned to the everyday world, everything seems different, everything paradoxically predictable and banal.

There is also a letter from Sister Adele. Amara opens it with feverish fingers. Something falls at her feet. She bends to pick it up: a photograph. It is her father Amintore as a young man. On a ledge in the mountains. He must have been scarcely twenty years old. A sunny day, cloudless. He is alone, up on a rocky ridge, on a peak at the top of a smooth perpendicular wall. Suspended in space, like a worker at the top of a skyscraper, calm, legs bent, one elbow on his knee, seen in profile, facing the horizon. A small man with regular features, with smooth black hair, a high forehead, prominent cheekbones, and big strong hands like the artisan that he was.

Dear Amara, your father died last night in his sleep. I don't think he suffered. His last words were for your mother, Stefania. He called her several times. For days he had recognised no one, not even me, though I was his daily companion. We dressed him in his best suit, the formal blue one, and new shoes, and smoothed down his still abundant hair with water. His expression was relaxed, not contorted at all. He died a beautiful death, even if we are sorry he could not receive Extreme Unction. But I believe Christ will have been indulgent and ready to open his arms to a man who had for so many years been the prisoner of a severe illness, by now almost completely blind, but a man with a good heart who never harmed a fly. I enclose a photo I found among his papers. I've put all his possessions in a box: his striped rug, his dressing-gown, his watch, some letters and books, a photo of your mother and some other small things, and closed and sealed the lot. I'll give the box to you next time you are in Florence. I've thrown away his slippers because they were in a terrible state, even if he was so attached to them and insisted on wearing them although we had given him a new pair.

I tell you sincerely that I am sorry he has gone, even if towards the end he had become very demanding to look after; he had to be fed like a child and have things put into his hands, because he couldn't see any more. Mostly he would sit with his head bowed and a sad expression on his face. Only one word would ever get any response from him. The name Stefania. When he heard it he would raise his head and smile. The smile of a child, really moving. I am sure he never stopped loving her, even when he hardly understood anything else. And this made him dear to me, because he was a loyal man and I have not known many loyal men.

All the sisters from the care home were there at his funeral. They loved him despite the fact he was so self-absorbed and latterly cantankerous. His gentle spirit inspired love. He was a courteous man and he trusted the sisters without reserve or suspicion.

When you are back, come and see us and I'll give you the box and show you his grave in the cemetery near our House. With my very best wishes, Sister Adele.

When she has finished the letter, Amara sits down on the bed with a sense of emptiness. She feels no pain, only a sort of meaningless exhaustion. Her legs are inert, incapable of walking, her arms lie by her sides unable to raise themselves, her head is stiff and will not turn on her neck, while her eyes stare fixedly into space.

Making an enormous effort she tries to take in her hand the photograph of Amintore on the ledge. She can't do it. Then, she doesn't know how, she finds it shining in the palm of her hand. Such a strong, agile youngster; how can he ever have been transformed into the mere shadow of a man with misty eyes and snot on the end of his nose? It is as if nature amuses herself by torturing human bodies, altering and deforming them. So you think this is you, with your figure, your face and your eyes? Well, I shall show you that it isn't, and that you aren't even someone else. You are only evidence of my power, which can stretch you, squash you, make you swell or smash you to pieces at my whim. Bodies that have been supremely beautiful, self-confident, cloaked in a kind of resplendent eternity, bodies that have played, leaped, loved, laughed and enjoyed, suddenly find themselves bent, deformed, dull and wrinkled, defeated by the world even though still alive and capable of feeling desire.

She and her father lived together for several years after Stefania died. Once, wanting to surprise her, he cut out some satin and made her a pair of shoes with upturned points, like the slippers of a princess from fairyland. 'I've made these for you,' he said, putting them on the table next to the schoolbooks and closing his big strong hands over her delicate little ones with such yearning that she could never forget it. Nothing more than a simple paternal gesture, but as if he was saying: I'm entrusting you with your own future; live it well because it's the only one you have.

Amintore had never accepted her love for Emanuele. 'Too rich. A spoilt brat,' he had said watching him walk down the street in his expensive but ill-cared-for clothes. Plus-fours made from English wool, a cashmere jumper. 'He's a houndstooth' her father would say, grimacing with contempt, 'a houndstooth and foie gras.' She had no idea what the words meant, but supposed they symbolised wealth.

Nor had Amintore approved in the least of the departure of the Orenstein family for Vienna at the most dangerous moment in the persecution of the Jews. 'She's mad, that Thelma Fink. A fine woman, a woman of spirit I agree, but what on earth can have induced her to throw herself into the lion's jaws? She's a miserable unfortunate woman, I tell you, and she'll come to a bad end. She and that weird son who hangs round her.' He would repeat this whenever he found her writing letters to Emanuele after the Orensteins had left for Vienna, or when the post brought a yellow envelope from him with a postage stamp of the Reich. He had never approved of her years of watching out in anticipation for the postman. Nor did he understand or share in her despair when no more letters came. 'What's happened to your houndstooth then?' he would ask, sniggering. But though he knew the Jews were being persecuted, it never crossed his mind that such rich and powerful people as the Orensteins might end up in a concentration camp. Nor had he ever approved of her marriage to Luca Spiga, the man of the caresses. He did not like the house where they went to live after their marriage, so full of books and records but with no proper bed. They had slept on a mattress on the floor between a wall and a wardrobe.

In fact, he had never approved of any of her life choices. Not even her decision to enrol at a school of journalism immediately after she graduated in Law. 'What has Law to do with journalism?' he would say. Then he criticised her when she started working for a pittance for a provincial paper. 'A trashy rag full of tittle-tattle, and you're getting less per hour than a waitress.' It was true, but it wasn't easy for a girl to find work. She was satisfied. They had a long discussion about it.

Now that he was dead memories, some of them comic ones, of the life they had shared came back to her in bursts. The kitchen at Via Alderotti with its rusty gas rings that sometimes got blocked and which he blew on as if to dust them, how he was the one who always let the milk boil over and block the holes the gas came out of. The refrigerator he was so proud of (it was one of the first) that made a sound like a cat in love, and how he would come into the kitchen determined to chase away 'that damned cat!' 'But Papà, it's the fridge making that mewing noise.' 'Don't be silly, fridges can't mew.' But the fact was their refrigerator with its big convex door did mew from time to time. And he was always the one who did the cooking. He only knew how to make a few dishes, but he made them well: soup with rice and peas, fried cutlets with egg and breadcrumbs 'alla milanese', and a boil-up of stale bread, red cabbage, potatoes, garlic, oil and black pepper.

They would eat in silence, listening to music on the radio. He hated the pop songs of the day like 'Mamma', or 'Se vuoi goder la vita' and 'Ba, ba, baciami piccina'. He loved opera: *Il Trovatore* and *La Traviata* but also *Don Pasquale* and *Manon*. He knew whole arias by heart and would sing them at the top of his voice while beating leather to soften it. Two or three times he bought tickets for the Pergola Theatre and they had gone there to hear opera live. One evening, she can still remember it, it was *La Traviata*. They were in the gallery and following everything from on high. Amara, leaning out over a low painted wall that prevented her from stretching her legs, had watched a massive woman running about on the stage pursued by a man called Alfredo. To her they had seemed scarcely believable, comic and ridiculous. But her father had been moved. As they went out she confessed she had been bored and he had answered that like all young people she was ignorant and insensitive to beauty. But he said this without malice, as a simple fact you couldn't do anything about.

Another time it was *Tosca*, and she was deeply impressed by the reconstruction of Castel Sant'Angelo. The stage was dominated by an enormous plaster angel with outspread wings and sword in hand, balancing on one foot as if about to take flight. Tosca was a slim, agile singer, and she had enjoyed listening to her arguing with Scarpia when he was trying to blackmail her. At the end Amara had seen her throw herself off the battlements, leaping into space. Leaning out dangerously over the little gallery wall, she had also been able to see beyond the stones of the castle a thick mattress, on which Tosca landed with an acrobatic dive. When Amara clapped in admiration, her father gave a couple of nods thinking she was admiring Puccini's music.

A timid knock on her door. From the rustle of clothing she realised it must be Frau Morgan.

'I'm not in to anyone!' she cried from the bed.

'Do you need a doctor, Frau Sironi?'

'No!'

'But surely you should eat something? Some good potato soup?'

'No, leave me in peace!'

'But you've been shut up here since yesterday, Frau Sironi. Are you sure you wouldn't like me to call the doctor?'

Since yesterday? She had never noticed the passing of time. She had been lying on the bed unsleeping without even managing to read, something most unusual with her. At one point she had heard herself talking. The little man had appeared before her, young and carefree, the lock of hair always falling across his fine brow, to tell her about his last trip to Monte Morello, and how he climbed Poggio all'Aia.

'But, Papà, do you still play with your trains?'

Her father, ridiculous in plus-fours and with a sly smile beneath his rakish moustache, started telling her about the new model locomotives now on sale.

'You really should see the Rivarossi 691, a masterpiece! Or the Coccodrillo, the 6/8s!'

'How can you know the names of engines when you're dead, Papà?'

Her father smiled behind his moustache.

'Are you teasing me?'

'Try the new Rivarossi. Just couple her to a few coaches and let her go. You'll see! Wow!'

Meanwhile Frau Morgan has slipped a note under her door. Hans wants to meet her at a bar called the Coffee House on Schweighofergasse. 'I'll expect you at three. Please come! Yours, Hans.'

Isn't it ridiculous that he is still addressing her formally when they've been friends for months? Suddenly she finds him grotesque, incomprehensible, irritating. I never want to see him again, she tells herself, and falls into a deep sleep.

54

Sitting in the Coffee House on Schweighofergasse, Amara is waiting for Hans. Outside large slow snowflakes are lightening the grey air of a December morning. Her stomach has contracted. She is not hungry. She has crunched a pretzel bought in the street and is now tasting heavily sugared tea. After her two days of seclusion everything seems new and different. The coloured festoons hanging across the windows for Christmas speak to her of mourning rather than impending festivities. And the trees with red rag balls hanging from their branches and silver balls made from cigarette wrappings hurt her eyes with their senseless glitter.

She slowly sips the tea they have placed before her: a little paper bag darkening hot water in a tall glass with a metal handle. After Budapest life in Vienna seems luxurious: peaceful crowded streets and clean well-kept fruit shops where shiny bright apples sit tidily in their boxes behind windows adorned with flowers that reach out invitingly from their vases. Every time a customer comes into the bar a tinkling is heard. In and out go men protected by hats and long coats and women by berets and galoshes against the snow. They sit down at tables of unvarnished wood and order a beer, a white coffee, a tea or a glass of wine. They have the air of people who are thinking of love and business, not war.

But wait, the door has trilled again. A man has come in. She recognises his threadbare coat the colour of a dead leaf, and the shirt open at his long thin throat. There is an affectionate smile on his dry lips.

He sits down beside her, timid and morose. He doesn't ask her how she is. For a while he doesn't say a word.

'I thought you'd gone back to Florence.'

'I didn't want to see anyone.'

'Your father's death?'

'How did you know about that?'

'Frau Morgan told me. I phoned several times.'

'So you knew I hadn't left.'

'I knew.'

Amara looks at him as she lifts the hot tea to her lips. This man has infiltrated himself into her life and little by little, timidly and almost unnoticed, has spread his roots. How deeply?

'Well, what shall we do?'

'Let's go and see the house in Schulerstrasse. They're expecting us.'

'Who are?'

'Ex-consul Schumacher and his wife Helga.'

'The people now living in the Orenstein apartment?'

'Exactly. Even if it seems they left it after getting it as a gift from the government then later took it back.'

'What sort of people are they?'

'Germans. He was in the Nazi diplomatic service. That's all I know.'

'Let's go.'

Amara and Hans catch a tram, then another, walk down part of the Kärntnerstrasse, enter the short Singerstrasse and cross Stephansplatz to reach Schulerstrasse. They stop for a minute or two to look at the building where the Orenstein family lived before they were deported to the ghetto at Łódź and then probably to Auschwitz. It is a large building from the early years of the century. Ten or twelve floors; pretentiously decked with Ionic pillars, windows with fake Gothic architraves and a gigantic main door reached by a flight of marble steps shaped like a half moon.

They go up the steps to face a locked door decorated with legendary and historical scenes. They look for the name on its brass plate. They find it and ring. A female voice invites them to come in.

The door opens suddenly to reveal a courtyard full of ornamental plants. On the right another entrance leads to a lift in wrought iron and glass. Hans and Amara slip into the great space which closes with a puff and slowly begins to climb. Frosted glass windows with designs in white on white reveal the stairs as they unroll elegantly floor by floor.

At the fifth floor, the lift halts with a dry hiss and they get out. They ring the bell. The door opens silently. On the threshold is a handsome woman with violet rouge, grey waved hair, and a fox fur thrown carelessly over a very elegant blue and grey wool dress.

'Please come in.'

Extremely polite, she leads them into a luxurious drawing room with long purple velvet curtains, Persian carpets to soften the floor, and armchairs and sofas covered in white linen and strewn with coloured cushions.

'Do sit down,' she invites them in a melodious voice. She is like a thirties film star. When she moves her blue and grey skirt dances round calves sheathed in transparent seamed stockings.

'So you are friends of the Orensteins ...' she begins lightly.

'Well, I never knew them, but Signora Maria Amara Sironi, who is Italian, was a close friend of Emanuele, the son of Karl and Thelma Orenstein who owned this building before ...' Hans looks around with embarrassment. He does not know whether to continue or not. But Frau Schumacher seems not at all put out.

'Yes, I know that before us the Orenstein family lived here. When the government assigned this apartment to us we were living in Tokyo. My husband is a diplomat. He goes where he is sent, as I'm sure you understand. We had a large house and garden and, can you believe it, ten dogs. My husband loves dogs. Do you love dogs, Signora Sironi?'

'Yes,' answers Amara in embarrassment. She cannot understand why this woman wants to keep the conversation on such a mundane and pointless level. At the same time she looks round thinking Emanuele lived here. Perhaps he once huddled with a book in the very armchair she is sitting on now. She can almost see him.

'It was just before Christmas, like now. We'd decorated the tree for our daughters Andrea and Margarethe. Wilhelm had already joined us,' continues Frau Schumacher undaunted, without making sure her two guests are following her. 'We were about to sit down at table. Our wonderful cook, Michiko, had roasted the stuffed turkey in the way my husband likes. Our dear butler, Yunichiro, brought me a letter. I opened it expecting Christmas greetings. Instead I read that the government was ordering us transferred within the week to Vienna to attend to administrative affairs, a move apparently decided by the Führer himself. So, instead of celebrating Christmas we had to pack our things. When we arrived we were told that the Reich's department for administrative affairs was not yet ready and that we must move into an apartment, a fine one certainly, but not what we had expected. We didn't even know that a family of Jews were living in our lodgings. We were assured the proprietors would move out within a few days and this is what happened. The house was in excellent condition, I have to admit that Frau Orenstein had kept it beautifully. There were flowers everywhere and elegant carpets and even valuable paintings. We would have preferred unfurnished accommodation; we already had so many possessions of our own. But the Foreign Ministry wanted us to take it just as it was, fully furnished with pictures, carpets and everything. Do you see those three men in dark blue against an azure background? It seems that Herr Orenstein probably bought that painting from the artist himself. Ottone Rosai, 1923. They say that Herr Orenstein was very well known as an industrialist in Italy, in fact they've told me that he owned a very fine villa in Florence, in the Rifredi district; and that unexpectedly, and, I have to say, most inadvisedly, he had decided to transfer his family to Vienna to reoccupy his house here, without considering the risks they would run.'

'But did you never ask yourself where the Orensteins had gone, when they left a furnished house complete with carpets on the floor, pictures hanging on the walls and flowers on the tables?'

'I would imagine they moved to another house. Or returned to Florence, to their beautiful villa at Rifredi. I've heard that they had dogs too and gave them German names, isn't that strange? I mean, to call a dog Wolfgang or Heinrich, I do wonder whether that might not have been a little disrespectful towards humans ... But unfortunately I never met the Orensteins. When we moved in here they had already gone. We lived here for nearly a year. Then we had to go back to Berlin. And there, in the bombing raids, we lost everything. Almost the only thing that was left of our house was the walls. The roof fell in and the whole block burned for a day and a night. Meanwhile my husband reached retiring age. So we decided to go back to Vienna where we had lived so well. Luckily the bombs had spared the old Orenstein house, so we were able to move in again. For a time an SS officer and his family had lived here, decent people who knew how to keep the apartment just as it was. Then he and his wife fled to Argentina leaving their small children here. I believe a grandmother took them. Anyway, the house was free so we moved back.'

Amara would have liked to ask many questions, but the woman gives them no chance to speak. She seems to want to tell them about Tokyo, about their houses and their dogs. Even about the apartment they are living in now, but as if the property had come to them in a normal way, through a contract. But Amara knows from Emanuele's letters that the house was confiscated fully furnished. Something about this elegant, self-confident woman, so utterly impervious to all questions, intimidates her. Only at the end does she decide to confront her, trying to be as laconic as possible.

'Frau Schumacher, I have a letter from Emanuele Orenstein in which he says that you knew the family,' she finds the courage to say.

'Oh, you should pay no attention to an over-excited child.'

Amara wonders how she can know he was an over-excited child if she never met him, but prefers not to argue and to let her talk.

'All the Jews whimpered at that time that they were being thrown out of their homes. In fact they were selling them for a good price and heading for places where bombs were unlikely to fall. This was very astute of them. Because their houses often ended up in ruins. But by then they had sold them. Do you see how cunning that was?'

'You said yourself that this house was not bought but was assigned to you.'

'Yes indeed, by the State, as is normal for diplomats. But the State had bought it from the Orensteins, I'm sure of that, and it will have cost a pretty penny. But why dig up these sad things from the past? The war was an ugly time for us all, Frau Sironi. We ourselves lost a son of twenty-two, killed on a bombing mission to Stalingrad. And you are still thinking of that child Emanuele Orenstein! Who today would be ... what? Twenty-two?'

'Twenty-eight.'

'He too will have died fighting. The best of German youth died in the war, my dear signora, and the same is true of the best Austrian youth; they fought side by side. Best to erect a stone over the past and begin again, believe me. When I heard my son Wilhelm was dead, I too wanted to die. And then, for years, I tried to find his remains, but never could. But do you know what my daughter Margarethe once said to me. Mama, you are more concerned with the dead than with those who are living with you. And I realised she was right: I was neglecting my husband and our two daughters to run after my dead boy. Since then I've built a little cemetery in my heart, where I constantly take fresh flowers, but I no longer search for his body to give him a burial worthy of our name. He is buried inside me and that should be enough, don't you agree?'

She is full of dignity and seems deeply sincere. Amara and Hans look at each other, discouraged. It is quite clear to them that they will get nowhere at all with this woman who has erased every doubt and every question from her past.

'Not every Austrian fought in the war, Frau Schumacher, some were shut up in extermination camps,' says Amara in a low voice.

'And is that not the same thing? You die how you die. War is a huge obscenity and causes damage everywhere. No one is best and no one is the winner. We are all equal in the face of death.'

'Is your husband dead?' asks Hans to gain time and to find another way of trying to get her to say something about the Orensteins.

'My husband is alive. He's in another room. Would you like to meet him?'

'Well, yes.'

Elegant and unembarrassed, Frau Schumacher rises from the sofa, and with great strides of her slim legs that set her blue and grey skirt dancing and her high heels tapping lightly on the floor, she opens a door and disappears.

'They have even appropriated the Rosai picture, have you noticed?' says Hans in a low voice.

On the white wall right in front of them hangs a large canvas showing three men in worker's caps, in a moment of rest from their work. A picture that evokes a distant world, telling of the friendship of three stone-breakers, sitting down for a chat and a smoke beside the heavy flagstones that they will use to pave the street. A fugue of colours containing light blue, green and sea-blue to enchant the eye.

'And isn't that a De Chirico?'

'Good lord! I really think it is.'

They both go up close to the little canvas with its clean colours, showing a triangular town square and, behind a clear arch, an approaching railway engine belching smoke from its large chimney.

'Wonderful.'

Amara can't stop herself going to the window. She wants to see if the pancake-seller Emanuele described in one of his first letters is still there. The stall and the itinerant salesman have gone. But the clockmaker whose clocks all tell different times is still there, on the pavement opposite. Amara's heart misses a beat.

Then the door opens and Frau Schumacher reappears pushing a wheelchair. Consul Schumacher is a tall, good-looking man with fine features and brilliantined hair. He occupies the wheelchair as if sitting on a throne. Under his elegant silk dressing gown can be glimpsed the striped trousers of a pair of pyjamas also undoubtedly of silk. At his throat is a frothy white scarf. He has just been shaved and is smiling like a child, with confidence and genuine warmth. As he advances he spreads a powerful scent of lavender.

'I knew Emanuele Orenstein,' he says at once, contradicting his wife who looks at him with irritation. 'An extremely sensitive little boy, extremely sensitive. I think he must have suffered a good deal at having to leave his home, but at that time the rules were absolute: no Jew could keep an apartment like this is in the centre of Vienna. I heard they were transported to the ghetto at Łódź. Where they are said to have led a life of dignity, even if obviously deprived of the comforts they were used to ... most unsuitable, I have to say, especially for the Orenstein family who had been used to every convenience. But I also heard that later they were able to get passports and returned to Florence where, I understand, they had a beautiful house, in the Rifredi district if I'm not mistaken. Civilised people. I heard no more after that, but I believe they may have ended up in Israel.'

'They were killed, both Herr Karl Orenstein and Frau Thelma. The only one we know nothing about is their son Emanuele. Signora Sironi here believes he must have survived. We are wondering how to find him.'

'Emanuele's last letter is dated May 1943,' adds Amara, looking firmly at the consul. She is beginning to realise that behind that air of infantile innocence is hidden a monstrous talent for dissimulation.

'I really believed they returned to Florence,' insists the consul, smiling sweetly.

'Have you ever looked for them? Have you ever tried to make contact with them?'

'Well no, actually not. We Germans were not allowed to have relations with Jews. And I was still a member of the diplomatic corps despite our change of home. It would not have been at all possible for me to ...'

'You know that all the Jews deported from Vienna to Łódź ended up in the death camp at Auschwitz?'

'If you say so, I believe it. But we knew nothing at the time. The Orensteins, and many like them, rich Jewish indutrialists, were said to have sold their houses for a good price before the buildings were bombed by the British and Russians. It said so in all the newspapers. Some repeated this with admiration. They always know where the money is, these people, don't they?' he added with a malicious little smile.

Amara blushed with anger. How can he allow himself to repeat the vile, stupid propaganda put about by the SS at the very moment they were plundering Jewish homes? But not wanting to interrupt the conversation which might lead to some useful bit of news, she forces herself to keep quiet.

'And how was Frau Orenstein when you met her,' she asks, pretending to be stupid.

'Very well. A beautiful woman of about forty. They had this one son of whom they were very fond. Every morning they would go and play tennis nearby, father and son. Or so I heard. Even when the bombing started they could be seen going out in their shorts with their racquets. Nothing seemed to frighten them. They were passionate about their tennis.'

'Is it really possible you never heard anything of what happened to them? You were a consul and ...'

'Consuls never know anything, signora. They concern themselves with high politics and international law. But they know nothing of what is happening in their own country. And then I was recalled to concentrate on administration.'

'Herr Orenstein was found mortally wounded in the Łódź ghetto, I repeat, and Frau Thelma Orenstein was hanged for internal sabotage at the factory where she was working, Consul Schumacher.'

'You shouldn't be so pessimistic. Have you any proof of their deaths?'

'Their own son wrote about them in his diary.'

'Pay no attention to him. He was a congenital liar. He even claimed he could fly. They will have undoubtedly moved to Palestine. Many Jews moved there, some of them secretly. My view is the Gestapo closed one eye when Jews wanted to escape to Palestine.'

'And my view is the Gestapo kept their eyes wide open. Anyway, if they had gone to Palestine, we would have heard from them.'

'And what happened to their house in Florence?'

'Confiscated.'

'Oh no, they will have sold that too. Canny people. Brilliant investors. I should have followed their advice instead of groping my way between Tokyo and Berlin.'

'Goodbye, Consul Schumacher. You've been a great help. Not with finding traces of Emanuele Orenstein, but in helping us in understanding what Nazism did to this country: how it was able even to corrupt honest folk and make them blind and deaf.'

'Why say such things, Herr Wilkowsky? Where were you during the war? Don't tell me you survived by playing hide-and-seek.'

'My mother died at Treblinka. I survived because I followed the advice of my family and went to Denmark, where I was hidden by decent Danish people.'

'Oh, Denmark!' intervenes Frau Schumacher as if it were nothing. 'Such clever people, I'd have so much liked to go there, but we never had the chance.'

'Thank you, Frau Schumacher. We really must go now. I wish you a happy future in this beautiful house so full of pictures and flowers!'

55

Christmas Day. Even though the city still carries the wounds of war, even though many of the vital necessities of life are scarce or can only be found on the black market, the windows of homes and shops are sparkling with festivity. Coloured paper hangs in festoons over front doors. Fir trees adorned with cheap ornaments stand in the squares. The crowded Naschmarkt with its curtains, lamps, acetylene lighting, stalls selling marzipan dolls, fake flowers, almond confectionery, sugar fir trees and ginger biscuits. Great fat Father Christmases circulate with long white beards and white curls over their brows and collars. There is even a noisy band and in front of the musicians four lines of girls in short skirts and stiff hats are beating their feet on the snow and brandishing tufted canes. The first time majorettes have been seen in Vienna; people say it's the influence of America. 'It's the war that has brought all these strange new fashions: boogie-woogie, blue jeans, chewing gum, Pall Mall cigarettes, Lucky Strikes, Camels in their pretty packets with a honey-coloured camel against a white background, and of course Coca-Cola, small chocolate bars and cans of Carnation condensed milk.'

Amara feels light-hearted as she walks among the stalls. It took her a few days to recover from her meeting with Consul Schumacher and his ineffable lady. Now she is waiting for her visa to be able to return to Italy. But she is in no hurry. After all, her father is dead and no one is expecting her. Her editor has told her that for the moment he doesn't want to hear any more about Eastern Europe. And he has even criticised her for being so slow in sending in her articles from Budapest. 'I published them but always late. That won't do, my dear Sironi, you had the luck to find yourself in the position to pull off a coup and you let it slip. Quite frankly, as special correspondent you've been a disaster.' She tried to get him to understand that the telephones were out of order, that the post office was closed, and that it was even difficult to find a typewriter, but he answered rudely that he didn't give a fuck for her excuses.

She is free until the first days of the New Year. Why not take a few days off in Vienna? – collecting material for possible further articles, enjoying the festive atmosphere, sleeping without having to wake in the night for fear of tanks.

She stops in front of a man struggling with enormous wads of candyfloss being churned out by a machine. It reminds her of when she was little. Once in the Piazza D'Azeglio Gardens with Emanuele, they had bought two balls of the stuff and watched spellbound as the machine pushed out the floss until it grew into a cloud. Increasingly slender threads piled up like cotton wool in the skilful hands of the salesman; they had watched him turn his little stick till the big ball was plump and round. The Piazza D'Azeglio candyfloss had been white; this in Vienna was a sugary pink, but when the man turned a handle, the skein turned purple.

She has an appointment this evening to dine with Hans and Horvath, who has gone back to his library and also put on several kilos in weight. Only his feet are still relentlessly bare in the friar's sandals he wears everywhere in Vienna despite the snow and slush, covering the pavements with the great strides of a mountaineer. But it's barely six now and their appointment is for seven. She decides to wander a little further among the stalls which she finds cheering. I shall buy myself a stick of candyfloss she tells herself, pulling out a coin and offering it to the man who looks at her with astonishment. Those he serves during the holidays are always children. Bur he gives her a smile and an extra ball of floss.

Amara lifts it to her mouth, but as soon as she smells the sugar and synthetic strawberry she no longer wants it. She turns it in her hand, thinking of Emanuele. Can she really have forgotten what they did that day after they bought the candyfloss? Perhaps they went on the merry-go-round. Perhaps they climbed onto the flying seats. Or was it the terrifying whirling wheel. But to please Emanuele she would have faced any sort of fear.

Emanuele, where are you? she murmurs, dropping the huge sickly-sweet mass into a rubbish bin. It's Christmas and here I am looking for you. Why don't you appear? She sees again the ravaged and lacerated face of the strange Peter Orenstein who claimed to be Emanuele. She couldn't believe him. Even so, thinking back over it, he did have some furniture very like that in the Orenstein home. How can it have come to him? This Peter is certainly over forty; how can he claim to be twenty-eight? We must go back and see him again, she tells herself. She will discuss it with Hans. Who knows whether he wants to go any further with this search that is becoming increasingly unreal.

Now it comes back to her: Emanuele made her go up in the flying gondola. She huddled on the floor the moment it started and held her head in her hands, such was her terror as it rose higher and higher before, reaching a certain height, it turned over and went down on the other side of the structure. A frightful sensation, almost as if her stomach was coming out of her mouth, and she asked herself why she had agreed to face it. But he had taken her in his arms and hugged her so affectionately that eventually her fear passed. She started laughing, then he laughed too. But how long had they been on that flying gondola laughing at each other? She can't remember. Certainly, when they came down it was dark and they had to go home. They had sworn never to be separated.

'Not even when we are old?'

'Not even when we are old.'

'But what if I catch an illness?'

'Then I'll catch it too.'

'And if I die?'

'Then I'll die too.'

Not true, because she was still alive and he was dead or at least had disappeared. Long ago, the gondola travelled on and on and they held each other close. Somewhere inside her that gondola was travelling still and something was contracting in her stomach like a fist squeezing her guts violently and wringing them out.

Where are you? she whispers, as she watches a little boy heading alone for the merry-go-round, squeezing an enormous ice-cream that is melting over his wrist.

But she grew up. She met the man of the caresses and married him despite the misgivings of her father Amintore. She was even happy with him for a while. Was not that already a terrible betrayal? Had she not repudiated the memory of her Emanuele merely because of a banal fear of the future? Even if now she tries to justify herself by saying the relationship between Luca and herself never had any depth. She never loved Luca. But she had still betrayed her pact with Emanuele. She had got married, like any ordinary girl who wants to feel safe and secure. But it did not take her long to learn that her husband was in constant need of new women to caress. So they separated. But could this have been a mitigating factor in her betrayal?

'I'm going, you know, Luca.'

'Where, darling?'

'Away.'

'For ever?'

'For ever.'

'You mean you're going to leave me?'

'Yes, I'm leaving you.'

'Why?'

'I need to be able to breathe.'

She never discussed the caresses with him. He wouldn't have understood. She just packed her bag and left, while he watched without moving a finger. He didn't seem to mind her going. Perhaps he had expected it, perhaps not. When she put on her coat he came up behind her and kissed her neck.

'Anyway, I know you'll be back,' he had said without conviction. To comfort himself. Or maybe just to fill the silence.

'I think not.'

'I'm sure you will. Do you need any money?'

'I have something set aside.'

'Good. And the house? Where are you going to live?'

'With a girlfriend, just for the moment.'

'And who would that be?'

'No one you know.'

'Okay; I'll be waiting for you, little one. Come back soon.' Which was worse than if he'd made a scene. His voice had been at the same time cold and exultant. She too had felt a strange bitter sort of relief. Was it mere pride or was it also a recognition of defeat?

Her friend Tonia had taken her in with great generosity, offering her a bed and her company even though she worked all day at a lawyers' office. In any case, Amara gave no trouble. All she had brought with her was a small suitcase containing Emanuele's letters, his photograph, a pair of check pyjamas and two or three blouses. She had decided from that day to concentrate on searching for Emanuele. She needed to know whether he was dead or alive. Never mind that years had passed since he disappeared. She seemed to have a feeling that he was alive somewhere and that if they met everything would be again like when they were little and had sworn to be together for ever. She knew now that they would make love. Closing her eyes she visualised Emanuele's body entwined with her own, feeling the sweet pressure of his hips and stomach and the happy and so long delayed union of his sex with hers.

56

Amara runs up the stairs two at a time. She stops after each flight to catch her breath. But how many floors does this building have? The bag with the champagne hangs heavy from her arm, together with her presents for Hans and Horvath.

She reaches the top floor out of breath and very hot. Though outside it's snowing and when darkness came it had got colder. She stops at the door. A bass voice is singing *Que sera sera, Whatever will be will be* … Doris Day's song from Budapest and the days of storms, cold and hunger. Happy, she rings the bell twice.

Horvath throws his arms wide to hug her and kisses her cheeks, her temples and her lips.

'Was that you singing, Horvath?'

'How happy I am to see you, Amara!'

'And I to see you …'

A tiny home. In one corner a dwarf Christmas tree, decorated with red bows and chestnuts wrapped in silver paper. Fixed to one wall a small bed covered with striped cloth. Next to it, a wooden plank propped on two trestles to serve as a table. A kitchen recess in one corner, a big cast-iron stove and four folding chairs, of which two are open. The table has been laid with a red cloth, three white plates, some mismatched glasses and cutlery with wooden handles.

'Where's Hans?'

'I thought he was coming with you.'

'I haven't seen him for days.'

'He must have married two or three girls by now.'

But here he is, arriving in his tailcoat. He seems taller and thinner than usual.

'You look good in tails.'

'One has to dress for a special occasion, don't you think?'

'If I'd thought, I could have made myself more elegant too. But instead ...' Horvath is wearing his usual old trousers at half-mast, with his usual friar's sandals and his usual stretched sweater with its overlong sleeves.

'I have to admit, I'm hardly up to your standard either,' adds Amara with a shrug. She's wearing the finest thing she has with her, a blue jersey in lightweight wool. With coarse woollen stockings and snow boots. 'But I did wash my hair this morning,' she states proudly.

'Elegant, don't you think?' Hans gyrates, showing off his hired tailcoat, well-polished shoes and white bow tie.

'I like you better in your sweater with the running gazelles.'

'That's in the wash. It was beginning to walk on its own feet like French cheese. Well, what are we eating tonight?' Hans rubs his hands and looks around, sniffing the air.

'Fish soup Neapolitan-style and Tyrolean strudel. I managed to get hold of some fresh fish. All stuff from the bottom of the net but still alive, and it gave me the idea of the soup. I was taught how to do it by one of my girlfriends, Maggie, who came from South Dakota. An American of Austrian extraction. She came here to look for her roots and found me. What bad luck. She was desperate to have a baby and I wasn't. It's immoral to bring babies into such an ugly, idiotic world, I told her; you'll just produce little criminals. But she was absolutely set on it. So I found her a wonderful boy, Willy Wüppertal, who was working with me in the library and dreaming of becoming a father. I introduced them and they became lovers. They produced four children, then separated. They nearly killed each other because he wanted to keep all four and so did she. Eventually they decided to go halves. Poor Maggie went back to South Dakota with two children in her arms. Before she left she came to see me. She told me Willy Wüppertal was scum, that he was desperate to have children but too lazy to look after them, leaving them all day in the street. True, but what can a man do when first his mother and then his father die within three years, when he loses his job for spending too much time off work, and when he finally gets another job in Africa, he comes back half-dead from malaria ... I mean, how can a man in such a situation care for his children properly? Life has been hard on him, poor Willy. But he does love his children very much, I assure you. He no longer loves his Maggie, but that happens. He called her 'the American stone-eater' in front of the children. She was furious. I've no idea what he meant by stone-eater. The fact was she had to live on boiled potatoes and cheap sausages because she wasn't making any money. But they both got it wrong and their children are neurotic. I occasionally see the two who have stayed with their father: they never stop hitting each other and trading insults, and they don't give a damn about poor Willy Wüppertal.'

'This fish soup,' says Hans, dipping his spoon into it. 'It's really good, you must tell me how you make it.'

'Put some garlic in a pan with a little oil and parsley, and as soon as it turns golden, slip in the fish, cleaned and cut up but complete with the heads which are the tastiest part, then pour on boiling water and let it cook for a long time. Then ...'

But Hans won't let him finish. The recipe immediately bores him.

'But how can this Maggie from South Dakota have learned how to cook fish soup Neapolitan-style?' he asks with curiosity, sucking the eye of a scorpion fish.

'Before she and I got together she spent a few months with a man from Naples. Even introduced me to him. His name was Salvatore, or Salvo, and he worked in an Italian restaurant on Heistergasse, near the station. A beautiful boy, with very black hair and light eyes. He had good manners and was an excellent cook. He said the northern countries drove him mad. I think he wanted a child too. In that respect they were on the same wavelength. But one day he vanished without a word. So Maggie from South Dakota attached herself to me because I comforted her. I'm good at comforting people, oh yes, I'm the best comforter in Austria.'

The three laugh as they thrust spoonfuls of hot soup into their mouths. Every now and then, a dangerous fishbone appears, transparent and as sharp as a needle, but the three are unperturbed, pulling out the bones with their fingers and laying them on the side of their plates. The peppery soup also contains little squares of crisp bread soaked in a fragrant sauce. Sheer delight.

Horvath fetches a bowl of warm water for their fingers and drops into it two slices of fresh lemon. Hans fills their glasses with wine.

'Müller Thurgau '46. Ten years old this month. It'll either be exquisite or vinegar. Let's find out ...'

Fortunately the wine hasn't turned to vinegar though it has taken on a rather disquieting brownish colour and leaves an occasional black clot on the tongue, but it has a good flavour of wood and must. Bells are ringing somewhere. It's nearly ten o'clock. Outside snow is spinning down out of a black sky, sticking to the windowpanes, sliding and drifting on the roofs. Inside, the room is cosy, as the wood-burning stove sends out waves of warmth. The wine attacks the palate and infiltrates the nose with its oaken fragrance.

As soon as they have finished the warm strudel and cream, Amara gives the two friends her presents: for Horvath, a book listing every library in the world that can be consulted free by phone. So the write-up claims and Horvath leafs through it with interest. For Hans a record of Verdi's *Rigoletto*, the opera her father Amintore so loved.

Horvath has brought an electric-blue beret for Amara and a new knapsack for Hans. While Hans has a portable typewriter for Amara; it is called Lettera 22 and is new on the market from Olivetti. For Horvath he has a pair of American naval shoes, in an attractive dark blue, with cloth uppers to enable the feet to breathe and heels well supported by leather and India rubber.

'I know you'll never wear them,' says Amara, watching Horvath turn them in his hands and inspect them from every angle.

'How about some excellent apricot grappa!'

'Gerard Haemmerle Schnapps. A special Christmas offer.'

The three friends drink sitting round the stove, in the warmth of a peaceful evening on the last day of the year 1956, remembering the uprising in Budapest and the friends they have left behind.

'I've had a letter from Ferenc,' says Hans, pulling out a folded sheet of squared paper. 'They haven't even got proper writing paper.'

'Will you read it to us?'

'That's why I brought it.'

Dear Hans, I'm in Miskolc at my sister's. All's calm here. We're buried in snow. They say it's twenty years since the last time it was so cold and there was so much snow. I wanted to go back to Budapest to put a flower on Tadeusz's grave, but moving about is dangerous. Every street, every corner, every cossroads is garrisoned and if you can't produce a hundred pieces of paper and a hundred permits they throw you in prison. We breathe a lurid atmosphere of clean sweep. Slander has become State truth. And woe betide you if you don't accept that. Yesterday it said in the paper that Nagy and his friends had plotted a coup together with foreign imperialists and internal counter-revolutionary forces. 'Do you know what this means? That very soon he'll be tried and sentenced to death. Kádár is now worse than Rákosi, whom we hated so much for becoming a pawn of the Soviets with his free use of political police and torture. The radio constantly repeats that the insurgents were working to restore to power the great landed proprietors, Horthy's fascists and the old capitalists. And who is to blame? Those who helped the insurgents. That is to say, practically every single Hungarian citizen: students, workers, imtellectuals, teachers, professionals. In effect they've started collective trials and sentences are falling on people like snow. All the directors of the factory Councils have been arrested. The Revolutionary Committee of Intellectuals started at the Petőfi Circle has been dissolved. The sentences handed down are extremely severe: nearly always death. Those who are spared end up without a proper trial or any specific accusation in the concentration camps Nagy closed. These are being reopened in their dozens throughout the land. Even a mere suspicion will land you inside for six months, easily extended to twelve merely by an administrative decision. But can they gag an entire nation? The ÁVH with their hated uniforms, badges and cudgels have started circulating again. And they hit people. They hit anyone who gets under their feet … Though Hungarians must have very hard heads, because resistance is continuing; desperate, sporadic, improvised but continuous. In a factory at Debrecen the other day all the workers came out on strike. The police arrived by the lorryload, arrested the leaders and carried them off to prison. A hundred or so other workers presented themselves next day in front of the prison to demand that their comrades be freed. Little by little the crowd grew bigger. By midday a thousand people had gathered. They were unarmed and did no more than shout. Do you know what Kádár's soldiers did? They fired on the crowd, indiscriminately and without warning. Fifty dead and more than a hundred wounded. Anywhere a crowd forms, the police come and fire directly at the people. On 12 December Kádár instituted special tribunals for political crimes. And what particularly saddens me is that on 8 December, at the Eighth Congress of the Italian Communist Party, the Soviet intervention in Hungary was approved, thus isolating the voices of any dissidents. The papers have been singing the praises of Italy in a big way these last few days. Tell Amara, if she doesn't already know it. This is the way the wind is blowing in this country. Oh, I forgot the censorship, which sticks its nose in everywhere and blacks out letters, even personal ones. If I had posted this to you I would now be in prison awaiting trial for high treason. Luckily I found a friend who has a friend coming to Vienna with all his permits in place and I gave the letter to him. We may be taking a risk, but I want you to know what's happening and tell the world about it. Tell Amara to publish it in her paper. Say hello to Horvath. With all best wishes from Ferenc.

57

Amara, Hans and Horvath are walking along the Wiedner Haupt-strasse. It's half-past nine in the morning but not a soul can be seen in the street. Only a few drowsy figures sweeping up broken glass and collecting waste paper, cigarette ends and beer cans. At Horvath's the evening before they ate and drank happily, with a toast at midnight while the city exploded with shots: fireworks that were a sinister reminder of the sounds of war. At one each returned home to sleep. But the explosions, drunken shouts and the dull sound of bottles thrown from windows continued till dawn.

Now the city is struggling to wake up. There is a smell of coffee, and here and there singing from behind closed windows. Soon the New Year concert will begin. The 1st of January 1957 opens on a cold but sunny morning. The three friends walk arm in arm, making a comic sight as they avoid the broken bottles, fried potato cartons and tin stars that fill the street. Two men and a woman. An elderly youngster, as his friends call him, with white hair cut short, dark trousers stopping short of his bare ankles, and huge feet enclosed in sandals. Next to him a small girl with nut-brown hair in a light blue coat, her red beret pulled well down on her head, her eyes half-shut against the cold. On her right another ageing youth, his thick brown hair streaked with grey tending to fall across his brow above intense and inquisitive chestnut eyes.

But where are they going so early in the morning on New Year's Day, trampling the remnants of the previous night's celebrations, in a Vienna still sleeping under the benevolent hand of the sun?

They do not speak. Each seems sunk in his or her own thoughts. But there is a subtle understanding in their linked arms. An under-stated and perhaps not even fully conscious friendship that has grown with time.

Reaching Karlsplatz they stop. The street they are looking for cannot be far away. They cross Ressel Park followed by a cat, its tail erect like a flag. But the moment they show signs of coming close it runs off severe and proud, tail scything the air.

Here's Brücknerstrasse. They follow the numbers: one to 32; 18 must be somewhere in the middle. A street that has more or less survived the bombs. Only two houses destroyed, their yards ready for rebuilding. Stacks of bricks covered with snow, a crane waiting for good weather to get back to work. A digger. A cement-mixer. All abandoned under the snow.

Number 18 is a red-brick house with a fringe of icicles hanging from its low roof.

'Here we are.'

'Sure? I can't see any number.'

'This is it, he even described it to me.'

'Are you absolutely sure we've got the right day?'

'Of course, don't worry. He won't eat you.'

Hans presses the bell. No answer. He tries again. A woman's voice from above. The three raise their heads to see an open window and a woman with two blonde plaits wound round her ears signing to them to come in. They push open the small gate and find themselves before a door of dark wood bearing a green ring covered with little silver bells.

When the door is opened all the little bells start tinkling together, each with a different sound. The woman with the blonde plaits gives a little bow of invitation and precedes them up some steep steps. The three follow. She seems extremely young, with an adolescent face above a solid, massive body. She climbs rapidly. On reaching the top she disappears down a small corridor to one side leaving them alone in a small sitting room panelled in light-coloured wood. On the rust-coloured wall-to-wall carpet are a small sofa and two small armchairs covered with white cotton decorated with obtrusive pink elephants and light-blue tigers.

They stand for a minute or two in the entrance uncertain what to do, then the door before them opens and the man they had met before comes in.

Peter Orenstein holds out his hand in his familiar clumsy and graceless manner. He seems to have changed since the last time they met. He is now wearing clean clothes, a fine red velvet shirt and an open grey wool cardigan. On his feet are plush slippers and under his arm a book. But his head is hairless, the hole in his cheek distorts his face and his parted lips reveal a set of dentures. He offers a sardonic grin.

'So you've moved, Herr Orenstein?'

'This is not my house, but my wife's. You've met her, Brunhilde, she's very timid. I come here when I want to see the child. And I have to say, she welcomes me with great courtesy. As she welcomes my friends. What can I offer you? I think Brunhilde keeps the drinks in here.' He bends to open a small cupboard of painted wood, pulls out a pot-bellied bottle with no label and pours into their glasses some white liquid diluted with water from another bottle.

'A little Pernod?'

He offers each of them a glass, and empties his own in a few gulps then refills it with quick, furtive movements.

'We would like to bring you our best wishes for a happy New Year, Herr Orenstein. Please excuse us for calling on you during a holiday but Frau Amara has to go back to Italy and before she goes she would like to have back the letter she left in your hands.'

'It was I who chose the day for your visit.'

'Yes, but today is New Year's Day.'

'That means nothing to me. For me holidays are a mere accident.'

'Well, that's all right then.'

'When you came before there were two of you, now there are three,' remarks their host slyly.

'This is our friend Horvath. We have no secrets from him. We were together at Budapest during the uprising. We all risked our lives together.'

'Oh yes, those awful friends of Horthy who tried to bring off a *coup d'état*.'

'That's not how it was. Perhaps you have been misinformed. We were there. It was a popular uprising.'

'The Soviets have done an excellent job putting them back in their place.'

Amara wants to argue, but Hans squeezes her elbow. They are there to understand and get the letter back, not to dispute politics.

'Herr Orenstein, last time you said that Emanuele Orenstein was yourself. Why did you say that?'

The man looks at them as though he doesn't understand. Meanwhile he has gulped down another glass of Pernod. Amara notices his hands are shaking as he pours the alcohol.

'Because it's true,' he finally says, grimacing like a puppet.

'But Emanuele was born in 1928 which would make him twenty-eight today. Excuse me, but how old are you?'

'Mind your own business,' says the man, suddenly offended.

Now his eyes are shining brightly. With stained, bony fingers he continues to pour Pernod, without even asking the others if they want more.

'Signora Maria Amara Sironi, who has been looking for you for months, would like to know a little more. Otherwise please tell us if you know nothing and we will leave you in peace.'

'Signora Amara, whom I knew as a child, is very sure of herself. Where does this presumption come from?'

'Presumption?'

'To know who I might or might not be.'

'She has been looking for you for months. And it was you who said that Peter Orenstein and Emanuele Orenstein are the same person,' interrupts Hans, trusting in logic.

'Have you been to Dachau?'

'No.'

'Precisely.'

'Why are you speaking in riddles, Herr Orenstein. What have you to do with that boy?'

'I am that boy.'

'Why are you teasing us, Herr Peter?'

They see him lean perilously over the carpet. At the last moment he saves himself by falling in a sitting position onto the sofa, leaning on one arm. Then he rises again painfully and stifles a retch. Grabbing the bottle with greedy fingers he lifts it straight to his mouth. The three watch in astonishment. They don't know whether to tear the bottle from his hands, to help him, or to go away. Everything seems possible and impossible at the same time.

'Are you Amara then? You don't seem to me the same person at all. I think you're trying to confuse me.'

'The fact is we're here to find out about Emanuele, not about Amara,' says Horvath, beginning to lose patience. But Hans holds him back. Perhaps, and Amara agrees, all this drinking will help to loosen a few knots, to draw out words buried for too long.

'If you really were Amara, you would have come to look for me before now. What have you been doing all this time? What have you been up to? Are you married? Screwing some foul Florentine turd?'

'Listen, I won't have you insulting the signora …'

'Shut up, you idiot! … As for you, woman, who do you think you are, you birdbrain! We're all cut from the same cloth, every one of us. Those who went through the war and those who didn't. Those who have been in a death camp and those who haven't. Shit is shit everywhere, even when it hides under camelhair coats and felt hats.'

'All right, we'll go …'

'Beginning to smell the stink of burning, are you? In a hurry to get away at the first whiff of shit, just like all the others, gentlemen with sensitive noses; well-dressed, well-fed gentlemen …'

He lifts the bottle to his lips again, but it's empty. Moving calmly, hands holding his armpits tight in a huge effort to control his shaking, he opens the cupboard again with a kick, pulls out another bottle that looks like whisky, holds it up to the light and sees that it's half full. Then he lifts it straight to his mouth.

'Now you two get out, you two drunks … get lost. I need to talk face to face with the Signorina Maria Amara Sironi here present.'

Hans bends his head in resignation. He takes Horvath by the arm and they move away. But Amara notices that they leave the door ajar and she sees them peeping through the gap. Hans signs to her not to be afraid, he will intervene if she is attacked.

58

Peter walks backwards and forwards. He takes Amara by the shoulders and forces her to sit down on the sofa. He suddenly becomes much calmer.

'I'm not the person you're looking for, and I never will be. So go away and leave me in peace.'

'Why won't you tell me what's happened, Emanuele, I'll believe you.'

'Don't treat me like an imbecile. You're not prepared to believe I really am Emanuele.'

'Your father and mother ...'

'Died in the ghetto at Łódź, you know that because I wrote to you about it.'

'And you ...'

'I've died and come back to life several times. Once it was tuberculosis. I don't know how I was cured, maybe it wasn't really tuberculosis but just my lungs spitting blood in desperation. I thought my life would end at Łódź. But I was reserved for something better: the drawing rooms of Dachau. There I died again.'

'So it was to Dachau they took you?'

'To Dachau, yes madam, a magnificent holiday location ... even with sulphurous waters and a brilliant medical facility ideal for conducting experiments.' He laughs and coughs, spitting.

'And how did you survive?'

'Always greedy for information, Amara, most bitter Amara. Digging and digging away like an old tapir ... Always anxious to stick your nose in the shit so you can say: oh no, that's not me, I don't know that shit. That's what you want, isn't it? But I've been in it up to my hair, get that into your head, you silly little Florentine cunt! And stop looking down on me with that superior air.'

'I'm trying to understand.'

'There's nothing to understand, stupid girl, nothing to

understand … Just things that are so real that they seem unreal, so real that they become sublime in their unreality. You will never understand, never …'

He stops and balances on one foot so that it seems he must fall full length from one moment to the next. But he recovers and again grabs the neck of the bottle. But this one is empty too. His eyes are shining with a livid, sinister light. Amara wonders whether it might not be better to go and leave him in peace. She seems only to have been able to dig up ancient, unbearable agonies. But when she gets up to go he takes her by the arm and forces her down on the sofa again.

'Since you're here I want you to know, little princess on the pea, I want you to know everything then you can go and fuck yourself wherever you like. And stop crushing my balls! Who asked you to look for me, eh? Who gave you permission to come ferreting about in this loathsome city trying to find out what happened to your beloved and incredibly stupid young friend Emanuele Orenstein? He's dead, got that? Dead and buried, and you make a serious mistake in trying to revive him. Because the dead don't speak, or if they do speak they spit, and if they spit they poison, remember that, you lousy little cow!'

Amara instinctively curls up, pulling her knees to her chin. She watches him, terrified and fascinated.

'Now you must listen, I want you to listen with your whole body because there are things I've never said before and I shall never say again. I want a little piss and vomit to reach you and wreck your style as a little girl of a good family, bloody hell, which I can't stand at all, are you listening?'

'I'm listening.'

'As soon as we got to Dachau, they separated us. My work-mates from the ghetto at Łódź, my carpentry shop friends, boys like myself, were all bewildered and understood nothing. Four days crowded together in the train. So many things thought and said! We kept close so as not to lose sight of one another. But as soon as we got to Dachau, those ever well-dressed gentlemen, those guards in their well-ironed uniforms, immediately split us up. A rapid and drastic process of selection. All the crippled, short-sighted, lame, sick, under-sized, and particularly the children to one side, please! Hurry up, *schnell*! The rest, a little bigger and capable of work, get moving, to the other side. Come on, what are you waiting for! I went spontaneously to the workers' side, I knew how to make out I was older than I really was ... intuition guided me but I was already thinking only of myself. I betrayed the others and left them to their fate without saying a word ... I'd learned a thing or two in that bloody ghetto! The next day I realised I'd been right ... Those on the right were immediately shut up in a lorry, made drunk on exhaust fumes and taken to Hartheim Castle ... A good way to rescue them from the problems of life, don't you think? I bet you don't even know what Hartheim Castle is: a splendid place, with well-kept flower gardens, where the SS gassed thousands of people, principally Germans: the crippled, the sick, the lame, the mad. Project T4, heard of that? No, of course you haven't. Memory is elusive and fleeting in people of your type. My friends never even reached the castle. They were killed at once, in the lorries. They died a disgusting death, writhing about in their vomit for a dozen minutes, climbing over each other to try to reach a bit of air, squashing the weakest, who cared a damn, so long as they could breathe. For what purpose? Just a few seconds more of life, among hundreds of others condemned to death in a hermetically sealed lorry into which poison gas was introduced through a huge pipe ... But those who had moved instinctively to the left, like me, off to work, hop hop, easy-peasy! Too simple for complicated heads like yours, it was so straightforward and simple ... Yet no one realised it, you see, not one of them, until it was too late. And me? How did you save yourself, I hear you ask? Just by work? Yes indeed, I worked half-naked with damaged hands and feet covered with chilblains in those damned clogs that were too broad and hard. I survived because I was strong in spite of my tuberculosis or whatever it was and having claimed to be older than I really was. I survived by stealing from everybody else. I became a daring and very clever young petty thief. I stole from the dead too. I was only caught once, when I couldn't tear bread out of the hands of a dead man. I'd been watching him. I knew he had a dry crust hidden under his pyjamas. But he was dying. I spied on him. And the moment he breathed his last I climbed onto his pallet and grabbed his treasure, but his hand was closed so firmly round that piece of bread I could not get it off him. He was dead but he still wanted to keep it. Madness! I needed to break his fingers but that took time and in the meantime the trusty came in. I got such a whipping that day that I still have the scars. Want to see them?'

Amara huddles up into herself. Something is collapsing inside her, reeling and drowning. Something sucking at her from the inside till she feels her face shrinking, her hands weakening, and her heart becoming a piece of calcified meat. Meanwhile he pulls up his shirt revealing ugly scars, red against his meagre white flesh. He strikes himself with flat, trembling fingers. Then angrily shoves his shirt back into his trousers.

'But I must tell you the truth to the end or I shall suffocate. Even though I already know you won't understand a damn thing … It wasn't just by stealing that I saved myself. I accepted the attentions of an officer to escape selection for the experiments. Do you get that, you stupid little tart? Experiments were a speciality at Dachau. Very useful for the pharmaceutical firms. Did a new drug need testing? Abracadabra, we have just the right bodies for that here. No complaints, no arguments. Why not inoculate the enfeebled body of an inmate with blood infected with malaria? His temperature would immediately shoot up to forty or forty-one Celsius. And Dr Schilling, solicitous as always, would be on hand to make you swallow the new medicine to see if it might help cure you from malaria. One subject's eyes would bulge from their sockets, another would be seized by convulsions and yet a third, the most fortunate, would go stone deaf but survive. And why not immerse a man in freezing water for ninety minutes to find out how to save any of their airmen who came down in the sea. Usually the victims died after an hour from cerebral haemorrhage. But in an attempt to bring them round, the doctor would give them injections in the femoral vein and in the belly and so forth. Most did not respond. Then as soon as they were dead, the hard-working camp doctors would open their cranium to find out what had happened. They'd find the brain soaked in blood and furthermore, something that surprised them, the heart transformed into an aubergine by the effort of trying to get oxygen. Dr Holzlohner was particularly able and occasionally even managed to restore the unfortunate victim to life. In his able hands the body would regain heat. But of course it would have suffered irreparable brain damage. So the drugs were useless. Who cared if eighteen out of twenty Jews died during these experiments? One survived, and that was me. A phenomenon of resistance. Another doctor from Hamburg, you should have seen him, a really able type, courteous, shrewd, with small hands, a handlebar moustache, and good kind eyes, came from Buchenwald where he had specialised in homosexuals. He got hold of those wearing the pink triangle, made them take off their clothes, grafted under the skin of their bellies a gland full of male hormones and stood back to watch. In the morning he would interrogate them: have you dreamed about women? Eh, tell me, what were they like? They would tell him what he wanted to hear and he would happily send in medical reports in beautiful handwriting that claimed that his experiments for the elimination of homosexuality had been successful. But what he didn't see was that around him, among the blond Aryan SS officers, there were dozens of homosexuals who amused themselves by picking out the best-looking young boys to use as slaves with duty as an excuse. Homosexuality was of course forbidden. Everything was forbidden in that place. But the officers knew how to bend the rules. I beg you, Herr Doktor, let him be no more than sixteen years old and in reasonable shape, he will have to keep the floor clean and look after the laundry. Herr Doktor would nod. But you had to show yourself clean, free of fleas and washed with soap or they were disgusted. I jumped into bed, actually not so much a bed as a latrine, but no matter. The thing was not to be caught and no place was safer than the latrines, which were flowing with dysentery. The SS never went there, they were afraid of soiling their uniforms. But the handsome Untersturmführer Rudolf Heinz did come there, at night, when no one else was about, to make love to me, you understand? I would have accepted this and more not to end up in that icy water again. Once you might survive, twice no. But d'you want to know the funniest thing? Coupling with the Untersturmführer served no purpose at all, because after a bit he got bored and passed me on indifferently to a friend of his, a medical officer who, not satisfied with the results obtained by Dr Schilling, was himself trying to discover an anti-malaria vaccine. Finding me in better condition than the others thanks to the scraps of food my friend Rudolf had secretly passed on to me, he injected me with infected blood. I became delirious with fever, my skin wrinkled and my teeth fell out. Doctor Müller was very fond of me; he was so happy I didn't die like the others and ruin his experiments. He wrote and wrote, long articles about his vaccine, using me and four other wretches as examples. But in the meantime I had become an old man at seventeen years of age, decrepit, bald, toothless and imbecile. I developed a festering abscess on my right cheek. Good, excellent, let's try a new type of anaesthesia, let's cut open the cheek and conduct an operation in acrobatic dentistry, that was how they put it. And here's the result: a hole that constantly fills with mucus. I could hear planes passing over and bombs falling and I knew the war was nearly over. I had to survive, I just had to hold out ... But what for? To bite into a slice of bread. Not just any old slice, no, a whole loaf, just for me, that was my dream. I didn't give a damn about the others who were dying like flies, about those hanged each morning at dawn, or still arriving in the trains. We were laying new railway tracks in a hurry, *schnell schnell* you filthy swine, damn bloody Jews! We must hurry with these new tracks to take the trains straight to the undressing rooms. A brilliant idea, don't you think? So that the moment they came out of the cattle trucks they could be stripped of everything, even their underpants, and the fittest ones be sent to work in pyjamas filthy with the shit and blood of those who had died. The rest would be either shot or gassed in lorries or sent on to another camp. *Schnell schnell*; no longer any time to cut off women's hair or strip gold teeth out of the old, the allies were barely a hundred kilometres away and no witnesses must survive, you understand, not a single one. Meanwhile in the offices they were burning papers, you could detect the smell over and above that of the crematorium ovens. Eight humdred, nine hundred, a thousand bodies a day, were thrown into those ovens. Their problem was they couldn't kill as fast as they needed to, so that with bayonets at our backs we were forced to drag the bodies of those just shot to a great ditch and throw petrol over them, for an SS officer to set fire to the lot with a burning torch. Some would still be moving, calling, slobbering or groping about. But if the rifles had not killed them, the fire would. What a grand spectacle: one more, one more, *schnell schnell*! What about that newborn baby saved and wrapped in a blanket? Throw it in the air so I can hit it in flight. Lagerführer Christopher Schöttle was an expert at clay-pigeon shooting. It would be easier still with a newborn child, wouldn't it? Meanwhile the big guns could be heard getting nearer and nearer. Those who understood German as well as I did could hear them discussing what to do with the surviving prisoners? Have Himmler's orders arrived yet? What was that cretin waiting for before giving precise orders! But then one morning the order seemed to have arrived, the actual order written by Himmler that stated in so many words: kill the lot. No witnesses, is that clear? Not a single survivor to say what happened in the camps, that's what the Führer wants. But how could thousands and thousands of people be killed in two or three days? There was no more petrol for firing the ovens. Meanwhile some officers had very quietly disappeared. There was no more ammunition for the machine guns and pistols, but the trainloads were still arriving and where to put the people they brought? How to dispose of them all. Then came another order: round them up and take them away. But away where? Where the hell you like, just away. By now the authorities were out in the open, they were nervous and discipline was suffering: all they wanted was dead people, more and more dead bodies. But didn't the order contain anything else? Didn't it explain where to take these damn Jews who were so pig-headed as to insist on continuing to stay alive? What did the order say? It said: since the allies are at the gates, and since it would take time to get rid of so many people, form up the remaining prisoners in fives and drag them to another camp, further away from the enemy front line. The death marches, do you know about them, little Alice in Wonderland? D'you know what they were? Luckily it was April by now, maybe that saved some of us: the temperature had risen five or six degrees, that was already something, wasn't it? Our clothes were still the same, French elegance: striped pyjamas and clogs. But at least our feet were no longer enclosed in a grip of ice. We had air to eat and rainwater to drink. We just had to march and move quickly. If you stopped, even for a moment, if you sat down, you were instantly shot. I don't know how I managed, I really don't know. I kept walking and thinking: look, I must get as far as that post, just to that post and then I'm there. And at the post I said: come on, one more post, keep going, one more post and we're there. That's how I did it, post after post, hundreds of posts, blinded by sleep, twisted by hunger. Every so often I heard a shot. Some couldn't make it, got out of step, or stopped a moment to catch their breath. Towards evening we would be given some soup: hot water with a few beans in it. And then, if there was a stall and some hay, fine; if not, lie along the road in the ditch. We collapsed and fell asleep anywhere, one on top of another to keep warm. Many never rose again next morning. So much the better, one mouth less! I overheard one SS man say to another, where the fuck are we supposed to take them, have you any idea? And the other said: they'll all die on the road anyway. But they hadn't taken into account the will to live of a boy of seventeen.'

59

Peter Orenstein laughs, attaches himself to the bottle and drains it in a few gulps. 'If I'm describing things as they are, Amara, it's only for you; the others disgust me, I don't know who they are and I don't want to know. You think yourself superior because you've never descended to the lowest dregs of self-disgust; we were all killers, the strongest against the weakest, even against those we should have helped and supported. There is no peace, there never can be any peace for us because they made us do things that will always make us feel dirty, horribly filthy and stained; but how they flew, those rapacious creatures, I saw them rise into the air with their great wings that cast gigantic shadows, I envied them their freedom to fly over the camp, their eyes always alert and if they caught sight of a prey even the least bit appetising, they would snap their wings shut and hurl themselves at the earth, expert at snatching up the right body in a single beakful ... some were too fat to rise again in flight, but others no, they cried out like falcons ... corrupt, you understand? Corrupt and degraded, that's what they enjoyed, reducing us to the same condition as themselves, robbing us of our self-esteem ... they tried repeatedly and they succeeded, at least with me they did ... the political prisoners survived better, they were united, had clandestine organisations, mutual solidarity, a network of informers, but isolated individuals like me, what could we do? Drag off the dead bodies of our friends, wipe away their faeces, fling them on the barrows, push them up to the ovens and shove them in three at a time. Do you know what they discovered? That if a woman's body was put in with two men, the men burned better. Because women's bodies have reserves of fat that we men lack, what a laugh ... fat hiding heaven knows where in all that starvation but it did exist ... all the more of course if the woman had just been brought by train from some city where she had been able to eat something ... and you can sit with your legs apart holding the head of a corpse and clipping off all its hair without feeling anything at all; you can open the mouth of some dead gaffer and wrench out a gold tooth with pliers before washing it in formalin, carefully removing any remaining fragments of flesh before cleaning it properly with a little brush specially made for the purpose and throwing it into a bucket for your fellow-worker to add to a collection for heating and melting down as part of a gold bar to be handed to the official camp treasurer to be forwarded to the Reichsbank, you understand that, lovely? A human being is capable of doing absolutely anything to survive and that fact is our most disgusting and unpardonable quality, that deadened us more effectively than anything else.'

He puts his hand up to his head, pulling his few remaining grey hairs with a horrible grimace as if to help him draw breath before continuing.

'My hair grew back to some extent when I came out and started eating again, but I had become bald inside, stripped of thought and feeling ... everything seemed to have changed with the end of the war: I was alive, you see, how could anything else matter compared to that? I thought I could distance myself for ever from that thieving whoring child who had performed disgusting acrobatics in order to survive, but how could I escape myself now that I was putting on weight and my hair was growing again, and I was even once more becoming a conscious being? I changed my name and way of life and went into a monastery but didn't take vows, everything I tried soon disgusted me ... I got married and had a son, and I thought that had solved the problem. But no, when my son was a year old I started kicking him, he horrified me ... my wife ran away with the child, even if she understood, she did understand me, but she could not leave the child exposed to my frenzy.'

Amara watches him with her eyes full of tears, and sees him run, staggering and bumping against the furniture, towards the bedroom. He returns immediately, holding a small piece of greasy paper.

He offers it to her with an awkward gesture.

'Here's the proof, Signora Maria Amara Doubting-Thomas ... You're incapable of believing in anything unless you can touch it, so here you are ... take this paper ... do you recognise it?'

Amara grasps with trembling hands the ragged scrap the man is holding. The crumpled remains of a letter she wrote in 1940, when she was writing to him at the Schulerstrasse address in Vienna.

'No more doubts, little sister?'

He plants his legs wide apart in front of her. Raises an arm and reaches her an open-handed smack. Not a violent slap. He is too drunk for his hand to have any more force than a wet rag. His red eyes bulging, he spits at her.

Amara gazes sadly at him with blood beginning to run from her nose. She cannot move. Tears pour down her cheeks uncontrollably. Hans and Horvath come back into the room and immobilise the man by pinning his hands behind his back.

'Let go, imbeciles! Let go or I'll kill you!'

Like a furious child, he fastens his teeth into the hand of Hans, who cries out in pain.

'Get out of here, you scoundrels, villains, out, out, out!' he screams at the top of his voice. The veins in his neck bulge and his eyes are bloodshot even if he is unsteady on his feet after all the alcohol he has swallowed.

'Please let him go!' says Amara, rising to her feet.

But at that moment Brunhilde enters the room. Strong, solicitous, competent, very young and beautiful, she grasps him passionately by his shoulders, and almost hoisting him onto her back, bears him away murmuring words of love in his ear.

60

Is it possible to die without dying? To lose oneself without losing one's body? Lying on her bed at the Pension Blumental, Amara asks herself how she will ever again be able to move her legs since each seems to weigh a ton, and reconciles herself to never being able to get out of bed again. Her head is somewhere else, watching her from a corner of the ceiling. Though the eyes so thoughtfully observing her are not her own. Dry tears are lacerating the skin of her cheekbones. She wants to vomit but cannot. She would like the window open but opening it is beyond her. Why are those cold, distant eyes fixed on her from above? Where are her arms? Her throat is trying to swallow something sticky that isn't saliva. Perhaps the blood that filtered from her nose when Emanuele slapped her.

What have they made of you? asks a voice she doesn't recognise as her own. She has no more tears, no more saliva, and her breath rises like a sob from her dry throat. Someone has placed an icebag on her head. There's a smell of onions.

They've stuck a needle into her arm. So perhaps she's not in Frau Morgan's pension, but somewhere else. A hospital? Her eyes are blind yet she is aware of a thick fog penetrated by other eyes which she could swear are her own. But how can she be up there fixed to the ceiling when she is at the same time down here nailed to this bed? What have they done to you? What have they done to you, Emanuele? she can feel her lips moving but no voice comes out. Blood is still oozing in her throat. And the eyes are bothering her because they are burning too brightly, as intrusive as lamps.

What has happened inside her head? Why can't she remember? Her temples are throbbing with pain. A pain she cannot chase away, but she has no idea what is causing it.

Then she gradually becomes aware of a boy slipping away between ruined barrack buildings. It's him, it must be him. She wants to tell him she understands him. She calls: Emanuele! He turns and limps slowly towards her and when he is really near her an enormous, cold, dirty open hand, heavy as a rock, strikes her mouth. Emanuele! she cries, but he moves quickly away. She sees him withdraw into a corner with an officer in a glittering uniform.

But the bicycle is still there, in the storeroom of the little house in Via Alderotti. And here he comes. He has just opened the gate of Villa Lorenzi and is running towards her steering his own bicycle with one hand. He raises the other in greeting. Smiles. And says something she can't understand. But here he is. He waits for her to step on the pedal and they're off! But where are they going? I'll take you somewhere you've never been before. They pedal on and on, sweating and laughing, up a steep slope. Then he stops, leans his bicycle against a tree and signs to her to follow. They set off bent double through brambles that obstruct an almost invisible path between fields and vineyards. The path narrows and it is almost impossible to go on. But he is not discouraged, ignoring the thorns scratching his legs. And she follows, also ignoring the vegetation grabbing at her ankles and tearing her skin.

Finally they arrive. But where? Emanuele pushes some branches aside revealing a sort of heavy iron lid blackened by time. He lifts it and signs to her to follow. Facing them is a narrow black well. He goes forward, carefully placing his feet on the iron steps. Suddenly it feels cold. The light gradually fades then disappears altogether. They are descending in darkness into what seems a bottomless well. Where are we going, Emanuele? she wants to ask but becomes aware that his throat is closed and he can't produce a single word. She can only follow him.

Now at last the steps end. He puts a foot on the ground and helps her down the last one. Where are we? She tries to speak but it is as if her mouth is walled up. Emanuele embraces her fiercely. For a moment they are again one single body, both lover and beloved. Two kids hugging tenderly. But something disturbs her. Animals are moving on the ground. Snakes? Mice? Something slimy and clammy touches her ankle. She jumps. Emanuele's mouth is against her ear and she can hear his voice saying softly: now we shall live together for ever, in here, safe from wars and the horror of wars. But I want to go back out, protests Amara silently, I want the open air! She extricates herself from his possessive arms.

Reaches a hand towards the stairs but feels the dark clammy wall slither under ther fingers. The stairs have vanished. Then she realises the body hugging her has no warmth, it consists of bones and darkness. She tries to shout. Wakes bathed in sweat. Frau Morgan is sitting on a chair, asleep with her mouth open and a book upside down on her lap.

The icebag slips on Amara's cheek and her tears begin falling again, no longer in her throat but onto the stuffed pillow that is squashing her hair.

61

Her luggage is on the floor. Too heavy to lift up to the netting rack. The carriage is empty. Six in the morning and the country-side coming awake under a luminous white carpet.

Amara's gloved hands are gripped tightly between her legs. She raises her coat collar. She has the carriage to herself but it is unheated. When she opens her mouth, vapour disperses in the cold air. The windows are encrusted with ice. The world all round is alien and frozen.

Too many things have happened in these last few days. The disastrous encounter with Peter or rather Emanuele Orenstein. Her illness, or rather her absence and delirium that went on for three days and nights, according to the worried Frau Morgan. The arrival of a letter informing her of the death of her husband Luca Spiga who, explains her sister-in-law Suzy, has left her two million lire in his bank account. Her decision to return to Florence. Her dinner with Hans who asked her formally to marry him. Her ina-bility to give him any answer. Her visit to Horvath at the library. He promises to come to Florence as soon as he has a visa in his passport.

The newspaper has written to tell her they no longer need her: she has been away too long and contributed no more than a dozen articles. Not good value for money. She missed her scoop on the uprising in Budapest, her reports all arriving later than the dis-patches of the international agencies. Appalling! The editor, after many hypocritical expressions of gratitude for her collaboration 'which I do understand to have been passionately committed if unfortunately at the same time extremely meagre' informs her that they have already replaced her with a 'quick and able' correspond-ent who will write from Eastern Europe and cost them less than she did.

This too is a new circumstance she will have to face. How long can one survive on two million lire? A year, two at most, then she will have to find another job.

She can't get the wrinkled, wicked, desperate face of Peter out of her mind and can't bring herself to call him Emanuele, even though she knows that's who he is. She found him, which is what she had wanted to do. But in looking for one person she discovered another. As if she had entered by mistake a place 'of cruel and absurd mysteries,' as Marlow describes it, 'not fit for a human being to behold.' She had been looking for an innocent little boy, persecuted and wounded. And she found a fury. Had the experiments damaged his brain, as he claimed? Or had the cost of survival been too high for him to be able to afford it? He could not trust her, or anyone else. What had been the point of searching everywhere for him? A boy who never had any opportunity to grow, who had married and then separated. Who had assaulted his own infant son. What did they have in common now? How could she ever have believed she could rediscover the Emanuele she had known?

The thoughts go round and round in her head. She must think of something else. Getting up, she opens a suitcase and pulls out a book. Conrad, as usual. 'He seemed to stare at me [...] with that wide and immense stare embracing, condemning, loathing all the universe. I seemed to hear the whispered cry, "The horror The horror!"' There is something lugubriously comic about the madness going round in her head. She would like to go on reading but cannot. Her eyes lift from the pages to rest on the windows and the frozen panorama unfolding behind them. Firs heavy with snow shake themselves as the train passes and drop white heaps on the already snowed-up countryside. Every so often roofs and a church tower like a proud plume rise above the mass of whiteness. Then a football field just cleared, with young men running about in shorts. One slips and tumbles and the others laugh. For a while a road runs beside the railway with women cycling, their heads in coloured scarfs, skirts lifted free of legs protected by thick woollen stockings. A farm-worker is leading an ox with gigantic half-moon horns.

It's like being on one of her father's model trains. In a perfect miniature reproduction of a carriage, travelling round and round on perfect imitation railway lines. But there is no one on board and the engine is pulling its coaches on tiny rails that come and go inside a single room. No stations of arrival or departure. Only a perverse racing towards something unknown, make-believe and unreal.

The absence of Hans, the man with the gazelles, torments her. Why could she not respond to his plea for love? Why did she not tell him to come with her? That was what had been expected. A generous, patient, good-hearted man. I'll write to him as soon as I arrive, she tells herself, and for a moment her heart shouts for joy. But something has been broken, has been spoilt. After the companionship of Budapest and their journeys together, the discovery of Emanuele hit her like an explosion. Causing another explosion inside herself. She can think of nothing else.

The future opens before her like a precocious flower touched by the first ray of the sun but still frozen on the branch. Because the spring is not yet here and the sun has deceived her.